Dear Reader,

Here we are, together again. Well, as together as we can be through the written word. Maybe you're standing in a bookstore, sneaking a peek behind the cover? Or have you just opened that box in your living room after ordering my book online? Perhaps you're waiting to check out, and browsing before you pay for your purchases?

Whatever way this book came into your hands, once again you've allowed me to work my magic spell and attempt to enchant you. For there's still fantasy in the world, here in my written words and the theater of your mind. You and I can journey to the Kingdom of Xy and the Plains of the Firelanders, to be drawn again into the lives of Lara and Keir.

For the Warlord and his Warprize have taken the first steps down a path that will lead to further adventures and a greater understanding of each other. But there is a saying on the Plains—and it's a universal truth—if you wish to hear the winds laugh, tell them you plans.

So why are you lingering here? Everyone has gathered to hear the tale. Marcus is waiting, with hot kavage and food. Hurry! I don't want to be on the wrong side of his tongue. Turn the page, and join us!

Elizabeth

WARSWORN

TOR ROMANCE BOOKS BY ELIZABETH VAUGHAN

Warprize
Warsworn
Warlord*

*forthcoming in 2007

Warsworn

Elizabeth Vaughan

tor romance

A TOM DOHERTY ASSOCIATES BOOK
NEW YORK

This is a work of fiction. All the characters and events portrayed in this book are either products of the author's imagination or are used fictitiously.

WARSWORN

Copyright © 2006 by Elizabeth Vaughan
Teaser copyright © 2006 by Elizabeth Vaughan

Edited by Anna Genoese

A Tor Book
Published by Tom Doherty Associates, LLC
175 Fifth Avenue
New York, NY 10010

www.tor.com

Tor® is a registered trademark of Tom Doherty Associates, LLC.

ISBN 0-765-35265-6
EAN 978-0-765-35265-1

First edition: April 2006

Printed in the United States of America

0 9 8 7 6 5 4 3 2 1

To Jane Lackey,
friend, neighbor, and sister

ACKNOWLEDGMENTS

First, to my readers. The last year has been a delight, getting e-mails and knowing that you are looking forward to the publication of this book. Your enthusiasm has kept me writing, and I thank you for it.

Thanks to Dr. Mary J. Gombash, MD, who patiently sat and let me ask her question after question over lunch. I think I 'what if' d' her to death. Thanks must also go to my cousin, Cindi Young, who shared her love of horses with me. She gave this city girl a bit of insight and I deeply appreciate it. To Barbara Doane, who shared with me her love of natural dyes and fabrics, and then found out the hard way why it isn't a good idea to loan me books. Sorry, Barb.

But for all the help that I've received, and all the research that I've done, any mistakes are my fault, and mine alone. I am perfectly capable of making horrible and embarrassing errors without any assistance.

The members of my writer's group, who told me all the painful truths that a writer needs to hear. This group consists of Spencer Luster, Helen Kourous, Robert Wenzlaff, Marc Tassin, Keith Flick, and Mike Szymkowiak.

Once again, Kandace Klumper, Patricia Merritt, and JoAnn Thompson were essential to the process, offering me constant reassurance and support. Tom Redding and Mary Fry read the final drafts, catching more mistakes than I care to mention. Phil Fry, Cathie Hansen, and Deb Spychalski are my long suffering co-workers, and I thank them for their love, support and patience.

I can't say enough about the contribution that my editor, Anna Genoese, has made to this book. Every time she makes a suggestion the story grows stronger and richer. And my deep thanks go to Heather Brady, my copy editor.

But once again, most of all, credit must go to Jean Rabe, who pushed me into the pool, and to Meg Davis, who found me there.

1

"Bloodmoss! That's bloodmoss, Marcus!" I leaned over, trying to get a better look. I was positive that the grubby little plant I was seeing passing under the hooves of the horse was the rare herb. "Let me down!"

The horse we were riding danced as my weight shifted and Marcus tightened up the reins. "If you don't stop wiggling, you're gonna tumble off, and embarrass Hisself and me." Marcus groused as the horse pranced under us.

I tightened my grip on his waist. "If you let me ride by myself, this wouldn't be a problem."

He huffed. "You can't ride worth a damn, and your feet remain sore. Now sit still! How would it look, the Warprize sprawled in the dirt?"

"Marcus, I am a Master Healer and my feet are healing fine."

"You know from nothing," Marcus growled. "I will judge if the Warprize is fit to walk."

I settled back, frustrated. I might be Xylara, Master Healer, Daughter of the House of Xy, Queen of Xy, Warprize of Keir of the Tribe of the Cat, Warlord of the Plains, but as far as Marcus was concerned I was little more than an unruly child. I sighed, and leaned my head on the back of his shoulder. "I can ride just fine."

Marcus snorted. "About as well as you tend your own feet."

Therein lay one of my problems. When I'd made the decision to follow the Warlord's army, I'd done so in the same garb I'd worn for the original claiming ceremony. Since tradition required that the Warprize accept nothing except from the hand of the Warlord, I had walked barefoot behind the army for some time before Keir had discovered what I was doing and reclaimed me. Following my Warlord, challenging his decision, had been the best choice, both for us and for our peoples.

Choosing to walk barefoot had not been quite so clever.

Joden, in training as a Singer, said that by choosing to honor the traditions of the Plains, I had made a powerful statement, one that would ring in the songs he was crafting. Marcus had arched his one eyebrow over his remaining eye, and inquired if the fact that my feet had sickened afterwards would be in the first verse or the second.

I straightened slowly, craning my neck to look around, careful not to disturb the horse this time. We were at the center of the Firelander Army, returning to the Plains. Not that Keir's people called themselves 'Firelanders'. That was a term my people used. Keir's people used 'of the Plains' which sounded awkward to my ears. In my thoughts, at least, they remained the Firelanders. Of course, I no longer add 'cursed' or 'evil' or thought that they belched fire. I still had hopes of seeing a blue one, though. There were brown ones, and black ones, and some even had a yellow tinge to their skin. Who knew what further wonders awaited me on the Plains?

Xy was really a large, wide mountain valley, that spread out all around us. I'd never been this far from Water's Fall before, never seen the furthest reaches of what was now my kingdom. The trees were starting to turn, their colors all laid out below us as we traveled.

Marcus and I were surrounded by horses and riders, which spilled out beyond the road as we rode. Keir had ordered that I travel at the center of this moving mass of warriors and horses. Even so, I knew that my guards would not be far away. Rafe and Prest were ahead of us, I could just see their backs. "Rafe!"

Marcus jerked his head under the hood of his cloak, and muttered. Fall was upon us, but the day was fine, and the sun warm on our backs. But not for Marcus. He'd suffered horrible burns at sometime in the past that had left him disfigured, taking away his left eye and burning his left ear completely away. So Marcus always rode cloaked, wrapped well lest the skies be offended by his scars. Yet another aspect of these people that I didn't understand.

Rafe turned and waved, and he and Prest slowed their mounts so that we could catch up with them. Marcus grumbled, but maneuvered his horse between them.

"Rafe, see that plant?" I tried to point it out to him as we moved.

"Plant?" Rafe looked in confusion at the ground. "Warprize . . ."

"The pale one; the one that looks like moss, but it's butter-colored."

Rafe shrugged. "Wouldn't it be easier to pick it yourself?"

I rolled my eyes in frustration. "Marcus won't stop!"

Rafe let his laughter ring out, then Prest reached over and grabbed the halter of our horse. Marcus exclaimed bitterly, but Prest guided us out of the crush. I had to smile, even in my frustration. Rafe always had a grin for me. He was a smaller man, thin, with fair skin and deep black hair and brown eyes. Quite a contrast to my other guard, Prest. Prest was much larger, and a quiet one, with skin of brown, and black hair in twenty thick braids that fell to the center of his back. More a man of action than words, he calmly guided the horses off to the side, where we could stop.

I started to wiggle off, but Marcus would have none of it. "You are to stay off those feet, you are."

"Marcus—"

Rafe swung down off his horse. "Point it out to me, Warprize and I'll get you handfuls."

Epor and Isdra came up beside us. "Problem?" Isdra asked, her long silver braid hanging down her shoulder. Her skin was a light gold in the sun, and her slanted grey eyes were quietly amused. Epor didn't bother to hide his smile. His bright gold hair and beard shown like the sun. He always reminded me of the paintings of the Sun God in the temple back home.

"Herself wants to be picking weeds." Marcus grumbled.

"Bloodmoss." I corrected him. "That's the one, Rafe. Let me see."

Epor snickered slightly as Rafe bent to the task of getting the plants. I noticed that Isdra gave him an amused look and reached over to nudge his leg. He caught her hand, and raised it to his lips. I look away, embarrassed at such a public display.

Rafe held up a handful of leaves and plants, their torn roots dangling. "Which one, Warprize?"

I heard a pounding of hooves behind us, even as I reached for the plants. Marcus heaved a sigh. "That'll be the young'un'."

It was Gils, all right, riding his horse at breakneck speed along the army, grinning like a madman. It cheered me to see his simple pleasure in racing his horse like the wind. Marcus grumbled, but the others smiled and made room as Gils galloped to my side.

"Cadr came to see me, Warprize! To ask for help with a bad boil." He smiled broadly at me, his curly red hair dancing in the breeze, his words spilling out. "I told him that I would ask you, that I had to consult with my Master."

I grinned back at him, the young Firelander who had declared himself my apprentice. While Keir had decreed that he had to keep his place as a warrior for now, his secondary duties were to act as my helper. At least until we reached the Heart of the Plains. I'd used every spare minute to give him lessons. "Good. With any luck I can show you how to lance it. But first, Gils, remember what I told you about bloodmoss?" Gils nodded, but I didn't give him time to answer. I grabbed the soft yellow leaves out of Rafe's hands, scattering the rest. "It's there, right there, Gils. Get some for me."

The army continued past as he swung down to join Rafe in picking the plants. The others had gone on alert, something I doubt they were even aware of, moving their horses to encircle us. Even though we were traveling in the center of the Warlord's army, their instincts were to safeguard. There was no danger in being left behind, since the army was moving at a walk, and was spread out over what seemed to me to be miles.

"Prest, do you have any ehat leather to spare?" Epor asked.

Prest cast him a look over his shoulder. "You have a need?"

"The handle of my club needs rewrapping."

"He fancies ehat for the grip." Isdra explained.

"Would take a piece the size of an ehat to wrap that fool weapon of yours." Marcus groused.

I glanced over at Epor, who had his club fastened to his back in a harness. It was a long thick piece of wood, half again as long as my arm, with metal studs along the length of the top and leather wrapped high on the handle. "What's wrong with his weapon?" I asked.

Rafe popped up next to my leg, bloodmoss in two hands. "Marcus doesn't approve, Warprize."

Marcus grunted. "Too slow and unwieldy."

"For you," Epor responded, as if this were an old argument. "I prefer a weapon where if I hit the enemy, the enemy goes down and stays down." Epor gave me a saucy grin and a wink.

I gave Rafe a questioning look, and he laughed at my confusion. "Warprize, a club is a two-handed weapon, best used by a big man with strength in his arms and chest. Like Epor or Prest."

"Not you?" I asked.

Rafe shook his head. "I'm one for speed. Quicker with a sword or dagger. Isdra, Gils or I would strike twice for every one of Epor's blows." His eyebrows danced as he gave Marcus a quick glance. "Or once for every three blows from Marcus with those daggers of his."

Epor laughed, his blond hair gleaming in the sun. "Ah, but in need, even you or Isdra could use it two-handed."

Rafe nodded. "Maybe. If I were desperate."

"Or insane," Isdra added.

Prest dismounted, and dug through his packs, pulling out a fold of dark leather. He handed it to Epor, who nodded his thanks. "I'll replace it, Prest, after the next ehat hunt."

"What exactly is a—"

Gils popped up and handed me a bunch of leaves, laughing up at me. "How much of this do you want?"

I smiled at him. "As much as I can get, Gils. Do you remember what it can do?"

He gave me a scornful look. "I's know, Warprize." He bent to his task, his voice taking on a chanting tone. "Bloodmoss is for packing wounds. It grows at the site of great battles. It will not bind to the flesh, will not stick in the scabs. It seems to aid healing, prevent souring of the flesh and will close the wound. It absorbs as much blood as it can, and when you are done with it you should scatter it about, for the plant will use the blood to take root and grow." He stood, his hands full of more leaves.

Marcus groaned. "A blood-sucking plant. More knowledge than I need."

I was pleased. But Gils's memory had never been a problem in his lessons. Firelanders were blessed with perfect memories, since they had no written word. No, it was the practical application of the information that had been Gils's difficulty. My feet had been a good example.

It's one thing to talk about cleaning and treating a soured wound. It's another to work on a wiggling patient who couldn't help but jerk her feet at every touch. Finally, in frustration Marcus had me lie on my stomach, and he and Keir held my feet as Gils cleaned them. The boy had done the best he could, but the right foot had become an angry, red, and pus-filled wound. Which forced poor Gils to try to clean it out with an angry and worried Warlord of the Plains hanging over his shoulder, watching his every move.

I leaned forward, holding my hand in front of Marcus's face. "It's wonderful, Marcus. Give me your knife and I'll show you how it works."

"Skies above." Marcus jerked his head back and the horse danced beneath us. "It's more like you'll cut your hand off. Not with my knife!"

Isdra laughed, and moved her horse closer. "Show me, Warprize." She pulled her knife and sliced deep into the meat beneath her thumb. Blood welled up quickly.

I took the leaves and twisted them, crushing their fibers. A strong scent of mold rose into my nostrils. "Take this and press it to the cut."

Isdra wiped her blade clean on her trous and sheathed it, then used her fingers to press the mass to the cut. The leaves turned color almost immediately as they drank up the blood, changing to a pale green. Gils craned his head to see, and Isdra lowered her hand to let him get a good look. At my nod, she pulled the leaves away. The skin was healed, with only an angry red line left to show she'd been hurt. Isdra held her hand up to show the others, and let the used leaves fall to the ground.

Prest and Rafe were clearly impressed, and Rafe started to gather the crop in earnest. Gils squatted, staring at the bloody leaves intently. I watched for a minute, then smiled. "Gils, I don't think it will take root while you watch."

"Oh." He was clearly disappointed as he started to gather more.

"And what do we have to be careful of when we use this plant?" I asked him gently.

He frowned a bit, then his face cleared. "Not to use it on a dirty wound. It will seal the dirt inside, if you are not careful." He bit his lip. "I could not have used it on your feet."

"That's right," I nodded. "And it's dangerous to use on a gut wound for the same reasons."

Marcus grunted at that. "Does it have to be fresh?"

"I was told that it works just as well dried, just not quite so quickly."

"I can think of other uses." Isdra smiled slyly. "It would be handy at moon times. Would it grow on the Plains?"

I flushed, uncomfortable even as I shrugged. She spoke so casually about something that wasn't discussed out loud by my people. At least, not in mixed company.

Epor had dismounted, and was looking at the leaves he was holding. His horse nosed his hand, but threw its head up when he offered it the leaves. "Would it work on a horse?"

"Why is it always about horses with you people?" I snapped, suddenly irritated.

There was an uncomfortable silence. The surprised looks on their faces made my pique vanish. I looked down at Marcus's back and mumbled. "I don't know."

Gils, bless his youth, was oblivious. "I's filled my bag, Warprize." His arms were filled with his pickings. "I's can fill another, if you want?"

"That would be good." I looked around, amazed to see that the little plant was spread through the grass as far as I could see. "Two handfuls in each warrior's kit would be useful in case of injury."

Gils quickly handed out his crop, making sure that each had at least two handfuls. Even Marcus took a supply. Gils placed his own in his saddlebags and then mounted. "I'll pass the word, Warprize. Two handfuls"

"Tell them to dry it well, Gils." I called after him as he galloped off. "We'll see to Cadr once we stop for the night."

Rafe mounted up as well, and Marcus headed us back toward the army at a more sedate walk. "Hisself will not like his warriors stopping to pick posies."

"They all have to pass water at some point, don't they?" I pointed out.

Rafe laughed, but Marcus just grunted.

As we returned to our position in the flowing mass of warriors, Marcus was careful to thread his way back into the direct center. Rafe and Prest rode ahead of us a little ways, and Epor and Isdra faded behind us. They didn't really try to maintain any kind of position, since there were warriors all around us. I shifted, trying to get comfortable, and tried not to sigh in Marcus's ear.

Marcus must have heard me, for he cleared his throat. "Epor meant no offense, Warprize, asking about the healing of horses."

"I know, Marcus."

I yawned, tired now that the excitement was over. It had been a brief change from the monotony of the days since Keir of the Cat, Warlord of the Plain, with his dark hair and flashing blue eyes, had taken me up on his horse and reclaimed me as his Warprize. I fingered the leaves that I still held in my hand. Eln would be so pleased to hear that bloodmoss thrived in this area. I could send him a plant with the next messenger, dig it up, roots and all, and wrap it in wet cloth. Even his dour face would crack with a smile at the sight. I'd laugh to see it—except that I wouldn't be there.

Suddenly, it all seemed too much. A flood of sickness rose up in my body, a sickness of the heart for which there was no cure. I was all too familiar with this feeling, for I was sick for my home, for the castle and the people that I'd left behind in Water's Fall. For Anna's stew and Heath's teasing, and my old room with its four familiar stone walls. I'd lived my whole life in sight of the castle of Water's Fall, and I felt sick at the idea that I'd never see it again. I sighed, trying not to feel sorry for myself and failing.

"You've not been yourself, Warprize." Marcus had his head turned, and I could just see his nose and lips under the hood of the cloak. His voice dropped to a low, gentle tone. "You're not eating, and I'm thinking that you're not sleeping either."

I watched the ground pass below us. "I'm fine."

"Are you pregnant?"

I dropped my head onto his shoulder and groaned. "Marcus . . ."

"It's a fair question." Marcus replied. "Our women take precautions in the field, but you Xyians have such strange ways . . ."

"I am not pregnant." I growled. I didn't want to think about that, although he was right. I hadn't taken any precautions. My courses were due any day. But the idea of being pregnant raised issues that I didn't want to consider. Of things that Keir and I had yet to talk about.

"Then what is wrong, Lara?"

The fact that Marcus was using my name, a rare event, told me that he was worried. I opened my mouth, but the truth would not come. "I'm fine, Marcus. Truly."

He snorted. "As you say, Warprize." He stiffened in the saddle, and I knew that I had upset him. This scarred little man had come to mean a great deal to me within a short period of time. He was fiercely loyal to his Warlord, and I was included in that loyalty. I wasn't sure that was by virtue of my own self, or the fact that I was Keir's chosen Warprize. Regardless, how could I confide my worries and fears to him? He already held Xyians in contempt on general principals. My fretful complaints could only heap wood on that fire.

I settled for an obvious question. "When do you think we'll stop for the night?"

"A few hours yet, Warprize. Hisself will keep us moving until we lose the light."

"Why is he in such a hurry?"

"Hisself has his reasons. You're to be confirmed when we reach the Heart of the Plains, and the sooner the better." Marcus's tone was a clear indication that the topic was now settled.

I looked about for a different distraction, and caught a glimpse of Epor reaching over to tug on Isdra's braid. "Epor seems sweet on Isdra."

"Eh?" Marcus growled. "Sweet? What means this?"

I floundered for the unfamiliar words. "That he cares for her."

There was an unnatural pause. I leaned forward. "Marcus?"

"They are bonded." He spoke grudgingly, almost as if the words caused him pain. "Do you not see the ear spirals?"

"Bonded? Is that the same as married?" I twisted about, trying to get a better look at their ears, but Marcus had apparently grown weary of me.

"Ask Epor. Or Isdra." His tone was curt and he whistled, somehow catching Prest's attention. Prest raised a hand, and started to move back toward us. Because I was a burden on the horse, I was traded off every hour so as not to tire any one animal. The elements forbid that a horse be over-tired. I was starting to feel like a package in a trading caravan.

Marcus spoke as Prest moved into position. "Joden is a good man, Lara, valued for his wisdom. He is heard in senel, although he holds no rank, and even by the Elders when he appears before their councils. He will make a great Singer once he is recognized as such."

Prest drew closer, preparing to transfer me to his horse, but I ignored his outstretched hand. I leaned closer, trying to figure out what Marcus was talking about.

"If you can't confide in anyone else, you can confide in a Singer." Marcus's voice was so soft, it was almost a whisper. "Words spoken to a Singer are held to his heart, where they cannot be pried free. Talk to Joden, Lara. Please."

With that, they transferred me to Prest's horse without breaking stride, and Marcus faded back and away into the crowd.

Prest was a full head taller than Marcus and easily twice as broad. I rather dreaded riding with him, since I couldn't see over his shoulders. That meant my stomach would be upset by the time I left his horse.

Prest also wasn't much of a talker, which left me free to dwell on my miseries. If Atira were here, I might be able to confide in her, but she'd been left in Water's Fall, under the care of Eln. Her leg would heal true, but the break would not let her travel. Even surrounded by thousands of warriors, I felt terribly alone. Keir had been absent now for two days, and part of me feared he'd decided that this Warprize no longer interested him. Maybe I could talk to Joden, confide in him. Joden had helped me so much when I'd been taken to the camp. He'd been the one to figure out that I'd been lied to by Xymund, my late half-brother. But I felt so very stupid and silly. Like a spoiled child with a broken toy.

Just how could I tell anyone how miserable I was? Firelanders already had a fairly low opinion of soft city folk, and if I started complaining it would only strengthen their beliefs.

I shifted my weight slightly and gripped Prest around the waist, trying to get comfortable. At least this much had improved. The first five days I'd ached so badly I'd thought to die. Spending day after day in the saddle had wearied my body in ways I didn't think possible.

"Gurt?" Prest held up a soft pouch.

"No," I replied softly, trying not to shudder as my stomach heaved. "Thank you."

Prest grunted and popped a morsel in his mouth.

'Gurt' is a kind of dried cheese, apparently made from some kind of goat-like animal. It looks like a small white pebble, which can be chewed, dissolved in water to drink, or melted over meat. Firelanders eat it at every meal. It stores easily, and never seems to spoil. They all carry a pouch of the stuff with them. While I had gotten to enjoy the taste of their kavage, gurt was another matter. It's horrid, bitter and dry, like a green apple in early spring. It was especially bad when they melted it over cooked meat.

An army on the move has a limited diet. At every

meal, it was cooked meat, gurt, and fry bread. Small bits of the dough were thrown into a pan of fat. That wasn't too terrible, but eating it day after day—well, I never really appreciated Anna for her skills. Or the marvels that Marcus prepared when we were in the camp outside of Water's Fall.

But that had been a full camp. While we traveled, we made an overnight camp, which was a completely different thing. We no longer had the command tent, which was almost as big as some houses, and took a full day to erect. Now it was tiny little shelters that you crawled into to sleep. Or not sleep, as was my case. I'd lay alone in the small tent, wrapped in blankets, and stare at the covering around me. Every little sound, every step of a passing sentry, every snort of a horse, every lump in the hard ground under me had my eyes open for most of the night.

It wasn't so bad when Keir was with me. For some reason I could sleep in his presence. Well, truth be told, I could sleep in his arms. But he had duties and had to travel from one end of his army to the other, and it spread out for miles. So there were some nights when he wasn't in our shelter, and I had not seen him at all for the last two days.

Firelanders could sleep in the saddle. If I tried that, I got sick. Firelanders, in the saddle, could repair tack, or sharpen blades or argue or, Goddess help me, talk.

Which was another thing. We had horses in Xy. I'd been taught to ride as a child, and have ridden many times. But in the city I rarely bothered. By the time a groom had saddled one for me, I could be halfway to where I was going. You had to worry about tying them to things and leaving them for long periods. I'd never been really enamored of the beasts; they were a form of transportation and not much more.

But I'd learned fast that Firelanders had relationships with their animals. Horses were treated like small children, acknowledged and admired. One of the worst insults imaginable was 'bragnect' which meant 'killer of foals'. Now that I knew what the word meant, I was much more careful about how I used it.

And just like proud parents are wont to do, they talk about horses. Constantly. Obsessively. They'd discuss the details of ears and mane and gaits until I wanted to scream. They had seventeen words for a male horse and could talk for *hours* about saddles. They loved to modify saddles with hooks and protrusions and supports, and talk out the advantages and disadvantages. Their world is very dependent on their animals and it was fascinating for about the first day. After that, I tired quickly of horses and horse talk.

And that was another thing. All this talk was out in the open where everyone could hear. They had no sense of modesty or privacy that I could see. I'd had one rider come up and start to discuss the state of his bowels without a qualm, in the middle of a moving mass of warriors. You couldn't really talk to anyone without being overheard.

Ahead of us there was a shout. I peered around Prest's shoulders to see one warrior launch himself at another, carrying him to the ground. The horses shied and shifted a bit, but everyone just kept moving as the two rolled on the ground, fighting. Their horses had moved off, to eat grass as their human riders resolved their differences.

Which was another thing. These people had such fiery tempers and they had no hesitation of attacking for any slight. It was only the exchange of a token that allowed safety for the speaker of offensive words. In Xy, challenge was made clear, with a chance to prepare. Not with these people.

So here I was, Warprize to the Warlord of the Plains, acclaimed before my people and his, praised and admired for my willingness to journey to a new and strange place, to be a bridge between his people and mine. What would they think, to find out that I was sick to my stomach, hungry, exhausted, dirty, alone and certain that the Warlord had lost interest in me?

I heaved a sigh, and tried to tell myself that I was being a soft city woman. That I had no right to complain over minor problems like this. That I was being foolish.

My stomach rolled over, and I focused my eyes off to the side, on the trees in the distance, and tried very hard not to cry.

Joden was broader than Prest, but not so tall. Once I was behind him, I propped my chin on his shoulder and looked ahead, which would help settle my stomach. Eventually.

"You look unwell, Warprize. Are you pregnant?"

Goddess, was every Firelander going to ask me that? "No," I spoke, my tongue sharper than I intended. "I am fine, Joden."

He was silent for a moment, then shook his head. "No, something troubles you, Warprize." Joden's deep voice seemed to resonate through his chest and right into my bones.

I sighed. This was the man who had helped me before,

by explaining the meaning of my title. Perhaps he could help me again. "Joden, words spoken to a Singer are private, right?"

Joden turned his head, trying to see my face. "Yes, if told to a true Singer under the sky. You need to confide, Lara? Something private?"

I nodded. "Just between us. You wouldn't tell anyone?"

He turned the other way, digging in the pocket of his saddle bag. "I am not yet a full Singer, Lara. But words between friends can be held as private." He pulled out a small string of bells and reached forward to tie it in his horses's mane. The soft bells rang with every step the horse took.

Without a word, the riders around us melted back and away, clearing a space around us. As I watched, I noticed that they didn't seem alarmed, or even curious as to what we were doing. "What are those?"

"Privacy bells." Joden seemed to understand my question. "For when you wish to talk or confide without being overheard. The bells are a request for privacy. Don't you have such?"

"No." I leaned forward and kept my voice down. "When we want privacy, we go off into a room alone and close the door."

Joden snorted. "Alone is not easy in the Plains. There are few doors in the tents of my people. Fewer still in the winter shelters. If you hear bells, it's because the person wants to be left alone or is speaking privately with someone."

I frowned, thinking. "Keir didn't use them in camp."

"A command tent carries with it its own privacy, Warprize." Joden seemed to settle in the saddle, as if making himself more comfortable. "Now, Lara, between friends, what is wrong?"

"Oh, Joden." I blinked back tears. "This is so much harder than I thought it would be!"

"Ah," Joden nodded. "You miss your home. That is norm—"

"No." A sob escaped my throat. "Oh, no, that's not—" I took a deep breath. "Joden, it's so boring!"

2

I told Joden everything. How hard it was to sleep with people moving around outside the tent all the time. How much my body ached from riding the long hours day after day. How Firelanders talked about nothing but horses, horses, horses. Their coats, eyes, gaits, their withers, for hours. The food was—well, it wasn't up to Anna's standards, that was for sure.

My voice sounded whiny, even to me, but I didn't let that stop me. I poured out all of my unhappiness into Joden's ear, as the privacy bells chimed.

Finally, the worst of all, was that I was afraid that Keir had lost interest in me. Thankfully, I couldn't see Joden's face as I confessed my doubts. Keir wasn't around, constantly moving here and there, and he didn't always return to our tent for the night. The Firelanders had very different ideas about things, and the women warriors were all tall, strong, confident, and . . . ample.

I lay my head down against his back. "I'm sorry, Joden. I've no right to talk like this. I sound like a fretful child. I mean, I did follow Keir, and I asked for this. It's just that . . ."

"It's not what you expected." I felt his voice rumble through his chest.

"My father used to tell me about his campaigning, and his travels. How hard it was. I just didn't realize that it was so hard and uncomfortable every single day!"

Joden laughed. I was offended at first, but couldn't help but laugh with him.

"So, you thought to become one of the Plains within the space of a few days? You, that have never ventured far from your home of stone." Joden chuckled.

"I guess I did expect that it would be easy."

"And it is not." Joden shifted a bit in the saddle and the leather creaked in response. "If Marcus has a flaw, it's that he believes that Keir can do no wrong. Have you talked to Keir, Lara?"

"No. I'm too embarrassed."

Joden fell silent at that, a silence that was all too much like Eln when he was trying to get me to think about what I had said. And when I did think about it, I flushed in shame. It was the truth, I didn't feel that I could talk to Keir about these things. He was so proud, so confident, so . . . perfect. How could I let him know that his Warprize wasn't? I heaved another sigh.

Joden turned his head slightly, as if to look at me. "This land of yours, this Xy, it is strange to us. Many have confided their unease to me."

"Really?" I looked around the valley, with its hills and trees. The sky above was a bright blue, and the air sweet with the scent of crushed grasses. "Why would they be uneasy?"

"On the Plains, one can see for miles and miles. A storm builds as one watches, and sweeps over the grasses with its rains." Joden looked up to where the mountains blocked our view. "Here, one can see nothing, and the trees block the stars from sight. It is uncomfortable."

"The Plains sound so big, Joden."

"As wide as the skies themselves, Lara." Joden spoke with a smile I could hear. "They hold their own special beauty." His voice was filled with a quiet pride. "But life there is hard, make no mistake about that. We are of the Plains and we accept the harshness, for it is also a life of freedom, and its taste is sweet."

His tone changed. "Keir seeks to change our ways, to ease the harshness, to improve the lives of all. But change is also hard."

I absorbed his words as he took a deep breath to continue.

"We are returning to the Plains, Lara, and normally our hands would be filled with the spoils from raiding. But this time, this army, although victorious, returns with but a Warprize. In your own way, you have more value to us than any goods or foodstuffs. But warriors sometimes only see the prey in hand, or the lack thereof."

Joden took a breath and continued. "Keir is making his way up and down the line, seeing to the needs of his warriors. But he is also reminding them that the bounty from this raid will come in the future, once the snows have cleared. Others work against Keir, pointing to empty hands and sagging saddlebags."

"Iften?" The large, blond man with a scraggy beard who had challenged Keir and threatened me was not one of my favorites. He looked at me like I was some sort of vermin.

"Iften." Joden confirmed. "There are those that heed him, not enough to break their oaths to the Warlord, but enough that they will have second thoughts to his new ways." Joden shook his head. "There will be trouble when we reach the Heart of the Plains."

"Trouble?"

Joden nodded. "But know this, Warprize. Keir has claimed you, and he honors the claim."

"Joden, I don't know what that means."

"We have bonded couples, Lara. Isdra and Epor are an example."

"What does 'bonded' mean?" I craned my neck, looking to see if I could find either of them in the crowd.

"They are sworn to one another, and have been so for many years."

"I didn't know."

"Yes," Joden's voice sounded like Eln's when I had missed something important. "Talk to Isdra, Lara. You must ask questions when you don't understand." He turned toward me again, and I leaned forward to hear him. "Keir has his reasons for the speed at which we travel. He is hoping to avoid some of the opposition if we can arrive quickly."

"Opposition? To me?"

"Yes. Messages were sent but the Plains are wide. He might be able to get you to the Heart of the Plains and confirmed before the major opposition can arrive. Talk to him, Lara. About your fears. This is something Keir must address. My reassurances will mean nothing to you."

I sighed, laid my head on his back and nodded.

"As to the rest, you are doing very well, Lara. For a woman of the city. Have no fear. All will be well."

"Why such a long face, Warprize?" Isdra took over for Joden, and had me on her saddle in a moment.

"Isdra, if one more person pats me on the head like a child and tells me not to worry, I am going to scream."

Isdra laughed. "You can't blame them. For us, one who bears no weapons is as a babe, to be protected and coddled."

I paused, uncertain. Isdra seemed so confident, so sure of herself. I wasn't sure that my confidences would be welcome or tolerated. "Isdra, Marcus said that you and Epor are bonded."

"Marcus told you that?" Isdra's voice rose in surprise. Next thing I knew, Isdra had bells in her horse's mane, and we were being avoided by those around us. "Warprize, I must ask for your token."

I blinked, taken aback, but I fumbled in my pocket for a stone I had learned to carry. "Have I offended?"

"No." Isdra took the token over her shoulder and held it in her hand. "At least, you have not offended me. Lara, I would tell you something that is known, but not discussed. Do you understand?"

"Yes. I think so. Something that everyone knows, but it's not talked about." I groped for words. "Like the people in Xy avoid talking about my brother's death. For fear of my grief. Or anger."

"Aye. You have it." Isdra nodded, then took a deep breath. "Lara, Marcus was bonded."

"Really?" I jerked my head around, to spot Marcus behind us. His chin was on his chest, and he appeared to be sleeping in the saddle as his horse walked along. "But his ear—" I stopped myself. His left ear had been burned away in the accident that left him scarred.

Isdra nodded again. "Aye, his ear spiral melted away with his flesh. I do not know the details, Lara. Don't ask him, even with token in hand, bells all around, and the Warlord at your side. Marcus is known to lash out when the topic is raised. Epor and I try to be considerate, but we know we cause him pain. I was surprised when the Warlord named us your guards, to be open to the skies."

"Oh, Goddess. Was she killed, Isdra?"

Isdra shook her head. "I will say no more, Lara. For lack of knowledge, and for courtesy. But if you wish to speak of bonding. I will chatter like the magpie I am." I could almost feel her grin as she handed back my token.

"Tell me about bonding."

"I'll say to you as I would teach a young one. Not to offend, but to inform." I could hear a rhythm in her voice, as if she were reciting it as she had been taught. She took my silence for assent, and continued. "Here is the way of the Plains. Once the required babes are birthed, and honor won through battle, one has the freedom to choose to enter a bond. Bonding binds two souls, and as with all bindings it can cause pain as well as pleasure. Where once one mind and body worked together, now so must two mesh. This is more of a challenge than the fiercest battle, for a battle lasts but hours, but the work of a bond is constant and never-ending. Adjusting to each other, the bond grows or withers with every breath. Rare is a bonding, but when it is found, it is priceless in the joy it bestows."

"You can't bond until you have had children?"

"And served the tribes as a warrior, yes."

"So," I licked my lips. "Bonded couples don't sleep with others?"

Isdra was silent for a moment. "I have heard that Xyians have different customs than we do. How do you mean, 'sleep'?"

My face grew hot, and I was just as glad that she couldn't see me. "For a man and a woman to lie together. To touch in ways that bring pleasure to both of them."

"Ah. Then yes, bonded couples do not 'sleep' with others."

"How does that—" I fumbled my words, unsure of what I really wanted to ask. "How does that feel?"

Isdra seemed to understand what I was asking. "Ah, Lara, Epor is my heart's fire."

She turned her head and my eyes followed. Epor was off to the side, riding about a horse-length in front of us. His blond braid was shining gold in the sun, and the light caught the beads and wire woven into his ear. One of the other riders said something, and Epor threw his head back and laughed. I felt Isdra sigh, as she looked ahead. "He's a fine-looking man, Isdra."

"Oh, yes."

"Was there a ceremony?" I asked.

"There can be. Depends on the bonded pairs." Isdra laughed. "I walked up to Epor at a dance and announced my intention. The look on his face . . ."

"Do bonded have children?"

Isdra laughed again. "Well, this bonded will not. My moon cycles dried up long ago." Isdra tilted her head to the side. "All bonded are older, Lara. They have served their people in the required ways, and are free to follow what paths they will." She paused. "This is our last campaign."

"Really? What will you do next?"

"Epor wishes to work with the herds. I'd thought of being thea to little ones." She twisted about in the saddle to give me a sly look. "Perhaps thea to your babes."

My face flushed again. "I'm not pregnant, Isdra."

She chuckled. "You're young, Lara. Keir is virile. There'll be babes."

I bit my lip, suddenly angry. Had she slept with Keir? I tried to push that little thought out of my head. Their ways were different, and I knew that Keir had probably been . . . active. But the thought of him with another woman burned in the back of my head.

"As to that," Isdra continued. "We need to make sure you understand our language completely, lest there be errors made. There are many words for 'sleeping' in our language. Let us go through them, starting with—" she broke off her words and looked to her right.

I turned as well, to see Keir riding off to the side. Dressed in his armor, his two sword hilts jutting over his shoulders, he looked every inch the Warlord. It lifted my heart to see his dark hair and those bright blue eyes that had captured my love the first time I saw him. Even covered in dust, and with a fine sheen of sweat on his forehead, he looked wonderful.

Keir rode a bit closer, with an apologetic expression. "If I can break the bells, I'd ask for the Warprize, Isdra."

She nodded, and removed the bells from the horse's mane. My rescuer rode closer, and swept me into his saddle, much to my great relief.

Keir took me in front of him, sideways across the saddle. As I settled in place, he claimed a kiss, a kiss that spoke of hunger, desire and our separation. Any fears that I had of his feelings for me were swept away by the heat that flashed through my body. I understood exactly what Isdra meant by 'fire of my heart'.

He broke the kiss off, and smiled ruefully at my flushed face. "Hold on, Warprize."

As I put my arm around his neck, he urged the horse into a trot, away from the main body of the army. When my normal bodyguards made as if to follow, he waved them off. As he guided the horse, it gave me a chance to study the face of the man who had my heart. It hadn't taken me long to learn that the Warlord of the Plains, the feared Cat, Ravager and Destroyer had an odd sense of the ridiculous. Sometimes when Keir was being stern, he was laughing deep within. This was one of those times, for he had the oddest look on his face, the look he gets when he finds something funny but doesn't want to show it. I looked at him closely. "What amuses you so?"

"Look behind us."

Puzzled, I pulled myself up, looked over his shoulder, and gaped in surprise. Every warrior had a clump of bloodmoss somewhere on his or her person, their hair, their cloaks, their horses. Gils had spread the word well. They had all gathered bloodmoss. I choked back a laugh.

"Now why do I think that you might have something to do with that." Keir's voice was solemn, but humor danced in his eyes. I couldn't help it. I laughed right out loud.

Keir held me tight, allowing his grin to escape. "Care to tell me why all my warriors have weeds adorning their persons?"

"It's bloodmoss. An herb."

"I gathered that." Keir replied, this time in Xyian.

I rolled my eyes and laughed again. Keir's command

of my language was much better than my understanding
of his.

Keir continued, mock growling at me. "It's hard for my
ravening hordes to strike terror in the hearts of the enemy
when they are adorned in weeds."

"It's very useful."

"How so?"

I explained, talking about its usage and offering to cut
myself to show him how it worked. That brought a bellow
of laughter from him, even as he declined my offer. I
didn't pay much attention to our direction until Keir
brought the horse to a stop. "Let's hope that you don't
need that much bloodmoss anytime soon."

We'd ridden a ways off from the army, to a large clump
of alders, their branches thick with small leaves just starting to turn yellow. A warrior held Keir's horse as he dismounted. Keir looked up at me, smiling with anticipation.
I look down into twinkling blue eyes. "What mischief are
you planning, Warlord?"

His smile grew. "None, Warprize. Shall I carry you?
It's not far."

"I can walk." I started to slide from my perch but Keir
put his hands on my waist and slowly lowered me to the
ground. The gesture by itself was not a suggestive one,
but my face grew hot at its implication as he placed me
gently on my feet.

Keir chuckled slightly, and took my hand. "Come, shy
one."

My feet were still a bit tender, but I could walk in the
soft slippers that Marcus had provided. Keir led me
through the bushes, keeping the lower branches off me
with his strong arm. Birds twittered and protested, taking

flight as we worked our way through the growth. We emerged on the shore of a small pond, surrounded on all sides by thick, yellow alders. A blanket had been laid to the side, with bundles piled next to it. I had that brief glimpse before Keir swept me off my feet. "Perhaps the shy Warprize would enjoy a bit of seclusion, for a bath and a meal with her Warlord."

"What? No guards? Just us?"

"Oh, there are guards." He placed me on the blanket and started to divest himself of his swords and daggers. "Beyond the alders, out of sight. I can raise them with a shout, if I need to." He placed his weapons on the corner of the blanket, close at hand in case of need. "Iften is my Second. Yers is my Third. The army will be safe with them for a time. I have something more important to do."

The blanket was soft beneath me, cushioned underneath with grasses. I lay back, and watched as he removed the stiff leather armor, stripping down the under-padding, leaving him in only his trous. My breath quickened as I watched him, and he knew it too, if the occasional flash of his blue eyes in my direction was any indication.

With wonderful grace he settled on the blanket next to me. "Oh?" I arched an eyebrow at him. "And what important task would that be?"

He gave me a knowing smile, and leaned closer, reaching out to pull me in to his body. I yielded willingly, loving the feeling of being wrapped in his strength. Keir nuzzled my ear, and whispered softly. "One that requires my complete attention."

His free hand worked its way under my tunic to stroke my waist. I caught my breath at his touch, shivering with need and anticipation. The alders danced over his head, the pattern of shadow and light all around us. Somehow all my miseries disappeared when I was in his arms. It all seemed clearer, easier. Perfect.

Keir moved his hands up my back, claiming a soft, warm kiss that went on and on. He sat us up, and it was only when my breastband was pulled over my head that I realized he'd left me with naught but my trous. I shivered, and Keir wrapped me in his arms again, easing me back down on the blanket, and I welcomed him into my arms, letting my hands explore those broad shoulders.

His skin was spicy and warm, and I nuzzled him behind his ear as his hands gently stroked my shoulders, stopping to hover over my upper arm. I pulled back and watched as his fingers traced the two pale scars that lay there. His voice was a soft rumble in my ear. "These are well?"

"Yes." The scars were from an attack that had come at my brother's behest. They would fade in time, but the memory would take longer for both of us. Mine, for the fear of the moment, Keir's for the guilt he felt, that I'd been hurt. I reached up to stroke his face, letting my fingers run through his hair.

"And your feet?"

"They're fine." I gave him a look as his fingers drifted down to the waist of my trous. "If we're to bathe, Warlord, why are we lying on this blanket?"

He tilted his head, smirking slightly. "Well, we need to get dirty first, don't we?"

I laughed. "Dirty?"

His hands moved again, burning the skin of my breast with his touch. "Perhaps 'sticky' is a better word?" He grinned at me then, his entire face lighting up.

I smiled back, pulled his head down, and kissed him. He responded, and within moments the alders, the sun, and the world around us melted away. All of my senses were wrapped in him, focused on the feel of his skin against mine.

His fingers drifted back down, under my trous to stroke the curve of my hip. I moved my hands to trail them up over his arm to rest on his shoulder. His eyes were half-closed and he nuzzled my neck, leaving soft kisses along my throat, down to the juncture of my breasts. His tongue traced the under curve, taking my very breath.

"Keir," I whispered, afraid to say more, wanting him to continue. As swift as I could wish, our trous were gone, and his legs were entangled with mine. I ran my foot up his leg, scraping the skin with my toenails. He groaned, then caught my leg in his large hand, pulling it up and over his thigh. But still he teased, denying me the contact I craved.

Instead, he moved his hand to stroke me deep within, responding to my movements and cries to insure my joy. I'd heard tales, of course, of men who took their pleasure and gave nothing in return. But to my lover, my bliss was as important as his own. Goddess knew, Keir was adept, and I tried not to think about how he'd learned those skills. Each time we loved, he proved that the hands that wielded a deadly blade could dance over my body, leaving me breathless and ready for more. This time was no different, as I cried out, grabbing at his arms as I exploded into pure pleasure.

As I returned to sanity, he rolled onto his back, taking me with him, sprawled over his body like a blanket. Now it was my turn, to touch and to tease, using his teachings against him. He let me explore with a will, allowed and encouraged my tentative touches. I knew the male body as a healer, but it was an entirely different thing to watch it respond as a lover. I tried to return the courtesy, letting his moans and movements lead me to bolder and stronger actions. My savage Warlord gasped and trembled beneath me, and that trust wrapped around my heart.

So we loved, under the shelter of the alders, skin sun-touched and shadow-dappled. And when Keir came into me, it was more than our physical bodies joining. It was our hearts and minds caught in a precious moment of shared passion. For an instant, Keir and I were one with each other and the elements that surrounded us, filled with light and joy. It left us gasping for breath, clinging to one another, and, well . . . sticky.

The sun moved quite a bit before we actually entered the water. Keir extended a hand to help me walk barefoot into the pond. The water was cold at first, but it warmed as we went deeper, to stand in water up to our waists.

Keir dived in, disappearing from view. I waited to see where he would surface, but I didn't see him come up. Just as I grew concerned, I felt something grasp my ankle. Before I could cry out, Keir surfaced before me, laughing and breathless.

"Keir!" I exclaimed, wiping the water from my face, laughing in spite of myself.

He chuckled, and strode back to the shore, returning to hand me one of the precious bars of vanilla scented soap. I thanked him, and started to lather my hands.

Keir moved closer, water streaming down his body. "Let me help you with that."

I cast him a sly glance. "Seems only fair, since you're

the one that got me sticky." He reached for me, but I pulled back. "But if you help me, we will never get out of the water."

He quirked his mouth. "I fail to see the problem, Warprize."

I laughed, and he caught me, kissing me soundly. I let my soapy hands trail over his chest. He took the soap, and soon we were laughing breathlessly as we teased each other both above and below the water.

Finally, he growled low, and pulled me toward him for a hard kiss. "Know what is even better than this, Lara?"

I kissed his nose. "What?"

"Food." He released me and headed for the shore, looking back over his shoulder with a wicked grin as I laughed.

I plunged deep into the cool water determined to get every inch of my skin and hair squeaky clean. Bathing from a bucket in a tiny tent is no easy task. Of course, the Firelanders all just jumped nude in the water, any water they could find, every chance they got, and washed each other. Maybe if I bathed under the bells? I broke the surface of the water, laughing at the idea of waterlogged bells.

Even as I washed my hair, I cast several glances Keir's way. Firelanders have no real understanding of modesty, and while it embarrasses me, there are times when I can appreciate its benefits. Keir was letting the sun dry his skin, not bothering to dress. The light through the leaves played over his strong back, and distracted me from my chore. I watched as he dug parcels out of the saddle bags, and laid them on the blanket. I returned to the task of rinsing my unruly locks. I didn't really pay any attention to what he was doing until I got a whiff of a familiar odor.

I was twisting my hair, trying to wring as much water out as possible. "Keir? Do I smell bread?"

"Come and see," he called. He was standing by the shore, with a spare blanket and drying cloth. I splashed through the water to the bank, shivering in the air that now felt cold. He wrapped me in the blanket, stole a quick kiss, and then carried me over to the 'nest' he had prepared.

"It is bread," I breathed, as I settled on the blanket. I took the drying cloth and wrapped it around my hair. "Where in—"

"Sal was buying stock for supplies, and the farmer's wife asked if you were with us." Keir reached for the loaf of bread and tore off a piece. "Apparently she was worried that you weren't being fed properly." He handed me the piece of bread, and a small crock of butter. My mouth watered, and I took the offered knife, and smeared the bread thick with butter and took a bite. I closed my eyes and chewed. The familiar food filled my mouth, and my senses with the taste of home.

"There's more."

My eyes popped open to see a baked chicken, bright apples, and a sweating jug. I grinned at Keir, and tore a leg off the chicken. Keir grabbed for the other one.

For many moments, we just ate, licking fingers and sharing the jug. Keir used his dagger to cut apples into crisp slices. They crunched in my mouth, tangy and sweet. The ale was light, cold and bitter. It didn't take us long to strip the carcass to the bones, and consume every bit of the meal.

I gave a great sigh of contentment as I padded to the edge of the water to wash my hands. I returned to the blanket, and dug through my bag to find my comb and a small bottle of vanilla scented oil. Combing the oil through my thick hair would help with the tangles. Keir tossed the carcass off into the bushes, along with the apple cores. There wasn't a bit left of the bread, or the butter. He washed his hands in the water, and returned to pull fresh trous from the bags. I knew that was more for my comfort than for his.

He rejoined me on the blanket, and lay back on one elbow to watch as I combed my hair. It was still damp, and I took my time working through the snarls. The light was still filtering through the leaves, but there was less of a breeze. The miseries of a few hours ago suddenly didn't seem so important. I smiled at my fears. Amazing what a real bath and a good meal can do for your spirits.

"Marcus told me that you spoke to Joden under the bells. All is not well with you, Lara."

I didn't look at him. "I'm fine. I just had some questions—"

"Look at me." Keir's voice was firm, and I obeyed, slightly resentful of his order.

"This has been hard on you." His voice was quiet, and he gave me an intent look. "Marcus has told me that you are trying to cope as best you can." Keir rolled his eyes. "I got an earful about the abuse I am putting you through."

I smiled, knowing very well the sharp edge of Marcus's tongue. "You're not abusing me. I'm doing fine."

"I'm sorry for this." Keir shifted to lay flat on the blanket, his hands on his chest. "I'd slow our pace, but I can't. We need to arrive at the Heart of the Plains as soon as possible."

"Joden tried to explain, but I'm not sure I understand."

Keir turned his head to look at me with his blue eyes. "I sent messengers to the Elders at the Heart of the Plains the very night I claimed you. They will have sent messengers of their own, summoning the other elders and warrior-priests. The ceremony will start when we arrive, under the open skies for all to see. If we hurry, the ceremony will be held before all can make the journey. There are some I would prefer to avoid."

"Can they deny my confirmation?" I leaned forward a bit, and the blanket that I had wrapped around me dropped slightly.

Keir's eyes fixed on me, but not on my face. "I don't want to talk about the future, Lara." His eyes grew sultry, and his voice roughened. "I don't want to talk at all." He rolled back on to his side, and reached over to tug on my blanket. "I'd rather talk about the way the sun is dancing on your skin. How you smell like vanilla. How the light is being caught in your hair, and kept prisoner."

I flushed up, put the comb down and moved toward him, letting him pull the blanket away from my body. His eyes were half-closed as he pulled me in close, wrapping me in his arms. He nuzzled my neck, and his hand drifted down to my buttock. "Too long apart, Lara. I've missed your touch, your heat, your—"

I opened my mouth in a jaw-cracking yawn.

Keir pulled back, looking into my eyes. I blinked at him, my vision suddenly blurry and tired. He shook his head, and then pulled me down to lay next to him, my head on his shoulder. "Sleep, Lara."

"Keir, let's not waste this haven. I can sleep late—" Another yawn cut me off.

"But you won't, and haven't, have you?" He stroked my back, rubbing circles softly on my skin. "Put your head down, and close your eyes, Lara. I'll be here, watching over you."

I yawned again, the warmth of his body and my full stomach defeating me. Keir chuckled as I relaxed, and I felt him pull the blanket up over us, even as I drifted off to sleep.

I woke to the odd feeling of something tugging my hair. Keir had spooned up behind me, and his arm was draped over my hip. The odd feeling was a robber jay, tugging on one of my curls that were spread over the blanket. I'd heard of them from my father, large grey birds that feared no one and nothing, and that stole whatever they could get their hands on. The bird tilted his head, looking at me, then jabbed at my curl again, trying to pull it away.

Keir's hand flipped out, and the bird took flight, scolding us in the process. I felt Keir nuzzle my neck, and I hummed softly at the pleasure.

Keir chuckled. "You smell wonderful."

I turned slightly, smiling into his blue eyes. His hand drifted up to cup my breast and I groaned at that simple touch. "One stroke of your hand and I feel such wonderful things."

"There's more," he whispered.

I kissed him, ready and eager for more when there was an outburst beyond the bushes. Horses, a lot of them, pounding up, with warriors calling out for Keir.

Keir sprang to his feet, with sword in hand. I fumbled for the blanket, pulling it to my chest to cover myself.

"Warlord!" The voice that came from beyond the thick alders was high and tense. "I must report."

"What news?" Keir sheathed his sword and grabbed for the rest of his gear.

"Rebellion, Warlord!"

3

The tradition of the Plains is that the Warprize takes nothing except from the hands of the Warlord. This was not, as I'd originally thought, to keep the Warprize subservient and dependent on the Warlord. Rather, it was to allow the Warlord to demonstrate that he had the ability and strength to provide for the Warprize.

This had resulted in some rather rigorous arguments with Marcus, self-appointed guardian of the tradition, once I'd returned to my Warlord's side. I had won on the issue of my healing equipment and supplies, since Marcus grudgingly acknowledged that Keir had purchased them for me while we'd been encamped.

Marcus had won on the issue of clothing, since that scarred little man had worked miracles in providing me with tunics and trous, and even one memorable red dress. While the clothing he provided was plain, it was also comfortable.

I'd won on the issue of undergarments.

Keeping the blanket around me, I struggled into my breastband as fast as I could, listening to the sounds of warriors and horses moving around our shelter. The leaves somehow didn't seem as thick as they had been a few minutes ago. "Keir, it can't be my people."

Keir grunted, reaching for his armor, called out in a strong voice. "Yers!"

"Warlord?"

"Call senel to hear the report. Warn Marcus, and find Joden as well. Summon the Warprize's guards."

Yers's voice was raised beyond the thicket, carrying out his orders, even as Keir stopped speaking. Keir continued to dress, his movements as fast and precise as a cat's. "We'll know soon enough, Lara." His face was grim as he rearmed himself.

I paused, my arms buried in my tunic, fear coursing through me. "And if it is?"

"It will be answered," was his gruff response. He gestured for me to continue, and I pulled the tunic on over my head, fighting to pull my hair free.

It had been one of my greatest fears. While I'd convinced Warren, the Lord Marshall, and the entire Council of the wisdom of accepting Keir as Overlord, we'd all known that the outlying areas might not be quite so accepting. Messengers had been sent to spread the word, but events had moved fast, even faster than the pace Keir had set for our return to the Plains. It was possible that one of the smaller villages had decided to defy the command, but I thought it unlikely. No single village had the wherewithall to close its gates and refuse to submit. The long summer of fighting before Xymund had conceded defeat had taken men from the villages. There was a question as to whether we had enough workers to take in what was left of the harvest, much less resist a foe. For in one thing, Keir was implacable: oathbreakers are punished absolutely, and completely. If a village or town swore fealty to him, and then rejected his control, he would raze it to the ground and salt the cinders.

I struggled with my hair, trying to free it from my tunic, as Keir waited impatiently. "I'm sorry. I should probably cut this mess off."

Keir stepped forward, and eased his hands under my hair, pulling it free for me. "Don't." His hands were warm and I shivered as he brushed my neck. I tilted my head up and he lowered his and kissed me. There was a sense of desperation, almost fear in him, and I brought my arms up to hold him close. He wrapped an arm around me as well and deepened the kiss until I ran out of breath.

He raised his head, and we stood in each others arms for a moment, until the sounds beyond the alders reminded us of the world around us. He stepped back with reluctance. I straightened my clothing, and he waited until I finished, but stopped me when I reached for the blankets. "Leave that." He turned, and started through the thick branches, again keeping the branches off my face as I followed. The birds protested again as we emerged from our haven to find Yers standing there, holding his and Keir's horses. Prest, Rafe, Isdra and Epor were coming up behind him.

Yers handed Keir his reins. "There's a large willow at the top of a crest down the road. I've called the senel to meet there, and have summoned the scouts."

I stood there, breathing hard, trying to braid up my hair. "What has happened?"

Yers shrugged, his crooked nose twitching. "All I know so far is that the scouts were attacked by Xyians."

"Injuries?" Keir asked.

"Unknown." Yers responded.

"Send word to Ortis that I want the scouts involved at the senel." Keir mounted, the leather creaking as he pulled himself into the saddle. "We'll go on ahead." He turned to speak to Prest and Rafe as Yers mounted his own horse. "Gather up the Warprize and her things, and bring her along. All four of you with her at all times. If they are offering challenge to me, they may well target her."

Epor nodded. "Marcus has gone ahead to prepare. Something about 'doing things right by Hisself'."

Keir gave a grim smile. "Marcus would serve drink in the midst of battle, if he could."

"Keir," I stepped forward, but he cut me off.

"Lara, there's no point discussing this until we know more."

"Keir, I—"

Keir shook his head, and his horse jumped forward. Yers was quick to follow, leaving me standing there in the dust. I put my hands on my hips, glared at their backs and called out to them as loud as I could. "The least you could do is let me ride my own horse?"

Yers had described it perfectly. The willow was old and bent, its long branches trailing on the ground, moving slightly in the breeze. I could make out people moving within its shade, and there was a smell of kavage in the air. As we rode up, Iften and Yers emerged from behind the branches, and Iften's voice was raised in complaint. "—wasting time, neglecting his duties, all he thinks about is plants and illness. Pah."

Yers responded mildly. "You'd not think it a waste, were it to your benefit."

They turned to look at us as we brought the horses to a stop. Iften had the usual sullen look that he carried whenever he saw me. I was riding behind Rafe. And saw him turn his head to look at Prest. Then they both seemed to glance at Epor, who nodded. The silent communication somehow also included Isdra, who rode up next to us and dismounted. Epor and Prest dismounted as well. Prest led off their horses, and Epor stepped to my side. "May I assist you, Warprize?"

I was about to protest the need for help, but something in his eyes stopped me. I accepted his assistance, and he lowered me carefully, keeping his body between me and Iften. Rafe moved off, and Isdra stepped up behind me.

"What is this?" Iften growled. "You have no place at senel, Epor."

Epor nodded, calmly accepting Iften's challenge. "True, Warleader. But the Warlord has trusted us with the safety of the Warprize, and commanded two of us at her side at all times." He said nothing more, merely adopting a neutral look. I took my cue from Epor, and remained silent. A quick glance behind me showed that Isdra was also keeping her face bland, looking almost bored.

"It's an insult." Iften spat, his cheeks flushing red under his beard. I wasn't sure, but I had the impression that Epor had managed to offend him somehow.

"It's a precaution, and a wise one." Yers countered.

"It's the Warlord's command." As if that was the end of the discussion, Epor inclined his head to the two leaders, and moved forward. They gave ground, moving with us under the branches. Iften's face was still red and angry, but Epor's remained bland, offering no offense.

There was a warrior there, holding a pitcher and a cloth. As I washed my hands, thanking the Goddess under my breath, I realized what the silent exchange had been about. Rafe and Prest had known that Iften would be difficult. Epor, older and with higher standing, had stepped in to handle the problem. Status was a critical part of Firelander life, although I had yet to really understand it.

Marcus had set two folded blankets at the base of the tree, and had arranged others in a pattern fanning out. He was waiting for me there, his cloak off, and frowning. "Sit here, Warprize. Kavage? Gurt? How are your feet?"

I sat, folding my legs under me. "Just kavage, Marcus, please. And they're fine."

He nodded, served me and moved off. Epor and Isdra took up positions behind me, but Marcus didn't offer them anything. I'd learned that they wouldn't eat or drink while on guard duty. But I noticed for the first time that he never really looked at them at all. Just past them, as if it was too painful to see them standing there. I looked into my cup of kavage and sighed. I'd been so lost in my petty misery. What else had I missed?

I could almost hear Great Aunt Xydell scolding me. "Pay attention, chit."

Keir was obviously taking precautions. The senel and the tree were surrounded by guards, watching over us and the horses. Rafe and Prest were beyond the branches, but had positioned themselves so that they could see me clearly. It was comfortable here under the tree, but a tightness had crept into my neck and shoulders. If some of my people were resisting, after they'd pledged their fealty to Keir, the consequences would be severe.

The area was starting to fill with the members of the senel. They stood, mugs in hand, as Marcus moved among them. I watched and considered.

Senels are basically councils for the army. I still hadn't figured out the details of the command structure, but I'd learned that the army had one Warlord, who had ten Warleaders under him. Each Warleader had command of a section of the army, and additional duties as well. Simus had been Keir's Second, Iften his Third. Their ranks were determined through a series of combats, not necessarily by the Warlord's choice alone.

I glanced to the left of Keir's 'seat', where Simus would normally reign. I missed Simus. His laugh, his smile, his eyes gleaming in his dark face, his overwhelming confidence. As Keir's Second and as his friend, he'd sat at Keir's left hand in senels before this. But Simus had remained behind in Water's Fall with half of Keir's forces to secure and protect the City, and be Keir's voice in Council. I'd had one letter from Othur, the Warden I'd left in my place, which indicated that things were going well. Beneath Simus's smile and good humor was a man of honor and wisdom. I felt the lack of his presence and voice.

I looked back at the others milling about. I was familiar with a few of the warleaders already. I'd met Sal when she'd come to me for advice on equipping the army and dealing with the Xyian merchants and traders. A stocky woman, with weathered skin and grey hair turned white by the sun, she loved to bargain for supplies. Yers, an average-sized man with brown hair and a crooked nose, had been Gils's Warleader, and had been involved when

Gils had surprised everyone with his intentions of becoming my apprentice.

Iften made himself known by being rude and obnoxious, something he was skilled at. He'd shown early on that he despised me and all things Xyian, and didn't hesitate to voice his opposition to Keir at every opportunity.

I smiled to see Joden enter the area, and he smiled back. Joden was not a warleader, but was acknowledged as the potential Singer that he was.

The others I was less sure about.

"Isdra?"

"Warprize?" Isdra took a step forward and knelt by my side.

"Can I ask you about the warleaders, without bells?"

She chuckled, keeping her voice low. "Yes, Warprize. You know Yers, and?"

"Iften." We exchanged wry glances. "Sal, I've met before. She takes care of supplies for the army."

Isdra nodded. "Aret is standing with Iften." She was referring to a tall, thin woman with short, curly brown hair. "She's in charge of the horses, and the herds when in camp, seeing to their well-being. Yers has the training and discipline of young warriors. Iften is now Second, so the senior warriors are also in Yers's care."

Iften had that position because Simus of the Hawk had remained in Water's Fall.

Isdra continued. "Wesren is the warleader in charge of encampments, Ortis, the large man at the back, is charged with the scouts."

Wesren was a short, thick man with thick black hair and beard. Ortis was a huge, lumbering hulk with a shaved head. He made Wesren look like a boy.

"Uzaina and Tsor are warleaders in charge of the army

when on the march. Uzaina takes the lead, Tsor works the rear."

I looked over, studying them. Tsor had skin the color of kavage with milk in it, and short black hair with traces of grey at the temples. Uzaina caught my eye, for she had her black hair in what looked like hundreds of small braids, each ending in a bead. They brushed her shoulders when she moved her head, making an odd clicking sound. Her skin was the color of dark amber, and the combination was very striking.

"So each has a duty beyond fighting. Right?" I asked.

"Yes. Except Seconds, who have the duties as the Warlord assigns. Duties do not change, ranking does. You understand? If Keir were to fall, skies forbid, Iften would lead."

"Become warlord?"

"No. That requires the Elders." Isdra made a slight snorting sound, which I interpreted to mean that event was unlikely.

Marcus approached, and frowned at Isdra.

Isdra made a face at him, but stood and stepped back, which seemed to appease him.

Marcus knelt to fill my cup. "Hisself will be here shortly."

I looked him in the eye. "And if it's true rebellion, Marcus?"

He shrugged. "It will be as it must." He rose, cutting off the conversation, and moved away.

I took a sip of kavage. Why would a village of farmers and their families defy the Warlord? Did they think to use pitchforks and hoes against him? It made no sense.

But then Xymund had shown me that there was little 'sense' to be had in war.

* * *

Keir strode in, signaling me with a hand to remain seated. He accepted kavage from Marcus, nodded to a few of the leaders, and then moved to kneel next to me. He shook his head at the question in my eyes. "I know no more. The scouts are outside, we will hear their report together."

I leaned forward, speaking in Xyian. "Keir, Iften is talking against Gils. I'm afraid that he will try to use him as a pawn against you!"

Keir frowned, and replied in the same language. "What is a 'pawn'?"

I blinked, then shook my head at my own stupidity. How could he know, since I doubted he knew the game. "It's a piece in a game. A pawn is an unwitting tool. An innocent person used against a friend."

"Ah." Keir stood and moved to stand before his blanket, waited until he had the attention of the group, and then sat, sinking down onto the pad. While Iften was second in command, there was no place made for him at Keir's side.

The rest seated themselves, and Keir waited a breath before calling them to order. There was less formality at this senel then there had been in the past, but I could see Marcus at the back, and he had Keir's token in his hands.

Keir spoke, silencing the group. "I have called for the scouts who met with violence, to hear their truths." Keir gestured to Marcus, who pulled aside the leaves. Two men entered, walked to stand before Keir, and knelt, heads bowed.

"Ortis."

At the sound of his name, Ortis stood. "Warlord, I assigned the scouts sent to cover the front. I sent these two warriors, Tant and Rton forward along the road to the village."

"A village sworn to us?" Keir asked.

"Aye. The headman, the leader . . ."

"The mayor?" I asked, using the Xyian term.

Ortis nodded. "That is the word he used, Warprize. The mayor had sworn fealty to you some weeks ago, Warlord. The walled village, where the goats roamed around the well."

Keir chuckled. "I remember. They called it Wellspring. The mayor almost soiled himself during the oath." There was a soft murmur of laughter at that.

A walled village meant that it was a remnant of my ancestor, Xyson. Few of those guard forts remained on the main road, fewer still had managed to retain a complete set of walls.

"Tant. Rton."

The other two men lifted their heads. I recognized Tant, since he'd been the scout that found me on the road, following Keir. His eyes widened to see me sitting there, and he looked down, clearly uncomfortable.

The other man, Rton, spoke first. "We approached the village to find the gates closed, Warlord. We hailed them with a shout, but there was no response."

Rton glanced at Ortis, and continued. "We moved closer then, and I dismounted to approach the gates, when someone started throwing rocks at us from the walls. A voice cried out, and then more rocks, and finally an arrow arched over the wall."

"What did the voice say?" Keir asked.

"I have no city talk, Warlord. But it sounded angry and defiant." Rton gestured nervously. "I mounted, and we moved off but there was no pursuit."

"Our orders are, we meet resistance, we retreat and report." Tant spoke up quickly, almost defensive. "So we circled round the walls and came back at a run."

"How many warriors were on the walls?"

Tant and Rton exchanged looks. Tant shrugged. "Didn't see any, Warlord."

Rton nodded his agreement. "They never exposed themselves to us."

"This wall," Iften spoke up. "How is it made?"

"Stone at the front and around the gates." Rton spoke with confidence. "Wood to the sides and back. They've built wooden structures inside, that sometimes take the place of a wall."

"Easily overcome?"

Tant nodded. "Easy enough, Warleader."

"Shouldn't we talk to them first," I argued, "before you make plans to destroy the village?"

"What else can this be, but defiance of the Warlord?" Aret asked.

"So much for their pledges and honor. Typical." Iften's voice was scathing.

Yers spoke, his face reflecting his conflict. "If they have defied the Warlord and broken their oaths they must be punished."

Keir looked grim. "Is there anything more to report?" Ortis shook his head, and Keir dismissed the two scouts. When they were beyond the leaves, he spoke. "Joden, what say you?"

Joden sighed. "Warlord, your path is clear. If this is defiance, and a breaking of their vows, they must suffer the penalty. But we know from experience that the different languages can cause problems of understanding." He gave me a look, and I nodded in return, sharing the memory. Joden continued. "I say, be on a war footing, but approach the village again with a speaker of their tongue. Be sure of the offense before dealing punishment."

"I agree." Keir glanced over at me. "We will give them a chance to explain their actions. But if they have shattered their vows, we will be ready. Ortis, what chance of ambush?"

"The scouts all report no activity, Warlord."

Keir turned to Iften. "Ready a warforce, Iften. As many as you think you need. If we are denied again we will attack, and raze the village to the ground. Any other truths we need to address?"

"A discipline problem, Warlord. The warrior Gils–" Iften scowled, but Keir cut him off.

"Now is not the time for a discipline problem, Iften."

"Especially when the man is my responsibility and not yours." Yers chimed in.

Keir stood, and we all stood with him. "The senel is over. Prepare to move out."

I moved closer to stand next to Keir, biting my lip. The warleaders left swiftly, as Iften called for them to get organized. Once the area was clear, I turned to Keir. "Keir—"

"No." He didn't even look at me.

"Keir, it has to be someone who speaks Xyian. It should be me. I am a Daughter of Xy. Queen of Xy."

"And touched by the moons if you think I will allow you to approach those walls." Keir focused on me, his gaze intent. Marcus, Epor and Isdra were glaring at me. Even Rafe and Prest, who entered the shelter of the tree once the warleaders had left, were glaring at me.

I smiled sweetly at them.

"This is going to be a problem, isn't it," Keir asked.

"Yes," the others chorused.

Keir growled. "Lara, if the village is rebelling, and if this is an organized response, they will try to pull others to their cause. Who would they want to kill first and foremost?"

"You," I answered promptly.

That stopped him, but he gave me one of those patient looks. "And after me?"

"Iften."

"No." He frowned, upset. "Do not play with me, Lara." He put his hands on his hips. "Perhaps the best answer would involve chains and a tree."

I glared right back at him. "Keir, you need someone who speaks Xyian. I am the best choice."

"You are not. A warrior, someone who speaks Xyian and can defend himself is. You would have me send a boy to do a man's job."

I flushed, but he held up his hand. "It's a saying of my people, Lara. Send the right person for the task the first time. I will send a speaker of Xy. We will give the village a chance to surrender and explain themselves. You will be kept back, until we know more." He fixed me with a look. "I will be obeyed, Warprize."

I took a deep breath and opened my mouth to argue, but the words never emerged. Marcus launched himself at my throat.

In an instant I was down on the ground, flat on my back, my breath gone from my lungs. Marcus's thin body was on top of me, pinning me with all the considerable strength in his wiry frame. Worse, he had a blade at my throat, the metal cold against my skin.

I opened my mouth, trying to gasp in air, my heart hammering in my chest. No one else moved.

"This is no child's game," Marcus hissed, his voice as harsh as I had ever heard. "You have no skill, none—and death comes in an instant."

I just stared at him, his disfigured eye, his puckered skin, frightened and wide-eyed.

"Do you understand?"

I nodded carefully and swallowed hard, very aware of the sharp blade pressed against the pulse of my neck.

Marcus pulled back and just as fast as he took me down, I was up on my feet and in Keir's arms. I clung to him, shaken. "That was harsh."

"And the elements are not?" Keir asked me softly.

"Better you learn at my blade than at another's." Marcus brushed off my back.

I shrank from his touch, trying not to cry. "Keir . . ."

"Harsh, but the lesson is true, Lara." He tightened his arms around me.

I buried my face in his chest and tried to get myself under control. "I'll do as I'm told."

Keir chuckled. "At least until the shock has worn off." He drew in a deep breath. "It won't stop you from flinging yourself to the aid of others, I know. All I ask is that you think before you do, and that you let us protect you. Yes?"

"Yes."

He leaned down and nuzzled my ear. "Ah, my Lara. I took you from your sheltered den, kitten."

"No." I straightened, wiping my face. "I left my den and chased you, remember?"

Keir smiled and kissed me gently. "I will send someone to speak to the village. You will stay with your guards, toward the center of the main army, back from the front."

Rafe cleared his throat. "I have enough of that tongue, Warlord. I am willing to go."

Marcus spoke up as well. "I can fill his place as Lara's guard." Keir looked at him and Marcus shrugged. "You will have no need of me, and it takes four to watch over this woman." Marcus gave me a wicked grin, but I looked away.

Keir lowered his head to speak softly in my ear. "Lara, understand this. I will send Rafe to the gates. But one rock, one arrow, one word of defiance and I will destroy the village."

"Keir, there are innocents there." I leaned back to look into his face. "Women and children who have no part in this. If we can talk to them, we can convince—"

"I will not take back an oathbreaker, nor will I leave one unpunished."

"But—"

He released me. "What would the penalty be, Lara, if a village broke its oaths of fealty to the King of Xy?"

I looked away. "I do not know. It hasn't happened that I know of."

"Because the penalty is severe. My hand can rest lightly on this land, but not on those who defy me. I will do what must be done."

With that Keir was gone.

I waited under the tree as Marcus hurriedly put out his small fire and two of the others gathered up the blankets. My feet were still tender, and I shifted my weight from one to the other as I stood there. They weren't really painful, but they reminded me that they weren't completely healed.

As we emerged from under the tree, one of Yers's men

approached me, leading a large brown horse. "For you, Warprize. From the Warlord."

I looked over to where Keir was standing, talking to Yers, Rafe and some others. Our eyes met and Keir gave me a small, hopeful smile. I smiled back, recognizing a peace gesture, and took the reins.

The horse was a glossy brown, with a brown mane. What caught my eye about it was a white line of hair that curved down its chest to run between its forelegs. On looking a bit closer, I saw that it was an old scar. The horse shook its head as I got closer, and buried its nose in my hair and took a deep breath. The hairs on its muzzle tickled my neck. I tried to move away, but the horse followed, breathing out and in again, filling my hair with its warm sweet breath.

"He likes you." Marcus had handed off the packhorse to another warrior, and now sat astride his horse, with a shield on his back and a sword at his side. He looked my animal over with a considering eye. "A good, steady animal. You shouldn't have a problem with him."

Which I took to mean that the animal would be slow, and one a sick granny couldn't fall off of. But at least I wasn't being toted around like a sack of flour anymore. I pulled myself into the saddle, noticing that this horse had a number of scrapes and scars on its legs and hindquarters. He'd seen quite a bit of action in his day. "What is his name?"

"Name?" Marcus gave me a funny look. "We call them 'horses'."

The others moved in around me. I noticed that Marcus placed himself so that his blind side was covered by Isdra. "I know they are horses, Marcus. What is this one's name?"

"I suppose you will now tell me that city dwellers name all their horses." Marcus rolled his eye, and the others chuckled.

I closed my mouth.

"Tens of thousands of horses," Marcus continued. "and we should name them all. Pah."

Rafe laughed out loud. "Now tell all, Marcus. We name stallions and mares."

"Lead stallions. Lead mares. Not entire herds." Marcus gave my horse a withering glance. Its ears were flicking back and forth, as if following the conversation.

"But how do you tell them apart? Or get them to come to you?" I asked as I mounted.

"What's to tell?" Marcus asked. "Rafe's black, Prest's brown with the notched ear, Isdra's roan with the scarred whither. And they come because that is the way of things. And while you might think so, they don't all look alike. Any more than people do."

I gave him a look, and would have asked more, but I was interrupted. "We're to move to the center, Warprize." Epor's tone was firm.

"I understand." We headed out to join the main body of the army. "How far to the village?"

"Not far," Isdra replied. "The Warlord will take the warforce and form up before they send Rafe to the gates."

"He will send word, Warprize." Marcus added.

Resigned, I nodded, and concentrated on guiding my mount.

We traveled for sometime before we passed a stone pillar, about waist high, with a hollowed top, which marked the boundary of the lands claimed by the village. A glint of light off the tip caught my eye. It could just be rainwater, but . . .

I tugged on the reins and started to work my way through the other warriors, urging my horse into the gaps between riders. He went willingly, shouldering aside the ones too slow to get out of our way. There was some loud swearing behind me, Epor from the sound of it, but I didn't stop. Marcus, too, was cursing, but it was too late for him to try and stop me. I broke through the line of warriors and turned my horse back. Urging him to a canter, I headed back to the pillar. Marcus and Prest were behind me, I could hear them urging their horses on.

I reached the stone to see that the hollow was filled to the brim. I didn't bother to dismount, just leaned over and dipped my fingers in the fluid. If it was water, well and good. But it hadn't rained, and . . .

Breathing hard, I lifted my fingers, and the tang of vinegar filled my nose, making my eyes water. Vinegar, one of the strongest cleansers known. Vinegar, which, when placed in the hollow of a boundary stone, turned it into something else entirely.

". . . *one rock, one arrow, one word* . . ." Keir's voice rang in my head. Goddess, I had to reach him before it was too late. I yanked my horse's head around, forgetting to be gentle. The horse fought me, tossing its head in protest, but it turned nonetheless. Marcus and Prest came up, their faces drawn into scowls, their horses snorting in protest.

"Warprize," Marcus started, but I cut him off.

"I need to talk to Keir. And that scout. Now, Marcus."

Marcus gave me an odd look. Prest turned a bit, scanning ahead down into the valley. Epor and Isdra galloped up, both frowning. "That was not well thought out, Warprize." Epor scolded.

"It was stupid," Isdra added.

"I need to talk to Keir. It's important."

"Do you see him?" Marcus asked.

"No," Prest replied.

Marcus tilted his head back, and warbled out a long, trilling cry.

A response rose from the mass before us, and Marcus responded again, making a slightly different sound. He turned toward me. "Come."

He urged his horse into a gallop, and I followed right behind.

Keir sat on his horse in the midst of turmoil, as the warforce prepared to move out. Yers and Iften were near by. The village was not yet in sight, for which I was thankful.

"Keir!" I called out as Marcus led me to his side.

Keir turned in our direction, frowning. "Lara, this is not safe—"

Iften was close at hand. "If she were a warrior, she'd be whipped."

Keir snarled, and lashed out at Iften, hitting him full in the face. Iften crashed to the ground. He jerked to his feet, hands curled into fists. Keir's hand was on his sword, his horse solid beneath him. "You take a hand to the Warprize and you die."

There was a pause for a breath, as everyone seemed to freeze. Then Iften bowed his head, and the moment was gone. The man remounted as Keir whipped his head back around to face me. "You will—"

Marcus interrupted him. "She says she needs to talk to you."

"Keir, I need to talk to the scout. This may not be what it seems."

Keir shook his head, visibly reining in his temper. "Lara, I know you don't want this to be a rebellion, but you must face the truth."

"Once more. Let me talk to him once more, then you can have Prest haul me off," I begged. "Please."

Keir scowled, but he called to Yers. "Find Tant and bring him here."

It didn't take long. I was talking before he drew his horse to a stop. "Tant, tell me again what happened at the village."

Tant looked at Keir, who glared at him, then turned back to me. "We rode up, Warprize, rode up to announce our presence and the army's. Only to find the gates closed against us. I stayed ahorse, but Rton dismounted and went to bang on the closed gates, and they threw rocks at us." Tant was clearly offended.

"Just rocks?" I asked.

"And arrows." He was affronted by my questioning him. "They fired arrows at us. They hit the ground at our feet."

"But didn't hit you?" I pushed.

"What's the point, Lara?" Keir asked.

"At us," Tant insisted. "They shot at us, but they missed. What are you saying?" Tant's eyes narrowed. "You doubt my word?"

"I think there was a different reason they drove them off." I looked at Keir. "A reason that has nothing to do with rebellion."

"They're defying him," Tant sputtered. "My word on it."

"Tant, I—"

"They even painted the gates with blood in their defiance," Tant rushed on angrily. "If that's not rebellion, what is it?"

My heart froze in my chest. "Blood? On the gates?"

"Aye, and fresh, too." Tant seemed proud of himself, at his final proof.

Keir's gaze was on my face, and I looked at him, unsure how to voice my fear. He frowned. "Lara?"

"Tant," I pushed the words through my dry throat. "Was there a pattern?"

"Pattern?"

"A design? Like a mark?"

Tant paused, thinking. "Aye."

"Show me," I demanded.

Tant shrugged, dismounted, and knelt in the dirt at our feet. He reached out and traced a 'P' with his finger.

I sucked in my breath, my worst fear made real.

"What is it, Lara?" Keir asked softly.

"Plague."

4

"Lara? What is 'plague'?" Keir's voice was sharp.

"Marcus," I jerked around in the saddle to look at him.
"I need Gils. My supplies, where are my supplies?" I'd
need fever's foe, more than what I had at hand. Gils could
make more, he'd learned that much.

"Xylara."

That jerked my head around, my eyes wide. Keir rarely
used my full name, and never with that tone before. He
was sitting on his horse, looking as if his patience had
gone. I swallowed hard. "I need Gils and my supplies."

"You need to explain, Lara. I have a warforce poised,
as you prattle about supplies. Tell me now, what is it about
this illness that changes things in any way?"

"It's plague. An illness that kills."

"Illness kills?" Keir ran his hand through his hair, frowning.

"Yes, of course it does." It took a moment to understand the full meaning of that question. But surely it was because he didn't know the word. Yet, my breath caught in my throat. His eyes were full of doubt, how could he not understand?

"There is no 'of course' in this." Keir responded in a voice that cut like a blade. "Are you telling me there is another explanation for the village's actions? A valid one?"

Holy Goddess. He didn't understand. "Keir, the villagers were trying to protect your men. It's not a rebellion." Keir frowned, but he listened as I continued. "Under our law, an afflicted village closes its gates and keeps to itself until the disease has run its course. They fill the boundary stones with vinegar as a warning, and warn off any who try to enter. It's not you they are fighting!"

"So." Keir thought for a moment, then gestured to Iften. "We'll position the warriors, but well back from the walls. No one is to attack except at my command. Full battle gear, I'll not have any warrior dead of overconfidence."

He pulled back on the reins, preparing to go. "Marcus, take her to the rear. Get her into some armor quickly, then come when I send for her," he glared at me. "And only when I send for her."

I opened my mouth, but he cut me off with a gesture. "And find Gils and get her what she thinks she needs. I will call for you when I am ready. Understood?"

My guards nodded, but it wasn't enough for me. "Keir, what are you going to do?"

"As I'd planned before. We will move into position, and send a messenger to the walls."

"Rafe. He needs to take precautions, I will—"

Keir didn't take his eyes off me. "Rafe, go with the Warprize. Epor . . ."

Epor moved his horse up slightly. "Aye, Warlord?"

Keir's gaze never wavered. "Keep her back, Epor. Within sight of the walls, but at a distance. And I order you to wrestle her to the ground and tie her to a tree if necessary."

I flushed up at Keir's words, biting my lip.

"Aye to that, Warlord." Epor responded, a bit too enthusiastically.

"No word for plague?" I asked.

I turned my head to look at Marcus, and my new helmet fell forward over my eyes, hitting my nose.

"It's too big." Gils said, a knowing tone in his voice. "Shall I get another one?"

Marcus moved forward, as I lifted the rim off my eyes, and I flinched as he drew closer. He stopped, and looked at me, then took a step back.

Isdra grunted as she worked to stuff me in a heavy leather jerkin, one that had been made for a warrior larger than I. "Take it off, and twist up your hair, Lara. We'll use the braid to help cushion it."

Gils took the helmet from me. "Perhaps some of the clean bandages would help."

"What is 'plague'?" Rafe asked. He was mounted, as were Epor and Prest, surrounding us and keeping watch. Epor had taken Keir at his word, and we'd moved to the rear to find the supply horses and Gils. While warriors were milling about us, we were far enough from the action to satisfy my guards. I was standing in the grass as they tried to fit me with various pieces of armor.

Once Keir had reclaimed me as Warprize, messengers had been sent to Simus and Othur at Water's Fall. They had in turn sent a messenger with letters of relief and joy and pack horses full of my healing supplies and equipment, all carefully packed for the journey.

Keir and Sal explained that with an army of this size, the best way to insure that I always had supplies at hand was to split everything equally between four pack horses and spread them out. No matter where I was, one of the horses would be close by.

"Plague is a kind of illness that kills, and kills many people very quickly. It spreads . . ." My voice trailed off as I looked up into Rafe's puzzled face.

"So, like winter sickness that spreads in the lodges. A misery, nothing more." Marcus said as he rummaged in a saddle bag, pulling out some long leather bracers.

"What is winter sickness?" I asked, running my fingers back through my hair to start the braid. The long sleeves of the jerkin were stiff and uncomfortable.

"A misery to be endured, for a time."

Gils cleared his throat, trying to interrupt. At my nod, he spoke. "It affects the body, Warprize, with coughing, and sweating and feeling bad."

I blinked in the sunlight as the mounted force seemed to swirl around us. The worst these people suffered was head colds? I looked back at Marcus. "No, plague is an illness that kills young and old, healthy and sick. It spreads quickly, and is very dangerous."

He gave me a doubtful look. "There are stories . . ." His frown deepened. "For us, injury kills. Accidents kill. Being cursed, or afflicted, those can kill. But the one afflicted takes themselves off, to live or die as the elements decree. But illness? Illness is uncomfortable, but not a matter of death." He let out an exasperated snort.

Prest looked over at him. "Tell her the rest."

"Rest?" I asked sharply.

Marcus shrugged. "There are tales told of city folk."

"What kind of tales?"

Isdra finished the lacings on my jerkin, and stepped back to survey her work. The thick, stiff garment hung on me like a sack. She considered me, frowning. "Maybe if we belt it around the waist."

"No need." Epor spoke from his horse. "It's not as if she has to fight in it, just ride."

"What tales?" I demanded, impatient with them. What hadn't I been told?

Rafe answered slowly. "We would not offend, Warprize."

"Oh for Earth's sake." Isdra snorted. "We have a saying. 'Raid them for their treasures, leave them in their filth.' There are songs of cities found with their gates closed, the people lying dead in the streets from their filth and corruption. Punishment for their sullying of the elements." She reached over to help me wind my braid on the top of my head, and put the helmet on. "I've walked the streets of your city, Warprize. While it was not perfect, it was not knee-deep in filth by any means."

The rags that Gils had padded the helm with slipped down to dangle in my eyes. I felt incredibly stupid, but my fear was stronger than my dignity. I focused on Rafe as Isdra stuffed the cloth up under my helmet. "Rafe, when you go up to the gates, touch nothing and no one."

"Yes, Warprize."

"Gils, tear some cloth into small pieces and douse them with the oil in the green bottle."

"Aye, Warprize." Gils started to work. Isdra accepted the bracers from Marcus, placed one on my forearm and started to tighten the lacings. I tried to stand still, but it was frustrating not to be able to move.

"Gils, now add four drops from the slender blue bottle." I watched him dribble the scented oil out slowly. "Let me smell it."

Gils lifted the bowl to my face with two hands, wrinkling his nose. Isdra turned her head, and sneezed.

"Good," It was strong enough. "Let them sit for a bit. Rafe, if someone comes out of the gates to talk, stay well away from them."

"Yes, Warprize."

"We'll give you some vinegar. Wash your hands and face with it after you return, before you come back to us."

"Yes, Warprize."

"Now, take two of those cloths from the bowl, roll them up, and put them in your mouth, between the gum and cheek."

Isdra had finished with the bracers, and she knelt to tie some kind of leather over my thigh and shin. Marcus, moving slowly, knelt at my other side and did the same.

"Er," Rafe looked at the oil soaked cloths that Gils held out to him. I could smell the sharp scent of ginger from here. "Warprize, is this necessary?"

I pointed at my helmet. "Is this necessary?"

"Yes," Rafe's answer was prompt. "Death comes in an instant. All it takes is a stray arrow."

"Then so is that." I pointed at the cloth. "Oil of ginger acts to prevent the spread of the contagion. Healers keep slices of ginger in their mouths when they treat people with the plague. This is the best I can offer."

Rafe nodded glumly, and stuffed the cloth in his mouth, screwing up his face at the taste.

"Now roll up two more pieces and put them up your nose."

They all stopped and stared at me in consternation.

I glared at them and tapped my helmet.

Rafe tilted his head back, and roared with laughter, startling the horses. The others laughed as well.

"So be it, Warprize." Rafe wiped his eyes and accepted two more pieces of cloth. "I will armor against your invisible foe. But I will wait until the enemy is a bit closer, eh?"

Marcus and Isdra stood and without thinking, I flinched back from Marcus. But this time I caught myself. "I'm sorry, Marcus. I don't understand why—"

"I do." He answered gruffly. "Think not on it, Lara." His eyes regarded me steadily. "The fear will fade. But not the lesson, eh?"

"I will remember."

Isdra had taken a step back, and put her hands on her hips to regard me. "It will serve."

I felt the fool. "The enemy will die laughing."

"So long as only the enemy dies." Marcus growled. "Up now. We need to be ready when the Warlord calls us forward."

We mounted up, with Gils scrambling to secure the pack horse with the healing supplies. The leather jerkin was chafing at the back of my neck, and I shrugged, trying to get comfortable. How did these people wear this all the time? But then I looked over at Rafe, wiping his eyes, probably from the fumes. I sighed, and resolved to live with the discomfort of my armor. At least for now.

As we moved out, Prest leaned over, and handed me a

small wooden shield. I took it, surprised at its weight. "What am I supposed to do with this?"

He grinned at me, his teeth white against his dark skin. "Hide behind it."

Iften had moved his warforce into position, ready to strike like a sharp knife. The warriors were poised, lances rattling in the quivers attached to their saddles. Their horses were churning the ground with their hooves, eager to run. My horse, on the other hand, was drowsing, his head hanging low.

From where I'd been positioned, I could see the village, with the 'P' on the gates, the blood now dried and brown. It looked small and vulnerable to my eyes.

"All right, Lara. I say again, what is 'plague'?"

Keir sat next to me on his horse, in full battle gear. Those blue eyes that had been soft and warm in our bower under the alders were cold and hard.

Having talked to the others, I was ready for Keir's disbelief. I described a plague, and told him the precautions the village would have taken. "To a Xyian, the 'P' on the gates is a warning of horror and death."

"We know nothing such as that." Keir offered, staring at me intently. Iften was seated next to him, but he said nothing, choosing instead to glare at me through his blackening eye. I returned Keir's look calmly, never so conscious of the gulf between us as that moment. Were we so very different? And if so, could we ever truly understand each other? My fears surged a hundredfold, for it meant that he had no understanding of what he faced.

I gestured toward the village, careful to keep my head still so that the helmet would stay in place. "Keir, the plague is a danger greater than any army, and your weapons are useless against it." I'll never know why, maybe the look on my face, but thank the Goddess, Keir listened. He turned his head and looked at Rafe. "Has she told you what to do?"

"At least ten times," Rafe flashed us a grin, his eyes still watering. "I've donned my armor, Warlord, against the Warprize's invisible foe." His voice sounded odd, what with the cloth in his nostrils and mouth. "I'm ready."

"The skies be with you."

With that, Rafe turned his horse, and started toward the walls at a walk. We'd gone over the various words for illness and plague, and Rafe had repeated them to me. He was to approach the gates, learn what he could, and report.

I shifted in my saddle, making the leather creak beneath me, startling my horse. He flicked his ears back, and I patted his neck to reassure him. I'd have to think of a name for him.

I looked out, and Rafe seemed to have barely advanced. Another fidget on my part drew Epor's attention. He had positioned himself on my right, by my horse's head. He turned his head so that he could see me from the corner of his eye. "Warprize, if an arrow flies, we'll head for the rear, away from the combat. Is that clear?"

I nodded, which just made the helmet tip forward and block my vision. I pulled it back into place. "I understand."

"A pity," Isdra's low comment came over my shoulder. "He's never tied a warprize to a tree before."

The chuckle from the others made me smile too, a bit ruefully. Somehow I didn't think it would take much on my part to get Epor to make good on Keir's threat.

As Rafe continued to amble down the road, fear clutched at my heart. What if I was wrong? What if the

villagers were defying the Warlord? If so, they were defying me as well. Queen of Xy, I'd made the decision to
bind our peoples together. Or at least to unite with Keir for
that reason. They could be resisting my decrees as well as
breaking their oaths to Keir.

If so, this army was poised to teach them the error of
their ways. I had no false notions as to the strength of the
village's walls, or their weapons. Keir would kill everyone, and burn the village to the ground, as an example as
well as a punishment. When word went back to Water's
Fall, what effect would that have on my people? My
Council?

Yet I almost prayed for a rebellion. Better that than
plague. Goddess above, how could I explain the dangers
to a people whose worst illness was a head cold? Plague
respected no boundaries, no rank, or worthiness. You
couldn't rush the treatment of plague either, forty days
being required to assure that the contagion was gone.
How could I tell Keir that he'd have to wait that long?

I shifted the shield on my arm so that it rested in a different place on my thigh. How did they carry these heavy
things all the time?

There was another factor, one that I didn't even want to
admit to myself. The last plague to afflict Water's Fall had
been the sweat some twenty years past. I'd been a babe at
the time, and been told that I'd had a minor case that I'd
recovered from quickly.

Could I deal with this on my own? Never mind that the
supplies I had with me might not be enough, that was an
entirely separate issue. Could I diagnose and treat an entire village?

My horse sensed my unease, shifted his weight and

stamped his front foot. I patted him again, letting him settle down. Maybe something from the *Epic of Xyson* would do. I frowned trying to recall what Xyson had named his battlesteed. Blackheart? Stoneheart? Something-heart. I had a copy with me, I'd look and see. Of course, that horse had been a warrior, a true battlesteed. I smiled as I felt my horse shift its weight, and lower its head, clearly about to take a nap.

I felt my shoulders relax a bit too. I'd learned at the hands of Eln, a true Master of the healing arts. I'd learned the symptoms of the four major plagues, could recall their history back to Xypar, some five generations back. We'd had warning before being exposed, messengers could be sent, help would arrive.

But like Gils, confronted by a living, breathing, wiggling patient for the first time, I had my doubts.

'The first rule is to never let them see your doubt.' Eln's voice whispered in the back of my head. *'You try. That is all you can do. All any of us can do.'*

I smiled at the mental image of my master, but the smile faded from my face.

Rafe had reached the gates.

He seemed so small, seated on his horse before the walls. He was staying at least a horse length away from the structure. I saw him tilt his head, and call out to the villagers, the faint echo of his voice reaching us on the wind. I held my breath, but no heads appeared, no rocks, no arrows. Just silence, and the sound of the warriors around us.

Rafe called again, and then set his horse to walking back and forth in front of the gates as he stared at the wooden structure. I held my breath, and then had to breathe again and again as he stood before the walls and called. My sorrow grew as the silence did. How many were dead? Or dying?

Keir signaled to Ortis, who put his head back and warbled a cry. Rafe raised a hand, turned his horse and headed back to us.

At the midway point, he stopped as instructed, took out the bottle of vinegar, and leaning over, washed his hands and face with it. I'd told him to repeat the action, and watched as he did it four times. I could just make out his lips moving at this distance, and I was sure he was invoking each of the elements.

Once that was done he rode up to us, his face red from the scrubbing. "Warlord, there was no response, no sound, no movement that I could see through the chinks in the gates."

Keir nodded. "My thanks. Return to your guard duties."

Rafe grimaced, spat the cloths out of his mouth and snorted them from his nose. "Warlord, I'd ask leave to go plunge myself in the nearest stream. The Warprize's precautions are almost more that a warrior can bear." He looked at me through swollen eyes. "That's a truth, Warprize, whether or not I hold your token."

Keir nodded his approval, and Rafe took off like a startled bird.

"So." Keir looked out at the village. "Iften."

"Warlord."

"Disband the warforce. Tell Wesren to make camp for the night, away from these walls. In the fields beyond that willow, perhaps. His decision."

Iften glowered, but made no objection. He turned his horse and left us, calling to his men.

Keir continued to sit, staring at the village as the warforce melted away. "Brave people, to enclose themselves within those walls and wait for death." A shudder went through him. "I doubt I could do the same."

"Wait for death?" I replied, sharper than I intended. "Not if I can help it."

"How so?" Keir asked mildly. I wasn't fooled, for his gaze was sharp. "How can you help them?"

"By going in there, of course."

Keir gave me a long, incredulous look. I returned it unflinchingly. There was no change in his expression, he just reached out and grabbed the reins near my horse's chin. "No." Without another word, he turned the horses and started to follow the warriors. Marcus and the others moved into position around us.

"Keir—"

"No, Lara." He didn't even look at me as he led the horses forward.

I threw my leg over, grabbed the saddle with both hands and slid to the ground. My horse's pace was enough that I stumbled back a step or two as I landed, enough to throw Prest's horse off his stride. Isdra got hers stopped and the look she gave me almost made me laugh out loud.

But Keir's face choked off my mirth. His face was a storm cloud building in the sky, dark and angry, and his eyes the lightning. He dismounted and stalked over to me, leaving the horses to stand where they were.

Prest leaned down to push a strip of privacy bells into my hand. I closed my fingers around them, but never took my eyes off Keir.

"There aren't enough bells in all the tribes . . ." Marcus let his voice trail off as he and Isdra pulled away, as Epor and Prest did the same. They gave us plenty of room, but kept their watch just the same. I wasn't sure why, since the biggest danger of all was standing, towering over me, the muscle in his lower jaw pulsing with his anger.

"What means this?"

"Keir, we have to help these people."

"Didn't you just finish telling me the dangers of this plague? Of the deaths it causes? 'A danger greater than any army' That is what you said." Keir ran a hand over his face. "Why would you even think to enter those gates?"

"To aid the sick, and care for the dying. To learn which plague it is, and where it came from. Keir, it may already be in the kingdom. We must warn Simus and Othur and Eln. The more information we have, the better prepared—"

"No." Keir cut me off and started to pace, moving with his usual grace. His horse watched us carefully. Mine had fallen asleep again, his head hanging, ears flopping over, eyes closed. He'd put all his weight on his left leg, his right hind foot cocked behind him.

Keir cut through my line of sight. "We must be at the Heart of the Plains as soon as possible. Your confirmation must take place as soon as possible. If we delay, we lose our advantage."

"Keir, these people swore an oath of fealty to you, an oath you demanded. Winning Xy as a fiefdom doesn't just mean taking the spoils. It also means taking responsibility for the people of Xy." I pulled the uncomfortable helmet off, letting the bandages fall to the ground and ran my fingers through my hair to untangle the braid. "The oaths flow both ways."

"We pass it by, flow around it as the stream flows past a stone. Acknowledging their sacrifice, but keeping clear of the danger."

"We can't do that. We need information. The army may already be exposed since you've traded with the farmers that we have passed. I am a healer; I have sworn oaths to aid those in need. I have to go in there." I smiled at him. "A healer goes where she is needed. To a Warlord's side or into a stricken village."

"That's insane. You are the link between our peoples; the only Queen of Xy and the only Warprize. I will not risk you."

"I swore oaths when I claimed my Mastery. As you did when you became a Warlord. They require me to serve these people."

"It's more important for your people that you become the Warprize."

"Keir, Xy was a nation of traders and merchants in my great-grandfather's time. But the plague swept through the land and decimated the people. It killed so many that the trade routes through the mountains were closed. The Xy you conquered is a far cry from the rich land of the past."

He turned, looking down at the gates, radiating fury.

I stepped next to him. "If plague has returned, we must give them aid, and learn as much as we can. We need to send word back to Water's Fall."

"What need?" Keir looked skeptical. "It will stay where it is, caught within those walls."

"No." I rubbed my hand over my sweaty neck. "If they are that sick, they can't even tend to the dead, Keir."

He grimaced, knowing all too well what that meant. "We will send for aid from Water's Fall. They can be here within five or six days."

"We can't wait that long. If we wait for help from Water's Fall, we may only have dead bodies and no one to tell us what happened and how. I must go, Keir, and now."

He glared at me.

"I am a healer, and these people, *your people*, need my help."

"These people are not worth one drop of your blood."

I looked at him steadily until he looked away. "You are thinking as a lover, Warlord."

His head snapped back, and his eyes flashed. "I am a lover, Warprize."

My cheeks flushed at that, but I didn't give ground. "If your people had the healing skills, you would aid them."

"Do you understand what you are saying?" Keir growled.

"I understand exactly what I am saying, Keir. My people need yours, for protection now that our forces have been exhausted, for links to trade, for our future. My people have enough to see them through this winter but they will need every bit of harvest that can be salvaged from the fields to survive. If it is plague, if it spreads from here . . ." I closed my eyes against that possibility. "Why do you send scouts out, if not to know what you are going to have to deal with? We have to know and the only way to know is if I go in."

"There must be another—"

I glared at him. "And if it gets to the Plains? What of your people? Will the warrior priests aid them?"

He stopped, jaw clenched, shoulders tight, his hands in fists. He started to curse and the words that poured from him at that point were not ones that I knew. He stopped, breathing hard. "There must be another way." He resumed his stalk, and started ranting. I'd not expected this to be easy, and it wasn't. As he paced, he repeated each of his arguments and I refuted them again, knowing that I was right. I started to work on the jerkin's lacings. These heavy leather garments were warm, and it was chaffing my neck. How did they wear this armor all the time?

Finally he spun to look at me, and jabbed a finger in my direction. "We can send Gils. He—"

"You'd send a boy to do a man's job?"

He flared like a fire doused with oil. "You are the last living member of the House of Xy. I'll not risk you. I'll not risk what we are trying to do for our people." He took a step closer, and I fought the urge to step back. "I'll not risk all this for a tiny village. Who will know? Who will see?" He turned, headed for our horses.

"The skies will know."

He stopped dead, his back to me, his hands clenched in fists.

My heart in my throat, I continued. "The Goddess will know."

The silence between us lengthened. There was no sound, not even the bells in my hand. Just the wind, whipping at the grass and my hair.

The tension left his hands first, as his clenched fingers slowly uncurled. Then his back and neck lost their stiffness as he took a deep breath. I moved the bells in my hand, letting them chime softly.

He turned and walked back to me, a rueful look on his face. "I should have known. From the moment you defied me in the marketplace, I should have known. There is more honor and stubbornness in one slight Xyian woman than in my entire army."

"Slight?" I raised an eyebrow.

He smiled, and raised a hand to cup my face.

"Keir, leaving these people would be as big a mistake as—"

"As when I plunged my sword in Durst's chest."

I nodded.

"I would not do this, my heart's fire." Keir stroked my lips with his thumb.

"All the other alternatives are worse. There is no choice, Keir." I stepped closer, and wrapped my arms around him. He enfolded me in his, and we stood for a long moment, a long moment of fragile peace.

I stepped back, finally. "I have to talk to Gils."

"We'll have him at the senel." Keir looked off in the distance, toward the army. "A few days delay will not be that great a loss."

I opened my mouth to correct him, but closed it as he turned back to me. "Come, Lara. Let us be about this as quickly as possible."

I took his hand without saying a word and we walked back to the horses.

If Iften didn't remove that smug look from his face, Keir was going to do it for him.

The senel had been called, under the same willow tree. The warleaders were gathered, and Marcus had managed a meal of warm gurt and fry bread. Kavage was brewing on a fire, and the smell of it filled the air. But I could barely choke down my food, my stomach was so tense. Now that Keir had made the decision I was eager to go, to find out what we were facing. If I left soon, I'd have daylight to take stock and talk to the remaining villagers. Please Goddess, let there be living souls within those gates. Xy had stories too, just as the Firelanders did, of whole towns filled with the dead and dying. Not here, Lady of the Moon and Stars. Please.

But before I could go, there were things I had to tell

them, had to teach them. I couldn't leave an entire army unprepared for the realities of a plague. But before I could teach them anything, I had to convince them of the threat. Gils was seated by my side, wide-eyed as he listened. His thin body trembled with suppressed excitement.

Keir's announcement that we would aid the village was met with puzzled looks by some and pure disdain by others. "Leave them to rot in their filth," was Iften's contribution and it was met with almost complete agreement.

But it was the statement that I would go into the village that caused that smirk on Iften's face. He remained silent as the others protested and argued, handing Keir's token from one to another. They made the same arguments that Keir had made to me, and Keir patiently went through everything again, refuting them as I had done to him. Only when Keir had finished, and there was an uneasy silence did Iften speak. "How brave and noble is the Warprize to go to the aid of the cursed." His tone was silky and insulting.

"Will you match her courage and offer to go with her?" Keir countered. There was an odd sound to his voice, and I was certain that swords were about to be drawn.

Joden's voice cut through the tension. "So it's true then, the songs of old, that tell of cities laid waste by illness."

"It's rare, Joden," I reassured him, making sure that my voice hid my fears.

"Can horses get it?" Aret leaned forward a bit, a worried look on her face.

"Not that I've ever heard of, Aret."

"But city folk do not live with their horses as we do," Uzaina countered.

"Maybe our people do not catch this illness?" Wesren asked, sounding wishful.

"The medicines of the Warprize work on our people. I fear that the illness will as well." Keir sighed. "I can't risk that. I will not risk taking this to the Plains. Can you imagine it among the children and the theas?"

Iften snorted, waving his hand over the group. "We are all hale and well, Warlord. There is no trace of this 'plague' among us."

"But we've traded with farmers along the way, and there was contact while we were encamped outside the city walls. The Warprize has said that there is a waiting period to insure that the illness is gone."

There was a stir toward the back, and Tsor rose. He was a big man, with long thick black hair. "Warprize, I would ask for your token."

I looked at him in surprise, startled that he'd feel that he needed a token in his hand. Gils nudged me, and slipped a small jar of fever's foe into my hand. I held it up, and Tsor stepped forward to take it. "I hold your token, Warprize. I give voice to one truth."

"I will speak to your truth." I said, curious to hear him.

"Warprize, I have seen the healing that you have done, and I have heard the words of the Warlord. I would not offend, but I am troubled. We of the Plains have a strong tradition of passing down our knowledge by the words of our theas and our Singers. But your people, they rely on words that are on 'paper' and in 'books'." He used the Xyian words slowly, as he played with the small jar in his hands. "You keep your wisdom in these things. And you do not have a 'book' here to tell you of the past." He cleared his throat, and shifted his weight, clearly uncomfortable. "Perhaps your memory is wrong?"

There were soft gasps around the gathering, and even Keir sucked in a slow breath. Marcus was glaring at the man as if he'd insulted me, and maybe to their way of thinking he had. Gils sat up straight, indignant. I put a hand on his shoulder, afraid that he would do something rash.

"Tsor, it's true that my people put their learning into 'books' in order to save it. But the lessons learned from them are well learned, especially on the subject of 'plague'." I let my gaze travel over the group. "My teacher was Eln of Water's Fall, and he insisted that we learn and know the—" I had to pause, they have no word for 'symptom'. "The signs to look for and how to treat them."

Tsor, still holding the jar, opened his mouth but I wasn't done. "I can't say that my memory is as good as yours. But my knowledge and my skill are from years of learning and doing. You understand?" I looked at him closely as he nodded. "Have I answered your truth?"

"You have, Warprize." He handed the jar back to me, and sat back down.

"So." Keir spoke. "We will aid the village. Wesren, this will be an extended camp. See to it."

Wesren was nodding, but Yers stood, his face thoughtful. "I'd ask the Warprize what to expect from the weather at this time of year."

I thought for a moment. "The Goddess's Lace won't be for a few weeks, Yers." I could tell that he didn't understand. "The first hard frost. We say that the Goddess is weaving the lace for her wedding. The snows start a few weeks after that."

It was clear that my explanation had confused him further. "So it will continue to get colder as the days shorten?" When I nodded, he grunted and sat down.

Sal spoke up. "Warlord, if we are to be here for any length of time, I must need supplement the supplies. How long will the time be, before we can safely move on?"

Keir turned to look at me. "Warprize?"

I licked my lips, and my eyes fell to my lap. "Forty days."

All I could hear was the beating of my heart in my ears. I looked over, to see that Keir's face had turned to stone. My breath caught in my throat, and a sick pit opened in my stomach.

Iften's smug look was an open grin. "You would delay forty days?"

Marcus frowned when Keir failed to respond, his gaze shifting from my face to Keir's. I froze, terrified that I'd gone too far. I'd lured him into this trap, but what choice did I have? The people of the village needed my help. But I'd seen his anger before. Would he support me, or—

"For the safety of our people." His voice a rasp, Keir turned his head to look at Sal, letting me see the small muscles in his jaw clenching. "Forty days. Plan accordingly."

Coward that I am, I avoided Keir and kept Gils at my side after the senel. Marcus had gathered all of the pack horses, and Gils and I split the supplies evenly between us. I talked to him as we worked, going through the various plagues and their treatments. I'd already prepared the letters for Othur and Eln and the messengers had left for Water's Fall at a gallop, with strict instructions to throw the letters to the guards at the gate. I was fairly certain that within a few days, a week at the most, Gils would have help.

Gils listened earnestly, his gaze locked on my face, absorbing my words. He nodded fiercely, and repeated things back to me, constantly reassuring me that he would be watchful and that he would remember what I said.

As we worked, I was aware of a brooding presence close by. Keir had not spoken to me, but I felt his gaze scorch the back of my neck.

Keir had gathered Marcus, Joden, Epor, Isdra, Rafe and Prest near him, and they were talking quietly. I didn't know what they were discussing, but there were occasional glances in my direction. I continued with my work, conscious of the tension in my shoulders and neck and that my feet were starting to throb.

It was only when Gils and I had finished that Keir stood, and stalked over to me. The others followed, their faces grim.

"I am ready to go." I had one of the horses. Gils had kept the others. Keir's eyes pierced me, but I kept my gaze steady. I'd come too far to break down now.

"You will not go alone." Keir gestured, and Epor and Isdra stepped forward. "They will accompany you."

"Keir, it's too dangerous. They—"

"No." He cut me off, leaving no room for argument. "We have seen no sick or dying. It could still be an ambush. You will have warriors by your side, or you will not go."

"We have chosen this, Warprize." Isdra's voice was reassuring.

"To face an invisible enemy? What songs they will sing of us, eh?" Epor smiled. "Joden is already humming under his breath."

Joden shrugged and everyone except Keir chuckled uneasily. Keir's face was still a stone, marred only by the tiny pulsing muscle in his jaw.

"There is one more thing." I paused, not sure how to phrase this request.

"Whatever it is, I am sure you will have your way, even if you have to lie to make it so." Keir spat.

There was a pause, and the others started to step back, as if anticipating the bells. But Keir raised his hand. "No."

Everyone stopped. Gils flushed a bright red, and was staring at his feet. My face was hot, but I didn't drop my eyes.

"Speak."

"We need to arrange signals. To let you know what kind of plague it is. To communicate what is happening. Because as soon as we know the kind of plague, we will need to send someone to Water's Fall to shout the news to them. Those warbling cries, maybe?"

Joden smiled. "They are used in battle, or in the hunt, Warprize. They are not meant for talk. But let us see what we can do."

Thankfully, with their memories, it didn't take long to assign new meaning to the calls. I thought up as many contingencies as I could, then cleared my throat. "We need one more. For if all three of us sicken and all the villagers are dead. We must set fire to the village and kill ourselves, to prevent the spread of the disease."

Keir's face was stark. The others were grim. Joden spoke softly. "I thought mercy was not your way, Lara."

"It is not, Joden. But I will not allow this illness to spread. To your people or to mine." I looked at Epor and Isdra. "Do you understand what you are risking?"

"We do." They spoke together.

"And do you swear to—"

Keir broke in. "You are not yet confirmed, Warprize. Do not exceed your authority."

I glared at him. "But I am a Master Healer. They have to promise—"

"They will do what must needs be done." Keir's look was chilling.

I dropped my eyes and tugged at the horse's reins. "We need to go. We are losing the light."

We rode in silence to the point where we could see the village gates clearly. There was no change, no sign that our presence had been noted or ignored.

We all dismounted, except for Keir. Isdra took the reins of the pack horse we'd loaded with supplies. I turned to my apprentice and smiled at him. "Gils—"

Gils launched himself at me, and squeezed me tight. I heard a faint whisper in my ear. "I's make you proud, Lara. I's swear it." He stepped back and gave me a smile, red hair gleaming in the sun. "Skies watch over you, Warprize."

Marcus stood there, looking unhappy and worried. "And now is when you stuff the cloths up your nose, yes?"

I nodded, too choked up to speak, and hugged him. "Take care of Keir."

"Always. But who will care for you?" He asked gruffly as I stepped back.

Keir was on his horse, as cold and remote as the mountains that surrounded us. He didn't look at me as he spoke. "Skies be with you."

I took a deep breath, and waited. Keir didn't look down.

Resigned, I turned away. I accepted the bowl that Gils held out, and Isdra and Epor and I stuffed the cloths in our nose and mouths. "Hope they leave this part out of the song." Epor grumbled as we moved off. I was thankful for the sharp ginger in my mouth, coming up through my nose as I breathed. It explained the tears in my eyes.

There was a noise behind us. I turned, only to see Gils take a few steps to catch my horse, who had started to follow us down the road. The horse protested a bit, but settled under Gils's hand. Keir didn't move at all, and I turned back toward the village. Isdra and Epor were right behind.

We were almost to the gates when I couldn't take it anymore.

I stopped and looked back.

Isdra and Epor gave me a knowing look, but kept walking.

Keir was off his horse, and Marcus was next to him, his hand on Keir's shoulder. Gils was leading my horse back to the other horses. As I watched, Keir raised his hand.

I smiled, and raised my hand as well. Then I raised the other, and slowly brought them close to intertwine my fingers to form a fist. I hoped Keir remembered when he had done that in the command tent, when he announced his intent to weave our people together. I hoped he understood.

He seemed to, since he raised his hand a bit higher in acknowledgment. At this distance it was hard to tell, but he looked stricken to me somehow. As if I'd taken all his hopes with me.

Which I had.

Tears in my eyes, I lowered my hands and turned away to follow the others. I didn't look back this time. I didn't trust myself not to run back and throw myself in his arms.

And I didn't trust him not to tie me to a tree.

5

Long before my time, King Xy had insisted that a main road be built from Water's Fall through the length of the entire kingdom to the border with the Plains. One of his great grandsons, either Xytell, or maybe Xykreth, had built watch forts along the road once the Firelanders had started raiding up into the valley.

Each watch fort had been heavily fortified, with stone walls and high battlements, modeled on the walls of Water's Fall. Each with a deep well and storage warehouses for food. They'd been designed to allow a contingent of warriors to be self-sufficient in times of battle. But they had all fallen victim to the one enemy they could not hold against: Time.

Walls collapsed, and the locals carried off the stone to

build huts and low walls to keep in their sheep and pigs. Only a very few remained intact, and most of them were closer to the border than to Water's Fall. While I'd read of them, I'd never seen one, since I'd never ventured more than a few hours from the city.

As we approached, I could see that this was one of the last remaining forts. Strong stone walls rose around the village proper, and the gates were logs, bound in metal. I could see the plague sign on the wood. The blood was dried. Epor watched our backs as Isdra stepped forward and pounded on the gates.

There was no response. We stood for a moment, hearing only the faint sounds of the army behind us, and the wind in the trees. I resisted the urge to look back again, to see if Keir was still watching.

Isdra pounded again. She stood with her hands on her hips, her head cocked, listening intently. "Nothing. I'm going in."

Epor grunted, and stepped forward to boost Isdra up and over the gate. Her boots scrabbled against the wood as she pulled herself over. Epor gestured me back, getting his weapon ready and facing the door. But there was only the sound of bars being pulled back, and then the one side swinging open slowly. We slipped through, and took stock of the situation.

The middle of the square was quiet, with no sign of any people. In the center was a large stone well with windlass, and spare buckets so that any could help themselves to the water. The square was surrounded by buildings, all wooden and built snug next to its neighbor to fit within the stone walls. Of course, not all of the walls remained, some sections had been replaced with wooden palisades. But what should have been a village preparing for the evening meal was silent. It was quiet except for some house swallows that were squabbling over something nearby.

Epor and Isdra were both on alert, weapons out and held high. Epor had his club, and Isdra had her shield and sword. They kept me up against the gate, ready to get me out at the first sign of trouble. But the silence continued, and no one appeared in the square.

"The scout said someone shot at him from the walls." Epor spoke softly. Isdra nodded, and I looked up. There were small battlements on both sides of the gate that were higher than the gate itself, with two wooden ladders leading up. "I'll go." Epor said.

I nodded. "I can check the—"

"No." Isdra interrupted me firmly. "You'll stay right here."

It was no more than a few steps to the ladder. Epor secured his club, and pulled a dagger before climbing up. He moved fast, choosing the one to our right first, and was standing up at the top in but a moment. He knelt, disappearing from our view, then his head popped up again. "There's a man up here with a bow, but I can't rouse him."

I took a step toward the ladder, but Isdra interfered. "No, Warprize. He'll bring him down to us."

I bit my lip in frustration, but Epor already had the man heaved up and on his shoulder. We watched as he carried him down and brought him to lay on the ground at my feet. I knelt and eased my parcels and basket down next to me. The man was older, his skin tan and weathered. I placed a hand on his forehead to find it cold and clammy. "He's sick."

Epor and Isdra had maintained their watch, focused

out, observing the buildings for any movement. "So, it's illness?" Isdra asked, without looking at me.

"One ill man doesn't make it so." Epor growled. "Let's wait a bit before we decide, eh? Let's check further."

"That house, the one with the shutters. It's close and it looks like it might be a—" I paused for the right word. "A warleader's home."

Epor snorted at my use of the word, but he got the idea. "Come."

"But this man—"

"Leave him." Epor's tone was hard, and I understood that he wasn't giving me an option. They moved carefully, keeping me between them as we headed to the structure. Isdra rapped on the door with her pommel, even as Epor guarded our backs. When there was no response, she kicked the door in.

"Isdra . . ." I scolded.

"Sorry." She shrugged, then stepped through the wide-open door as I peered over her shoulder. It was a sitting room, with a hearth, and chairs. There were stairs up, and a back door into what appeared to be a kitchen. There was no outcry, no response as she strode across the room and through the opposite door. I took a step, but Epor stopped me with a gesture.

Isdra reappeared immediately, with a grim look. "There's a dead woman on the floor. No wounds." She moved to the stairs, and disappeared. I could hear her footsteps on the floor above. She was back down in a moment. "A boy, dead in a bed."

Epor grunted. "Illness, as you said, Warprize." He was fussing with the cloth in his nose, trying to get it to stay in place.

"I wish I'd been wrong."

He nodded his agreement, and stepped out of the building, back into the square. He put his head back and warbled a long cry. That was the signal to let Keir know that it was indeed plague that we faced. As the cry ended, we heard a response from over the wall.

Epor turned back to me. "They understand. Joden asks what kind of illness."

I shook my head. "I don't know yet."

Epor warbled again, as Isdra joined me in the doorway. "Do you wish to look at the dead?" she asked.

"In the morning. I'm more worried about the living." We hurried back across the square. Epor heaved the man into a sitting position as we gathered our parcels. "I need to get him in a bed and tend him." I looked up at the sky. "You two need to start checking the buildings before we lose the light."

Epor frowned. "Where?"

"There's a shrine to the Goddess over in that corner, Epor." I stood, and gathered up my parcels. "I can use it as a healing house. I'll be fine there."

"I don't like leaving you alone. I will go and—"

Isdra snorted out a laugh. "Takes longer to argue her out of it than it will to search."

Epor shook his head, but he pulled the man up and back over his shoulder. "As you say, Warprize."

Thankfully the shrine was empty and quiet. It was a large space, with movable benches, used as a place of worship and a meeting area. In the back was a small sleeping room, with a hearth. No priest in residence from the looks of things. I had Epor deposit the sick man on the bed, and placed my packages on the side table within easy reach. Quickly, I stripped him of his clothing, then paused. There was a strong odor that not even the ginger could disguise. I pulled the cloth from my nose and was met with a foul, rank smell, coming from the body of my patient. Confused, I replaced the plugs and continued with my work. That was not a symptom of any plague that I knew of. What could this be? The Sweat? The Swellings?

I vaguely heard Epor and Isdra as they searched the shrine, but my focus was on my patient. He was unresponsive to my touch, cold and clammy skin, his breathing rough and uneven.

"Warprize."

His armpits weren't swollen, nor his neck. I reached for his groin to check—

"Warprize."

His groin wasn't swollen, nor did he react as I pressed down. I'd start him on fever's foe and—

"I swear an ehat could charge though this room and she'd never note it."

Epor's voice cut through my thoughts. I looked up to see him standing in the door, holding a bucket of water. Isdra was kneeling at the hearth, feeding a small fire, smiling at Epor's jest. Epor placed the bucket beside the hearth. "The back seems secure. It's surrounded by walls, and there's but a small house back there."

"Privy." I corrected, turning back to my patient.

Isdra leaned in to look at the man. "Do you know which illness it is, Warprize?"

"No." I got up to put some water to heat. "Not yet."

Epor scratched his beard. "Makes sense that an invisible enemy is hard to track. But there's no bolt on the door, Warprize. Isdra will remain, and I will search."

"You don't lock the doors of a shrine, Epor." I answered absently, still intent on my patient. Then his meaning sunk in, and I snapped my head around. "Don't be foolish. You can move faster if there are two of you." They both got a mulish look on their faces, and I stood up. "Fine. I will put a bench before the door. If anyone comes in, I'll scream. Will that satisfy you?"

Epor frowned, but it was Isdra who spoke. "Remember Marcus's lesson, Warprize. Death can come in an instant."

For a moment I remembered the touch of the blade at my throat, and the fear that went with it. He'd moved so fast. The fear was real, but I wasn't going to let it stop us from rendering aid. "It will have to do. The quicker you leave, the quicker you will be done."

Isdra looked at Epor, who shrugged. "We will do as much as we can before we lose the light."

"Remember the phrases I taught you?" I followed them out the door.

"Do not be afraid." Isdra spoke slowly in Xyian.

"We will take you to a healer." Epor had the words down, but his accent was terrible. Still, it would work. I closed the door behind them.

"I'm not leaving until I hear the bench." Isdra's voice floated through the door.

Irritated, I dragged a bench over, and dropped it down in front of the door. "There."

"We'll check the nearest buildings and return. Stay safe, Warprize."

I'd already forgotten them as I hurried to my patient's side. No swellings, no boils. No signs of vomiting or flux. I wiped him down with damp cloth, and tried to get him to drink but it dribbled from the side of his mouth. He never roused as I examined him, and his strange lassitude disturbed me. Still, from all appearances, I was dealing with the Sweat. He wasn't coughing, although each of his breaths seemed an effort. I listened to it as I set my supplies in order, praying that I'd have enough to minister to those in need.

Blankets, we'd need blankets. And something to eat, a broth if I could find something to make it from. Porridge, if nothing else. I should have said something to Isdra, so they'd look for them as well. There were no supplies to speak of here. I tried to relax, take a breath and ease the knot in my stomach. Once the villagers knew that a healer had arrived, we'd have help aplenty.

A pounding at the door jerked me up. I let Isdra in, her arms filled with a squirming bundle, her face grim. "I found this one on the bed next to her thea." The blanket fell back to reveal a baby, squirming and fussing in the cloths. Isdra brushed past me. "Ward the door, Warprize."

"Isn't Epor bringing her mother?" I looked out into the square.

It was the silence that made me turn to look at her. Isdra had an odd, cold look in her eyes. "No."

I bit my lip, and turned back to secure the door. By the time I entered the bedroom, Isdra had the babe by the fire, cushioned by the blankets, and was digging in her saddle bags. The baby was crying, kicking its feet in the air. "I've gurt here," Isdra said. "We can soften it in water and feed her. She's a mess, Warprize. Her thea must have been dead for hours."

I knelt down, and smiled at the little one, checking her over. "There's no sign of fever in this one. Just hungry and unhappy."

"Skies be thanked." Isdra started looking through the blanket. "I grabbed some extra swaddles." She pulled forth some clean diapers, and the few stalks of lavender fell to the floor. The babe opened its eyes and looked at us with sweet brown eyes framed by dark curling lashes. Then the little face squinched up and a howl filled the room.

"What are those flowers?" Isdra asked as she started to work. "They are lovely."

"Lavender. Her mother must have freshened her diapers with it." I cleared my throat. "I'm not sure gurt will be to her liking. Hopefully we can find a nursing mother among the other villagers."

Isdra's voice was cold, even as her practiced hand worked to clean the child, a little girl. "I doubt there will be others, Lara." She made an odd clicking sound with her tongue, and the baby opened its eyes wide, staring at her. "We've been in half the buildings and this is the first we found someone alive."

My throat closed. "No," I croaked. "Please, tell me it's not true."

She kept her head down, focused on the babe, who grabbed at the end of her braid and bawled, kicking in the air. "They are dead in their beds, Warprize. Dead in the halls and doorways. Some are laid out, some died where they fell. Some for days, others just hours from the look of them."

I sat there, numb, staring at the babe as it tugged at her hair, threatening to loosen the leather strip that held it. Dearest Goddess, the entire village?

Isdra turned her head slightly, careful not to pull the braid from the babe's hands. "We need to feed her." She picked up the crying child and cradled her to her shoulder with both hands. She seemed to chant something under her breath, and her hands were gently tapping out a rhythm on the babe's back. The child hiccupped, and looked at me with wide eyes, tears clinging to her eyelashes.

I smiled at the babe and reached for my baskets. "I

have a feeding cup we can use. We can sweeten the gurt."

"Trust me, Lara. This little one won't care. As long as it's warm and filling she's going to drink it." Isdra continued to use her fingers and hands to beat softly. The babe yawned, and let her head fall onto Isdra's shoulders. Isdra, on the other hand, gave a critical look at the ceramic cup with its long spout. "Are you sure that will work?"

"Yes." I reached for the water and gurt. "What do you use on the Plains?"

"We use a dried animal teat," Isdra frowned. "It's more like a breast than that cold dish."

"It works, trust me." I mashed the gurt into the warm water. "Where did you learn that?" I nodded at her hands.

She chuckled softly. " 'Tis what we do to comfort a child. We drum a pattern on their backs and chant to them. It calms them, and as we slow the pattern, they usually fall asleep. We use it to wake a sleeping child as well, at need."

Isdra was right, the babe sucked the gurt up with no complaint, falling asleep with the narrow spout still in her mouth. Isdra smiled at the lax child in her arms. "I should go. Epor will need help . . ."

There was a pounding at the door that broke our fragile peace. I started for the door at Epor's call, even as Isdra settled the child down in the blankets we'd placed by the hearth.

Epor came through, carrying a gray-haired woman wrapped in blankets. She was conscious, and had her arms about his neck. Epor headed for the back room. "Here's one with breath still in her body, Warprize. There is one other that I have found, but I will need Isdra to chase him down." He eased the woman down in the chair.

The woman held the blankets close around her, and seemed to sink into them.

"Chase him?" I asked as I put a hand on the woman's shoulder to steady her. She looked up at me through reddened eyes, and I could feel her tremble even through the blankets. Even through the ginger I could smell the foul odor of her sweat.

Epor grinned. "He's running loose, thinking we are the enemy." He gave me a sly grin. "Of course, we were." I gave him a look as he chuckled. But he turned serious in an instant. "I tried the phrases you gave us, but it's no use. I want to secure him, for his safety and ours."

Isdra frowned. "I should have been there to help."

Epor gave her a grin. "Ah, but you had a babe in your arms. I knew you were lost to me, the moment you heard the squawk from the bed." He turned back to me, his eyes taking on a sad, woebegone look. "Warprize, are these cloths up my nose really necessary? They will not stay in!"

"Yes, they are."

"What if I did this?" He took a strip of bandage from my supplies and tied it over his nose and mouth. "If we dip this in the oil? Please?"

I had to smile at his pleading tone. "That would work."

"Epor, you are my hero." Isdra sighed with relief as they quickly rigged the masks and made ready to leave.

The old woman struggled out of the blankets and clutched at me with her thin hands. Her palm was cold and clammy on my arm. "Are they going after Kred? Tell them, please, not to hurt him. Kred is raving, he's mad with the Sweat. He doesn't know what he does."

"They'll not hurt him," I assured her. I focused back on Epor and spoke his tongue. "She says he's ill."

Epor nodded, and looked at the old woman, and spoke

Xyian with his terrible accent. "Do not be afraid." She just stared at him. He straightened, and returned to his language. "Isdra has told you? Of the dead?" At my nod he continued. "We will continue to search and find the crazed one. Pile three benches in front of the door, Warprize, and scream if any try to enter."

I nodded as I followed them to the door. "We will need supplies, too."

"There is kavage in my saddle bags." Isdra nodded toward the pile. "A pot would be welcome."

"Oh yes," Epor agreed as they headed out. "It will be a long night."

I returned to the back to find the old woman standing by the bed, looking down at my other patient. She looked up, her sorrow clear. "He's dying."

I took her arm, and guided her back to the chair. "He's ill, certainly." She sank down into the chair, trembling with exhaustion. "But it's too soon to—"

"No." Her voice was sharp. "You think I don't know? When they lay there, breathing rough like that, it's the end, the—" She cut off her words, shuddering, hugging herself, sobbing and rocking. "It's changed," she whispered. "It's not what it was." She stared past me, the sweat beading on her brow, her thin hair matted to her forehead. "All of them, all . . ."

I pulled the blankets up around her. "Take the word of a healer, it's not certain he'll die. With proper care, he'll—"

The old woman closed her eyes, her hair plastered to her face, sweat or maybe tears running down her cheeks. "I'm a healer, and we'll all die." She covered her face with her hands, and wailed.

* * *

It was dark when Epor and Isdra returned.

"No sign of the crazed one. If there's more, they're hiding." Epor placed his load of blankets by the hearth. "We've lost the light. We'll look again in the morning."

I ran my hands over my hair, brushing back the loose tendrils. They'd hauled in supplies as I had tended to our three patients. We'd done quite a bit in the last few hours.

Isdra had a bucket of water, and a crock jug tucked under her arm. "The babe?"

"Sleeping." I took the water from her and placed it with the others. "I fed her again, so she should nap for a while."

Isdra nodded absently as she went over to the child, sleeping on a cushion of blankets. Epor and I exchanged an amused glance as she checked her, not satisfied with my reassurance. Isdra smiled down at the child, her angular face softened in the firelight. "I found a goat with milk." She put the jug down, then stood, stretching out her back as she did so. As I handed Epor some kavage, I caught him looking at her, and quickly looked away.

Isdra accepted kavage as well, and settled down on the floor not far from the child. She arranged her weapons at her side, close at hand. They had raided the nearby homes for supplies, so instead of the rations that we'd brought, there were two chickens on the spit, a broth simmering on the hearth, and bread and cheese. The well had provided the water, there was plenty of wood out back and they found bedding and blankets for all. Epor had even carried in another bed for the healer. It was cramped quarters, but it would serve for tonight. They hadn't been able to catch the one man, and Epor was determined that he and Isdra would stand watch through the night.

Epor settled by the fire opposite Isdra, arranging his

weapons close at hand, too. He looked tired, and I had to admit that I was feeling worn myself. He was reaching for water to wash with when I spoke. "Did you cry out to the others, Epor?"

He looked up at me, his eyes wide, then laughed. "We would say 'signaled', Warprize. Aye, I did, gave the 'All's well' cry." Epor moved an empty bucket between himself and Isdra, and poured the water for us to wash.

"Who replied?" I tried not to look like I cared about the answer.

But nothing got past those two. Isdra flicked a glance at Epor, but his gaze stayed on my face with a knowing look. "Joden."

I said nothing, just settled down with them. We washed, and they pulled their masks down just enough to be able to eat. I removed the pads from my mouth as Isdra reached for the chickens. Epor broke off a chunk of bread and handed it to me. "The others?"

"Sleeping." I looked about the room at the quiet figures around us.

"Do you know the enemy yet?" Isdra had a chicken leg and was tearing into it as she passed me part of the bird.

"No." I bit into the warm meat. The old woman had broken down after she revealed that she was the healer. I'd managed to get her on to a pallet and calmed to the point that she'd fallen asleep. I'd save my questions for the morning. She'd mentioned the Sweat, but the symptoms that I was seeing were nothing that I'd ever heard of. Tomorrow I'd go to her home and see what she'd been using, and take any supplies that I could.

I'd taken to calling the man that we'd found on the wall 'Archer'. He was so deeply unconscious I hadn't been able to get him to swallow any liquids. I'd settled for scraping a small amount of fever's foe on the roof of his mouth, hoping that it would melt down his throat. His breathing was rough, but there was no cough and the fever seemed to have vanished.

Thankfully the babe glowed with health. Isdra was smiling at the sleeping child as she ate. Epor passed me more food and urged me to eat. We sat quietly, eating and enjoying the peace of the moment.

After we'd picked the bones clean, Epor settled back, and gave a quiet belch. Isdra poured more kavage. I drank some of the bitter liquid before I spoke. "Tomorrow, I want to go to the healer's home, Epor. She will have supplies that I will need."

"We must also start to deal with the dead or the filth of this place will overwhelm us." Epor responded.

Isdra wrinkled her nose. "It already does. I have seen enough that I will never live in a tent of stone. Dirt and mouse droppings in every corner." She waved her hand for emphasis. "A tent you can clean, shake free and be off. How can you think to keep a 'house' clean?"

Epor chuckled, but I admonished her. "Isdra, they have been sick. Maybe they haven't been able to clean."

Isdra shrugged. "Still, Warprize."

"Warprize, you give your dead back to the earth, yes?"

I turned toward Epor. "Yes, we bury our dead. What is your tradition?"

"We give ourselves back to the elements, as do all. Some by fire, earth or air. It is rare to give to the waters, but it is done. Each according to their preference."

"Air?" I tried to imagine how that would work and failed.

"The body is lifted on a platform, left naked to the sky. Over time, the platform decays, and falls to the ground, usually pulled down by the snows." Isdra gave me a look when I tried not to show my disgust. "Cleaner than giving back to the earth. But if earth is your custom, we will follow it."

"I suppose." I responded politely. "Epor, you and Isdra alone can't bury the bodies. From what you say, there are too many."

"We can start. A shame we can't let the army know to dig for us. But none of the cries are designed to carry that message."

"We can't risk exposing them."

Epor shrugged. "We will do what must be done. We can use fire as well, if we can find a clear clean place to build a pyre. Fire is my preference. We will finish our search tomorrow, then start on the dead." Epor drained his kavage. "You will stay in here, with them?"

"Yes." I finished mine as well. "I will tend them through the night, catch sleep when I can."

"Then I will take first watch. Isdra—"

"Needs a bath." Isdra stood, securing her weapons. "There is a well and buckets and I am going to bathe."

Epor laughed softly. "As you say." He stood. "I will watch . . . to keep you safe."

Isdra smirked at him, and reached over to scratch him under the chin, her finger rasping in the hairs of his beard. "As you say."

Epor acted offended. "I must keep an eye out for the crazed one. What other reason would I have to watch?"

I had to chuckle, even as Isdra rolled her eyes. She rose, with a last look at the babe, and headed for the door. But Epor did not move. I looked at him, curious.

He sighed, and lowered his voice. "Lara, I would ask for your token."

Startled, I fumbled in my pocket and pulled out a stone. He took it gravely. "I would speak a truth, Lara."

"I will hear your truth, Epor. And answer it."

He shook his head. "No answer is needed. This is a truth of our ways, that I would tell you, and have you consider, yes?"

I nodded.

He focused on me, holding my gaze with his. "Bonding is not an easy thing, Lara. It takes a lot of work for a couple to maintain a bond." I nodded again, and he continued. "One of the things you cannot do is lie to your bondmate."

I flushed, embarrassed, and looked away. I opened my mouth to retort, but Epor touched my knee and silenced me with his words. "I do not know your ways in this, for I have learned that those of Xy bond early, and for life. Maybe this is the way of your people. But Keir is of the Plains, and for us, the bond must come first, the bondmate being due your first thoughts, eh?"

I nodded, still looking down at my hands.

"So." Epor reached over and tucked the stone back into my hands. "I ask that you think on my truths, Lara." He stood and stretched as I fidgeted with the stone. "Now I will go and watch Isdra's back, yes?"

I nodded again. He put his mask in place, gathered up his weapons and left without another word. I waited until he left to wipe my eyes. I'd been right to stay silent. If I'd told Keir about the forty days he'd never have allowed me to enter this village, never have stopped on his way to the Plains. I plucked at a rough spot on my tunic and tried not to hear the tiny voice in the back of my head, the one that was pointing out that I'd never given Keir a chance.

* * *

Once I'd checked everyone and set up my pallet, I realized we'd need more water. With empty bucket in hand, I eased the door open and slipped into the main room.

Shrines to the Goddess are designed with small, high windows to allow her light to shine within. The moon was not full, but the soft beams of light filled the room with a silver glow.

The doors out to the square were open. I stepped out into the doorway, and stopped.

The same silver light made the square glow, casting faint shadows. Epor was seated on the well, his club in one hand. The light made his hair seem an even brighter gold. He'd lowered his mask again, I could see the gleam of his smile.

Isdra was naked, a slim silver figure in the light. Her braid shone in the moonlight. She was using one of the buckets to splash water over herself. I couldn't make out what they were saying, but Epor's eyes held a light that needed no explanation.

Captured by the sight, I watched as Epor stood, caught Isdra with his free arm and pulled her close. She moved eagerly, plastering her wet body against his and pulling his head down to hers. Their kiss was long and deep and—

I stepped back and hid behind the door, embarrassed. A longing blazed within me, for Keir's strong body, for the taste of his lips in my mouth. I bit my lip. And took a step further away from the sight, for I wished so very much that it was Keir and I by the well, in the moonlight.

Yet, here I was alone and by my own choosing. Events demanded that I do this and I had made the right choice.

These people were ill, and needed my help. It had been the right thing to do, of that I was certain.

The emblem of the Goddess gleamed on the far wall, the Lady's calm face serene in the light. I sent a silent prayer to her, for the lives of my patients and the people of this village. Legend has it that the Goddess, the Lady of the Moon, is wed to the God, the Lord of the Sun. Their relationship is a fierce one, filled with storms and rumbles.

He'd been so angry. So furious with me. But I'd done the right thing after all. There was illness here, deadly illness and it could not be ignored. We'd help those we could, bury those we couldn't, get the information we needed, stay isolated for the required period and then be on our way. All would be as it was before. Keir would forgive my actions. Wouldn't he?

I gnawed at my lip, suddenly filled with doubt. What had seemed like such a small thing before now seemed—

A sound came from the other room, and I hurried back to my patients.

"Those barbarians will kill us in our sleep."

"No, they won't." I was trying to sooth the old woman as I wiped her face. She'd woken, drenched in sweat, the heat and stink radiating off her body in waves. I'd added rose oil to the water, and it seemed to help with the smell. Her weak eyes were wide with fear, and she clutched at me with what strength she had left as I bathed her face and chest. "Can you tell me what happened here?"

She squinted up at me, confused. "Who are you?"

I decided to keep my explanations simple for now. "Lara, Master Healer, trained by Eln of Water's Fall."

Isdra entered, hair damp, but fully dressed, carrying more water. The old woman tensed, sucking in a breath. "That's a Firelander!"

"It is, but she will not harm you. She is my friend." I tried to block her vision with my body. "Who are you? What happened here?"

"Rahel, Healer, trained by Thrace of Lake's End." Rahel answered me almost absently as she tried to see what Isdra was doing.

"What happened here, Rahel?" I repeated.

Her eyes moved back to lock on my face. "It's changed, the Sweat. Too fast, too fast!"

"Tell me."

"Three days ago, two strangers were found on the main road, ill and feverish."

Three days? These people had all sickened and died in the last three days? My throat went dry.

Rahel grasped at my arms, her gaze fixed on my face. "We had no warning, no time to act. There's those that left for the city two days past, but all we could do was close the gates and pray to the Goddess. My fault, all my fault that they died . . ." Her voice rose in a shriek, waking the baby who started to cry. Isdra moved to pick her up, and soothe her.

The babe's cry seemed to clear some of Rahel's confusion. "Whose baby is that?"

"We don't know. We found her next to her dead mother."

"How old?"

I rinsed my cloth out in the cool water. "Some six months is my guess."

Rahel lay back against the pillows and stared unseeing at the ceiling. She drew in a long shuddering breath.

"Meara's get, then. So Meara's dead." Her eyes filled with tears. "I birthed her with these two hands. My babies, all my babies. I tried so hard." Her voice trailed off in sobs.

I wiped her face with soft strokes. "Tell me about the illness, Rahel. I must know."

"First the sweat, where water pours from the body in rivers. Then the madness, a delirium like I have never seen. The soul raves and rants with unseeing eyes and horrible anger." She closed her eyes, and took a deep breath, as if reciting a lesson she'd forced herself to memorize. "Then a sleep so deep that they respond to nothing, not pain nor noise. Deep, deep, past any hope or will to live. They are just . . ." She opened her eyes, and clutched at my arm. "They all died. I tried everything I knew, but they all—"

"Hush now, all will be well." I assured her. "A good broth, a strong dose of fever's foe and you will be—"

"Fool girl," she snapped. "Trained of Eln? Have you not heard what I said? Tried them all, there's no remedy, no cure, they just fall over. There's only cold, cold death." She cried out, sobbing as through her heart would break. "I failed them all. My babies . . ." Her fingers pulled weakly at the blankets.

"Fever's foe—"

"Tried it."

"Dittany."

"Tried that."

"Watermint."

"Tried that, too." Anger flashed over her face, but she was too weak to hold the glare. "Fool girl, tried them all, but there's no remedy, no cure. There's only cold and the grave." She put a hand to her forehead. "It's come for me, death has, and it's welcome. All my babes, and their babes . . ." She started to wail, sobbing out her despair.

Isdra was trying to feed the babe, and comfort it at the same time. Epor stuck his head in. "What's amiss?"

"The woman woke, and her cries have frightened the babe. She thinks you are going to eat her."

Rahel stopped crying and stared at Epor, wide-eyed.

Epor smiled at her, showing his teeth. "I wouldn't. Too scrawny."

I smiled at the jest, and Rahel demanded to know what he said. She looked at me with suspicion, but seemed to relax a little, especially when Epor leaned against the doorpost, watching Isdra make a bed by the fire for herself, with the babe nestled down beside her. In the quiet, Rahel closed her eyes, and whispered something. I leaned closer. "What did you say?"

She opened her eyes. "Bind me."

"I don't think—"

"Bind me, girl."

"Rahel, you're no threat."

"The fever has me. Bind me now."

"What does she say?" Epor asked.

I explained and he nodded. "Even a weakling with a knife is dangerous. Take no chance, Warprize."

Rahel seemed to sense his attitude. "He knows. Healers know the way of pain. Those that heal can hurt in need. Tie me, I say."

I rolled my eyes, and in the end I secured her wrists to the frame, but only after I had her drink some broth. She lapsed into an uneasy sleep. Epor went outside to stand watch, Isdra rolled into her blankets and I settled in for a long night.

* * *

By dawn, Rahel could not be roused. She lay silent, still, and unresponsive.

I was exhausted, and filled with chagrin at my folly. I should have listened to her, forced her to tell me everything while she was conscious and talking. I should have heeded her warnings, but I had not believed that a disease could kill so very swiftly.

I knelt by Epor, sleeping in the blankets that Isdra had vacated. They'd traded off during the night. A touch of my hand on his shoulder, and his eyes were open. He sat up when he got a good look at my face. "Warprize?"

"We need to go to the healer's home, Epor. I need to see what she was trying to do before you brought her here."

Epor glanced at the beds. "The man?"

"Dead." I refused to look at the body. I'd covered his face, and my failure, with a blanket.

Epor stood, gathering his weapons. His eyes flicked to the corner where the babe rested. "She's well, at least?" he asked gruffly.

"So far."

Epor led the way, and I followed him out into the main room. Isdra was just inside the door, seated on one of the benches, positioned so that she could see out into the square. She made no comment as we approached, just lifted an eyebrow.

"A scouting run." Epor spoke softly, tightening his mask. "Anything?"

"All's quiet." Isdra stood. "The others?"

"The babe is well. The woman still lives. The man is

dead." I didn't really want to discuss the details. Thankfully, Isdra was content with my response.

"We'll finish the search when we return." Epor looked out over the square, and the light that was growing steadily. "No sign of the crazed one?"

"None."

"Heat some kavage for us, eh? We won't be long."

Isdra gave him a smile, and a nod. "I'll see to the babe."

Epor stepped to the doors, and I moved to stand next to him. The light was growing brighter, but the walls and the house made deep shadows around the edge. Epor put his hand on my shoulder. "You will stay with me, and do as I say. If I say run, you will come back here, yes?"

"I will."

He moved then, at a fairly rapid pace, around the square, staying in the shadows as much as he could. He'd stop every few paces, listening. I'd stop too, but my heart was beating so fast that I would not have heard an army approaching. It was scaring me, that he thought this was necessary.

The healer's clinic was off the square, in a small alleyway. Epor went in first, urging me to stay pressed against the wall next to the door. It was a small area, just the two rooms and a loft above, much like the house we'd gone in the day before. Epor returned quickly, and gestured me into the back room. "This is it, Warprize. The room above has only beds with the dead in them."

It was her stillroom, filled with familiar scents and the cloying odor of death. The room was in disarray, as if it had been used in haste. There were pots of fever's foe over by the fire, still in the cauldrons. I found half-ground dittany and watermint on the tables. She'd tried them, as she had said.

Epor stood at the door, shifting his gaze from me to the other room and the outer door. He was making no secret of his impatience, but I wasn't to be rushed.

The old schools of healing taught that you kept your best recipes and discoveries to yourself, calling them the secrets of the trade. Eln took a different approach, teaching that all knowledge must be shared to make us all better healers. If Rahel was of the old school, she'd have hidden her notes and recipes somewhere. I only hoped that Rahel had not guarded her secrets too well.

It took a bit of poking around, but I found rolls of notes in a canister on a high shelf. I put that in my satchel, along with the notes. With any luck, she'd taken some notes about the process of this plague.

Epor coughed. "Warprize . . ."

"One last thing," I moved to his side. "I want to see the bodies upstairs."

"Quickly."

I moved up the stairs as quickly as I could. It was warmer here and the smell was that much stronger. I was grateful for the ginger cloth over my nose and throat, but even that couldn't cover the smell. I stepped to the nearest bed and pulled back the blanket. There were no visible wounds on the body. He lay on his back, as if asleep. The cups and jars on the table between the bed held fever's foe and dittany. I looked at the other man, and had to pause, thinking for some reason that I had seen him before. I studied the face, but death had left his mark and I wasn't sure if—

"Warprize."

I replaced the blankets and moved to leave when a pile

of clothing caught my attention. Quickly I held up the top garment, then shuffled through the rest of the pile. These were priestly garments, worn by the priests of the Sun God. What were they doing here?

"Warprize."

This time, Epor was at the bottom of the stairs, and not to be denied. I turned to go and took a step, when a noise came from behind me.

From under one of the beds.

I froze, holding my breath. At the bottom of the steps, Epor frowned at me. "Lara, we need to—"

"I think—" I turned to look, but I was too slow. The man sprang from under the bed, barreled into me, throwing me to the side. As I fell to the floor, he leaped down on Epor with a snarl.

"Epor!" I called out as I staggered to my feet. There were sounds of a furious struggle below, with grunts and howls from the sick man. I clattered down the stairs, to see them rolling together on the floor. "Epor, don't hurt him!"

Epor gave me an exasperated look, even as he tried to pin the man down. The man put up a furious struggle, using fists and teeth to win free of Epor. Epor had him pinned when the man craned his neck and bit Epor on the arm.

Epor spat a curse. The man escaped, scrambled to his feet, and ran into the still room, with Epor right behind. I winced at the sounds of breaking crockery.

By the time I got to the door, Epor had the man on the ground, and pinned. "Get some rope."

"Rope?" I looked about wildly.

The man heaved under Epor, trying to break free. Epor panted with the effort to keep the man down. "Get something!"

I reached for a pile of cloth, and handed him some ban-

dages. Epor muttered something under his breath, flipped
the man over, and hit him in the jaw. The man collapsed,
moaning.

"Epor."

"Sorry." His eyes crinkled in a smile that proved he
wasn't. "He may be sick, Lara, but he's strong. As well
for me that he's no warrior, eh?" Teeth flashing, Epor
heaved the man over his shoulder. "Let's get him bound
to the bed before he wakes."

As we crossed the square, a warble rose from outside
the walls. Even I knew that Joden was asking our status.
Epor tilted his head, and warbled what I assumed were reassurances. He looked at me with a question in his eyes,
and I knew I had to make a decision. "Tell them to send
the message that it is the Sweat."

Even as he raised his voice, I prayed that I was doing
the right thing.

It was no problem to secure him, the man was still unconscious from Epor's blow. The bite had just broken the
skin on Epor's arm, but I insisted that I clean and bandage
the wound. Isdra made a few pointed comments about the
difference between helping and hurting my patient. Epor
protested his innocence, asking if anyone was concerned
about his welfare. They bickered a bit as they carried out
the body of the archer.

The new patient was still sweating heavily, rank with
the stench. For the first time, I was considering drugging
a patient into cooperating with me. If the lotus kept him
asleep, perhaps I could get water into him to replace the
fluid he'd lost. Re-balance the elements in his body, as
Keir had told me once. I flushed at the memory. But to

give lotus to someone could also cause the deep sleep I was trying to avoid.

Deep in those thoughts, I checked on Rahel. She was still unresponsive, but I managed to get her to swallow some broth. Not much, but it was something. With that faint hope, I turned back to the man. Maybe a very small dose would aid him.

Epor and Isdra returned. They obviously washed before coming in. Isdra shook her head. "He's still out?"

"Yes." They started to settle by the fire, and I frowned. "Aren't you going to finish the search?"

"I don't want to leave you alone with that one." Epor responded.

"From what Epor says he could awaken and break his bonds." Isdra replied. "Best we stay here."

"No, you need to finish the search." I reached for my bag, digging for the lotus. "I will scream if he looks like he is breaking free."

Epor shrugged. "I'm too tired to fight you, Lara. We'll be as fast as we can."

Isdra stood as well. "We'll scrounge for breakfast as well."

I looked up with a guilty start, and Epor laughed. "See? Does the Warprize consider my empty belly?"

"I didn't think—"

"Don't let him tease you, Lara." Isdra rolled her eyes. "Like he doesn't have a pouch of gurt on his belt?"

"If it were up to the Warprize, I'd starve to death!" Epor led the way from the room. "Nothing but skin and bones, yes?"

Isdra made a comment that I couldn't hear, but I heard Epor's laughter ring out in response. It made me smile.

But that faded when I turned back to my patients.

* * *

The lotus helped, but not as much as I'd hoped. He woke eventually, but he remained crazed, yelling and crying out. He fought the bonds until the skin on his wrists was rubbed raw with the effort. I could get no medicine or water into him, for he'd spew out anything I poured into his mouth. I talked until I was hoarse, but all he could do was curse me, in anger and fear, and for the most part his words were past understanding.

Epor and Isdra returned before the worst of it. There was no one with them, and their faces told me the horrible truth. Rahel, the babe, and the man were all that were left of a thriving village. My eyes filled as I turned back to my work.

For hours, we worked together in the cramped room, trying to rouse Rahel and break the fever of the man she had called Kred. Despite our struggles they were both slipping through my fingers like sand, and faded with each breath. Kred lapsed into the lassitude just as Rahel breathed her last quiet breath. I pulled the blanket over her face, and settled back on my heels by her bedside. All her knowledge gone, all these people gone. I'd risked our lives for nothing. Tired, I lifted my hands to rub at the ache in my temples, knowing that I had failed these people.

The babe chose that moment to cry out, unhappy about something. Isdra was there in an instant, but Epor scowled. "Can't you keep her quiet?"

The irritation in his voice cause both of us to look at him in surprise but Epor already had a hand up in apology. "Sorry. Tired, I guess."

Isdra accepted it, and turned back to the babe. But I fo-

cused on Epor and really looked at him. At the furrow between his eyes, and the stiff way he held his head. "Epor?"

He straightened, empty buckets in his hands, and gave
me a weak smile. I took a step closer to see the sweat on
his forehead.

Goddess, no . . .

6

"So. I will be the first of the Plains to face this enemy."

Epor put his warclub on the bed, his movements slow and deliberate. He began to fumble with the buckles of his armor, but his hands were shaking badly. Isdra stepped close, reaching out to help him. He was already sweating heavily, and I could see the pain in his eyes from the headache. I ground a dose of lotus as fast as I could. Isdra was grim as she released the straps, and helped him off with the heavy leather. Epor used his finger to lift her chin and forced her to meet his eyes. "You fear this."

Isdra moved her head aside. "I fear nothing." She tugged his tunic up and over his head.

"You fear this, Isdra." Epor spoke again, his voice soft and insistent.

Isdra stopped what she was doing, and looked at him. "I am Isdra of the Fox, warrior of the Plains. I fear nothing."

Epor put his hands on her hips to pull her close. "But you fear this."

Isdra sighed, and her hands grew still. "Epor—"

He put his finger over her mouth and gently rubbed it on her lower lip. It was a private moment but I could not look away. Finally, Isdra let out a puff of air against his finger. "I fear this," she admitted.

Epor nodded, and sat down heavily on the bed. "Is that so hard to say?" Epor looked at her calmly. "A true warrior faces the very thing he fears, yes?"

Isdra growled. Epor pulled her close, laying his head on her breast. "I will defeat this enemy, and Joden will craft a song to my glory."

"You'd best. Or Joden will sing only of our deaths. That will please Iften no end, and hurt our tribes and our Warlord."

"How so?" I asked.

Isdra hesitated for just a moment. "We are bonded, and as such are valued by the tribes. We spoke of this before. For Keir to lose us in less than honorable combat would shame him."

"Truth." Epor hung his head down, as if gathering strength. He lifted his head, and looked at Isdra. "But all will be well, fire of my heart."

"Shut up, and help me get these clothes off of you." Isdra snapped.

Epor chuckled. "Heyla, Lara. Would you hear a tale of the strength of my bonded?"

Isdra flushed as she knelt at his feet to unlace his boots.

Curious, I paused in preparing the doses. "Tell me, Epor."

"Well, this one, she says to me that we're to bond. Being a wise man, I agreed to her demands, not eager to face her anger."

Epor grabbed the bottom of his tunic, but got it stuck trying to pull it off. Isdra rose to help him. "So, on the day of bonding, Isdra sat first for the spiral to be woven in her ear. All had gathered, and my Isdra sat, so beautiful and so determined not to utter a sound."

Epor's head disappeared as Isdra pulled off his under tunic. His voice was muffled by the shirt.

"Does it hurt, Epor? The weaving?" I asked as I mixed the lotus in water.

"The piercing hurts, for it takes time for the ear to heal. Once the holes are in, it's not so bad. But my Isdra didn't flinch or cry out, for she is a Warrior of the Plains, strong, tough, and proud."

Isdra knelt at his feet to finish removing his boots. "It was to honor you."

"And I was honored." Epor took a deep breath, and I gave him a sharp look. He was suffering, I could see that. I offered him the cup. He took it, and drank it down quickly, with only a light wrinkling of his nose at the taste and continued where he'd left off. "It was then my turn. I sat before the weaver, and at the first touch of his needle . . ." He paused dramatically, "I screamed like a baby."

I laughed at the image. "Really?"

"Oh yes," Isdra sat back on her heels. "He carried on, weeping and wailing, saying that to bond with me was worth any pain, any suffering. He had the weaver and the watchers and the witnesses all laughing so hard they cried."

"Who can I mock, if I cannot mock myself?" Epor asked hoarsely.

"I will let no one mock you, my brave warrior." Isdra's voice broke as she stood and finished stripping Epor. His energy was waning before my eyes. Never before had a patient weakened so visibly, so fast, even as the beads of sweat gathered on his face. I'd lost the others. I'd not lose him.

Isdra folded his clothes off to the side as I helped Epor settle into the bed. She went to place his weapons at his side, but Epor stopped her. "No."

She looked at him, startled, then over at me. I shook my head as well. "If he raves . . ."

She gave a sharp nod, and placed the weapons, all of them, in the far corner by the hearth. The warclub she set down last, as if to guard the others.

"You must bind me." Epor's voice was low and rough.

Isdra balked at that. "I can control—"

"No. Take no chances with this enemy. Remove your own weapons, Isdra. For I am a dangerous and clever opponent."

Isdra nodded, unable to answer. My own throat closed as we tied his wrists to the bed frame, down at his sides. He insisted that we secure his feet as well. Only after testing the strength of the bonds did he relax onto the bed, his eyes closed. We covered him with a blanket.

Isdra moved off, removing her own weapons as instructed. I gathered the necessary vials, and pulled two buckets of water closer to the bed. I wrung out a cloth and started wiping his face and chest. Isdra did the same. We were silent for a few moments, when Epor's eyes fluttered open. They were vague and unfocused, telling me that the lotus was starting to work. He focused on Isdra and smiled. "You are my bonded, my heart's fire, and I am yours, to the snows and beyond."

"Do not speak of the snows." Isdra whispered as she wiped his chest.

"You must promise me . . ." Epor cleared his throat. "You must promise me to remain at the Warprize's side for as long as she needs you."

Isdra looked off, caught my eye and looked at the floor.

"No." Epor tugged slightly at his bonds and Isdra reached out to cover his hand with hers. "Promise me."

She leaned down, her lips close to his ear. "You must fight this, Epor."

"I will." He gave her a smile, a far shadow from his normal grin. "But you must promise."

Isdra closed her eyes. For a long moment, the only sound was Epor's breathing. Then her grey eyes opened, and she nodded slowly. "I promise."

I should have listened to the old healer, should have heeded her warning. She was right. It was too fast. Too fast for the medicines to take effect. Too fast to break the fever. Too fast for us to be able to balance his humors, replace his fluids.

It started well. The lotus seemed to calm him. But the Sweat was a vicious enemy, and as fast as we eased his fever the heat would rebuild in his skin. We labored hard, changing bedding, and using fresh water and rose oil to wipe him down. At first he'd respond to both of us, obeying our commands to swallow. But as the fever built, his eyes would only open at Isdra's call, and they held no awareness. Even that reaction failed in time and Isdra could no longer rouse him.

But worse was to come.

"Where is Isdra?" Epor mumbled, testing the restraints.

Isdra leaned closer. "I'm here, Epor."

Epor's eyes opened a crack, but his gaze slid right past her to me. "Where is my bonded? Why isn't she here?"

Isdra sucked in a breath, but I moved forward to answer. "She's right here, Epor."

"No, no, she's gone, my bonded has left me," Epor started to fight the restraints with a passion, shaking the bed. "Where has she gone?"

Isdra was speechless, white and shivering. I touched her arm. "It's the fever, Isdra. He's raving."

"His eyes are open . . ." She looked at me in doubt.

"But he does not see." I reached for the water and cloths. "Keep talking to him, Isdra."

She jerked her head in agreement, but the pain never left her eyes. We kept talking, both of us, trying to convince Epor that Isdra was there, that she would never leave him. But he couldn't be comforted or reassured. He became very agitated, demanding that we release him so that he could find her. It broke our hearts to hear the pain in his voice.

Worse still, he fell into the stupor without realizing that she was there. Isdra's tears did not start until Epor lapsed into the lethargy and would not wake. Still, we tried to force liquids into him, with no success. In the end we sat in silence, each holding a hand. Every breath was a painful rasp, each inhale a victory, every exhale a fear.

At the last, Epor opened his eyes as he drew in a final rasping breath. Isdra leaned over, stroking his head. He focused on her face, and gave her a weak smile, closed his eyes, and exhaled. The beat of his heart under my fingers stopped even as his breath faded.

Isdra stared at me, the knowledge building within her until her face crumbled and her eyes closed.

I sagged back on my heels, sweat beading on my forehead, weak with anger and fear and a headache pounding between my eyes. What killed a healthy man in so few hours? What had I done wrong?

"Epor." Isdra's voice cracked. I looked over as she took his right hand in hers and waited for a response. When none came, she reached over for his left hand. "Epor of the Badger."

"Isdra, he's—"

I cut myself off as she nodded, and moved so that she could grasp his left foot. She called his name again, tears running down her face. The silence echoed as she grasped his right foot, and drew in a deep breath that ended in a sob. "Epor, my soul's delight, beloved, please."

My weeping was her only answer.

She knelt at his feet, her head bowed, for a long moment. When she finally lifted her head, her face was streaked with tears. With effort, she rose and went to her weapons and pulled her dagger, sharp and bright. She returned to cut his bonds, freeing him from the restraints. Once that was accomplished, she eased down to kneel by Epor's head. She stroked his hair and placed her lips at his ear. "I'll see you beyond the snows, my heart's fire."

She sat back, and turned her streaked face to me. I offered a cloth, but she refused. "The wind will take them, Warprize."

I used the cloth to wipe my own tears, trying to bring myself under control and then sat working the cloth between my hands.

We might have sat like that for hours, awash in grief, but the babe wailed from her blankets, and kicked with her feet. Isdra turned her head dully, then rose to see to her needs. I remembered my other patient, and turned to his bed, only to find that he had died as well, unnoticed and untended. Guilt brought more tears to my eyes as I pulled the blanket over his face. I'd never once looked at him after Epor had taken ill. Some healer I was. All my patients, dead at my hands. An entire village, gone. I lowered my aching head into my hands and wept for the loss and my incompetence.

I could hear Isdra chanting to the babe even as I cried. Those low tones were a comfort, and I managed to get myself under control as I listened. My head hurt too much to think beyond the horror of the last few hours. But eventually I felt cool fingers on my neck, and I let Isdra pull me up and over to the hearth. She settled me in the chair, and wiped my face with a cool cloth, Once I'd had something to drink, she sat back on her heels and looked at me solemnly.

"The babe?" I croaked.

"Well." Isdra continued to study me silently.

I let my gaze drift over to the bodies on the beds. I felt so helpless, with no energy left to deal with the tasks ahead. I slumped in the chair, and closed my eyes in despair.

"The enemy has you, Lara."

It took me long moments for Isdra's words to sink in, and even longer for me to open my eyes and face the truth. I stared at her, numb. She reached over, and wiped my face with a cool wet cloth. I put my hand up to feel my own forehead. "I'm sick?"

She nodded, her eyes resigned.

So. I drew in a deep breath and straightened in the chair. "You are well? And the babe?"

"Yes."

"You must take the babe and go. Bathe both of you in vinegar. Stay away from the others for forty days, Isdra.

Forty days. If you and the babe are still well, it will be safe to rejoin the others after forty days. You understand?"

She tilted her head. "And you, Lara?"

I drew a breath, then used my sleeve to clear my eyes. "You leave, and set fire to the village. That will take care of the dead, Isdra. Forty days, you understand?"

She stared at me, not asking the question I had not answered.

I sobbed, the pain in my head building. "Isdra, I ask for mercy. Kill me."

"That is not your way, Lara." She frowned, clearly unhappy with my request.

"I'll not risk you or the babe, or any of the others. Grant me mercy, Isdra, then burn the village and leave." I drew in a shuddering breath. "I command it. As the Warprize, I order—"

Isdra stood. "I will do what must be done, Warprize." She helped me out of the chair. My head had started to pound, and it was hard for me to think. I leaned on her gratefully, my feet made clumsy by the pain.

She took me out into the square and sat me by the well. The cold stone felt good on my back. I blinked in the sunlight. Isdra knelt at my side, reached out and pulled the damp hair off my face. "You must be sure about this, Lara."

"Isdra, grant me mercy. Kill me, take the babe and flee. But promise me," I clutched at her arm. "Promise me that you will stay apart. Keep Keir safe for me, Isdra. Please?"

"So." She set her shoulders back, as if relieved and grateful for the task. "You will be wild with fever soon. I will bind you here, to keep you from wandering." She gripped my wrists firmly and I watched as she bound them together with a bandage. Once that was done, she lifted my bound wrists to the windlass and secured them

to the stout wood. I closed my eyes, holding my wrists
high to make it easier for her.

She knelt before me again. "I must prepare the village,
Lara and then do what must be done. You understand?"

I bit my lip. "Do you promise?"

She nodded. "I will keep to my oaths."

I closed my eyes and leaned my head back against the
stones, listening as her steps faded off. The only sound
was my ragged breathing. Even the larks were gone. But
in the back of my head, I could hear the litany, a prayer
for the dying and the dead. It seemed to ring in my ears as
if I could hear the words echoing in the temple as they'd
been chanted at my father's bedside . . .

*Gracious Goddess, Lady of the Moon and Stars, be with
me in the hour of my death* . . . Oh, I was going to die and
never see my Keir again, never ask his forgiveness or feel
his body moving in mine. Tears overcame me, and I wept
at my loss, the loss of his love, of what might have been
between us, he was so angry with me, so very angry . . .

*Gracious Goddess, Lady of the Moon and Stars, full of
forgiveness, forget my offenses and my flaws* . . . I'd made
so many mistakes, and my pride had made me think I
could deal with this illness and treat these people and now
they were all dead and it was all my fault, my fault, oh
forgive my arrogance and . . .

A sound and I blinked open blurry eyes to see Isdra
place a large basket at my side. The babe lay sleeping inside, tucked in with extra swaddles and her feeding cup.
Such a lovely babe, whose name was lost now, because I
didn't want to think that I could fail. I blotted my tears
with my sleeve and let my head fall back again.

*Gracious Lady of the Moon and Stars, full of mercy,
see my true repentance* . . . for I deeply regretted my er-

rors. Don't let anyone else suffer for my mistakes, oh please, keep Marcus and Keir, oh my Keir, and Othur and Anna safe, dearest Goddess, please . . . my people and his people . . . safe . . . the pounding was getting worse, my clothes were drenched yet I burned. I closed my eyes for what felt like hours, but dragged them open to see Isdra as she moved from building to building, opening doors and arranging fuel of any kind in the entryways.

Gracious Lady of the Moon and Stars, full of kindness, incline your ear to my plea, and She was, for I could see in the gathering dusk the first twinkling of a star over the mountains. But I couldn't keep my eyes open to see Her gift because the sweat was in my eyes and burning them. I tried to wipe them on my sleeve again, but the cloth was soaked.

Gracious Lady of the Moon and Stars, full of glory, guide me to a place in your garden and let me dwell there in peace. There'd be problems, I knew. My death would create such problems for Othur and the Kingdom. The cousins would try to claim the throne, and all would suffer thereby. But I couldn't find the strength to care, I'd be in the garden of the Goddess with Father, and we'd abide in the peace of that place together. And Keir, my Keir, would be safe, wild and free on his Plains. I smiled as I saw him mounted on his black horse, galloping in the sun, wild and free and safe, oh Goddess, please let him be safe and well.

At some point, I faded out and awoke to find Isdra arranging Epor's body on a pyre that she had made of a table from one of the homes. She placed him close to the well, as if in a place of prominence. She was arranging his hair, and seemed to be speaking but I wasn't sure. What I could see was that she had strapped Epor's warclub to her back. I caught my breath at the sight.

Finally she came to my side, and knelt to offer me water, and wipe my face. She took a long drink as well. "Almost done, Lara." She stood, and seemed to look around with satisfaction. "A fitting tribute to my Epor." She looked down. "I have only to light the fires, Lara. Be ready."

"You . . . you are sweating." Fear bubbled in my chest.

"With effort, nothing more."

Gracious Lady of the Moon and Stars, full of glory, embrace my soul. I closed my eyes, content. All my beloved family and friends would be safe, and Keir, my beloved Keir, he too would be well and strong. Tears flowed and I gave up fighting my sobs. He's been so angry.

Isdra stood before me, a silver figure in the moonlight. It was darker now, and I couldn't really see her face. But I could see the pitch torches in her hand as she stood over me, burning brightly. She ran off, the flames leaving a trail of light and sparks behind her. The flames flared from the buildings as she passed, throwing the torches into the building. Flames danced on the edge of my vision.

Sweat stung my eyes, and I struggled to keep them open to see her standing by Epor's pyre. She threw back her head, warbling a cry, perhaps the cry of a hawk, or maybe just of her sorrow and threw the torch.

The pyre exploded with light, and the smoke was fragrant with herbs that she must have found in the healer's home. I coughed as the smoke reached me, closed my eyes. Almost over. Safe, they were safe. *Gracious Lady of the Moon and Stars, full of glory, embrace my soul.*

"Warprize."

I found the strength to open my eyes to see Isdra kneeling next to me. Epor's dagger was in her hand. My eyes focused on the bright reflections dancing on the blade.

"I'm ready, Isdra."

She gave me a sad smile, and a nod. I closed my eyes as I felt her hand on my arm, and tilted my head to expose my neck. *Gracious Lady of the Moon and Stars, full of glo—*

7

Except Isdra had other plans.

The blade sliced the binding that tied me to the wind-lass. She had me tossed over her shoulder and the babe's basket in her hand before I understood what she was about.

The flames were rising all around us, crackling at the dry wood, sparks jumping to the sky. Smoke was filling the air. I was gasping from the smoke and the realization that I was still alive when Isdra spun on her heels and ran for the main gate.

"Isdra, NO!" I cried out, struggling against her hold, beating on her back with my bound hands. She didn't understand the risks, she had to stop. Isdra grunted when I struck, but her pace never faltered.

The gate must have been open, for she took me through it with ease. The light of the flames was replaced by a cool, velvety darkness. I couldn't see for a moment, but I didn't have to.

Keir was there.

All I could see was the ground, and Isdra's legs through blurry eyes. But I sensed him, standing there, waiting just beyond the gate. I blinked through the sweat as he took me from Isdra's shoulder and held me in his arms. For a timeless moment I rejoiced at the feel of his body as he drew me in close. Joy filled me at the sight of his face, but only for a brief instant before horror followed in its wake. "What are you doing?" I whispered.

Keir didn't answer, just looked at me, a strange light flickering over his stone face.

"Oh no, no, Keir, beloved, why?" The sickness in my heart had nothing to do with the fever that racked my frame.

The light came from torches that Marcus was holding, one in each hand. Isdra had put the basket down and was dragging brush in front of the gates. Keir moved back a few steps as Marcus began to set fire to the tinder.

The babe fussed, and Isdra saw to her before she took the other torch from Marcus and moved off to fire more brush that was off to the sides. Even in my fevered state I could see that tinder had been set along the length of the walls.

Frantic, I struggled to get Keir to release me, but he just tightened his hold. His strong arms didn't budge, impervious to my struggles. "No, Keir, don't do this." I tried to push at him with my bound hands. "I wanted you safe, please, please—"

"Hush." His voice was soft, but firm. He tucked my

head under his chin. I sagged against his chest, taking comfort from his strength for just a moment. But guilt and anger made me renew my struggle. He didn't understand the danger, didn't know what he was doing.

"Hush," he repeated, his voice warm and solid in my ear. His grip tightened to hold me still. "Save your strength, Lara. Fight the enemy, not me."

I cursed him then, using every phrase and word I could think of.

"What does she say?" Marcus's questions made me realize I was yelling in Xyian. I slumped back, all my strength spent, struggling to catch my breath. The heat of the flames, of Keir, no, of my own body was building and I burned. I put my head back against Keir's chest, too exhausted to even weep.

"She is displeased." Keir's voice was dry. "Isdra, report."

The voices around me continued as we moved. I wasn't strong enough to care. Everyone in the village had died, and now Keir had condemned himself and Marcus.

Isdra's voice rose and fell as we moved. I could feel Keir's muscles tense, holding me tight as he covered the ground with his long stride. The scent of his skin eased my headache. His voice would reverberate in my ear as he questioned Isdra, but I couldn't concentrate enough to understand what they were saying. Just as well, I didn't really want to hear a retelling of events or of the deaths. I kept my eyes closed so that I couldn't see Keir's face as he learned of my failure.

Then we were within a tent, and I was lowered onto a bed. Warm hands moved over me. I opened my eyes to see Keir beside me. Isdra was still talking, repeating the portion of her tale that spoke of the steps I had taken with my patients.

"Lotus? You are sure it was lotus?"

I jerked at the sound of Gils's voice. It couldn't be, and yet when I slowly turned my head, he was there, with his red hair and gangly arms, with healing supplies on a table next to him and a very determined look on that freckled face.

"No . . ." I whispered, and turned back as Keir removed my boots. "Oh, Keir, why have you done this? Why?"

Keir looked up, his eyes glittering. "I will not lose you, Lara." His voice was strong and urgent. "Fight this, Lara. Fight for me. For us."

A sound came from Isdra, and I shared her grief at hearing the same words she'd spoken to Epor but hours ago. I looked at her with eyes clouded with tears and sweat. "Isdra, why? Why do this?"

"My Warlord commands, and I obey."

Anguished, I dropped my aching head to my chest and let a sob escape me. Keir knelt down beside me, and cut the binding on my wrists. "Oh Keir, you should have listened. You stupid man."

But Keir simply continued to undress me. "I listened, Lara. Iften has charge of the army, and they are about a mile off. We will remain isolated from them. We will care for you until you are well enough to continue to the Plains. All will be well, fire of my heart."

"Drink this."

I looked into Gil's face. He stood there with a cup, trying to look so firm and competent. As I had felt the first time I'd dealt with a patient by myself. I licked my dry lips, looked at the cup, and then back at his youthful face.

"It's lotus." He gave me the best stern look he had. "Drink."

I raised a trembling hand but Keir took the cup, sat next to me and urged me to drink. Not that it took much urging. I welcomed the drowsiness that the lotus would bring. As soon as the cup was empty, Keir finished stripping me, and urged me flat on the bed beneath a rough blanket. "She's sweating, Gils."

"I will see to her." Gils replied, the barest trace of trembling in his voice. "We will need more water."

"The stream is close. We can get more easily." Marcus answered, gathering a few buckets. He paused to look at me with concern. "If the Sweat is as bad as you say, maybe we should cut her hair. It will be hard to keep clean, and will tangle."

"No," Keir answered softly. He was beside me, running his fingers through my hair, pulling it off my face. "No need. I'll braid it for her. I'll not see it cut."

Marcus snorted, and left the tent. Isdra followed, but not before I caught a glimpse of her face, and saw her naked grief. Gils was busy getting his cloths ready. I stared up at Keir as he worked his fingers through my hair, and cradled my head in his hand. His fingers gently massaged my scalp, easing the headache even further. Or maybe it was the lotus starting to take effect. I seemed to be floating slightly, but I wanted to tell him. Sorrow filled my heart, and my eyes welled with tears. I'd killed him, my strong, handsome lover, killed him with my pride and arrogance. I reached out blindly, and felt his cool hand grasp mine. I concentrated, trying to focus as he lowered his face to mine. "Lara?"

"It's all my fault." I whispered carefully. "I'm so sorry, so sorry."

"Lara," his voice was soft and urgent, but the lotus pulled me away.

"Papa? Papa!" It was so hot, so dark, where was Papa? The garden was withered and the sun seared my skin. I ran along the path, trying to find Papa. Xymund was behind me, so angry, so furious. He was going to kill me. I cried as he caught me, and struck out at my attacker. Papa's voice cut through the fire, but he wasn't talking to me, wouldn't hold me. What had I done, that he was angry with me?

"Papa? What is 'Papa'?"

"A name they call male theas. She thinks you're her father."

"Her thea?"

"Talk to her. Get her to drink something."

"Hush, Lara." Papa's voice sounded odd somehow, but it was deep and gentle and his cool hands touched my face. "Be easy. I am here, little one." A cup clinked against my teeth. "Drink."

I swallowed as the water flowed into my mouth, easing the dryness within. I let myself relax back into Papa's arms, soothed. I was safe, safe, Xymund couldn't get me here. The flames could still hurt me though, and Papa rocked me in his arms.

But when had Papa been so badly burned?

I stood by the well in the village square, which was silent and dark. As I looked about, I saw the morning larks laying on the ground, their little legs stiff, their songs silenced. As I covered my mouth in horror, the doors of the buildings opened, and the dead began to emerge. They were moving slowly, murmuring over and over, stumbling toward me, their eyes glittering with rage.

The door of the shrine opened and Epor stepped out, his gentle, smiling face easing my fears. I called out to him, and he started toward me. But as he grew closer, his face contorted into a snarl and he joined the villagers in their chant. "You killed us. You killed us."

"No, no, no, oh, Goddess, forgive me, please forgive me, Epor."

I pressed against the well, feeling the windlass cut into my back. They kept coming, pressing in, chanting their accusations. Rahel stood there, her arms raised, cursing me in a voice that rose to the skies.

I turned, looking into the well, seeking escape. But the dead were there, too, their arms lifted as if to pull me into the depths. I cried out again, terrified and looked back to see Epor before me, his club raised to strike me down. "Epor, please don't hurt me!"

"Epor would never hurt you, Lara."

"She can't hear you, Isdra."

Terrified, I sought a way to the gate. But the dead had piled themselves at my feet, their dead and dry carcasses pressed against my legs like cord wood. Xymund stood before me, the madness dancing in his eyes, with a flaming brand in his hand. "Die, whore."

He threw the torch at my feet, The flames flared up, I cried out . . .

I burned.

The castle was dark, but the stones were cool under my feet. I welcomed the silence and the quiet. But as I walked

*the halls the very stones began to warm, blistering my
feet. The familiar halls became a maze where I wandered,
lost and confused.*

"She's stopped drinking."

*I stumbled into the kitchen. Anna was there, lying on
the floor, sweating and moaning. Othur was seated at the
table, a mug of ale in one hand. When I touched his
shoulder, he collapsed to the floor like a broken doll.*

"Her eyes are so sunken, like Epor's."

*I fled, running, crying out to the Goddess for aid. When
I burst into the chapel, the benches were filled with the
dead and dying victims of the sweat.*

*Archbishop Drizen and Deacon Browdus stood before
the statute of the Lady, their vestments drenched in sweat,
dragging on the floor as they went about the service. Two
acolytes, the men in Rahel's loft, were assisting with the
offering.*

"Can you think of anything else to try, young'un? From
her teachings?"

*They all ignored my pleas and cries as they moved
about the base of the marble statue. The cool peace of the
chapel filled me then, and I sank to my knees. The Goddess reached out to me and with a glad heart I stretched
out my hand to touch hers, wanting nothing more than the
peace of her gardens, there to dwell forever.*

*But her hand withdrew before it touched mine and it
was only when I looked up into the Lady's face that I realized that she was sweating too. Suffering as Her people
suffered. The marble moved then, the Lady raised her
arms and called out to her husband, the Sacred Sun, and
the flames rained down on my skin.*

"I's have an idea."

I burned.

* * *

"*. . . Death of earth, birth of water . . .*"

I burned.

The heat within my body was all encompassing, and there was no escape. It was in my blood, in my lungs, and every limb of my body. I tried to lick my lips, to find some precious moisture in my mouth, but there was none. My tongue was a dry and lifeless thing, and my lips cracked and stung. I could feel the sweat under my breasts and behind my knees, but it dried as fast as it appeared. There was only heat and I burned. I tried to open my eyes, to see what was happening but there were only blurs about me. Nothing seemed to have any substance except the pain behind my eyes and the flames that licked my flesh. I tried to reach out but my hands grasped nothing but dry air.

"*. . . Death of water, birth of air . . .*"

I was flying beneath a field of blurry stars against a clear black sky. My eyelids rasped, dry and itchy, but still I stared at the blooms of light above me. There were figures around me, moving with me, chanting softly. I flew, but my hair hung heavy, seeming to brush against the tall grass. The heat was still with me, the hearth located in my chest. It was impossible to move with the weight that pressed me down. Each breath was an effort. All I could do was hold open my weary eyes and stare.

"*. . . Death of air, birth of fire . . .*"

The chanting was muted, soft, as indistinct as my vision. It seemed somehow to first raise me closer to the sky, then lower me to the earth.

I cried out as something cold bit my skin, surrounding me, covering me, stealing my breath and the heat from my body. My mouth opened as the flame died, and I sucked in great gulps of air, even as I rose high in the air.

"... *Death of fire, birth of earth* ..."

Keir. It was Keir beside me, Marcus on the other side. I blinked as the water ran off my face. I was in their arms, cradled, being lowered back into water as cold as death. Keir was letting cold water trickle from his cupped hand onto my face, and I blinked as the drops hit my eyes. I felt clean. Clean and cold and alive.

"... *Death of earth, birth of water* ..."

They lowered me again, into the stream, letting the heat flow from my body with the water. I was wrapped in a blanket and Isdra and someone else were holding my legs, chanting as they lifted me, dripping and gasping. Wet cloth clung to my body, as the hands supporting me lowered me into the water once again.

"... *Death of water, birth of air* ..."

The waters flowed over me, driving away every breath and thought. My hair grew heavy, drawn away from my head as the current caught it, fanning it out in the water. My parched lips softened, and I ran my tongue over them, trying to get moisture into my dry throat. Keir used his cupped hand to dribble water into my mouth. I shuddered in relief even as the cold seeped into my very soul.

"Enough."

Gils? Was that Gils? There was a reason that thought was important, a reason that it was wrong to hear his voice. But my concerns were wispy and I couldn't keep them. They were pulled from me even as I was raised from the water. Before I could gather them back, I was dry and under warm furs and a hand was pressing softly on my heart. My eyes refused to open. A cup at my lips, a few swallows and the warm darkness welcomed me back.

* * *

I opened my eyes, and stared into the darkness. It seemed familiar somehow, to lay so, in a tent where the only light came from braziers. I was too weak to move, or do much more than simply breathe. It felt good, and it took long moments for me to understand that I was feeling better. Utterly drained of any strength, but I wasn't hot, wasn't sweating. My breath came slowly and I enjoyed the sensation for a while in the quiet warmth of the tent.

A soft sound drew my attention. I thought about that for a moment, then slowly turned my head toward the noise.

Keir was sitting on the floor, leaning on the bed. His one hand braced his head, the other lay close to mine. He was asleep, and snoring, something I hadn't heard him do before. He looked so tired, so haggard. Hair mussed, his chin rough and unshaven. If he slept like that for much longer, he'd have a sore neck. With some effort, I managed to move my hand enough to brush his fingertips with mine.

His head snapped up, eyes wide. He stared at me in the dim light, then joy flooded his face, and he grabbed my hand. "Lara?"

I tried to smile, but it became a yawn instead.

"My heart's fire." Keir's voice was soft, and I blinked at him. "Are you well?"

My curiosity forced me to make an effort to talk. "How . . . long?"

He stroked my hand, gently. "Three days."

I stared at him, trying to make sense of the images and memories in my mind. It was all so jumbled.

There was a sound of someone stirring, but I couldn't lift my head to look. Marcus moved into my line of sight, with Gils right behind, looking anxious. When he saw that I was conscious, his face split into a toothy grin.

"How?" I whispered.

Keir glanced at the others. "We were losing you. Gils came up with an idea, to place you in the stream to quench the fire within."

"You . . . were . . . chanting."

Keir nodded. "A ritual. We wanted you to be prepared if . . ." Keir's voice cracked and he swallowed hard.

Marcus cleared his throat. "For mercy, Lara. If the stream had not returned you to us, we were prepared to grant you mercy."

I looked into Keir's face, so tired, so full of pain. "Oh, my Keir."

He crawled onto the bed, and pulled me into his arms, which trembled even as they crushed me close. Voices spoke, but it was too much effort to try to understand. I closed my eyes, let my head rest on Keir's chest and concentrated on breathing, content. It was so comfortable to be held, listening to the rapid beat of his heart.

Eventually, Keir eased me back, supporting my head and neck, and a cup of cool water was placed at my lips. I swallowed gratefully. It was replaced by a bowl, and I recognized the scent of the broth that Marcus makes so well. I managed a few sips, to the delight of someone.

Then someone put a dose of fever's foe in my mouth and I crinkled my nose, recognizing the taste as it flooded my throat. I heard Marcus snort. "Don't like the taste of your own, eh?"

Keir chuckled, and I pulled my eyes open again to focus on him. He still looked tired, but the crinkles at the corners of his eyes were back. I took a deep breath, and then made a face. He leaned in, "What is it, Lara?"

I had to take a deep breath to get the words out in a croak. "You stink."

The laugh burst from him, his entire body shaking, and he pulled me in, holding me tight to his chest. "Ah, my Lara." He lowered me down to the bedding, eyes bright with what looked like tears. "I suppose I do, at that."

"She'll sleep now." Marcus growled. "Gils and I will watch over her. You need to care for yourself. I'll have food ready when you're done."

Keir made as if to protest, but I frowned at him. He sat back with a sigh. "Fair enough." He reached over and stroked my cheek with his hand. I closed my eyes at his touch, and fell back into sleep between one breath and the next.

The fever had broken, but the lethargy held me in its grasp. I lay in the tent for the next day, with barely the energy to draw breath.

Gils kept forcing liquids into me, regularly appearing with a cup of sweet, cold water, or a bowl of Marcus's broth. At first I was eager, since I was wrung dry by the fever. But after a while, it was an effort to drink and swallow, more exhaustion than inability. Keir was beside me constantly, bracing my head, encouraging me to drink. I slept more often than not, awakening to a cup or a bowl.

As my exhaustion continued everyone's faces grew grim. They were worried, and had I the strength, I'd have been as well. But with each passing moment, the life seemed to fade from my body, bit by bit after the last bout of fever.

"Out."

I opened my eyes to find Marcus shooing Keir and Isdra from the tent. Keir made as if to protest, but Marcus cut him off. "She'll feel better for a bath. The young'un is all the help I need, and none of your prying eyes."

"We'll help." Keir frowned.

"No such thing," Marcus insisted. "Go out and do something useful."

"What?"

Marcus threw up his hands. "Chop wood. Carry water. Sharpen your sword. Anything to get you out from underfoot."

Keir made a growling noise, but he and Isdra cleared out of the tent. Marcus and Gils fussed for a bit, with Gils going to fetch a bucket of warm water. I appreciated his efforts to honor my 'shyness', although I wasn't sure there was a point to it anymore. Everyone had seen me in all my glory at some point. But I couldn't even muster the energy to be embarrassed.

Marcus moved to the side of the bed, and pulled back the bedding. "We'll wash your hair, Lara. You will feel better, yes?"

The idea had appeal, but I'd no energy to contribute to the effort. I sighed as Marcus helped me roll closer to the side of the bed. He must have heard me, since he made the same kind of soothing sound that I'd heard Isdra use on the babe. I smiled weakly, even as he beat a gentle rhythm on my back, just as Isdra had done.

I coughed.

Pain gripped my chest, and I went into a spasm of coughing, a horrible deep racking sound. It left me gasping, hanging over the edge of the bed, trying to clear my throat. Marcus was holding me, calling frantically for Keir and Gils. I stared at the mess I'd made, and gasped for air, trying to make sense of what had just happened.

Keir and Gils came running in, demanding an explanation. Marcus sputtered an apology, even as he tried to push me onto my back. But I resisted, sure that I knew what was happening. The fluids were in my chest. Building slowly, instead of sweating out, drowning me. The exhaustion had masked it, but Marcus had . . .

"Again. Do that again." My voice wasn't more than a rasp, but it cut through the babble about me. Keir had his arms about me, and Marcus was pale as a cloud.

"What did you do?" Keir asked sharply.

"I drummed her. I thought to offer comfort . . ."

"Again." I struggled in Keir's arms. "Do it again."

"It hurts you," Marcus objected.

"Have to . . ." I coughed again.

Gils knelt by the bed. "She's purging her body of the bad water, when she coughs. Is that right, Warprize?"

I nodded. "Again."

Marcus flinched back, but Keir adjusted his hold on my body. "I'll do it." His warm hand gently tapped on my back.

It worked, although I almost wished it hadn't. The cough was harsh and rough, and my chest ached. Gils wanted to give me one of my cough remedies, but everything in my supplies would sooth the cough, not encourage it.

We settled into a routine of having someone drum my back every hour. That gave me time to recover enough for the next bout. With every session, I could feel an improvement in my well-being. But it was an agony, and Keir took to bribing me with treats to get me to cooperate. Not that there were many treats to be had in our little camp. But I took great pleasure in watching him play with the babe, making faces and silly noises. Odd how a War-lord, so fierce in combat, could make a baby coo.

"Letters have come. From Water's Fall."

I looked over at him, standing in the entrance of the tent. He seemed pleased with himself for some reason. Marcus was behind him.

"They threw them to us, Lara, so no contact, as I prom-ised. Gils is trying to read Simus's for us." He moved closer, pulling back my bedding. "But first you must cough."

"I'm so tired, Keir."

"I know. But each time there's less pain, less water. You are doing better." Keir opened his arms and I moved into them. He helped me into position, and I rested my head on his chest for just a moment, enjoying his strength. He paused, and pressed me close to his heart.

"You're still well?" I asked, worried that he'd start to sicken before my eyes.

"We are all well, Lara." Keir's hand rubbed a warm cir-cle on my back. "Marcus, Isdra, the babe, Gils, we are all well. Stop fretting so."

With that, he started to drum my back, and I began to cough. Maybe it was his warmth, or his soft words of en-couragement but this time seemed easier than the others, and it was over quickly. Marcus came in to help settle me back into the bed. Keir eased in behind me, to help prop me up, and Marcus fussed over the bedding.

Once I was established, Marcus provided hot kavage. Isdra stepped in, the babe in her arms. The child was gur-gling and kicking, happy and well. That alone put a smile on my face. But I frowned as well. How was it that the child was so healthy?

More to the point, how did she stay healthy? She'd spent hours next to her dead mother, time with us in the

village, and had been in this tent with me during that
time. Yet here she was, plump and pink, and no trace of
fever. In my experience, children were the first to suc-
cumb to illness. What was different here?

Keir interrupted my thoughts. "Is he ready?" Keir
asked.

Isdra smiled, and stepped aside to sit next to Marcus on
a stump. I looked at Keir questioningly, but he simply
pointed to the tent entrance.

To my surprise, the flap was pulled roughly aside, and
Gils leaped in, striking a pose, his fists on his hips, his
legs wide apart, and his chest puffed out. I smiled, recognizing Simus in the stance. But what looked powerful on a
tall, muscular man with black skin looked terribly silly on
a gangly youngster.

"HEYLA, little healer." Gils boomed out, trying to
deepen his voice. "These are the words of Simus the
Hawk, and they are written even as I speak them!"

I had to laugh out loud at that, and looked up into
Keir's face. While there was no smile, his eyes were crinkled in the corners, and I could see the laughter hidden
there. I leaned back, safe in his arms, and watched as Gils
struck another pose, gesturing with one hand.

"All is well within the stone tents of Water's Fall. Have
no concern for your people. Although your Council talks
too much, and have sent you many dry words on paper.
Do not read them. I have told all that their senels waste
breath and sunlight. Othur turns bright red when I say so,
and Warren laughs and laughs."

Gils started to pace, swaggering back and forth in
front of the bed. I covered my mouth not wanting to hurt
his feelings, but from the side glances he gave me, I

knew that he was trying to make me laugh. So I did, loud and clear, as he continued.

"One of the council is worth her words, one Mavis. A fine woman. She fancies me."

Keir snorted.

"Our people have settled here with not too much trouble. The stone walls make us all uneasy. There have been only a few fights, and no deaths that I know of, although Eln of the Healers has sharp words for me each time I see him.

"Othur rules well. Anna makes good food. She fancies me. Warren is a strong warrior and we have tested our blades against each other. Eln has said that Atira is fine. I was forced to share my kavage with her, as her pleas were pitiful. My own leg heals well.

"I have attended a High Court and am not impressed. We of the Plains can teach your people much about senels and celebrations. The women dress in drab colors and act oddly. They pretend to fear a warrior such as I, but they admire my strength and prowess. They all fancy me."

I laughed so hard, I started to cough, and Gils waited until the spasm passed.

"Send word of your lives to me. Send kavage, for I will grow ugly without it. I have sent words for Joden's song. Read them to him."

Gils came to stand at the end of the bed, his hands on his hips, chest thrust out. "Tell that Warlord of yours that all is well, and that he could have no better voice than I. Fare well, little healer, Xylara, Daughter of Xy, Warprize and my friend." Gils bowed, and I laughed, looking up into Keir's face again to share the moment. His eyes softened as he returned the look.

Gils approached, his eyes alight. "Warprize, here are the others. I could only read that of Simus. The words in the others are too hard."

"You did very well, Gils." I smiled at him, and he blushed.

"Now." Marcus stood. "Isdra and I have to wash the babe's things before we are overcome with the stink." He fixed his good eye on Keir. "You are getting flabby. Go spar with Gils. Leave her to her letters."

Gils went pale, his eyes wide.

Keir raised an eyebrow at Marcus, then looked at me. "Do you need anything?"

"She's fine." Marcus started to push him out of the tent. "Are we not within calling distance? Go. Work out your frustrations, yes?"

"Why me?" Gils protested, as they all filed out.

Simus was right. The formal letters from my council were dull and dry. They'd all been sent some time ago, so there was no mention of the plague, or its effects on the city. Simus had included another letter for Joden, with his version of the events that had reunited me with Keir. I tucked that one away to read to Joden once we were all together again.

The parchment of the various missives crackled under my fingers. Othur had included a short, private note to tell me that he and Anna were well and that Lord Durst was still recovering from the blow that Keir had dealt him.

The next set of letters would tell me what had happened. If the plague had hit the city. If Eln had gotten my warnings in time. As much as I longed for word, I dreaded it as well. Eln would want the details of what had

happened, and how I had managed to survive an illness
that killed a warrior in his prime and the entire village of
Wellspring. How Isdra and the babe remained healthy
when everyone else succumbed. I had no answers.

From outside the tent I could hear the sounds of sparring, and water being sloshed in buckets. Probably Marcus and Isdra washing the babe's cloths. The guilt rose in
my chest, and my eyes filled. The entire village, the
babe's mother . . . the babe's name . . . we'd lost all of
that. Rahel's remedies and cures, her stash of notes, all
gone in a matter of days. What kind of illness was this,
that some lived on for days, and others suffered for a few
hours, but all die? All except me.

Of course, they hadn't had Gils. I smiled, wiping my
tears. I couldn't ask for a better apprentice. He was so
passionate about his new skills. He'd taken an old saddle
bag, and was using his spare moments to make it into a
kind of satchel, stitching on a wide strap, and adding
pockets for 'lots of useful things'. He'd offered to give it
to me, but I'd told him to make me another one when he
was done with his.

My smile faded slightly. Gils had found a way to
break my fever, which had left me with enough strength
to fight the lethargy and the fluids that had built up in my
lungs. But I doubted that Eln would be satisfied with my
new remedies. He'd want an herbal cure and I'd nothing
to offer.

All I had to offer was a desperate way to bring down a
raging fever, and a touch that caused the body to do what
it should do on its own. Those were not the weapons with
which to defeat an invisible enemy.

The tent flap opened and Keir stepped in, sweating in
his armor. He gave me a gentle look, and I flushed a bit,

conscious that this was the first time that we'd been alone since the fever had broken.

He came to stand at the foot of my bed. "All's well?" He nodded toward the letters.

"It was." I gathered up the documents. "I need to send a message to Eln and tell him what has happened."

"Good. We'll do so before we leave for the Plains."

Startled, I looked up at him. "Surely before that. We can't leave for some forty days."

It was amazing how those blue eyes could change in an instant. They sparked like flint as his body tensed. "Another day will see you well enough to travel. We'll leave for the Heart of the Plains the day after tomorrow."

"You can't be serious." I gaped at him. "Keir, we have to stay isolated from the others for forty days. I have explained this to you—"

He cut me off, raising his voice to drown me out. "With the elements favor we will make up the lost days on the journey. We will rejoin the army, and depart this place."

The letters scattered over the bed as I struggled up out of the blankets. "This illness killed an entire village, not to mention Epor. For the love of the Goddess, Keir, you must listen to me!"

The sound of our voices had attracted attention. Marcus came into the tent, with Gils peeking around the flap. Isdra stood behind them, considering us carefully, a serious look on her face.

"You survived. Isdra and the babe survived. We are well." Keir threw his head back, his nostrils flaring. "I will not be denied in this, Warprize."

I struggled to get out of the bed, but the blankets defeated me. Marcus moved to my side, but I was so agitated that I fought him off. My anger flared for the first time in days. "You stupid man. Why am I here, if you won't listen to me?"

That was a mistake. Keir's face closed. "You are here because you will bring the gift of healing to my people."

I sucked in a breath, bit my lip, then lashed out. "So the very thing that I bring to your people is what you ignore. If you do this, it will bring only death."

Keir glared. "Rest. Gather your strength. Tomorrow night I will give the orders. We leave on the morning after next." He stomped out of the tent, practically tearing the flap from the tent as he left.

The fight fled my body and I grabbed at Marcus's arms to support myself. "Marcus, he can't mean it. Can he?"

Marcus eased me down. "Hisself is determined, Warprize."

Gils crept into the tent, avoiding my eyes. Isdra came in, bringing the sleeping babe. She sat on the edge of the bed, and showed her to me. "She does well, Lara."

"It takes time to know that the illness is gone." Worried as I was, I smiled to see the babe's sweet sleeping face. Isdra lay the child on the bed next to me. "She's thriving, that's true. With a strange fondness for gurt."

Isdra nodded. "She'll need to be marked soon."

"Tattooed?" I looked at her in horror.

Gils laughed. "Not one so young, Warprize. We use a stain to mark babes with their tribe."

"You must design a mark for your tribe, Lara." Isdra seemed to be studying the floor of the tent. "The tribe of Xy. The Elders will require such before our blood combines in children." Isdra stood abruptly. "I have some things to see to, Warprize. I will leave the child with you."

I smiled. "Of course, Isdra. I am well tended here."

She gave me an odd look. "That you are, Lara."

* * *

Needless to say, the air in the tent had turned frigid since Keir and I had argued. Gils was very clever in avoiding any contact with Keir and I, especially when our tempers flared, and flare they did over the course of the evening. Marcus just grumped at both of us. Isdra kept her distance as well. I wasn't so occupied with arguing with Keir that I didn't notice the distant expression on her face. I thought she was thinking on Epor's death, and Keir's folly, but I couldn't have been more wrong.

Later the next day Isdra walked into the tent, her face so sorrowful, it scared me. She looked different somehow, but it was the reaction of the others that brought me up short. Keir sat up a bit straighter, and Marcus stopped what he was doing. Gils looked up from the book of herbs that I had him studying and closed it slowly. At their reactions I looked again. Isdra wasn't wearing any weapons or armor, just a plain tunic and trous. Although she carried Epor's warclub in one hand, she looked naked to me, as if the warrior had been stripped away somehow to reveal the vulnerable woman underneath. She looked at each of us in turn, then focused on Keir. "Warlord."

"Warrior."

"It is time, Warlord. Past time. I've completed our tasks, Epor's and mine."

Keir stood. "A task well done, Isdra of the Fox. I thank you for your service, and wish you well."

I looked from one to the other, puzzled. "What's going on? Are you leaving, Isdra?"

Isdra looked at me, but then looked back at Keir. "I'd ask that you give this to Prest, Warlord. He'll wield it with honor." She held out Epor's warclub.

Keir stepped forward, and took the weapon with a nod. My heart started to pound in my chest. "Isdra?"

"Safe journey to the snows, Isdra." Marcus spoke softly. "And beyond." The sorrow in his face and eye reflected hers.

Gils stood as well, his face a mask of stoic pain.

"No." I cried out, certain now what she intended. I pushed the blankets off my legs and tried to stand. "No, Isdra, you can't." I stood, swaying and reached a trembling hand toward her.

Isdra stepped up to grasp my fingers. "Warprize, I've seen to your safety. Epor awaits, and I'm eager to join him." She hugged me tight. "Lara, this is our way. Try to understand and accept."

I pushed her back, holding on to her arms for support. "No, I don't accept it. Keir, tell her not to do this. Command her—"

"Lara."

I looked over my shoulder to find Keir shaking his head. "In matters of bonding, I cannot command." His gaze flicked over to Marcus then back to me. "The choice is hers and hers alone."

I turned back to her. "Then choose to stay. I need you, Isdra." A soft cry rose from the blankets, which caught my attention and hers. "The babe needs you, too."

With a patient look, Isdra gripped my forearms and lowered me to the bed. "Lara, you are well cared for, as will be the babe."

"I am the Warprize. I can—"

"You cannot." Isdra stood. "None have the right to interfere in a bonding, Lara. Not even a Warprize." She took a step back, and bowed her head to Keir. "Warlord."

"Warrior."

Isdra turned, but before I could protest, the tent flap opened. Chill air flowed into the tent and Joden appeared, his broad face grim.

Keir spoke first. "Joden? What is wrong?"

"The plague. It's in the camp."

8

My father loved to dance. On impulse, he'd command the musicians to play, and would join the lords and ladies in cavorting around the throne room, anything from a stately promenade to a sprightly jig. One of his favorite dances was where everyone held position when the music stopped unexpectedly. It reduced his normally stuffy court to giggles and guffaws when they tried to keep still until the music started again. Due to Father's illness, and my less than popular position at court under my brother's rule, I hadn't seen that dance in years. But that was the memory that swirled in my head when we all froze as Joden's words sunk in.

Keir was the first to react, sweeping up his swords and strapping on the harnesses. "Horses?"

"Outside." Joden stepped further into the tent. "Enough for all."

"We'll go." Keir jerked a blanket from his bedroll and moved to my side. He snapped the blanket out, and wrapped it around my shoulders. I stared at him, numbed at the idea that this might have made its way to the camp, but he gave me no chance to speak.

"I's got the supplies." Gils started packing even as Marcus moved toward the babe.

Keir had me bundled up and in his arms before I could say a word. I wrapped my arms around his neck and used them to pull myself higher so that I could look over his shoulder. "Isdra?"

As if my voice had cut off the music, everyone froze again.

Isdra stood in the center of the tent, weaponless, looking naked and vulnerable. I'd never seen such pain as I did on her face. She was torn right in two, longing pulling her in both directions. She hesitated, licking her lips, indecisive for the first time since I had met her. Joden's face held a puzzled look as his eyes took in the scene, until a brief look around the tent answered his unspoken question. He closed his eyes in pain, and the loss of Epor stabbed at my heart all over again.

In that suspended moment, Keir's lips brushed my ear with the barest of whispers. "I can't ask. You can." He turned slightly so that I faced Isdra.

"Isdra." I made my voice firm. "I need you. You've been through this, can speak of it to the others. I need you to stay. Please."

The pain was still in her eyes, but the uncertainty vanished. "For now, Warprize."

As if the music started again, we moved. I tightened

my grip as Keir spun for the tent entrance, with Joden right behind. Marcus and Gils scrambled to follow. Isdra calmly stepped into the corner of the tent and grasped Epor's warclub as the flap fell to cut off my view.

There were seven horses waiting outside. One, a big black horse, neighed a welcome, and advanced to meet us. He was followed closely by my own brown mount, with the scarred chest. Keir handed me to Joden, then swung up into the saddle of the black. I opened my mouth to protest, since there was a horse for me to ride, but one look at Keir's face and I decided it wasn't the time to press the issue.

I did take advantage of the slight delay. "Joden, how many are sick?"

"Ten, Warprize. The longest for half a day."

"Half a day?" Keir growled. "Why wasn't word sent?" He leaned over to take me.

Joden said nothing until he was sure Keir had me safe in the saddle. "Iften's orders."

The black stamped, reacting to Keir's sudden tensing. Keir shifted in the saddle, easing the beast, adjusting me in his arms, even as his eyes glittered with rage.

Joden stood there, his face bland. "I would have brought others with me, but none could disobey."

"Except you?" I asked.

"There are benefits to being almost a Singer." Joden's teeth flashed as he gave me a rare smile. "Almost the same as being Warprize."

"Where is Iften?" Keir ground the words out. Even in his fury, his arms cradled me gently.

"In your command tent." Joden's face was a polite mask once again, but I knew that his choice of words was deliberate.

I shivered, fearing Keir's reaction. But he surprised me as he snorted, more amused than offended. He gave me a look, and I caught a glimpse of impish humor lurking in the back of his eyes just as he called out. "Marcus!"

Marcus opened the tent flap. "We're packing as fast—"

"Leave it. I will send others to aid Isdra and Gils. I need you with me."

"Eh?"

"Iften set himself up in the command tent."

Pure rage danced over Marcus's face. He disappeared, only to pop out a breath later, fully cloaked, heading for a horse, muttering something under his breath. Isdra looked out, even as Joden and Marcus mounted.

"Isdra, I will send others to break this camp. Bring Gils and the babe to the command tent as fast as you can."

If she replied, it was lost as the black horse surged forward.

The wind whipped around us as we moved at a gallop. The camp was in the distance, spread out by the shores of a small lake, its waters a clear, cold blue. I was glad of the blanket and the warmth of Keir's strong arms. But he was grim and silent as we rode. Joden and Marcus followed, and to my surprise, my horse was behind them, riderless, but following his herd.

Once we entered the encampment, the warriors about us started to react, calling greetings to Keir, and making those warbling cries. Keir didn't slow the horse, but he responded to the calls, calling out names, summoning warleaders. I had glimpses of people scrambling for horses and running off, obeying his commands.

A familiar voice caught my attention, and a smiling

Rafe rode up next to us, seeming almost to dance in his saddle. "Heyla, Warlord!"

"I call you back to duty, Rafe."

"Good." Rafe turned in his saddle to look behind. "Prest and I can give Epor and Isdra a rest, yes?"

"Epor is dead." Keir's voice was flat, but Rafe's head whipped back in shock, his eyes wide. "Find Yers, Rafe. Bring him to the command tent."

Rafe turned his horse off. "I'll find Prest as well, Warlord."

As we raced closer, I could see more and more tents around us. Keir had split the army, leaving about half of his troops in Water's Fall with Simus, but he still had a large number of warriors with him. If the plague had truly reached the camp, the deaths here would make the village seem like nothing. I swallowed hard as the horse came to a stop in front of the command tent.

Joden and Marcus rode up behind us as Keir dismounted. He wouldn't let me walk the few steps to the tent, lifting me without even asking permission. I opened my mouth to protest, but he cut me off. "Save your strength for what lies ahead."

The guards at the entrance held back the flaps, and Keir strode into the main room of the tent. Without stopping, he headed for the sleeping area. As he pushed through that flap, I heard an odd grunting sound. I caught my breath at the sight of Iften bare-assed and plowing a woman in our bed.

Our bed!

Thankfully, the glimpse was brief. Keir spun on his heel, taking me back into the meeting area even as I let out an exclamation. Marcus, on the other hand, stepped right into the smaller room and I heard voices raised in anger. I peeked over Keir's shoulder to see a woman warrior leaving the tent, her gear in hand, naked as a babe.

Keir seated me on the platform. I glared at him, but he used his body to shield me from view, and placed a finger over my lips. In the background, I could hear Marcus yelling at the top of his lungs. A few more warleaders had entered the tent, listened and smirked. There was anger in Keir's eyes, but there was also a glint of humor there. I gave him a questioning look. He leaned a bit closer. "Marcus does with words what I'd use a sword to accomplish."

Marcus's voice was sharp as a dagger and Iften's defensive. Iften was trying to justify his actions without much success. Of course, Marcus was giving him no quarter, no chance to put in a word edgewise.

I snorted softly, but then reason reasserted itself as I remembered our situation.

Keir sensed the change. Even though I was already wrapped in a blanket, he pulled off his cloak and swirled it out and over my shoulders. It settled on me gently, wrapping me in his warmth. I reached to pull the edges closed, but Keir knelt and did it for me. His head was close to mine, his breath warm on my cheek.

I clutched at him. "Keir, I—" I couldn't continue for the fear that clogged my throat.

He gathered my cold hands in his strong warm ones. "What happened in the village will not happen here."

I swallowed hard, and stared at him, unable to speak.

Keir kept his voice low. "You lived, Lara. Isdra and the child never sickened. Take hope from that."

Marcus was bellowing at the top of his lungs, something about Iften using his cooking pots. The meeting tent was still filling with warleaders, much amused by the scene. I took advantage of the distraction to lean into

Keir's arms, hugging him in return. He pulled me close, wrapping his arms around me, holding me like something precious. I drew a deep breath of leather and the scent of his skin, seeking a small comfort before facing what lay ahead.

Keir waited, seemingly willing to sit there all day if necessary. But I pulled back, and he released me. "There's so much to do, Keir. I need—"

"First things first." With that Keir stood and called out over the noise. "Marcus. Enough."

Marcus got in the last word. "Clothe yourself. The Warprize will be offended by your naked ass."

Iften emerged, still struggling into his trous, carrying a sheathed sword, his face red with anger. But everyone's attention was now drawn to Keir.

"The enemy is in the camp. We must take action before it claims lives." Keir stood at my side, his hand on my shoulder. "The village is dead, leaving only one survivor. Epor has fallen as well." The response to this was immediate, with warriors stiffening all over the room. Keir didn't pause. He turned slightly. "Joden. Where are the sick?"

"Spread out in camp." Joden replied.

"We will gather them here. Set up the Warprize's still-tent, and—"

"Why?" Iften stood, some of the red fading from his face. "They are afflicted. Let them crawl off, or better still, let us leave this accursed place and return to the Plains." Wesren was standing next to him, and nodded his agreement.

"They'll die without treatment." I pointed out.

"So?" Iften looked at me, honest surprise on his face. "This is our way, Warprize."

"Then our dead will dribble behind us, as water from a leaking skin." A voice spoke from the tent entrance and we all looked to see Isdra standing there, with Gils behind her holding the babe's basket in one hand, satchel of healing supplies on his hip.

From the look on Gils's face, he hadn't known of the meeting. To his credit, he didn't pause for long. He stepped past Isdra and walked through their midst to stand by my side. The babe was kicking at her blankets, waving her arms around happily.

What astonished me was the reaction of the warleaders. Even Iften's face seemed to soften at the sight of the child, kicking and cooing. "Is that the only survivor?" Tsor asked softly, craning his neck to get a better look.

"Yes." Keir smiled at the basket as Gils set it down next to me. "The babe and Isdra did not sicken. The Warprize became ill, but she survived."

Isdra had followed Gils, to stand next to me. Without their speaking, I could see the various warleaders considering her with long looks. Was it because she lived? Or because of Epor's war club, still strapped to her back.

Iften's eyes narrowed. "Why have you not joined your bonded, Isdra of the Fox?"

Isdra's eyes were dark and cold and something in my stomach clenched. But she merely stood straight and still, tilting her head up a bit to look Iften in the eye, and responded in low tones. "Be wary, Warleader. For you do not hold my token, and I might take offense."

Marcus chose that moment to emerge from the sleeping area, his arms full of weapons and armor. He moved next to Iften, and dumped it at his feet. Before the blond could react, Marcus had ducked back under the tent flap. Iften had a snarl on his face, and took a step as if to confront Marcus, but Keir stopped him. "There is no time for this." Keir's voice cut through us all. "This is no senel, and no truths will be addressed. The old ways of dealing with," he hesitated slightly, "of dealing with the sick will not work, for all of us have been exposed to the enemy. Alone, we will all die. Together, we will defeat this enemy. This is battle and I will be obeyed."

That was that for most of the warleaders, although Iften scowled and a few others looked uncertain. But all focused on Keir's commands.

"All who are ill are to be brought here, to the shore. The lake will be used to cool the fevers."

"Ortis, pull the scouts in. Set a guard within the camp, with no warrior alone. The rest of the scouts, send to the Warprize, to learn the signs and treatment of this illness. They will spread the word in the camp so that all learn the enemy."

"Food, Warlord." Sal spoke up, grim and anxious. "How can I send out hunting parties if they may die at any moment?"

Isdra spoke up. "The village had animals. We released those we found outside the walls. And there were herds beyond the walls, to the south. Cows, sheep and goats."

"There'd be pigs in the woods as well." I added.

"That will work well." Sal relaxed slightly. "But I'll save a milk goat for the babe, eh?"

There were a few brief smiles at that statement. But the smiles faded and faces grew grim when Isdra spoke, her voice flat and hollow. "Some must gather wood. There will be a need for pyres." No one drew a breath in the silence after her words. Isdra continued, relentless in her honesty. "The village still smolders. We can burn the dead there."

"That is as may be." Keir looked at her with understanding, not offended by her comment. "We will start by teaching everyone what Gils and the Warprize have learned about this illness. Set up the Warprize's stilltent as quickly as possible. Until then, use this area. Fill the tent with messengers to learn from them and spread the word." Keir continued speaking, issuing orders to all, but I was already considering what had to be done. It was only when he took my cold hands into his that I realized he was kneeling before me, and the tent had cleared of all but us and Marcus.

His eyes were clear and grave, the blue of the early morning sky. "I must go, Lara. There will be trouble over this, and I must be seen and heard to counter the rumors that will be spread."

"See to the army." Marcus placed a hand on my shoulder. "We will see to her."

Keir cupped my face in his warm hand, letting his thumb stroke my cheek, feather-soft and gentle. With a swirl of his cloak, he was up and gone.

Within moments of Keir's exit, warriors crammed into the command tent to listen as Gils and I explained how to treat the ill, what to watch for, and what to expect. We sent them out all over the camp to repeat our words. Thank the Goddess for their memories. That, and their strict obedience to Keir's authority.

As the messengers left, more warriors filled the tent. Gils and I started them on the hunt for willow bark, as much as they could gather. Luckily, the army had cut down a number of willows to make their camp. I sent warriors off to strip bark from all the firewood and tem-

porary tables and chairs. A small army of warriors would
stir pots and pots of the stuff, boiling it down for fever's
foe. We'd need every jar we could fill.

Again the tent filled. I sipped some kavage that Marcus
forced on me, then Gils and I started the herb lessons. I
already knew that the supply of lotus wouldn't be big
enough to serve the entire camp. We needed alternatives,
such as sleepease, tree butter, or comfrey. So these warriors became the gatherers. We held up the herbs we were
seeking, and gave examples to them so that they knew
what to look for. Rahel may have had a healing garden
outside the walls, so I set them to searching for whatever
they could find.

When gathering herbs the general rule is that you never
strip an area of all of the plants that you are gathering.
You try to leave enough that the spring will bring new
growth and renew the area. But I didn't have the luxury of
leaving anything behind. I told them to bring me everything they could find. Should I pass this way again, I'd re-
seed the area myself, to make up for the damage. But we
needed those herbs and we needed them now.

Within hours we had a hundred sick. By the end of the
day the number tripled. Men and women fell dead as the
wheat falls before the scythe. It struck with the sweat, the
headache, and the stench as it had in the village.

The fever was the worst. Using the cold waters of the
stream or the lake only seemed to work if the fever had
built to its highest point. Too soon, and the fever returned,
prolonging the illness and exhausting the patient. Gils ran
himself ragged, helping to make the decision of when a
patient was ready to be immersed. He gained far too
much skill over a very short period of time.

Outside, the shores of the lake filled with people using

its cold waters to bring down the raging heat of fever. And the sick kept coming as more and more fell victim. I could see no reason to its effects, either. One would be sick for days or hours, each with as likely a chance of dying as the other. But we learned, Gils and I, that if the person made it through the initial fever, his chances of survival were much higher. Once past the coughing stage, the individual recovered strength fairly quickly.

I'd enough strength to manage supplies, and train warriors to tend the sick. So I commanded from the stilltent, checking the quality of the fever's foe and using the gathered herbs to make an alternative to the lotus. One of the draughts, the one based on sleepease, was milder than the lotus, and seemed to work better, so I concentrated on making that mixture. The familiar scents and surroundings of my stilltent were a comfort in those dark hours.

Poor Gils was the one to actually tend the sick, wearing himself to the bone with the patients, making sure that the right doses were given, that the fevers were brought down, that the drumming on their backs was done on a regular basis. His was the hardest task, for since he was out and about, everyone turned to him for advice, or when a patient took a turn for the worst. He'd return to my stilltent frequently, to ask questions, and restock his satchel, and then he'd be off again.

The raving seemed less of a problem than it had been in the village. Perhaps because of our use of the lake waters to bring down the fever, perhaps due to the use of the other sleeping draught. Or maybe it was the presence of warriors at the bedsides, well able to subdue any crazed by the fever. Still, I insisted that those who were ill not sleep with their weapons. This was resisted strongly, not that they'd disobey exactly. It was as if I had attacked their pride, that their weapons be taken from them. There was disagreement as to how far away the weapons were put, but it only took two incidents for them to start obeying me.

In many ways, I felt disoriented during those hours, since I had limited contact with the patients. Gils and Joden would report to me regularly, or other warriors would appear with questions, or asking for supplies.

It was a heady feeling, to have such power, to see my commands obeyed, a feeling that I wasn't used to. I'd never commanded a large staff, and had only truly been Queen for a few hours before I followed Keir. This was a new experience for me, to be obeyed absolutely.

Yet, it had its drawbacks as well. They did exactly as they were told. I'd set a group of them looking for a weed, and they'd bring me all the weed they could find. But they didn't have the ability to tell me if there were other plants in the area that I could have used as well. So I went through a range of about ten plants and herbs that I could use, trying to insure that I covered every possibility.

Keir was absent during these long hours, moving about the huge camp, explaining, issuing orders, sending us information about the state of the warriors. His presence insured that the ill were helped and that supplies were distributed where needed. He was the calm at the center of the storm, and the reason the warriors didn't mount their horses and head for the plains. But I feared for him, exposed to all and sundry, and working tirelessly among his warriors. I'd tried to have him wear a ginger mask, but he pointed out that it hadn't worked for Epor and I. Worse, I didn't have enough ginger to mask the entire camp. Keir refused a protection that wasn't available for everyone. Since he was absent more often then naught, I took to sleeping in the stilltent, to be quickly available to any that needed me.

Marcus was everywhere, aiding where needed, and somehow keeping us fed. He and Isdra shared the care of the baby, trading off when necessary. What amazed me was the ease with which the warriors dealt with her, for there was no shortage of volunteers. The rare smiles I saw were at the antics of the babe, who kicked and cooed and laughed, the one sound of joy in a camp filled with despair.

For there was little joy in our hearts. There were so many deaths, regardless of the care we took or the medicines we doled out. The darkest moments came when the ill outnumbered the healthy. At that point, we were all exhausted. Whenever I emerged from the tent, I tried not to look at the horizon where the smoke rose from the pyres. Instead, I tried to focus on the living.

Goddess love him, Marcus still found time to make sure that I ate. One morning, during the time when the days blurred together, he was coaxing the morning meal into me when we looked up to see Prest standing just inside the tent, his face grim.

"Prest?" I put my bowl aside and stood.

"Please come, Warprize."

"Who's ill?"

"Rafe."

Prest led the way, and I followed. Marcus came behind, carrying a basket of my supplies, refusing to let me carry anything. I protested, until the walk itself left me breathless. My strength was still not fully returned.

A few of the smaller tents had been cleverly fastened

together to form a larger shelter. Prest held the flap as I bent to enter. The tent was filled with people, but my eyes went to young Rafe first.

He lay on a pallet, already covered in sweat, his black hair plastered to his forehead. His face was pale, far paler than normal, and his eyes were huge and glittering as he looked at me. His lips moved and I heard a faint "Warprize."

This caught the attention of the other people in the tent and they turned to look at me with wide eyes. Four girls, well, warriors . . . but girls to my eyes. They couldn't be that much older than Gils. Their surprise was only for a moment, then the one closest to Rafe's head wrung out a cloth, and placed it on his forehead. She gave me a veiled look of mistrust, bright green eyes flashing through long black hair.

The girl closest to me was dressed in brown leather armor, with her brown curly hair cut very short. She inclined her head. "Warprize, I am Lasa of the Horse. We are tending to Rafe." She straightened, a confident look in her clear brown eyes. "We have talked to Gils, and we know what we must do."

"And we will do it well." The honey-blonde girl kneeling by Rafe's shoulder pounded a stake in the ground with a fierce blow. But she looked up with hazel eyes flecked with fear.

"I am sure that you will." I smiled, trying to reassure her. "But Rafe is one of my guards, and I'd like to check him myself. Would that be acceptable?"

The hazel gaze flicked over to Lasa, but she must have gotten approval. "Of course, Warprize." She got to her feet. "I am Soar of the Deer."

Marcus handed the basket to me, but remained outside

with Prest, given the crush. The girls arranged themselves carefully, leaving me to kneel by Rafe's head. He gave me a weak smile as I put my hand to his forehead. "I'm sorry, Warprize."

"You've nothing to be sorry for, Rafe." He was warm alright, the fever flushing his face. "How long have you been ill?"

He blinked, looking at me, lost and uncertain. As he had looked the first time I met him, in the healing tent in the castle gardens. His head injury had been bleeding, and he'd been the first of the prisoners that had let me treat their wounds. He'd talked to me in a form of trade talk that our people had in common. It had taken time to win his confidence, but Rafe had been the one to ask me to treat Simus, and had reassured Joden of my skills. "Never you mind. Sleep, Rafe."

He closed his eyes, and relaxed. The scar from that old wound stood out, thin and sharp against his skin. The green-eyed girl wet her cloth and began to stroke his face and chest. "He's been ill for a few hours now, Warprize." Her gaze flashed at me again. "Gils has told us all that we need to know."

"Fylin!" Lasa scolded. "Earth's sake, you have no courtesy!"

The green gaze disappeared, as Fylin bowed her head. "Forgive me, Warprize." The tone was sullen. "I am Fylin of the Snake."

"And I am Ksand of the Cat, Warprize." The new girl knelt and held out a half-full jar of fever's foe for my inspection, her brown hair in a braid. "Gils has dosed him with the sleepease. And left this fever's foe for us to use."

"We have taken his weapons, and removed ours as well. We are ready to bind him when the raving begins."

Soar sounded almost eager. I heard a snort from outside the tent, and knew that Prest was listening.

I suppressed my own smile. "You are ready for the battle, then. Let me give you another jar of fever's foe, just in case." I rummaged in my basket. It seemed that Rafe would be well taken care of by his friends. I wanted to stay, but I knew that I didn't have the strength, and that I was needed in the stilltent. Besides, I would insult the honor of these women if I tried to take their duties from them. "I know that Rafe is in good hands, and that you will see him through this."

I heard a grunt from outside, and knew that Marcus approved.

The women seemed pleased at my response, and even Fylin unbent enough to reassure me. "We will send for Gils if we have any doubts or questions, Warprize."

I nodded, and bent down to brush the hair from Rafe's forehead. "May the skies be with you, Rafe."

His eyes opened then, and cleared, truly seeing me. "You must take another guard, Lara."

All four girls went wide-eyed and sucked in their breaths, clearly impressed.

"No, Rafe. I am safe. Prest and Isdra will see to me until you can return to your duties."

"I will return as soon as I . . ." He sighed, and his eyes drifted close.

"Win this battle, Rafe." I stood, and left the tent before he could see my tears.

Outside, Marcus and Prest waited for me, their faces grim. We walked in silence for a moment, as I got my emotions under control. When I felt I could, I turned and looked at Prest. "Four women?"

Prest smirked.

Marcus gave a dry chuckle. "Rafe has always been popular. A charmer, that one. To rival Simus."

I smiled at the comparison. But my smile was short lived as I lifted my head and saw the black smoke still rising from the pyres that burned where a village used to be.

"Rafe was right, we need another to ward you." Marcus spoke from behind me.

I looked down at the ground as I continued to walk, wishing for the security and comfort of my stilltent. "No, Marcus, don't disturb Keir. I have Prest and Isdra, and that's enough." I felt the disapproval radiate from him and cut him off before he could speak. "The healthy care for the sick. The sick try to reclaim their health. Who has time or the strength to threaten me?"

We returned to the stilltent in silence.

The next day a slight noise outside my tent caused me to peek through the flap to see Marcus working his familiar magic on yet another warleader. This time his victim was Joden, being told in no uncertain terms to sit down and eat. Poor Joden looked drained of all his strength as he plopped down onto the stump.

Marcus returned to shove the baby into Joden's arms, wrapped in a blanket and fussing loudly. "Make yourself useful and see to her."

Startled, Joden took the wriggling handful as Marcus stalked off. The babe was kicking and crying as Joden started to make funny noises, trying to distract her. But I could see her tiny feet moving and knew that she was not to be soothed by such a trick.

So that clever, exhausted man patiently reached into

his pouch and brought out a strip of privacy bells. At the sound, tiny hands reached out of the blankets and clutched them tight. The fussing changed to happy laughter; a happiness reflected in Joden's face. A happiness that I had seen in the faces of others that Marcus had played this trick on, using one tiny baby to restore their hearts. I turned back to my pots with a lighter heart.

When Marcus returned with soup and kavage, Joden was relaxed, singing a quiet song to the babe. I emerged from the tent as Joden put the babe back in her basket. When he tugged at the bells, she let out a squall, and tugged right back, putting the leather strap in her mouth and gurgling with joy.

"A warrior's grip, Warprize." Joden accepted the food from Marcus. "What have the elements named her?"

I pushed my hair back behind my ear as the wind caught it. "Her name was lost, Joden. We found her next to her dead mother. Her thea."

Joden drank soup, and studied the child. "A serious thing, to lose a name." Isdra walked up with a load of firewood as he continued. "We listen to the elements to find a child's name. She is young yet, the loss will not harm her. We should have a naming ceremony for her."

Isdra brushed her hands off. "She is of Xy. We should follow their ways in this."

Joden looked at me.

"We name our children for their ancestors, or we choose a name that we like. Rahel said her mother's name was Meara."

"Name her for her thea then," Isdra knelt by the basket.

"Meara, it is." Joden reached out to tickle a waving foot. "She should be marked. Stained."

I had a sudden vision of Anna's face on seeing this child with a tattoo, no matter how temporary the mark. "We can see to that later." I stated firmly.

Joden sighed and picked up his kavage. "It is good that she is named."

Meara shook the bells and laughed, letting us share a rare smile as well.

Her laughter reminded me of something else. "Joden, I forgot to tell you, Simus sent a letter for you. He asked that I read it to you, so that you had his words for your song."

I expected a positive response, but Joden didn't even look at me. He stared at the babe, his face grim. "Joden?"

"I do not think I can craft that song, Warprize."

Puzzled, I studied his broad face, trying to figure out what he meant. "Of course. You're tired. Now's not the time to create a song. I will save the letter, Joden. For later."

Joden ignored me, addressing Marcus instead. "My thanks, Marcus. I have the strength to continue in my task."

"No need of thanks, Singer." Marcus gave him an odd look, but didn't press the matter.

"What are you doing, Joden?" I asked.

"I am seeing to the dead, Lara. Someone must sing for them, even if just a snatch of song." Joden straightened his back and stood. "Give me some good word, one that I can carry in my heart."

"It's slowing, Joden." I answered. "The number of newly ill is falling off."

He took a deep breath, nodding. "That is good, Warprize. I will take that with me." He looked down at the child, still shaking the bells. "The Warlord was right to hold us all here. I can't imagine this horror in the Plains."

"Among the children and theas." Marcus's voice was hushed. "It would destroy them."

"Destroy the very future of the tribes." Joden spoke with a cold voice. "With a city-dweller affliction."

"Joden?" His tone puzzled me. But Joden only gave me a curt nod, and then turned and left.

So the hours flowed, with no real sense of time. Warriors came and warriors died, and jars of fever's foe and sleep-ease passed through my hands. I worked, slept when I couldn't keep my eyes open any longer, and ate when Marcus put food in front of me. There was an occasional glimpse of Keir, as he worked to keep his army together. Which is why I cannot say when Marcus appeared at the entrance to the stilltent, babe in hand, his face mottled and pale.

"Lara? She won't eat."

"Perhaps she's finally noticed just how bad gurt tastes." I kept my voice light as I moved to his side.

"I thought she was sleeping. I checked on her regularly, but she slept on. I didn't think to touch her."

I placed my hand on the babe's forehead. The heat of her skin burned my fingertips. She didn't open her eyes at my touch, just whimpered slightly.

"Goddess. The lake, Marcus. Now."

Marcus turned and ran into the sunlight.

I grabbed a jar of fever's foe and followed, gasping for air as I ran behind him. My legs trembled, but I forced them to move. Others raised their heads as we passed, curious.

Marcus never stopped. He splashed right into the lake, up to the waist, submerging himself and the babe in his arms. He was balancing her on one arm, stripping away her blanket and swaddles, letting them sink as I entered the water. I ran to him, the cold water pulling at my legs. The little one kept her eyes closed as the cold water hit her skin, but there was no cry, just a slight whimper. Hands trembling, I got a dab of the dark brown paste on my finger, and placed it in the babe's mouth.

Those dark eyes opened, and hope blossomed in my chest. She looked so sad, but I held my breath, waiting for her to protest the taste of the medicine.

Instead, she hiccupped once and closed her eyes.

A crowd had gathered on the shore as word spread that the babe was ill. Marcus continued to bathe her, cupping water in his free hand and pouring it over her head. He held her carefully, keeping her eyes and nose above the waterline.

The sound of running feet brought my head up, and Isdra burst through the crowd, splashing into the water. "Meara?" She asked as she came close.

"She's sick." Those were the only words I could force out. The babe lay so limp in Marcus's arms, her entire body flushed, as if burned by the sun. Isdra, breathing hard, held her cold, wet hands to Meara's cheeks. "She's on fire."

"Lotus?" Marcus asked.

I shook my head. "Not for babes. Too dangerous."

I'd brought the feeding cup, and Isdra filled it with water, trying to get her to drink. But the little lips were limp, and she did not swallow.

"Here, let me try." Marcus switched Meara into Isdra's arms. The wet tip of Isdra's braid, Meara's favorite toy, brushed against her cheek. Meara opened her eyes to look at Isdra. The woman warrior crooned to her. "You'll be fine, little one."

Meara closed her eyes, hiccuped and drew a last breath.

I knew, oh Goddess, I knew. One so small, so tiny. I reached out and grabbed Marcus's arm as he lifted the feeding cup. He looked up startled, staring into my face as I shook my head, unable to speak the words. Then he knew as well, and the pain tore though him. "Skies, no." He raised his head, and let out an anguished cry.

Isdra threw her head back as well, wailing to the skies.

An answering lament rose from the shore. The crowd that had gathered raised their voices as one, sending a mournful cry like I had never heard into the air. For all the warriors that had died, I'd seen no outward grief. But for a tiny baby of a Xyian village, these hardened warriors raised their voices in sorrow, tears in their eyes.

But the sight of Marcus's head thrown back, his neck taut, his pain raw filled my soul with rage. I snatched Meara from Isdra's arms and flipped her over, cradling her chest in one hand. "No, no, no." I denied this was happening even as I slapped my hand down on her tiny back. This can't happen, I won't let it happen, Goddess, please, Skies, *please*.

I struck her again, and again, turning as Marcus reached to stop me, calling out to any power that would hear, begging—

Meara took a breath.

I froze as I felt the movement of her chest, holding my own breath as I waited for more, turning again to avoid Isdra, hoping—

Meara took another breath, and then my heart leapt as a cry, a wonderful, angry cry filled the air.

Isdra and Marcus were beside me, and helped me lift

Meara up onto my shoulder, crying and coughing and spitting her outrage.

Joyous voices rose from the beach, and we staggered back through the water, supporting each other. Many hands reached out to help us as we drew near, pulling us onto the shore, taking great care not to disturb the crying babe in my arms. As one, we sank to our knees, as those around us knelt as well. I lay my head on Isdra's shoulder, crying, as Meara's keening continued and the crowd swirled around us.

Meara was furious, her eyelashes thick and dark with tears. Someone handed us a drying cloth, and Isdra took the babe to get her dry. I reached to cradle her cold foot in the palm of my hand, trying to warm her perfect little toes, never so happy to hear a baby cry. With one arm around Isdra's shoulders, I closed my eyes, and we rocked her gently. Just a babe, the last of her village, whose name I'd lost. The scent of lavender still lingered on her skin. So close, so very close.

What's a babe, amidst all the dead about us? Yet all hovered about, enjoying the miracle of a child almost lost to us. I drew a ragged breath, wishing I could voice my joy. But I was so exhausted, all I could do was lean against Isdra, and try to stifle my sobs.

"So this is what comes, of being accursed." Iften's voice cut through my sorrow. He was standing there, outside the mourners, his hands on his hips. "This city-dweller's filth threatens children."

Marcus glared at him. "We are not accursed."

"Cover yourself, cripple." Iften's lip curled in a sneer. "You offend the skies, and the very waters of this lake."

I caught my breath, expecting an explosion. But Marcus flinched back, and sagged to the ground, flinging one arm up over his head.

"We are not accursed." Isdra spat. "It is an illness, as the Warprize has said."

There was a rustle in the crowd about us, and from nowhere a cloak appeared. Marcus grabbed for it, and was soon wrapped in its folds. He said nothing.

"As the Warprize has said." Iften scoffed, pointing off in the distance to the smoke rising on the horizon. "Such a comfort, her brave words. But one less body to add to her tally, eh? One more she sickened so she could claim to have healed?"

Marcus struggled to his feet, but I grabbed his arm, holding him back. Isdra glared at Iften, clutching the babe to her shoulder.

"For myself, I will offer to the elements to protect what is left of this army. And leave you to your business." Iften turned, and stalked off.

Marcus collapsed back onto the ground, and I leaned into him. He wrapped his arm around me, sharing his cloak. We sat in silence for long moments, the crowd about us quiet, as if in shock.

Warm hands touched mine and I turned my head to find Ortis kneeling next to me, that huge, lumbering man with the deep voice. His hands were a warm contrast to mine. "Joden is not here. May I do the honor?"

I didn't know what he meant, but Marcus and Isdra both nodded, so I did too. Ortis sat back on his heels, and spoke. "The fire warms you."

The crowd responded, their voice in such unison that it raised the hairs on the back of my neck. "We thank the elements."

"The earth supports you." Ortis said, his voice a bit louder and stronger.

"We thank the elements."

"The waters sustain you."

"We thank the elements." I joined in, stumbling over the phrase.

"The air fills you."

"We thank the elements."

Ortis stood. "We thank the elements, for the life of this child and the power of the Warprize."

A loud cry of triumph and thanks rose as people stood and somehow made their way to Isdra's side, to touch the baby's foot or cheek in farewell. There were no open smiles, but many faces filled with a quiet joy and tears. Many nodded to me as well, although I was too numb to appreciate it. When the crowd was down to just a few, Ortis spoke again. "You are exhausted, Warprize. Let us tend to her."

"She needs to be upright, Ortis, and her lungs kept clear." I looked up at him, my tears falling down my face.

Meara's cries were softer now, and her coughing was mere hiccups. Isdra had her on her shoulder, patting her back gently. Someone provided a warm blanket and Marcus draped it over Meara carefully. My tears spilled as they worked, watching as Isdra made sure her tiny feet were well covered against the cold.

We stood, but when I reached for the babe Marcus put his hand on my arm. "No, Warprize."

"You have been ill." Ortis used the Xyian word. "Many hands will care for her, Warprize. It will raise our spirts to tend her."

Isdra looked over at me, the bundle in her arms. "I'll make sure she is cared for, Lara."

I nodded, biting my lip, noting the lines of pain on her face. As she turned I managed to croak out her name, unable to voice my true fear. "Isdra?"

She stopped, but did not turn for a moment. Then she turned her head and gave me a grim smile. "I've given you my word, Lara."

Marcus stood, and wrapped an arm around my shoulders as she and the others carried Meara away.

"Strip. You need to be out of those wet clothes." Marcus urged me into the stilltent.

I was so numb it was all I could do to stand there. "You're just as wet."

Marcus chuffed at me. "I'll send for clothes for both of us." He stepped outside the tent for a moment, calling to someone. I managed to lift my hands to the collar of my tunic, but stopped there, unable to move. Marcus entered, and without a word lifted the tunic off and over my head. "The living need you, Warprize. More than the dead. You should return to the command tent. I've cleaned any trace of that fool."

"I need to be here, Marcus." I wanted the familiar surroundings of my medicines and herbs, more comforting by far. I shivered, and he pulled a blanket from my pallet and wrapped it around me. The rough blanket warmed quickly against my skin.

Without a word, Marcus reached under the blanket and pulled down my trous, then sat me down on a stump so that he could remove my boots. He didn't give me time to be embarrassed, just matter-of-factly removed my wet things from around my feet. "Kavage. Kavage, soup and sleep. Best thing for you now."

I clutched the blanket tight around me, knowing that his fussing covered his own exhaustion. "You're tired too, Marcus."

"I have not been ill." Marcus pulled off my boot. "And have no plans to be, either. What will Hisself be thinking, if he sees you like this?"

Tears filled my eyes at the thought. He'd blame me for the babe, blame me for all of this and rightly so. "We should send word. Tell him what happened before someone else does."

"I did, Warprize." Marcus's voice was soft. "He will be told."

There was a noise at the tent entrance. Marcus intercepted whoever it was quickly. "Here now. Herself has rules about privacy, yes? Don't come barging in without asking, eh?"

He returned with a bundle of clothes and hot kavage. He poured a cup for me, and placed a bowl of soup close at hand. He watched me take my first sip. I frowned at him, standing there in his leathers, soaked to the skin. "Change, Marcus."

"Here?" He asked, oddly hesitant.

" 'Nothing there I've not seen before,' " I quoted to him.

He rolled his eye, and stripped off his tunic to reveal pale skin beneath. It struck me as odd, since all the other warriors, Keir included, were browned by the sun. Marcus was pure white, except were the healed burns mottled his skin. He was whipcord thin, the muscles taut. There were scars too, more than Keir had on his body. The scars of one who has seen many battles.

Marcus reached for his trous and I dropped my eyes. I stared into my kavage instead and tried not to think about anything. But all I could see were those tiny cold toes in the palm of my hand. It was hard to believe that she'd survived. I closed my eyes, and yawned again, my jaw cracking.

"Soup will have to wait." Marcus pulled the kavage from my hand, and settled me down onto the pallet. I was so tired, so weary that it felt like the softest bed to my aching body. Marcus pulled up the bedding over me, tucking me in carefully.

I blinked up at him and protested even as my body sagged into the warmth of the bedding. "I should check the fever's foe. And on Rafe, to see how he fares."

"Rest, Warprize. I've been cooking many a year. I can watch a few pots. I'll send for word on Rafe."

I blinked at him, my eyes gritty. "But you're tired too."

"I'll sleep as soon as Isdra returns."

He moved a stump so that he could see the pots through the flap. I blinked a bit and yawned again. "Marcus?"

He turned almost all the way around so that he could see me.

"What does it mean? When you say 'Beyond the snows'?"

He looked at me for a long moment, then turned back to look at the pots. I thought he wasn't going to speak, but then he folded his arms over his chest. "We of the Plains believe that our dead travel with us, ride along beside us, unseen and unknown, but knowing and seeing. Not . . . not their bodies, you understand? Their—" He used a word I didn't understand.

"Their spirits? Souls?" I asked. I used the Xyian words.

Marcus hesitated, then nodded. "Until the longest night, in the winter. You know this night?"

"Solstice." I snuggled deeper into the blankets. "The shortest day, the longest night."

"Just so. On that night, we mourn our dead, who are released to journey to the stars."

I thought about that for a while. For us, the Solstice marked the Grand Wedding of the God and Goddess, the Lord of the Sun and Lady of the Moon and Stars. A long night of bright laughter and celebration. Our people were so different, in so many ways.

I yawned again, my ears popping with the effort. Marcus shifted on his seat, and the light caught his left side, where the ear had been burned away. "Marcus?"

He looked at me again, frowning. "Not yet asleep?"

"You're not offensive, you know."

For a moment, he was so sad, then he gave me a slight smile. "In your eyes, Lara. Sleep now."

I nodded, and closed my eyes. "Please, Marcus, please tell me that in the morning, this will be over. That everything will be all right?"

There was a very long pause, and the despair rose in my throat. Then his voice came, quiet and low. "All I know for certain is that the sun will rise, Warprize. I can offer no more, and no less."

Oddly enough, it was a comfort. I drew a breath and sought the peace of sleep.

I awoke at dawn when Gils showed up, looking tired and needing a fresh supply of fever's foe. Yawning, I put my hair up and sent Prest for kavage and food for all of us. "When did you last eat?"

Gils blinked at me, and yawned. "I's not sure, Warprize." He dropped his satchel at his feet.

I pushed him down on my pallet. "Well, you are going

to at least eat now. Tell me how things are going. And how does Rafe?"

He drew a deep breath, and started talking. First, with the good news that Rafe was doing well. Then he reported on the sick and the dying and those that were recovering. I puttered a bit, to keep my hands busy, arranging the contents of the tables, just listening to his voice get slower and softer. It didn't take long. By the time Prest returned, Gils was fast asleep on my pallet, oblivious to the world around him.

Marcus entered with Prest, carrying food. He glanced at Gils and nodded as he set the kavage down. "Good for him, to get some rest." Prest took his food outside, but Marcus handed me a mug of kavage, and a bowl of soup, and pointed to the stump. I sat, and started to eat, looking at Gils sleeping so soundly. He looked even younger, his tousled red curls falling about his face. My gaze wandered about the tent, coming to rest on the large basket under one of the tables.

Meara's basket.

The soup in my mouth turned to ashes, and I choked it down as I remembered. How could I have forgotten?

Marcus followed my gaze, and sighed when he saw the basket. He reached under the table and pulled it out. "I should have said. She is fine, Warprize."

"You were just as exhausted, Marcus."

He grunted, pulling the blankets from the basket. "Eat something, then we will go and check on her." His tone was gruff, but I noticed that he smiled gently as he folded and smoothed the small blankets as he removed them from the basket. A few pieces of dried lavender fell to the ground, and I gathered the dried flowers up, and held them to my nose. The scent was sweet, and I put them aside. We could use them to freshen the clean swaddles.

A noise made both Marcus and I look at the entrance. Prest was standing just inside the tent, his face grim.

"Prest?"

"You must come, Warprize."

"Who's—"

"The Warlord."

9

"Keir?"

My heart in my throat, I entered our sleeping area, blinking to adjust to the cool darkness within. Marcus had followed me, and he paused behind me as well, trying to catch his breath.

Keir was seated on the bed, head hanging down, bracing himself with his hands on his knees.

I jerked to a stop, my stomach clenching. Keir looked up, and gave me a weak smile, a fine sheen of sweat on his forehead and cheeks. I forced myself to slow my breathing, and calmly moved to sit next to him on the bed. My nose picked up the familiar stink and I placed my hand on Keir's forehead. "How long?"

"Not long." Keir answered.

"You think." Marcus knelt and started to unlace Keir's boot. He pulled off the boot with a jerk, letting Keir's foot fall to the floor. "You've been working yourself ragged for days. Who's to say how long?"

Prest spoke from behind us. "I'll wake Gils."

"Iften must be told as well." Keir's voice was rough. I looked at him in horror, but he frowned at me. "With Simus gone, he is Second. He will have command."

With a nod, Prest left the tent.

"Should have killed him when he challenged." Marcus grumbled, working at the other boot.

"Who's to say that would have been best?" Keir sighed and closed his eyes. I moved closer and placed my hand on his shoulder. He looked up at me. "Lara, I heard. About the babe." His eyes crinkled slightly in the corners. "So now you raise the dead?"

I shook my head, choking on my tears. How could he jest when—

Keir continued, clearing his throat, trying to strengthen his voice. "We must discuss what happens in the event that—"

"Nothing is going to happen to you." I snapped, cutting him off. "If Meara can live through this, you can."

Keir chuckled at that, but I wasn't laughing. My fingers trembled as I unbuckled his armor.

"The best of warlords plan for all possibilities." He paused for a moment, gathering strength. "I will plan for the worst, yes? Then it will not happen."

I pulled his tunic over his head. His head emerged, that dark hair all rumpled and mussed. I ran my fingers through it, feeling the heat of his damp scalp. He grabbed my hand and held it to his cheek. "If it turns to the worst, I want you to leave this camp before I draw my last breath."

"I will not leave you." I whispered.

"Stubborn. So very stubborn." He closed his eyes for a moment, rubbing his cheek against my palm.

"Your head hurts." I leaned forward, seeing the pain in the lines etched on his face. He murmured agreement softly.

"We'll get you into bed and get you some sleepease. It will help with the headache."

"Not until I have spoken with Iften and Isdra." Keir tried to raise himself up, to help Marcus remove his trous, but his arms trembled with the effort. Marcus made no comment, merely went about his business. When all was done, I lifted the bedding and Keir settled back, his hands reaching to place his weapons at hand.

Before I could say anything, Marcus covered Keir's hand with his own. Keir's face held a particular look of pain as he realized what had to be done. Marcus murmured something I didn't catch, and Keir seemed reassured, pulling his hand away from the swords. Those blue eyes, cloudy with fever, watched as Marcus left the tent.

Keir looked at me with a grimace. "You must restrain me."

I sat at the side of the bed, and put the back of my hand against his forehead. The heat was starting to rise. "Not just yet, Keir."

Keir brought one bare arm out from under the covers and curled it around me, trying to pull me down onto his chest. I went willingly, taking comfort from his closeness.

"So. You are cursed."

The smug voice came from behind us. I turned my head to see Iften standing there behind me, Isdra and Gils just visible behind him. Isdra was glaring at the back of Iften's head, and Gils did not appear to be pleased with him either. I stood slowly, feeling uneasy with my back to the man. Iften stood there and oozed his glee, making no secret of his pleasure at Keir's condition.

Keir had his eyes closed, his hair plastered to his head. He didn't bother to open his eyes. "Iften. You have command until I am through this."

"But not the tent." Marcus growled as he entered from his quarters, bring a bucket of cold water, and cloths.

Iften shot him a hateful look. "As if I need the tent, crip—" He cut himself off, then—pasted a satisfied smile on his face. "Have no fear, Warlord. I will summon the warleaders and inform them of this." He turned, and moved to push past Isdra.

"Hold, Iften." I snapped. How dare he treat Keir that way?

Iften stopped, then turned slowly. "Yes?"

"You may summon them, but I will speak to them for Keir."

Iften's brown eyes flashed. "I am Second."

I drew myself up straight, and gave him a glare right back. "I am the Warprize, Iften."

Iften's eyes were filled with hate, but he bowed his head, turned and left, pushing past the others.

"May the elements afflict him." Marcus muttered.

Isdra nodded her agreement as she and Gils entered. Gils was fumbling in his satchel, pulling out the items that we would need.

"This is not an affliction. Or a curse." I reminded him gently. "It's an illness." The cold cloth in my hand, I sat back down and began to wipe Keir's brow.

Keir turned his head and opened his eyes to look at me, catching my hand. "Singers will praise my Warprize for a thousand years to come." His eyes were shining with the fever.

Guilt rose in my breast. It was more likely I'd be known as the woman who killed an entire village and army with her arrogance and pride. "No. No, they won't."

Gils handed me the cup with the dose of sleepease, but Keir pushed it away, and turned to Isdra. "I have no right to ask this of you, but I am going to. Not as Warlord, but as a friend. Please—"

"There is no need to ask." Isdra cut him off, putting her hand on her sword hilt. "I will see her safe before I go to the snows."

"As will I." Marcus added.

"As will I." Gils echoed, his voice cracking. Keir looked at him oddly. "No, Warlord, I do understand. Better than you think."

Keir nodded. "My thanks." Nothing more was said, but I let my confusion go as Keir reached for the cup with shaking hands. I helped him, and he drank it quickly, grimacing at the taste. Something about that teased at my memory as he smiled at me and spoke.

"I will fight this."

The bile rose in my throat as he repeated Epor's very words. I jerked my head up, meeting Isdra's eyes, which held the same horror that mine did. But the others did not know and I managed to control my face before they could see.

Keir was relaxing, letting the sleepease do its work. "Warprize."

I leaned over him. "Keir?"

"As Warlord, and Overlord of Xy, I command your obedience to my will. Return to Water's Fall."

I lowered my lips to his ear. "My heart's fire, there is only one way to make me obey your command."

He turned his head slightly, his eyes unfocused. But I could see the question in his eyes.

"Live."

That heady feeling of command that I'd had a few days before had been replaced with bone-chilling terror. The warleaders, or their representatives, were looking to me to make decisions that affected an entire army. I felt the weight of that responsibility press down on me, knowing for the first time the burden Keir carried with him every day. I'd asked Joden to attend as well, hoping that his presence would help. But he stood to the side, and kept his eyes fixed on the ground before him.

The wind blew my hair into my face, and I pulled it back with one hand. We were outside the command tent, standing in a loose circle, as many as could gather. Iften stood to the side. Prest was behind me, as was Isdra. I'd insisted that we meet here, because I didn't want Keir disturbed, nor did I want him to try to participate. He needed every bit of strength to fight his battles with the sickness. Marcus remained with Keir.

I was frozen with fear, standing before them. My teeth wanted to worry my lower lip, but I stopped myself. I needed to be confident and strong before these warleaders. Or, at least, to look the part. Why hadn't I asked Marcus who to trust, or paid more attention during the senels Keir had called?

I'd managed to convince the Council of Xy that being Warprize was best for my country and myself. But I'd understood the motives and desires of the Council members, and managed to learn enough, fast enough, to make a strong argument. But I felt lost in this military setting. What did I know about the command structure, or who did what? I cursed myself for a fool, and vowed to pay more attention in the future.

If I had a future.

A mug of kavage was placed in my hand. All had been served, and now all eyes turned toward me as silence fell. *Blessed Goddess, please help me.*

I'd start where Keir would start. "The Warlord has taken ill." No looks of surprise on any face, so I took a breath and continued. "So let us consider the status of the army and what needs to be done. Where is Sal?"

A woman took a step forward and inclined her head to me. "Warprize, Sal has been ill. She is in the coughing stage and sends her regrets. I am Telsi. Supplies are holding, although I fear we've come very close to stripping the area."

She started to go into detail, and I blessed the precious moments it gave me to think. I looked casually about, but I couldn't seem to remember anything about anyone. A sense of panic rose, then in my mind's eye I saw Master Eln, standing in his still room, stirring a pot. *"If the Kingdom were ill, what would you do?"*

"What?"

"If the kingdom were to somehow stumble into the clinic, weak and ill, what would you do first?"

I'd look at the symptoms and diagnose. I blinked, thinking it through. I'd determine the extent and the nature of the illness and I'd cure it.

I shifted my gaze to the side where Iften stood, a smug look on his face. No doubt there, of all the warleaders he was the sickest, his hatred of Keir an oozing, pus-filled wound. Wesren stood next to him, shoulder to shoulder. He had the illness as well, but not quite as bad. It was more like Wesren agreed with everything Iften said, instead of opposing Keir.

Something eased in my chest. I could do this.

Telsi was finishing her report. "We will be fine for at least a few more days, but Sal asks that you advise when she can send out hunting parties further afield."

"My thanks, Telsi." I said, and she inclined her head with a smile. I decided to treat that as a sign of support, and took strength from that.

Aret took a step forward, and inclined her head. "The herds of horses are well, Warprize, and have plenty of feed and water. We've watched them carefully. There's been no sign that the 'illness' has touched them."

I smiled at her, but she merely inclined her head again and stepped back. I'd take that for a neutral position. I was glad to hear her report; it hadn't occurred to me to worry about the horses but it made me feel good to know that Keir's black and my brown were safe.

Wesren stepped forward, and spoke rapidly, without looking at me. "The encampment has been maintained as well as can be expected, but I fear problems if we remain for much longer." He stepped back, and darted a glance to Iften, seeking approval.

No surprise there, he was firmly mired with Iften.

Ortis stepped forward, and inclined his head. His voice rumbled as he spoke. "My scouts are pulled in, as ordered, and we keep watch at the perimeter. There have been no problems, and no sightings of any potential enemy."

I remembered him from Meara's ceremony and hoped I didn't imagine the look of support on his face as he stepped back.

Uzaina and Tsor stood, and they both glanced at Iften before Tsor stepped forward to speak. "There is little to report, Warprize, since our duties involve the army on the march." Tsor looked at Uzaina, who shrugged. "We've been helping with the sick at the shore."

I nodded to them both, and Tsor stepped back. I wasn't sure, but I had a feeling that they were both waiting before making a decision. Why show support for Keir if he was dying? I swallowed hard.

Yers spoke then, stepping forward and inclining his head. "The warriors are maintaining discipline—"

"For now." Iften interrupted.

Yers glared, but I spoke first. "Then let us continue on as we have. Keir will be well within a few days."

"And if he is not?" Iften asked smoothly.

I ignored him. "I will see to Keir, with Marcus's help. Gils will see to the rest of the sick. Come to me with any questions, but I will give my attention to Keir."

"What a surprise, that you will ignore the others for the Warlord."

I focused on the others as Iften spoke. For the most part, it seemed I was right in my diagnosis. Telsi, Yers and Ortis scowled at Iften's words, but Wesren, Uzaina and Tsor were clearly considering their import. Aret had an odd look on her face, as if undecided.

I wanted to slap that smug look right off Iften, and make him take back every oily, ugly word. Thank the Goddess Marcus was inside with Keir. He'd have had his daggers plunged into the man's chest. I held my temper hard, biting the inside of my cheek. "I ignore no one. He is the Warlord, and I am his Warprize. My place is at his side."

"Warprize only so long as he lives, Xyian."

All in attendance stiffened at the insult, but I ignored it. "You are Second, Iften. But I am the Warprize."

He bowed that handsome blonde head, smirk firmly in place. "As you say, Xyian. But as Second, I shall return to my tent and keep myself from the contagion that you have brought among us. So that when a leader is needed, I will be ready." He turned and walked away without another word.

Silence fell as he moved off. The warleaders exchanged glances, but I'd learned one thing from Keir. I cut off any comment and dismissed them. "Thank you all for your reports. I will send word when Keir has recovered."

There was a pause at that, and I waited a breath, but then Aret moved, returned her mug, and left. The others followed suit, leaving Joden and Yers standing before me. Gils popped out of the tent, so quickly that I suspected he'd been listening.

Isdra was focused on Iften, seen disappearing into his tent. "That one dares much, with Keir unable to silence him."

Gils jutted out his jaw. "I's think he denies the Warprize, yet uses her medicines secretly."

"Yet, is it not true that we need a leader to be healthy, and stay ready to lead?" Joden asked. "If Keir dies, we will need someone to lead this army."

Yers gave him a searching look. "You side with Iften?"

Joden sighed deeply. "I have no love of Iften. But don't let your bias against him blind you to his actions. Perhaps what he is doing is a wise precaution, given the way things are."

The way things are. From where we stood, I had a clear view of the lake shore. People being immersed in the water in a desperate attempt to bring down their fevers. I watched for a moment, then asked a question I didn't really want an answer to.

"How goes it?" I asked, turning my head to focus on Gils.

Gils shifted his weight nervously, adjusting the strap of his satchel, looking everywhere but at me.

"The truth, Gils." I said.

"Tell her." Yers said.

Gils sighed. "The deaths continue. About one dead for every ten sick."

I lifted my eyes in the direction of the village, where black smoke rose into the sky. One for every ten, in an army of thousands.

"But, Warprize, I's thinking that there are fewer new sick in the last few hours." Gils spoke quickly, trying to offer reassurance.

Yers nodded. "I agree. And the warriors are all cooperating to aid the sick. We will fight on, Warprize."

"Joden," I turned to the large man, his broad face grim and unsmiling. "Would you continue Keir's work with the army? Keeping their spirits and minds focused as he did?"

Joden was silent for a moment, staring at the shoreline. He spoke, but would not meet my eyes. "I would decline, Warprize. My place is to assist with the dead."

"I will take up that task, Warprize." Yers covered an awkward silence with his words. "It should be mine anyway, since I am now Keir's Third."

I nodded, then watched as they both walked off. Not once did Joden look at me.

"I's never thought I'd witness anything like this." Gils's voice brought me back.

"It only happens once in a lifetime." I responded.

"Once in a lifetime will be enough, Warprize." Gils

heaved a deep sigh, then adjusted the strap of his satchel. He looked me up and down with concern. "See that you eat and rest, Warprize."

Prest snorted and I laughed out loud at the gangly lad with his red curls, freckles and oh-so-serious face who stood before me, looking offended. It seemed he was trying to sound like Marcus. My apprentice, who learned so much so fast in the short time we'd been together. He'd grown before my eyes, older suddenly, with an air of confidence that he hadn't had before. "I will, Gils."

"See that you do." He huffed.

"I promise."

He grinned then, like the boy he was.

"Prest, I want you to help Gils. Be sure to check on Rafe."

Prest frowned at me.

"You'll do more good among the sick. Isdra and Marcus will aid me."

Prest gave one of his shrugs in response. "Very well, Warprize. Call if you need aid."

Marcus and I had our work cut out for us. With Keir, the fever took hold, built and then broke, each time worse than the last. We knew the time was coming when he'd have to be restrained, but we both put off the moment, delaying it as much for our sakes as for his. Isdra said nothing, but I saw that she'd prepared leather straps, setting them out of Keir's sight, but where she could get to them quickly.

The sweat poured off Keir. I gave up changing the linens, and concentrated on wiping down his chest and limbs, trying to keep the fever down as much as I could.

Instead of rose oil, I used my precious vanilla. More for myself than for Keir's comfort. The rose oil brought back too many memories of my father's illness and death. The vanilla offered better comfort, and as rare as it was, I could think of no better use.

"I first saw you in the garden." His voice whispered into my ear.

"What?" I started and looked up into those blue eyes, sane for the first time in days. He stared at me for a moment, then let his eyelids drift down. His hand tried to lift from the bed, and I snatched it up and clung to it. "Keir?"

"The night you helped Simus." His faint voice cracked, but his eyes fluttered back open. I knelt next to the bed, bringing his cold hand to my cheek. He focused on my face with effort. "I was in the castle garden."

I didn't know whether to laugh or cry. "You were?" I sat on the edge of the bed. "I thought we first met in the marketplace."

One corner of his mouth turned up slightly. As sick as he was, he was proud of himself. "Knew Simus had been hurt. Tried to find him." He turned his hand in mine to rub his fingers on my cheek.

"You took a terrible risk."

"Skies favor the bold." But there was a spark in his eye, the look of a little boy who'd gotten away with something. I couldn't help but smile in response, and reached out to run my fingers through his hair. The thick hair was oily with sweat, and I moved the clinging strands off his damp forehead.

Keir looked up at me, his eyes glittering and bright. "You walked down the path, with that basket and jug. The next thing I know you're bossing everyone around and taking care of Simus." Keir chuckled weakly, leaving him breathless. I placed my fingers on his lips to stop his speech, but he pulled his head away. "I was glad that you had warned the guards as to what you were doing. Else I might have rushed the tent at the sounds of Simus's cries. It sounded like he was being killed."

I smiled at the memory. "It took a lot of men to hold him down." I frowned slightly, thinking back. "I didn't see you."

His face took on such a smug look that I laughed out loud. Marcus walked in, his eye wide at the sight. But Keir was focused on me. "When Joden threatened you, I decided to kill you when you came out."

I blinked. Marcus let out a bark of a laugh as he put a bucket of clean water at my side. Keir ignored us, his eyes focused on something beyond us. "I stalked you as you moved down that path." He moved his hand slightly, and touched my hair. "You stopped on the path by the roses, like some air spirit, standing in the shadows and starlight, looking around. And when you reached up and fixed your hair . . ." Keir's fingers gently tugged one of my curls. "I wanted you then and there."

My eyes filled as I looked at him. Marcus moved off, giving us some privacy. I leaned down, and brushed his lips with mine.

He smiled weakly, then closed his eyes. "Tired."

"Sleep, my Keir." I placed his hand on his chest, and rinsed my cloth with the fresh water. He nodded slightly, and sighed as I wiped him down.

"Isdra?"

Marcus had left us for the moment, muttering something about making broth. Keir was asleep, curled in the center of the bed. Isdra and I were keeping watch from the corner, scooping fever's foe into smaller jars as busy work. Warriors were still boiling the medicine down, under Gils's watchful eye.

Isdra looked at me with a raised eyebrow, waiting for my question.

I kept my voice low. "What did it mean, earlier? When Gils said that he understood more than Keir knew."

Isdra focused her eyes on the fever's foe, as if it were critical that her work was performed to an exacting standard.

"I knew what you meant, when you said that you would see me safe before going to the snows. But why did Marcus and Gils say what they said?"

I didn't think she was going to speak, and for a long moment she didn't. But I just out-silenced her, waiting for my answer.

Finally she sighed. "Lara, if Keir dies, the next death will be Marcus's."

I sat for a bit, scooping up the thick fever's foe. "Because of his scars?"

"In the Plains, to be so crippled is to be considered afflicted and useless. An offense to the elements. Normally, such a one would end his or her life." Isdra set the full jar aside and reached for another. We no longer bothered to seal them.

"He's not useless or an offense." I snapped. "That is so stupid, to think that way."

"I would not have agreed with you before this campaign." Isdra responded. "But knowing Marcus, having seen his worth, well . . ." She shrugged.

"But Gils is whole. Why—"

"Gils proclaimed his desire to learn the healing ways publicly, for all the warleaders to see, rejecting our ways."

Isdra reminded me, giving me a sharp look. "I wasn't sure he understood what he'd done, but apparently he does. A bold stroke, in its own way."

"So he'd suffer, if Keir . . ." I couldn't bring myself to finish the thought.

Isdra was content to work in silence, but I had to say something. "Isdra: Meara, how is she?"

She stopped. "Well, Warprize." Her voice was steady, but the spoon in her hand smeared fever's foe on the side of the jar. Isdra looked over at Keir, pain in her eyes. "She's more theas than she needs. Worry more for your Warlord." She reached for a rag. "I will finish this. Get some sleep." Her voice was gruff.

"The last of the dried ehat." Marcus said. "I've hoarded it 'til now. Do not waste it." His voice was stern, but Marcus gently supported Keir in his arms and helped him with the bowl of broth, patiently waiting as Keir took small sips. It took awhile, but Keir managed to drink the whole bowl.

At the end, Keir closed his eyes and licked his lips. "That was a good hunt."

"One of the best." Marcus agreed softly. "More?"

Keir shook his head and shivered. Marcus pulled the bedding up around his shoulders then turned to me. "Warprize? Can I tempt you with a bowl? Can't have the young'un upset with me, eh?"

Curious, I accepted a bowl, and recognized the taste right away. It was the same broth he'd fed me the night Keir had claimed me in the throne room. "Marcus, what is this?"

"Ehat."

"What is an ehat?" I asked, taking another drink.

Keir chuckled weakly from the bedding. Marcus gave me a small smile. "An animal of the Plains, Warprize. A fierce one whose horns are as large as its meat is sweet. Taller than a mounted man, and dangerous to hunt. Hisself is known for his skill in planning ehat hunts."

Keir, shivering under the blankets, gave us that smug look again, but it faded fairly quickly. "It's getting worse."

I sat on the bed, and reached to stroke his face. "Keir, you're doing—"

"No." He shook his head. "Each time, it gets harder to stay . . . I would die if I hurt you."

I went to protest, but Marcus made the decision for me. "I'll get Isdra." He left the tent.

"Lara, I . . ." Keir swallowed hard, his eyes cloudy, looking lost.

"I'm here, beloved. You are not alone, Keir." I turned so that I faced the entrance, and pulled him close, so that he could put his head in my lap.

With his eyes closed, he nodded. Marcus and Isdra entered, and Isdra pulled the straps from where she had hidden them. With grim expressions, they bent to their task.

Keir was right. The raving started soon after, with Keir screaming and fighting his bonds.

Marcus was asleep, and Isdra was pulling more water when I ran out of clean cloths. Keir was unconscious, the sweat starting to build again, and the scent was so rank . . . it only took a moment to duck out to my stilltent and return with a handful.

I returned to our sleeping area to find Iften standing over Keir, his dagger in his hand.

10

I dropped the cloths, too astonished to cry out.

Keir didn't react, still unconscious, bound to the bed, helpless. Iften turned toward me, and laughed, sheathing his dagger. "You think I would advance myself through his death?"

I nodded.

He laughed again, a cruel harsh sound. "Why take that action when the elements will take it for me, eh?"

I took a step forward, my anger overruling my fear. "He is not going to die."

"But you are not sure, are you, little healer?" He mocked me. "You, who claim the power to heal all."

"I never claimed that, Iften." I stepped closer to the bed, sweeping my gaze over Keir, making sure that he hadn't been hurt. But I didn't take my eyes off Iften for long. Oh, where was Isdra?

Iften folded his arms over his chest. "With his last breath, your status changes, *Xyian*. You will be as nothing to us. It will be my charge to return the army to the plains and report his failure. And in the spring, when the challenges are issued and won, I will return to this valley as Warlord, and—"

"Keir will not die. Leave us." I was of half a mind to scream out, to attract attention. But what would they think of a Warprize cowering before him? I grit my teeth.

Iften opened his arms, as if making a peaceful gesture. "It is you that should leave. Ride out now, return to your people. All will be as it was." His voice was smooth and sure, as if offering the friendliest of advice. "No need to place yourself in jeopardy. No need to face attacks, such as in your own marketplace. No need to face the Elders or the warrior-priests."

His face changed, and I had to stop myself from taking a step back. "Go, Xyian. Prepare your people for the army that will come in the spring, to ravage—"

Something broke the fear inside me. With swift steps, I moved toward him, my fist raised in anger, swearing at the top of my lungs. "I curse you, *bracnect*. May the skies deny you breath!"

Iften's eyes went wide, and his breath caught. His hand went to his sword hilt.

I glared at him, took another step forward and shook my fist in his face. "May the earth sink below your feet."

There was a gasp from outside, I wasn't sure who, but I didn't let it stop me. "May the fire deny you heat, and the very waters of the land dry in your hand."

Iften didn't draw his sword. His face went pale and he

stepped back quickly, stumbling out into the meeting room, heading for the main exit. As he retreated through the flap, I followed right behind. "May the very elements reject you and all that you are!"

Marcus and Joden were outside, their eyes wide as plates. Others within hearing distance turned horrified faces toward us. I just kept my eyes on Iften, and took another step to jab my finger into his chest. "May your balls rot like fruit in the sun, and your manhood wither at the root!" I spit in the earth in front of Iften's toe.

Without another word, I stomped back into the tent.

By the time Marcus and Joden stepped into the tent, I was sitting calmly by Keir, wiping his chest down with water that I had added herbs to.

Marcus spoke first, softly. "Warprize? How did you know such a curse?"

"She overheard it?" Joden said.

"How? When? None would say it in her presence without my knowledge. And none have cursed so in this army that I have heard word of."

I responded calmly. "I didn't know it. I made it up. He was standing there, prating about the elements and bragging about what he was going to do and I just got so very angry."

"A strong curse, Warprize." Marcus's voice carried a note of pride.

"I don't care, so long as he stays away from me and Keir."

Joden's tone was dry. "No fear of that, Lara."

* * *

"MARCUS!"

I jolted up out of my pallet from a sound sleep.

Keir had broken one strap. With his free arm, he was fighting the very man he was calling for. I stumbled up and over, and placed my hand on Keir's forehead. Marcus was doing his best to secure the loose arm, and he grunted with the effort. I raised my voice, calling out. "We need help!"

"Help him, you maggots! It burns, oh Skies, he burns!" Keir was screaming the words, the muscles of his neck taut with the strain.

"For sure they heard that," Marcus muttered, forcing Keir's arm down onto the bed.

"Keir, it's Lara. It's all right—"

Keir strained at the strap around his other wrist, trying to break it. He cried out again, summoning unseen help. "Bring water! Douse him with water, bring buckets—" Keir relaxed for a moment, moaning as if in sorrow. "His ear, oh his ear."

I glanced at Marcus, and knew where and when Keir was.

Keir's voice dropped to a snarl. "Damn you to the snows forever, Warrior-Priest. He will live, and I will use my last breath to break you, do you hear me?" He threw his head back against the bed. "Heal him now, or I will kill you."

"Is this what happened?" I whispered.

"Don't know, Warprize. I was not aware at the time." Marcus looked grim. "Where are those fools?" He looked toward the tent flap, then back at me. Marcus growled. "Do not dwell on it. He called me back from the snows. I answered. There is no more to say."

"Fear the day Keir of the Cat is named Warking." Keir howled.

Prest, Isdra, and to my surprise, Rafe poured into the tent, with Isdra stepping forward to help Marcus. At the word 'Warking', all of them flinched in shock, but only for a moment. Marcus darted to Keir's side, and put his fingers over his mouth. "Warlord, the enemy is near. Be silent."

The others exchanged worried looks. I opened my mouth to question them, but Marcus caught my eye, and shook his head, putting a finger to his lips. So I suppressed my curiosity.

"Rafe, are you well enough to be up and about?" I asked.

"Well enough, Warprize." He gave me a faint smile. "Seems I didn't sicken as much as others did. Didn't even need the aid of the lake waters."

I frowned, considering him. He'd lost weight, and there were smudges under his eyes. He was pushing too hard, I was certain, but for now I had a greater concern.

Keir had fallen silent, still a prisoner of the fever. The others started to rebind Keir, but I stopped them. "Prest, call Gils. It's time."

I followed them down to the shore, the moon providing enough light to see by. Gils, Prest, Marcus and Isdra carried Keir, who struggled in their arms. Marcus had insisted that they bind Keir to take him to the water and he'd been right. They set him down on the shore to give themselves a chance to strip out of their own clothing. Once they picked him back up, I followed them right into the water, catching my breath at the bite of the cold against my skin.

I supported his head, using my hands to pour the water onto his forehead. His bronze skin looked so pale, his hair so dark as the water trickled through it. He didn't open his eyes, but his lips opened slightly, and I trickled water into his mouth, remembering how sweet it had tasted when I'd been in the same position. The others chanted the same ritual of purification that I'd heard in my fever.

I knelt down, and whispered his name into his ear. A slight turn of his head, and I knew I had his attention. "Fight, beloved. Remember that you are my Warlord, Keir of the Cat. You are mine, and I am yours. Fight for us, my heart's fire."

Keir blinked, but gave no other sign.

They dipped him in and out, letting the water and the slight breeze chill his naked form to the point where he was shivering. Only then did we return him to the command tent. Rafe had stayed behind, warming the bed with heated stones under the bedding, keeping the warmth within the covers. He used a dagger to cut Keir's bonds as the others gathered drying cloths.

Once we had him dry, we slipped Keir into the warmth, keeping him upright just long enough to get a bowl of broth into him. He looked so pale, laying there, so still. My heart was in my throat, although his pulse beat strongly under my fingers.

To my surprise, Keir's eyes fluttered open after we settled him down. They were foggy with sleep, and when his fingers moved, I took them into my hand. He felt so cold, so I sat on the bed, and tried to rub some warmth into them.

"You need to get out of these wet things and get some sleep." Marcus moved behind me, and put his hands on my shoulders. "I've sent the others off to rest."

"You need sleep more than I do, Marcus. I'll change, then take the first watch."

Marcus sighed, but he didn't argue.

How many sickbeds have I watched over in my time? More than I can count or remember. Yet, this time was different.

Eln taught that a good healer was dispassionate. Objective. I tried to follow his teachings, and with most patients I succeeded.

Not with my father.

Not with Keir.

My father's illness had been a long slow process, and his death had been a release. But this man was a strong warrior, in his prime, and my emotions swayed from despair to hope and back again. I'd done everything I knew to save him, and it lay within the Goddess's hands. All I could do was sit and watch over him, taking in each breath as if it were my own. Hours passed, and Keir still slept, with no sign of the fever's return. The light was faint in the tent, with the braziers burning to provide warmth.

Marcus had curled up on a pallet at the foot of the bed, exhausted. I checked on him as the hours wore on, to make sure that he was sleeping easily, and that no sweat formed on the scarred forehead. I'd everything I needed close at hand, thanks to him, including a pitcher of kavage as thick as mud. All that was left to do was wait and watch.

Watch and worry.

What would happen if Keir died?

What would happen to my life? The others were

pledged to see me home, to the safety of the castle at Water's Fall. In the face of Iften's threats, I knew that Keir's dream of uniting our peoples would die with him.

But, Goddess forgive me, my concern was not for our people. For Keir's death would shatter the very heart in my breast. It would die, or the largest part of it would. As I looked ahead to that future, I knew for an instant Isdra's pain, and the release that she sought.

I flushed, ashamed for what I'd asked of her. The priests of the God, Lord of the Sun, condemn suicide. But my own pain showed me this very truth—that it wouldn't be far from my thoughts if Keir took his last breath.

Yet, as another hour passed, Keir's breaths came steadily, one after another. And I gave thanks to the Goddess for each and every one.

I was trying to remember what Keir had told me, about balancing the elements in the body using touch, the night he'd comforted me after Xymund had burned my books. Keir's skin still felt cool to me, but perhaps it was more my fear than truth. I cradled his right hand in both of mine and started caressing it, tracing each finger slowly, and moving my fingertips over his palm. I tried to remember what Keir had said when he had done this to me. "The breath is made of air, and sits within the right hand." I whispered, continuing my movements until the warmth returned to his hand.

I reached over, to take his left hand, and did the same thing until the flesh was warm and pink. "The soul is made of fire, and sits within the left hand."

Keir seemed to be breathing easier. I tucked his hands back under the bedding, and then went to the foot of the bed, reaching under to feel his toes. "The flesh is made of earth and sits within the left—"

"No . . . wrong."

The sound was faint but I looked at Keir to see blue eyes looking back at me.

"Keir?" I scrambled up onto the bed to lean over him, and cup his face in my hand. My hair fell around us. His cheeks were bristly under my fingers, but there was no trace of excess heat. I smiled at him, calling. "Keir?"

His lips moved, forming a faint smile.

"Keir." I whispered softly, my heart full of joy. The worst had passed. My warlord would survive.

Keir smiled softly, and turned his head just enough to brush his lips over my palm. With a soft sigh, he fell back to sleep.

If there is a universal truth, among both our cultures, it is that men of the sword have no patience with their healing bodies. They always seem to think that the body's humors should balance quickly. But a body heals in its own time, and there is no rushing it.

Keir's chest was big and muscular. It took more force and longer periods of drumming to clear his lungs of the water within. So the warriors were the ones that had to drum for him as he hung over the side of the bed, coughing. I didn't have the strength to be effective, but I was the only one that could bully him into cooperating. At one point in the process, Keir had swivelled around and glared at Gils. "You're enjoying this too much."

"Keir," I admonished, and he turned back around to let Gils continue.

"Me? Enjoy beating on my Warlord and helping him?" Gils asked cheerfully as he thumped on Keir's back. "Not I, Warlord."

Keir coughed, then spat to clear his throat. "Say that to the naked sky?"

"Well, looks like we are done for now." Gils backed off, smiling and moving toward the exit. "I's chores and patients to see, yes I's have." He bolted out of the tent, grabbing his satchel by the strap.

I snorted back a laugh.

Keir pulled himself up, and gave me his best glare, but I shook my head. "Oh no, my Warlord. I seem to remember someone insisting that I do this. Fair is fair."

Keir was a horrible patient. Whiny as a babe, cranky as a grandfather—he wanted this and needed that and why couldn't he get up out of that bed? We tried letting him care for Meara, or giving him small tasks, like sharpening blades, but his strength just wasn't up to it. Keir's mind was racing, but his body could not follow.

When Marcus threatened to smother Keir in his sleep, and stomped out of the tent, I knew it was time to resort to desperate measures. I started reading long passages to him from the *Epic of Xyson*.

The Epic had been written about the battles of the second King of Xy, and it was one of the dullest pieces of history that had ever been written. But Keir lay curled under the covers, listening with rapt attention as I droned on and on about military matters, army maneuvers and planning. " 'Upon the dawn, King Xyson mounted his warhorse, Greatheart and . . .' " I paused, remembering. That was the horse's name. Greatheart.

"You name your horses?" Keir asked, looking puzzled.

I rolled my eyes and continued, but other than that the tale bored me to tears. There was only so much I could take, reading it aloud.

There had to be another way to keep a Warlord busy.

"This is a playing board."

"The squares?"

"Yes." I set the board by his side and sat on the edge of the bed. Keir curled onto his side, studying the board. I held out a piece in my hand. "This is the King. He is the tallest piece on the board. He moves one square in any direction."

Keir studied the piece of wood. "There are two kings."

"Yes. Yours and mine." I positioned the kings on the board. "They start here."

"Always?"

"Yes."

Keir grunted. "So. A war."

I nodded as I reached for the next piece. "The smallest pieces are the pawns. They go here, forming a line." Keir reached out to help me place the small black and white river stones that I'd gathered. Black for him and white for me.

Slowly, I took him through each piece, their names, how they moved, what power they had. I explained the board and the colors. The problem occurred when we reached the bishop. I tried to explain their role in the church, but all I got for my trouble was a grim look of doubt. "So. They are warrior-priests."

A brief vision of the florid face of Archbishop Drizen covered in tattoos had me speechless for a moment. "No, not exactly."

"But these bishops, they act to protect their king? Their people?"

"Yes, of course." I bit my lip, re-thinking my words. "Well, some care more for their status than their people, but the good ones—"

"Ah." Keir nodded. "Warrior-priests." His tone was one of disdain as he clutched the stone tight in his hand.

I reached over, and touched his fist, gently pulling the piece from his fingers. "You hate them, don't you? Because of Marcus?"

His jaw clenched, and there was a pause before he answered. "It goes beyond Marcus, though that alone was enough. I will see them broken and destroyed."

"Keir," There was so much I didn't understand. "If they are as powerful as you say they are—"

He gave me a tight smile, and shook his head. "That is for another day, Lara. This piece here, this 'castle'. Castles do not move." Keir frowned at the piece on the board. "Why do they move?"

"They just do." I sighed, resigned to the change of subject.

"It should be called something else." Keir looked at me intently.

"Whose game is this, anyway?" I asked. "Let's go over the moves one more time." With his memory, it took no time at all. Once he had them down, he looked at me expectantly.

"The best way to learn is to play." I moved one of my center pawns out.

Keir gave the board a close look, and then lifted an eyebrow at me, his eyes sparkling for the first time since he'd gotten sick. Father had taught me chess long ago, and we'd played many games during his illness. I knew myself to be a fair player. Father usually won, since he'd had an uncanny knack of holding all the possible moves in his head well in advance of the actual turns. I knew that once Keir learned the strategies behind the moves, I'd never be able to beat him. Best to take full advantage while I could.

Keir made his first move carefully. I reached out and advanced another piece, and then watched as he committed a classic beginner's mistake.

A few more moves and I had him. "Checkmate."

"What?" Keir frowned, glaring at the pieces. "What did I do wrong?"

I stood up. "When you figure it out, call me, and we'll play another game."

He was muttering under his breath as I left the tent.

I was doomed.

It had taken most of a day for Keir to pick up the basics. I'd gone about my business at the stilltent, returning when Keir would bellow, make my move, smile and then leave to let him contemplate the possibilities. This frustrated him to no end. But once he learned to avoid the basic mistakes, he started to take great childish glee in seizing my pieces and hiding them in the rumpled bedding, chuckling over my pending defeat. I spent the next morning barely avoiding the capture of my king. I hadn't lost to him yet, but it was only a matter of time.

Keir was gaining strength, but he was still weak. He'd manage a trip to the privy area, and then I'd insist that he return to the bed. He made a token protest, but he leaned heavily on Marcus for the few steps back to the bed.

But he felt and I agreed that he was strong enough to

receive the reports of his warleaders. So there was a great
deal of coming and going as the warleaders prepared to
make their reports to their Warlord. For Keir needed to
see and hear as much if not more than to be seen and
heard. The warleaders needed the reassurance that he had
survived the illness.

I could feel the burden of command lift from my shoulders as we crammed into the sleeping area, even Sal,
looking thinner and weaker, but determined to participate. Iften stood by Keir's bed, shooting fairly nervous
glances in my direction.

No one had the strength to talk long, so all kept their
words short. Keir listened intently, asking few questions,
sometimes only grunting in satisfaction. Yers's report
took the longest, as Keir questioned him as to the minds
of the warriors. Keir's eyes flickered with surprise when
Yers began to speak, and his gaze traveled over the room
before settling back on Yers, concentrating on his words.
I suspected that Joden's absence had been noted.

My heart lifted as Gils stood confidently under the
scrutiny of his superiors and reported that the number of
the newly ill had fallen off dramatically. As proud as I
was of Gils, I also felt a guilty sense of relief at his words.
Relief, that it was almost over. Guilt, because so very
many were dead, and I still had my Warlord.

Gils's report put new strength into everyone. Keir gave
Sal permission to range the hunting parties further afield,
and resolved a few other issues before his strength
started to wane. And not just his—the others were tired
as well. The warleaders departed quickly, with Iften in
the lead.

Keir reached for the chess board, but I beat him to it,
removing it from his grasp. "Sleep, Keir."

He sighed dramatically, but the effect was spoiled when it changed to a yawn.

Marcus had put together a meal of fry bread, kavage, and gurt. As tired as I had grown of those foods while on the march, they were a welcome change from the soups and stews that we had been eating. Isdra and Gils joined us in the stilltent, and we all dug in, eating in silence.

It was only after we were full to bursting that Gils spoke up. "Warprize, I's thinking that Iften is saying that the illness was spread on purpose by the Xyians."

Isdra muttered something under her breath, and Marcus gave her a sharp look. "Careful, warrior. Iften is Second, and earned that rank through challenge. Twice your size, and the better warrior."

I stiffened, surprised to hear Marcus say something like that without a token, but Isdra merely shrugged. Marcus scowled, and opened his mouth for a blistering comment, but there was a noise outside the tent. Isdra took advantage of the interruption. "That's Pisila, returning with Meara." She left the tent.

I looked after her, but Marcus shook his head. "Young'un, you at least listen to me, yes?"

Gils nodded. "I's staying out of his way." Gils also stood, grabbing for his satchel. "There's all that fever's foe that we might not be needing. Maybe Sal will have wax for the sealing, Warprize."

I nodded. "Keep track of the new cases, Gils. We have to stay isolated for forty days from the last case."

He nodded, looking serious. "I's remember, Warprize. Forty days."

Voices rose outside, Isdra's the loudest, with a sharp

exclamation of anger. We all rose and went out to find Isdra yelling at Pisila, a younger girl, of fair skin and a serious look on her face. "Isdra, I did no wrong. She had to
be marked!"

"You had no right to make the decision without the
Warprize's approval!" Isdra was outraged, her hands on
her hips.

Between them lay Meara in her basket, her little arms
waving about, playing with a wide strip of privacy bells. I
took another step and bent down to look closer, and
gasped.

A tattoo. Goddess above, *a tattoo*.

Marcus and Gils moved and we all stood there, looking
down at the smiling babe, with two thin tattoos on her
tiny upper arm. I confess, my voice was a shriek. "YOU
TATTOOED A BABY?"

Everyone looked at me in horror, but it was Pisila that
answered. "Earth, no! Warprize, I used–"

"A stain." Marcus knelt down, holding out a finger,
which Meara grabbed with glee. He stretched out her arm
for me to see that it was a stain, two thin parallel lines on
her pink skin. I remembered now, Isdra had mentioned
that to me. As I looked closer, I could see that the lines
were really thin willow leaves. "With a fair hand." Marcus added, clear impressed by the work.

Pislia's smile was smug. "My thanks."

Isdra was not appeased. "You had no right, warrior.
The Warprize has not chosen a design."

Pislia looked confused at that. "She has not? But I
thought—" she gestured to my upper arm and I realized
she'd mistaken my scars as tribal marks. "I thought that
was the mark of Xy."

Isdra proceeded to tell her how stupid she was as I

stood there, stunned. I couldn't blame the young woman, I could understand her confusion. The scars on my arm were from when I'd been attacked by Xyians in the Firelander's camp outside of Water's Fall. How ironic that she would see it as my tribal marking, as was their tradition.

Meara waved the bells in the air, gurgling with laughter, as Isdra and Pislia argued.

I put my hand over my mouth, but I couldn't keep my shoulders from heaving.

They all looked at me, worried, and Pislia spoke anxiously. "Warprize, forgive me. The stain will wear off."

"Eventually," voiced Gils.

That was it. I lost control, laughing so hard, I thought to wet my trous.

After they'd departed with the babe, a wave of weakness came over me. Marcus fixed me with a look. "Bed for you. Hisself sleeps, you sleep." He gave me a long look. "You could sleep in the command tent, yes?"

"I don't want Keir disturbed, Marcus." I stared into my kavage. "I'll sleep here."

He frowned as he gather up the dishes. I shrugged, and played with the hem of my tunic.

"What is wrong, Warprize?"

It was my turn to sigh. "I feel guilty, Marcus. Why did it never occur to me that their lungs were filling? If I'd realized that in the village, maybe they would have lived and none of this would have happened."

"Don't you think that Isdra wonders why she failed to offer Epor comfort in that fashion? If she had, maybe he would have lived. No one knows the wind's way, Lara. And you will make yourself mad trying to predict or say 'what if'."

I had to smile. "You sound like Eln."

"A wise man." Marcus chuckled, and picked up the pile of dirty dishes. I watched, but stopped him when he would have left. "Marcus? Would Isdra . . . ?"

He sighed and gave me a long look. "She made you a promise, Lara, and Isdra is not one to give her word lightly." He looked off at the tent entrance. "But the breaking of a bond is a painful thing."

"Like yours?"

He turned on me, the dishes in his arms rattling. "What do you know of that?"

I took a step back, surprised at his sudden anger. "Someone told—"

"No business of yours, or any other. Say no more of this to me." Marcus spat out the words, and left.

I stared at him, bewildered at the sudden change. Suddenly, it all seemed too much, and I sagged, tired in body and spirit. We all were short of temper and energies.

A voice caught my attention, and I stumbled over to the entrance, to hear Keir calling my name. Goddess help me, that man was supposed to be sleeping.

I walked over to the command tent to find Rafe and Prest there, guarding the entrance. As Keir bellowed yet again, I looked at them and smiled. "Anyone interested in learning a game?"

Of course, I'd forgotten about their memories.

Not their memories, exactly. It never occurred to me

that they could hold the picture of the board in their minds, telling each other the movement of the pieces without having an actual board in front of them.

Rafe and Prest took to the game like ducks to water. They cheerfully learned the moves from Keir and then started playing. This had the added benefit of keeping Rafe from trying to do too much. I'd worried that he'd put our security before his well-being. Sitting and studying the chess board wasn't as good as sleeping, but I would take what I could get.

Thankfully, Marcus had grown curious, and had started asking questions about the moves and the pieces. I made sure that they had the moves right, and left them to their own devices. I'd thought to kill two birds with one thrown stone, since Keir would have others to play with and I might be able to get him and Marcus to rest while playing. But Marcus grew adept at calling out his moves to Keir as he worked.

As the day wore on, they all kept themselves amused for the most part. I would go over to check on Keir regularly, but all was well, except for an odd feeling that I had. Both Keir and Rafe seemed worried about something, but what it was I couldn't get them to tell me. Rafe in particular seemed always on the verge of asking me about something, only to change his mind at the last minute. Keir was just cranky about something.

Finally, when Rafe gave me that odd glance for about the tenth time, I confronted him. "Rafe, is there something you want to ask me?"

Rafe straightened, and gave Prest a beseeching look, as if asking him for help. Prest just shrugged.

"Warprize, some of the warriors, they are worried."

"Worried?" I frowned, concerned. Perhaps there had been complications that hadn't been reported.

"Worried." Rafe nodded. "Especially the male warriors."

Male? I thought about that for only a moment before the answer hit me. Of course. Male warriors not used to illness and its effects. I put a hand over mouth to cover my smile, thinking of Rafe and his four 'nurses'. I only spoke when I could do so with a serious tone. "Rafe."

"Warprize?"

"Rafe, sometimes, with this kind of illness, the male warriors may have other problems, lingering effects, that might worry them."

Rafe looked at me, his face intent. "Problems?" His eyes drifted down slightly, then returned to mine.

"Problems." I said firmly, giving him a steady look. "Such as maybe their . . . bodies . . . not working as they did in the past. But it is passing, and will return to normal when their full strength returns."

"So." Rafe thought for a moment. "Can I spread word of this?"

"Please." He stood, as if to go, and I raised my hand. "And please spread the word that any can come to me when they have . . . problems."

He paused. "Are you sure? It's hard to know, Warprize, your ways are strange to us. No one wishes to embarrass you or to anger the Warlord."

"I'm modest as to my body, Rafe. But not as to my patients. I have a token. I know what it means. Tell them to use it."

"I will, Warprize."

I watched him walk off to spread the word, and then turned and contemplated the command tent. Seems I might need to have a quiet word with one very cranky, and very worried, Warlord.

"It's called a 'draw'."

Keir and Prest glared at me. I remained calm, looking down at the playing board. "When neither player can maneuver the other into checkmate, it's called a 'draw'. The game is over with no winner."

"There is always a winner." Keir declared.

"And a loser." Prest agreed.

I rolled my eyes. "Not always. Keir, you weren't a clear winner against Xy."

Keir flashed that boyish grin of his. "Ah, but I claimed my Warprize, didn't I?"

I blushed. Luckily, Prest was studying the board. He grunted, "But I've no piece to offer as warprize."

Somehow, they'd assigned sexes to the various pieces. They didn't like the fact that the Queen was the only female piece on the board. I wasn't sure how they'd assigned genders but they managed to their satisfaction. So now they both looked at the remaining pieces intently. Finally, Keir sat back. "With no Warprize to offer, I suggest we regroup our troops and meet in battle again."

Prest nodded, and they started to rearrange the pieces.

I opened my mouth to argue, then closed it again. I suspected by the time we returned to Xy, the rules of the game would be so changed as to be unrecognizable.

Ortis entered the tent, ducking his head to avoid the top. "Papers from Water's Fall, Warlord."

We both looked up, startled to see a bundle of letters in his hand. He spilled them out on the bed at Keir's feet. "Exchanged at a distance, as commanded."

I looked up at him, and he smiled and nodded. "I sent your papers back the same way, Warprize."

"Thanks, Ortis."

Prest had moved when Ortis had entered, and he now moved the board away from the bed and took his leave. I started sorting through the various letters, looking for familiar handwriting. Most all were formal missives from the Council, but I found one from Eln, Othur, and what looked like another one from Simus.

I paused, feeling the heavy paper crackle in my hands, looking at the wax seal. I wasn't really sure that I wanted to know their contents. These would contain word of the plague and its effects. I glanced up to see Keir looking at me, patiently waiting. I broke open Othur's seal.

Lara,

All is well, dearest girl. Eln's letter and the reports of the Council will give you the details, but the Sweat seems to have passed us by. Thanks to your warning we were able to close the gates, and isolate the few that sickened. Eln was surprised by the change in the disease, but I am sure his letter is filled with that information. I do not know of its effects in the outlying manors and villages, but we are well. Send us news of yourself as soon as you are able.

Would that all was as well within the castle. Alas, that you have inflicted me with one Simus of the Hawk.

Never mind the fact that Simus strides from his chambers to the mineral baths naked as a plucked chicken, smiling and greeting all and sundry with a cheerful smile.

Never mind the fact that he and Warren have

taken to weapons practice in the Great Hall, jumping from table to table swords in one hand, flagons
in the other, fighting and laughing, and cursing each
other, causing ladies to swoon and leaving heel
marks on all the tables.

Never mind that half the lords want to kill him,
the other half want to befriend him and that all of
the ladies seem entranced. Which includes my own
Lady Wife, thank you very much.

Oh no, the worst of it is that Simus is having rela-
tions with Dye-Mistress Mavis, or so the sounds
echoing in the castle halls at all hours of the night
announce to all and sundry.

By his tradition, Simus does no wrong, or so
Dye-Mistress Mavis has informed me, Warren, and
the Archbishop. Further, when we confronted her,
she told us in no uncertain terms that she is an adult
and Master of her trade and that her behavior is
none of our concern. She added something to the
effect that you aren't the only one willing to make
sacrifices for her guild. Which had the Archbishop
clutching for his holy symbol.

I think Dye-Mistress is only after the cloths that
Simus wears like a peacock. I have tried to explain
that to Simus, but he just smiles that wide smile of his
and indicates that he sees no harm to being 'used'.

The entire Court and Council is scandalized.
They all come to me and complain, taking the
greatest pleasure in going over every juicy detail.

Durst is recovering, gaining strength slowly. Eln
is uncertain that he will ever recover his full vigor. I
think his health suffers more from the hate that fes-
ters within than the wound itself. He holds all of the

Firelanders responsible for his wound and the death of his son. Which places Durst firmly in the camp of those who wish to kill Simus of the Hawk and any other Firelander that he can get his hands on. Although he hasn't moved from his bed, he foments trouble with the other lords. He has been warned, but his temper flares every time he hears of the Firelanders. I'd send him to his estates, but I'd rather have him here under my eye.

The official letters will hold more of the details, Lara. Send us word as soon as you can. We are terribly worried about you.

Your Warden,
Othur

My Lady Wife begs that I add this note and sends her love and best wishes and wonders if perhaps you are pregnant? She asks that you send word as soon as you can.

O.

I fell back on the bed, laughing in delight at the image of Simus wreaking havoc in the Court of Xy.

I'd returned to the stilltent, after I'd read Simus's letter to Keir, along with the rest of the letters from Water's Fall. Eln had written of his dismay over the disease and its severity, but he'd come up with no alternative remedies. I took comfort from the fact that I had already sent a letter to him outlining our treatments. But I took far more comfort that the Sweat had not reached the City. It would be months before we knew its true effects.

The Council reports were dry, but Keir seemed interested, so I read them out to him. I'd left him with a firm promise that he'd sleep. I decided that the time was right to clean and reorganize the stilltent. It had been sometime since Gils had reported a new fever, and I prayed that we'd seen the last of it.

I had a bucket of jars and bottles to clean when I was done, and I took them outside and sat on a log to start cleaning them. There was still a bit of sunlight to enjoy, and I wanted to take advantage of it. Isdra was off some ways, supervising some warriors doing laundry. Rafe and Prest were at the command tent, sitting outside, playing chess from the looks of it.

I was content with my small chore, setting the clean items on a cloth to dry when Gils stumbled up and sat next to me, his satchel in his lap. The strap fell off his shoulder. I smiled, then frowned as I saw how tired he appeared.

"Gils, you are exhausted. Let me get you some kavage."

He sighed softly. "Just had some, Warprize." His face was turned, and he was looking at the sunset. "I's just very tired."

"Gils?"

Without another word, his satchel slipped from his fingers, and he collapsed against me, his head on my shoulder. I put my fingers on his warm forehead and cried out for help.

11

People poured out of the tents in answer to my cries. I'd clutched Gils in both arms, trying to keep him from collapsing. Clean bottles and jars rolled everywhere as I tried to get purchase to support us.

Yers reached us first, Isdra a breath behind. They lifted Gils off me, cradling him in their arms. As I stumbled to my feet, my gut clenched to see Gils so pale and still, as the baby had been before she . . .

Others came, even Rafe and Prest gathered about us. Keir was coming as well, walking slowly with Marcus hovering at his shoulder.

I reached my hand out, intending to feel the extent of Gils's fever. He had run himself to exhaustion helping others. Would he have enough strength to survive the Sweat?

Gils convulsed, limbs jerking in spasms, his head thrown back, gasping for air.

Yers staggered, almost dropping the lad in horror. But Isdra stepped closer to Yers, taking more of Gils's weight. They both managed to hold steady as Gils stopped thrashing as quickly as he had started.

I froze, dread deep in my bones. Convulsions? Goddess, what was happening to him? There'd been no others with such symptoms—

Isdra's voice broke into my thoughts. "Warprize? The lake?"

I moved then, my hand on his forehead. Gils was warm, but not extraordinarily so. Had his work weakened him to this point? "Gils?" I called his name, but there was no reaction, no indication that he was aware. I placed my fingers at his neck, feeling a slow, weak pulse.

Quickly, I checked for any kind of head wound, or perhaps he was choking. But his head showed no sign of injury and his throat was clear. There was no sign of other injury, it had to be the plague, and yet there was no odor, no real sweat on his body. But the headaches could cause these kinds of problems, if they were severe enough. A new fear gripped me. Had the Sweat changed again? Or had the Sweat came on him so fast that it was causing convulsions? I spent precious moments checking every possibility I could think of, but I had no answers. Gils's breath was rapid and labored, perhaps . . .

With Yer's help, Isdra and I got the boy in the position that we could drum his lungs. If I could just clear his lungs of the fluids there—

Again, Gils jerked in spasms. Those around us stepped

back, looks of fear on their faces. I had no comfort to offer, and what was worse, I knew that no amount of cold water would cure this ill. His breathing was slowing, as was the beat of his heart. I looked around, finally focusing on Keir's face, a question in his eyes. I met his gaze, and let my tears fall, answering with a shake of my head.

"You can do nothing?" Keir rasped as he reached us.

"No." I ran my fingers through Gils's red curls. He didn't react, and I was desperately afraid that he was dying. "He's in the hands of the Goddess now." I stepped back, and gestured to Yers. "Bring him into the tent."

"Grant him mercy." Keir said firmly.

"What?" Shocked, I watched in horror as Yers and Isdra lowered Gils into a patch of thick grass off the path. Yers unlaced Gils's jerkin, as Isdra stepped over to stand next to me. Rafe and Prest each knelt, and took hold of a leg, removing Gils's boots. Joden took Gils's left arm, and pinned it over Gils's head. Marcus left Keir's side, pulling his dagger as he drew closer.

"No!" I cried out, leaping to stop this. But Isdra grabbed me from behind, pinning my arms, and bore me to the ground.

"We'll not let him suffer, Lara." Keir looked at me, his eyes blue sparks under grim brows.

"The fire warmed you." Joden began, his voice trembling.

The others responded in unison. "We thank the elements." They pressed Gils to the earth as he convulsed again. He seemed to be fighting them, even as I fought Isdra. They couldn't do this. They couldn't!

"The earth supported you." Joden's voice was firmer now.

"We thank the elements."

Marcus drew closer, but as he did, Yers looked up, and said something I couldn't hear. Marcus handed him the dagger, and they traded positions.

"The waters sustained you."

"We thank the elements."

I cried out, denying their thanks, begging them to stop. Isdra pulled me back and wrapped her arms around me. "Would you let him suffer?" she whispered in my ear. Bile rose in my throat even as I cried out again, trying to deny this, trying to deny that I was helpless to stop his death, from the plague or from the dagger.

"The air filled you."

"We thank the elements."

Yers leaned forward. "Go now, warrior. Beyond the snows and to the stars."

He thrust the dagger between Gils's ribs and into his heart.

I screamed, and collapsed sobbing in Isdra's arms. I turned in toward her, hiding my face on her shoulder. Her face was damp as well, and she rocked me as I wept. Why hadn't I kept a better watch over my own apprentice? How had he sickened to such a point under my very eyes?

"Is this my fate? To sing dirges and laments for days unending?" Joden asked. Silence was the only answer. He sighed, lifted his face, and began to sing.

I hid my face again as they began to prepare the body. I only looked up when Marcus placed Gils's satchel by my feet. I reached out to take it, my arm trembling at the effort. Had I ever told him how proud I was of him?

I looked up at Marcus. "I couldn't heal him," I swallowed hard. "I failed him."

Marcus knelt, and wrapped his arm around both Isdra and I, saying nothing.

Joden's chant ended. Within the warmth of their arms, I looked up to see Keir standing over us, looking at where Gils lay, his jaw clenched. He looked down and met my gaze and looked about to speak, when another voice rose, angry and scornful. "This is what comes of Xyian ways."

We all turned to see Iften standing with Wesren and Uzaina next to him. "The death of our best and brightest, through their filth."

Keir growled deep in his throat. "Iften—"

"No." Iften cut him off. "Once before I challenged, and stepped back. Not this time. I call senel to witness and hear my challenge and see you answer with your blade. Summon the warleaders, summon those who can still walk and all will hear my truths." Iften spun, striding toward the command tent.

Isdra helped me to my feet. Marcus stood next to Keir. "If there is a challenge, he will win."

Keir nodded, a resigned look on his face. "He will."

"You can't!" I wiped my face of its tears. "You can barely walk, much less fight. Iften can't. Simus said that the rules—"

"Normally." Keir stepped closer to me, reaching to tuck a stray curl behind my ear. "But the situation is hardly normal. He will use that to his advantage." Keir straightened a bit, and used his hands to adjust the leather harness of his swords. "Your pledge still stands?"

"It does." Marcus answered.

"I will do what must be done." Isdra responded, looking off after Iften.

Keir gave her a long look, but didn't push the matter.

"We'd also see to the Warprize's safety." Rafe spoke quietly, with Prest nodding his agreement.

"This isn't right." I looked over at Joden, but he looked away and said nothing.

Keir reached out, and enfolded me in his arms. My eyes still red, I buried my face in his neck, trying hard not to weep. The soft brush of his lips against my ear had me desperate for more, and I took his face in my hands and kissed him.

Keir broke the kiss and stepped back. "Let us face Iften's truths."

"Gils," I turned back, to find that Gils had been lifted from the ground unto the arms of some younger warriors.

Yers spoke. "They will see him taken care of, Warprize."

I stepped over by them, to look into that dear face one more time. Gils seemed asleep, as if he'd awaken if any but called his name. I arranged his curls with a quick gesture, saying a silent prayer to the Goddess for him.

"Go with them, Lara." Keir urged. "You do not need to attend this senel."

I took a step back, and turned to face Keir. "My place is at the side of my Warlord. They will care for his body. Gils is safe in the hands of the Goddess." I walked over and took Keir's hand.

Keir smiled with pride, and we walked toward the crowd together.

The warleaders had gathered by the time we arrived, forming a circle outside the command tent. Iften was speaking, almost shouting, to the crowd, his sword and shield in hand. "We are cursed by the elements, and this foul Xyian is to blame."

Many heads were nodding in agreement, and I shivered at the implication. Keir moved to stand before us, standing at the ready. I moved up beside him, with Prest and Isdra at my shoulders. Rafe was a step behind, watching our backs. Marcus was behind Keir, and to my surprise and relief, Yers was there as well.

"Her filth strikes deep, and leaves its taint. Even a child of her own lands falls victim to her corruption. A child that carries the corruption now within her!"

This remark was met with scowls, a negative reaction that surprised me, Iften saw it too, and hurried on. "Keir of the Cat has brought this upon us, by bringing his Xyian into our midst. He is to blame for what has happened here, and he must answer for it." Iften was shouting now, spittle flying from his lips.

Keir had not yet pulled his sword, but I could tell that he was prepared, a cat about to leap upon its prey. My heart seemed stuck in my throat. He'd not refuse this challenge but—

Iften pointed his sword at me, his face full of disdain. "Gils had the new knowledge of healing and the elements killed him because of it. Epor was curse—"

A scream split the air, freezing the blood in my body. Isdra launched herself from behind my shoulder, her face a snarl, Epor's warclub in her hands.

Iften moved fast, his sword out and his shield up to meet the blow. But he'd been facing Keir and Isdra's attack forced him to shift slightly to meet her. What precious moments she gained Isdra used, the warclub a blur of motion in her hand. The blow fell on Iften's forearm, and I thought I heard the crack of bone.

Everyone scattered, trying to give them room, forming a loose circle around the fighters. It was a large circle, showing a healthy respect for the reach of those weapons.

Isdra never paused, never let up, pressing Iften with a series of blows to his shield. She had eyes only for her target, grim and calculating.

Keir stood, unmoving, watching the fray. Yers was standing next to him, his sword in his hand. Marcus was slightly behind Keir, his gaze scanning the crowd for any threat.

Prest was behind me, and Rafe stepped to stand in front of me, a little to one side. They too were tense, but they did no more than place their hands on their weapons and wait.

I clutched at Rafe's shoulder. "She's smaller . . ."

Keir understood. "He insulted her bonded," was his soft reply.

Iften was bigger, his sword flashing in sure strokes that surprised me. But he seemed to have the use of the arm still. Isdra parried, the blade skittering off the metal studs that lined the top of the warclub. She seemed to move well, but she was breathing hard. Iften, in contrast, seemed able to stand where he was and wield his weapon with ease. His face was triumphant. He fully expected to kill Isdra.

Isdra's next blows hit Iften's shield dead center, with Iften grunting under the impact. Iften would wait, lunging at Isdra each time he sensed that she was vulnerable. But each time she danced back, away from his blade.

Iften smirked, and lowered his shield. "You are no Epor, woman."

Isdra's grim face never changed. She took a step and swung for Iften's knee.

Iften moved, dodging that blow. But Isdra somehow used the momentum to take a step closer, and drove the handle of her warclub into Iften's jaw.

Iften's head snapped back. He staggered, dropping his shield. Isdra cried out in satisfaction, taking another swing at his unprotected head and connecting.

Iften crumpled to the ground, unconscious.

Isdra swung the warclub high over her head, as if to crush Iften's skull. "For Epor!" She shouted, and started the blow.

"STOP." Joden stepped forward.

Isdra caught herself in mid-strike. She glared, her chest heaving, never taking her eyes off Iften's unmoving body. "Who dares?"

"Do not kill him, Isdra of the Fox." Joden took another step forward.

"He insults Epor, my bonded, the first to meet the enemy and the bravest of all that have died in this battle." Isdra spat out her words, trembling with anger. "He held no token of mine, or any other." Her anger shifted. "It is my right, Singer!"

The crowd shifted, uneasy. I glanced at Keir, but he was intent on the drama before us.

"The skies are clouded, Warrior, and full of turmoil." Joden stepped forward. "I do not know the truth in this. So I will claim Singer status long enough to declare Keir's illness is in the nature of a war wound, although the enemy is one we have never met before." Joden turned to look at the crowd, seeking out the warleaders. "As such, he is not to be challenged in the field, and remains Warlord until we reach the Plains. It will be a question for the Elders then."

Relief flooded through me. There'd be no further chal-

lenge from Iften or any other, at least until Keir had his
strength back.

Isdra snarled, furious. "What has that to do with the insult given to Epor?"

Joden raised his hand. "If the truth is to be known, then
Iften's truth must be told as well, and I would preserve his
words for the Elders to hear."

"You are not yet full singer, Joden." Isdra's voice
rasped in her throat. "It is my right as Epor's bonded."

"That is true, Isdra of the Fox, and I answer to your
truth by saying that I only ask this. I can not, and do not,
command."

There was a long pause as Isdra stood there, breathing
hard, glaring at Joden. No one seemed to breathe. I risked
moving just enough to look at Iften, to see if I could determine his injuries. He lay like a broken doll, clearly unconscious, but he seemed to be breathing.

Finally Isdra lowered her weapon. "Epor honored your
wisdom, Joden. I will do no less." Isdra drew in a deep
breath. "But this carrion will answer for his insults as
soon as the Elders have heard his words."

"Iften must answer to you." Joden acknowledged.

Isdra sheathed her warclub in its harness, turned, and
walked out of the circle.

Keir stood, and spoke. "It shall be as the Singer has
said. This senel is over."

I took advantage of the distraction, and pushed past
Rafe, headed for Iften. With careful hands, I moved him
into a prone position.

Joden had picked up his sword. "He will not thank you,
Warprize."

"I did no less for Simus." I didn't bother to look up. "I

will do no less for him." I pressed my fingers gently to his jaw, but it wasn't broken. The bruising had started, and I was certain that the arm would be badly bruised as well. I started to unlace the armor from his forearm. "Marcus, would you fetch my bag?"

There was no response, and I looked up to see quite a few people looking very unhappy. I returned scowl for scowl. "I have my sworn oaths, as you all know. He needs my aid. I will give it to him."

Keir's face was grim, but he nodded. "We remember, Warprize. And honor your oaths to heal all in need."

I bit my lip, conscious that I had quite an audience around me, conscious that Keir was making a point. But my attention went back to my patient in an instant as Joden knelt beside me, and reached to unlace Iften's bracers. Iften's breathing was even, and I'd seen no blow to the chest or ribs. I concentrated on the head blow, and his sword arm. Without shifting him too much, I pried back first one eyelid and checked his eyes. They were unfocused and dazed, with no sign of awareness. Probably for the best right now.

Joden had his sword arm bare, and the forearm was beginning to blacken and swell, but the skin wasn't broken. I took his arm carefully in my hands and felt along its length, using a firm pressure. There, right in the center, where the blow had landed. The top bone was badly cracked, but still in one piece. The bracers had probably kept the bone from shifting, but it needed to be set.

Someone placed Gil's satchel by me. I turned to it quickly. "Splints. Gils, I need—"

There was a silence about me, and I closed my eyes as the loss of Gils coursed through my heart all over again.

There was silence all around me. I didn't look up, I just wiped my tears, and cleared my throat. "I need two pieces of wood, flat and straight if possible. Bandages and a length of leather."

"I'll see to the wood." Marcus growled. "Hie to the tent, Rafe, and get the rest."

Rafe set off at a run.

Iften groaned, moving his head slightly. He was going to be in a lot of pain shortly from that blow to the head. I was tempted to dose him with some of my remaining lotus, so that I could set the bone in peace, but I resisted the urge. Besides, I was fairly sure the medicine would be wasted if I did.

"Broken?" Joden asked.

"Yes." I rummaged in the bag for the bandages that I had there. "Help me hold his arm still."

Joden reached over, and we got the forearm in the right position for binding. I started at the base of the thumb and began to wrap. Marcus and Rafe returned at the same time, and aided me to bind the arm, secure the splints, and then protect it with the leather over all.

I finished as Iften began to come around, which gave me a chance to place him on his side before the inevitable happened. Sure enough, after a bit of moaning and groaning, he vomited into the dirt.

"Move slowly. You'll be dizzy from the blow." I cautioned.

I was ignored. Iften struggled to right himself, trying to crawl onto all fours. I managed to steer him away from the mess, but he struggled up to his knees, hissing when his arm came into contact with the earth. He knelt there, clutching his head with one hand, holding out his sword arm and staring at it. "What happened?"

Joden put his hand on Iften's back. "I'll explain once you are in your tent."

Iften's eyes were dazed, but he managed to focus on his arm. "What is this?"

"A splint." I stood, brushing off my knees. "Your arm is broken."

Iften blinked, taking in the crowd, all eyes on him. Keir in particular was watching closely. Iften's eyes widened as his memory returned, and he snarled, swaying as he tried to get to his feet. Joden offered support, and Wesren moved in to help as well.

Iften shrugged them off, and took a tottering step toward me. "I want no aid of yours, Xyian." He tore at the bindings, and ripped away the leather. "The elements will heal it. Or I will seek a warrior-priest when we reach the Plains."

It was my turn to glare. "Don't be stupid. The bone must be—"

He swayed again as he ripped the bandages off, flinging them down to the dirt. "May I wander the snows forever if I accept your filthy ways, Xyian."

I scowled, offended by his foolishness, and opened my mouth to argue the point. But Iften took a few steps away from me, staggering like a man in his cups. Joden took Iften's good arm and pulled him toward his own tent, and Keir was shaking his head. So I stood, amidst the bandages and watched the idiot walk away.

Gils was the last to take ill.

It took me the better part of two days to confirm it, but the plague claimed no new victims since his death. Once I told Keir we could start counting the forty days, he called for a senel. Joden attended without being asked. He wouldn't take a seat, but he stood at Keir's side, a silent sentinel over the meeting.

The warleaders were uneasy and uncomfortable at first, but Keir made his normal inquiries and they relaxed. Having received satisfactory answers, Keir spoke. "I feel that we have the need to purify ourselves after this war that we have fought. For make no mistake, this land of Xy has challenged us in ways that no warrior of the Plains has had to deal with in hundreds of years, if ever. We have fought a war and our dead have fallen honorably," Keir raised a hand when Joden opened his mouth to protest. "Although I understand that the Elders will make the final determination concerning that matter."

Joden relaxed, satisfied.

"So, for a ten-day period, we will purify ourselves. Not because I believe that we bear any curse, or the ill will of the elements. I call for purification to ease our spirits, and to balance the elements within us. However, I forbid any warrior to fast, for fear of weakening those who recover."

That had been my condition when we had discussed the matter.

Keir continued. "After the ten days, we should all be back to our regular strength. I would offer a contest then, to determine a new bodyguard for the Warprize. Epor has gone to the snows, and I would honor his memory by offering all a chance to combat for the position. I reserve the right of final approval of the winner. All combats to the first blood."

There were nods at this, and looks of approval. I bit my lip, but kept silent. I'd resisted this strongly, not liking the idea that Epor could be replaced. But Keir had overruled me, and when I'd turned to Isdra for support, she'd agreed with Keir. Three guards were not enough, and someone had to be chosen to work with Isdra.

Keir had promised that he would consult Isdra on the final candidate, making sure that it was someone she could work with. He'd pointed out that the combats and eliminations would take about twenty days and keep the warriors well occupied as we waited. Isdra thought the idea of the competition was a tribute to Epor. So I'd been forced to agree. But it would seem odd to have someone else at Isdra's side.

"Further, I propose that we have what the Warprize calls a chess tournament, to determine a champion within our ranks." Keir's grin was positively wicked. "Open to all, just as the combat."

I tried not to roll my eyes. The game was sweeping the entire camp, and every warrior seemed to have at least one game going on in their head at all times. If Keir thought the combats would be good for morale, then I was sure that a tourney was an even better idea. Certainly, there'd be less injuries as a result.

Iften looked sour. As far as I knew, he hadn't learned the game, which came as no surprise. I was also not surprised to see that he was holding his sword arm at an odd angle against his chest, as if protecting it. I narrowed my eyes, trying to see how bad the swelling had become. Iften caught me at it, and gave me such a glare as might curl my toes if I cared for his opinion.

Keir released the senel, and all rose to mill about. Iften and Wesren were talking with Uzaina. Others lingered to speak with Keir, and I used the opportunity to talk to Joden. He gave me a grave look as I moved closer, his broad face troubled.

"I wanted to thank you, Joden. For—"

He interrupted me with a gesture. "I am not so sure I did you any favors, Warprize."

"But—"

"Had Iften challenged Keir, I would not have interfered. I am not sure I was right to stop Isdra, either." He looked away. "All I've done is delay these matters until we are before the Elders."

"But Keir will be able to speak for himself. And you will support him."

Joden didn't meet my gaze.

"Joden?" I asked, suddenly aware of a change in my friend.

He looked at me, his normal serenity gone. "I will not support Keir before the Elders, Warprize. I will speak against him."

"Against him? A-a-against me?" Stunned, I could barely get the words out.

His face softened. "No, Lara, not against you. But," he looked out over the area, as if gathering his thoughts. "It seems like a lifetime has passed since I crouched at Simus's side and saw to his wound. Tradition demanded that I grant mercy, to prevent his suffering and evade capture."

"But you didn't kill him."

"No," He turned then to look me in the eye, his gaze filled with pain. "I tried to bind his wound, and we were captured."

"Which brought Simus under my care, and to my meeting Keir." I smiled. "We should thank you for that, Joden."

"Would you thank me for these deaths as well?"

His question sucked the very breath from my body. "Joden . . ."

"You saved the life of my friend," Joden continued, his voice cracking. "You became the Warprize, bringing gifts of your knowledge. But all I see as a result is death. Ugly, dishonorable death."

"You blame me." I whispered.

Haunted eyes looked into mine. "You are a gentle, caring soul, Xylara. I can lay no blame on you." His face hardened and his hands formed fists. "I blame Keir's ideas of combining our peoples and their ways. What happened here speaks to me of the dangers of his leadership."

I swallowed hard. What had happened here . . . I blinked back tears.

"What can I say to you, Lara?" Joden's voice, his lovely voice cracked. "You gave me hope when you saved the life of Simus, and more hope when I understood your willingness to sacrifice yourself for your people."

"But now my people lie dead, and the smoke rises to the skies. Precious lives have been lost, and I can't but think they are lost because Keir is trying to go against the elements themselves."

Joden shook his head. "Keir asks that you become of the Plains, and demands that we be of Xy. No good has, or will, come of it." Joden took a breath. "My decision is made. Excuse me, Warpr—" He stopped himself. "Excuse me, Xylara. I must tell the Warlord of my truths." Joden's voice was soft, but he turned and left me without another word.

* * *

I returned to my stilltent to find Isdra sitting inside, re-working the leather on the handle of Epor's warclub. Her hands stroked the smooth leather, as if it was precious.

With leaden steps, I moved to stir the coals in one of the small braziers, adding fuel, losing myself in the task of warming kavage. I said nothing, and Isdra was silent as well, both of us lost in memories of a golden-haired man with a ready smile.

I dropped on a stump and watched the pot, numb and tired. For just a few moments, the only thing I wanted to think about was kavage. Not sickness, or challenges, or failure . . .

Or death.

Isdra finished the wrapping and secured the ends of the leather strip. She sat for a moment, her hands resting lightly on the weapon in her lap.

Isdra quietly started to cry.

I knelt beside her, leaned my head against her arm, and offered what comfort I could.

The rattle of the pot forced my attention back to the world around us. I poured kavage as Isdra wiped her face. She took the mug I offered, and we drank in silence.

I broke the silence. "The other day, Marcus told me 'the sun will rise. I can offer no more, and no less'."

"It should not." Isdra whispered, staring into her kavage. "It should hide itself in sorrow and mourn." She lifted her head to gaze at me. "My life is broken, yet the world goes on around me. As if it had never happened. As if he had never been." She drew a stuttering breath. "Never to hear his voice again, or feel his touch. Not until I—"

I looked down at my hands, suddenly ashamed of what I had asked of her. "Isdra, I don't know what to say. You are a warrior, and my guardian, and my friend." My voice hitched, and tears welled up. "I don't want to lose you too."

She sat silent.

"Besides," I tried to smile. "Who will raise Meara? Or the babe I hope to have? Who will teach them in the ways of the Plains besides you, Isdra?" I put my hand over hers. "My babe will be a child of both worlds and will need guidance in all ways." I hadn't thought of that before, but it was true. Any child I bore would need a thea. In my mind, I could see Anna and Isdra arguing over some point of child-rearing in the castle nursery.

Isdra's hand moved to clasp mine. "There is that, Lara." Her face darkened. "And my Epor to avenge." She looked off, her eyes distant. "But there are many sunsets between now and then. Many long moments of—" she cut her words off and stood, her face taut with sorrow. "I would take my leave, Warprize."

I stood, and watched her take up her position outside by the fire, then I turned listlessly to plop down on a stump, facing the tables with their various bottles and jars. The kavage was bitter in my mouth. But the ache in my chest grew until the grief and the guilt welled up, and fat tears started to fall, hard and fast.

I moved, pulled the flaps down and tied them closed. I had enough sense to wrap a strip of bells in one of the ties. I wanted no visitors, well or ill.

Stumbling, I crossed to the stump furthest from the door, and sat down. Through my tears, I reached for some cloths and buried my face in them. I didn't want anyone to hear, or know. The material stifled my sobs, and I let go, releasing all the pain. I hunched over as my shoulders shook, and I cried.

I wanted Anna, wanted home, wanted Father. It was a true pain, deep in my chest, the longing to run home. I should never have left those safe walls, never stumbled out on the road after Keir. It was all my fault, all of it, and the pain of that truth cramped my heart and closed my throat.

I pulled the cloths back just enough to suck in a deep breath, rocking a bit to ease my anguish. But the pain and horror of Epor's final breath wouldn't let me go, and I pressed the damp cloths against my face and moaned.

Why had I insisted that I enter the village? Why had I let Epor and Isdra go with me? My arrogance was to blame, for his death and all the others that lay burning in the ashes of the village.

It seemed as if nothing was right. Everything was tinged with a deep blackness, and I could see no hope. There was despair everywhere I looked, or turned my head, and nothing I could do would solve anything. In fact, my actions seemed only to make things worse.

Meara, that sweet child, almost lost to us in a breath, her cold toes in the palm of my hand. Gils, oh, Gils, had I ever told him how proud I was of him? He'd collapsed at my feet, convulsing helplessly, and nothing in my power could save him. Oh, they'd been right to grant mercy, and maybe that was the only cure for my pain, for I knew of no other way to end my sorrow and grief.

All the dead, offered up in flames on the ruined village, hundreds of men and women. All taken by a disease that I was powerless to stop, for all the talk of my so-called skills of healing.

Now Iften was stronger, much stronger in his actions against change, for he had new support, including Joden.

For Joden had lost faith, in me, in Keir, in the elements themselves.

He wasn't going to call me Warprize any more.

My stomach clenched in a knot and I swallowed hard. I'd complained about everyone using the title but Joden had been one of the first to call me that after Keir claimed me. For him to renounce me hurt terribly. And I'd poured out all my petty fears and problems in Joden's, exposing myself to him. How would he use that? To hurt Keir? To hurt me? And Keir . . .

A decimated army, his warleaders turned against him, his plans for the future in ashes around us, I wouldn't blame Keir if he turned his back on me in anger. The depression crashed down on me and I pressed the sodden cloth even harder against my face and wailed.

Oh Goddess, why had I lied to him?

He'd never forgive me for that, never. How could he, in the face of the damage I'd done to his people?

To us?

There'd be consequences, seen and unseen. Nothing I could do would bring back my friends, or repair the damage I'd created. I shook with sobs that I couldn't stop. I'd lied and everything had gone so very, very wrong . . .

It was the touch of a callused hand on mine, gently tugging the cloths away from my face that brought me back. I knew it was Keir even as he knelt by my side, by his touch, by the spicy scent of his skin. I couldn't look, couldn't raise my swollen eyes to his face. For I knew what I would see there, knew what I deserved. Anger, contempt—at the very least he'd hate me for all that had happened.

I sat, shivering, trying to stop crying, looking at my lap

where his hand covered mine. He said nothing, and I tried to get my ragged breathing under control, to face the disgust that I'd see in those wonderful blue eyes. If I was lucky he'd just go away and leave me to drown in my despair.

But those strong fingers moved and lifted my chin and I raised my gaze to face my Warlord.

12

What I found was understanding and love in those bright blue eyes.

I broke into fresh sobs, ~~and~~ threw myself into his arms. Keir drew me close, pulling me to his chest with strong arms and allowing me to cling like a child. As I wept, he rocked me, drumming my back gently with his hand, which made me cry that much harder.

"I'm so sorry, so sorry . . ." I snuffled my nose, and tried to breathe but I could only gasp out the words. "It's all my fault that—"

"Hush." Keir stroked my back even as he pulled his cloak around us. The warmth of his body enfolded me and I sagged into his strength, continuing to cry.

Keir held me for long moments, then pulled away, stepping to the tent entrance. He closed it again, entwining more privacy bells into the ties. He returned to my side, coaxed me down to the pallet, and proceeded to wrap us in blankets, covering us with his cloak. With soft, comforting sounds, he arranged us so I was cradled in his grasp, supported by arms and legs. The bedding started to warm around us, and I finally caught my breath. He wiped the tears from my face with his hands. I lay silent, within his protection, and felt my body loosen and relax against his.

I breathed deep, taking in the scents of the stilltent, and the spicy smell of his skin. The warmth of his body was a comfort and I let him support me, feeling my bones melt under his touch. He murmured something about the elements, but what he said didn't matter. What meant more was his touch, his strength, his love, all pouring into me without a single word. Just the sound of his heart beating under my ear, and the feel of his breath on my skin was enough.

His fingers started to work their way through my hair, gently carding out the snarls and tangles.

"You broke the bells." I kept my face buried in the blankets as he continued to stroke my hair.

"I did."

"Isn't that rude?" My breath hitched as I knotted my fists in the blankets.

"Yes." His voice was the barest whisper. "But I'll let nothing stand between me and my Warprize."

Another sob escaped me. His hands shifted and he rubbed my back, soothing me. I lay silent, trying to collect my scattered wits. I could hear the faint sounds of the camp around us, but I didn't care. Didn't want to care. I was so tired.

"Talk to me, Lara." Keir's voice was deep and soothing and brought fresh tears to my eyes. I let them come, not trying to suppress my sorrow.

"It's all so horrible, the sickness, so many dead and Epor, oh Keir—" I gasped for breath, and pulled my head back to look him in the eyes. "Isdra's pain is so deep. And Gils, he was just a child, he tried so hard and he's—" I couldn't finish the sentence. "I keep seeing him convulse, and the dagger—" I wailed, burying my face in his tunic. "Goddess help me, and so much worse, I lied to you, Keir. I didn't tell—"

His fingers covered my lips and I cried until I was exhausted, so tired, my head pounding, my nose so clogged I couldn't breathe. His leather armor was smooth under my cheek, and I was sure I was getting it messy with my blubbering. Keir seemed not to care, but I did. I forced my head up, trying to ease out of comfort I had no right to. "It's all my fault, Keir."

He didn't let me out of his arms. His long arm snaked out of our cocoon and grabbed up a clean cloth. He held it out to me. "Blow."

I obeyed, and used the cloth to clean my face and wipe my eyes. He tossed it off to the side and brought his arm back into the warmth to hold me. His breath was sweet and warm on my cheek. The ache in my heart eased slightly, within the shelter of the bedding.

"So." His voice was a soft whisper. "You are responsible for all? The illness? The deaths?"

I closed my eyes and nodded.

"How so?"

I opened my eyes, to look into the calm blue of his. "I shouldn't have insisted that I enter the village. Shouldn't have lied to you about the waiting period." I swallowed hard, and forced the truth out. "Shouldn't have thought I could deal with the plague on my own."

He shifted then, arranging us so that he was on his back, allowing me to curl at his side. Once we were settled again, he sighed. "You are not the only warrior to take on overwhelming odds."

I lay my head on his chest.

"Maybe you are right, Lara. On the other hand, maybe the enemy was among us, silent and invisible even as we argued over what actions to take. The wind blows, and no one can hinder it or dictate its path. If I had overruled you . . . if we had sent messages back and continued on, we may have taken the enemy into the Plains . . . who can say?"

"I'm so sorry."

"Such slight shoulders to take on the weight of all our sorrows." Keir paused for a moment. "Think on this. What would have happened had you not been here, and we'd no warning, no lessons in illness? If Gils had not listened and learned so well?"

I thought for a moment, then answered honestly. "I don't know."

"That is the hardest truth of all, Lara. That we do not know what might have been or what could have been. We only know what is." His arms tightened slightly. "I say to you this truth—that all our actions, all of them, led us to this place and no one person bears the blame."

"Joden and Iften blame—"

"Iften would name the grass red if I called it green." Keir heaved a sigh. "Joden has come to me in honor and spoken his truths. He is a man that I respect and I must hear him and consider his words carefully. He must make his own decisions and come to his own conclusions."

I rubbed my gritty eyes, and lay my head back down on his chest. "I don't understand, Keir. How can Joden support Iften?"

Keir snorted. "Joden does not support Iften, Lara. Joden opposes me. There is a difference."

"There is?"

Keir's hand caressed my hair again, long, slow strokes. "Iften tries to undermine my authority, working in the darkness to turn my warleaders and my army against me. He treads a fine line, trying to provoke me into something stupid. Joden's opposition is honest and true, in the open for the skies to see."

I drew a breath. "Xymund would have killed Iften."

That brought a chuckle from my Warlord. "Your brother did not listen to the counsels of men of wisdom. He listened only to those who agreed with him. A fatal flaw in a leader. We of the Plains do not silence our opponents, for they keep us strong. It is the stone against the blade that hones the edge. A good leader does not silence those in opposition; they listen and consider. Sometimes they are right, yes?" Keir settled himself a bit more comfortably in our bed. "Joden will tell me his truths and I will listen."

"Keir—"

"I am disappointed that you hid the truth from me, before you entered the village."

My breath hitched in muted sobs, my tears returned, and I raised my head to look at him, opening my mouth to respond. But Keir shook his head, stopping my words. "I am also disappointed in myself—that you thought it necessary. That is my failure."

He drew me in closer, and pressed my head to his shoulder. "Your brother's lies almost destroyed us, but we won through together. We will work our way though this as well. Although I confess that I did not think you one to manipulate people in such a way."

My throat was tight, but I managed a whisper. "I thought I was doing what was best."

"For our people, perhaps. But not for us. For what lies between us." Keir sighed, hugging me tight. "Marcus warned me of this. Told me that bonding was harder than I realized, more effort than 'throwing a woman over your shoulder and claiming her'."

I nodded. "Epor said the same. He told me that you were 'due my first thought'. Keir," I strained my voice, trying to convince him with all of my heart, "I promise I will nev—"

"No." Keir shook his head. "Trust is not so easy to mend. It will take time and deeds on both our parts, eh?"

I hugged him, nodding my head. My sorrow was still there, but there was a spark of hope as well.

"Let us pledge that we will have faith in each other." Keir continued. "That will see us through."

"Oh yes, my Keir." I kissed him softly, and nuzzled his ear. He lifted my hand to his lips and kissed my palm. Wrapped in those blankets, both of us fully clothed, I some how felt more intimate with him than if we'd been naked. "I could stay like this forever." I whispered.

"So could I." He whispered back. "Sometimes, I think of us taking two horses and riding away, as far and as fast as we can."

Surprised, I studied his face. He returned the look steadily. "We could run, Lara. Far and fast and free, with only the skies as a witness. We'd have each other, no worries beyond our own needs, no burdens, no—"

"No Iftens?"

"No Iftens." He growled. "It would be perfect."

"It would be."

He heaved a sigh, and we lay in silence for some time, until I shifted slightly and spoke into his ear. "But that is not who you are, Keir of the Cat, Warlord of the Plains."

I felt his head move, nodding his agreement. "It is not who you are either, Xylara, Daughter of Xy and Master Healer."

I nodded, but stayed silent.

"Now, Marcus will be worried." Keir smiled ruefully. "If I could, I would rise from this pallet, sweep you up and carry you to the command tent. But I fear that if I try, I will fall and take you with me."

I smiled through my tears. "Let us lean on each other, then."

From what I could tell, 'purification' was just another way of saying 'clean everything'. Everything in camp was cleaned to even Anna's exacting standards. Tents were shifted to new ground, and even the horses were washed. If it couldn't be washed or boiled, it was burnished or polished, until the entire camp glowed. Braziers were set up at central points, and something called stargrass was burned to cleanse the air and the spirits. It made me sneeze.

This took a great deal of time and effort. At first the warriors moved slowly, almost all recovering from the illness. But as days passed, their strength and spirits started to rebuild. Keir reached the point where he could walk through his warriors again, and it wasn't long before he was moving about with his old confidence.

Meara too, made an enormous difference in the camp.

She of the melting brown eyes and dark lashes, had each and every warrior wrapped around her little finger. I didn't see much of her, as she was being passed from warrior to warrior, each acting as thea for a part of the day. At first I was concerned, but when I made a point of checking on her regularly, she was always smiling, waving her arms and legs in the air from her basket. She thrived and her presence raised the spirits of everyone around her.

After the purification, almost everyone had regained their normal strength, but the planned contests had everyone pushing harder to get into the best condition possible. The camp rang with the sound of sparring weapons clashing, and the grunts of fighting warriors. Keir participated as well, claiming the need for practice. But as far as I could see, he was in excellent condition. I loved to watch him in the practice circles, as graceful as the cat he was named for. He seemed to enjoy that I watched him every chance I got, and yet all was not the same between us. Although he seemed fully recovered, Keir had made no move to resume our . . . physical relationship. I wasn't too worried, since he was still mending, and yet . . .

The other sound that rang through the camp was the constant sound of warriors announcing their chess moves to one another. Everyone was determined to enter the tourney and win the honor of champion. I had quite a few visitors to my stilltent, with vague complaints of stomach troubles and sly questions about chess strategies. I cheerfully answered their inquiries, dosed them with my worst-smelling, foulest-tasting flux remedy and sent them on their way.

There were very few repeat visitors.

More letters arrived from Water's Fall, with reassurances of the conditions in the city. Othur continued to complain of Simus's behavior, but now he mentioned additional problems with the Lords, including some border disputes that he felt would never be resolved without bloodshed. Which told me that things were fairly normal within the Kingdom of Xy.

Simus demanded, rather loudly in his missives, that we give him all the details of events and that more kavage be sent. He also gave some rather pithy details of his sexual adventures. I could barely contain my laughter at the sight of the scribe's handwriting. I was certain sure that the poor man had nearly fainted during the 'dictation'.

I was pleased to read Eln's letter that Atira's broken leg was mending, and that she had demonstrated the 'drumming' technique for him. He'd used it successfully on his patients, and had been pleased with the results. Of course, he was still searching for an herbal cure to combat what he called the Savage Sweat, but he'd no new patients to try it on. I sensed a degree of regret in his words, but I sent up a brief prayer of thanks to the Goddess for the lack. Both Othur and Eln told me not to return to Water's Fall. There was nothing I could do to make a difference there, and my Council wanted me to secure my position on the Plains.

Keir called an evening senel to discuss the combats and the chess tourney. This one was far more comfortable, with the warleaders more relaxed. Even these experienced warriors had succumbed to the lure of chess, and I could hear a few muttered moves being exchanged as they entered the tent. Ortis had the gleeful look of a man who'd just achieved a checkmate.

Marcus had help with the serving, and was determined to do well by this meeting. There was kavage and fry bread and mutton stew with gurt melted over the tops of the bowls. The stew was good, but I discreetly pushed the melted gurt off to the side.

Once everyone had eaten their fill, more kavage was poured and Keir opened by asking for suggestions for the combats. Elimination rounds were quickly organized and a schedule set up so that everyone could watch some portion. It was embarrassing that guarding me was a coveted position, but I could see that this was important to everyone's spirits so I endured in silence.

Sal was there, looking much better. Her recovery was going well. Tsor had lost quite a bit of flesh, as the fever had burned it off of him. Marcus gave him two servings of stew with extra gurt, which he quickly devoured.

Iften was present, as was required. I noticed that he was eating with his offhand. He was acting as if all was well, but he couldn't fool me. He'd worn a long sleeved tunic, with leather bracers on his forearms. While he managed to avoid my gaze, I could tell that the fingers were swollen. Goddess only knew what the arm looked like. He'd been fairly quiet of late, and spoke only when Keir asked him a direct question. Keir was instructing Yers to supervise the combats, and while there were a few side glances at Iften, no one made any comment.

I stared down at my plate. What would happen to Iften if his arm didn't heal? I glanced over to where Marcus was pouring kavage for Keir. Marcus's injury was not crippling as I defined it, even if the loss of his eye meant he couldn't fight. He'd certainly proved his worth when he'd saved me from my half-brother's blade. But his position was only secured by Keir's support. If Iften's sword arm went numb, and his fingers curled into a useless claw, what would he do? Kill himself?

I took a bite, and chewed thoughtfully.

Keir looked over at me with a smile. "Once the combats are done, and a new guard selected, we will start the chess tourney. This too, will be stretched over a period of days."

Aret stood. "Warlord, I have a suggestion."

"Speak."

"These games will not be easily seen by a large number of people. I propose a living chess board, with warriors taking the roles of the various pieces. So all may see and enjoy, even at a distance."

There were many grins at the plan, and Keir nodded in approval. "I like that well, Aret. In fact, once we are down to eight players on the field of wood, let us begin the living boards. Aret, it's your idea. You may direct it as you will."

Aret grinned.

Keir drew a deep breath. "Our dead ride with us until the snows, but the living carry burdens of pain and sorrow. As the day of our departure grows closer, I would call for a mourning ceremony, for we have much to grieve. Joden, I would ask that you plan the ceremony, and sing for our dead."

Joden sat, hands on his knees, his head bowed. I swallowed hard at the sight.

Keir leaned forward. "This has nothing to do with what lies between us, Joden. Only with singing the dead on their way."

We sat in silence for what seemed like forever before Joden spoke without lifting his head. "There are many dead to sing for."

"There are." Keir's voice was quiet but firm.

There was another long silence as Joden studied his feet. I shifted on my stump. "Will there be a pattern dance?" I'd loved the patterns I'd seen danced before. But even before the words left my lips, I realized it was a foolish question. Pattern dances were so full of joy, they'd have no place at a funeral.

"No, Warprize." Keir spoke softly, confirming my thoughts. "There is a special grieving ceremony."

"It seems the only songs I know are laments." Joden sighed, and nodded. "I will sing. We will mourn."

"My thanks, Singer." Keir dismissed them, and stood with me as they left the tent. Joden left as well, never once looking at Keir. I could see that he was a man torn between duty and friendship and I wished that I could help him somehow. Keir said that he must make his own decisions, but maybe if I talked to him privately.

I bit my lip at that thought. I'd confided in Joden, as a friend, confided all my doubts and fears. The details of the conversation flashed through my head. Would he use that information against me? A knot formed in the pit of my stomach at the idea that he would. My imagination gave way to a delightful tune about the complaints of the city-dwelling Warprize. Unobtrusively, I slipped my hand into Keir's. He grasped it in a tight grip, his fingers warm in mine.

Yers lingered, and once the others were gone, approached us. "Warprize, I would ask for your token."

Startled, I fumbled in my bag for a jar. "You hold my token, Yers. What truths would you voice?"

Yers held the jar in both hands, rubbing his thumb over the surface. He didn't look me in the eye. "Warprize, I want to make sure that you bear me no grudge for giving Gils mercy."

My throat closed, and my eyes stung with tears.

Marcus came to stand beside me. "He would not let me do it, Lara. For fear that you would hate me."

Keir gripped my hand, and I drew enough comfort to speak the ritual words. "I will answer to your truth."

Yers held the jar out to me, a gesture of trust. I took it back from him, and used the fumbling to replace it in my bag to clear my throat and my thoughts. When I felt I could speak, I looked him in the eye. "Yers, you did the right thing. Once he went into convulsions, I," I had to bite my lip and stop for a moment, "I could do nothing but wait for the end." I gave him a weak smile. "At the time, I confess I was angry and upset. I do not give up easily. You were right to act."

Yers nodded. "I am pleased to hear it, Warprize, for I would have no ill will between us. I thank you for your truth." He gave Keir a nod, and left the tent.

"That was well done, Warprize." Marcus started to clear the various mugs that had been used, and any remaining dishes. "I've some of that stew left, and I think I will take it to Tsor's tent. He looks to need fattening up. While I'm about it, I'll check on Meara as well."

Keir sighed. "I should walk the tents."

I turned slightly, and shook my head. "I think not, Warlord. I have a different task for you this night."

Marcus snorted, and left.

Keir raised an eyebrow. "Oh? And what is this task, Warprize?"

"One that requires your complete attention, my Warlord." I stepped closer, close enough to feel the heat of his body. Close enough that he could smell the vanilla I'd put on the back of my neck. I watched, pleased, as his nostrils flared.

He arched one eyebrow, and I could see the humor lurking in his eyes. "Perhaps I can assign this task to one of my warriors?"

"No, my Warlord." I reached out to take his hand, and entwined our fingers together. I smiled, took a step toward our sleeping area, and tugged on his hand.

"Are you certain?" Keir pulled me so that my back was pressed to his chest. His arm wrapped around my waist and held me close. He nuzzled my neck and I titled my head so that he could reach the tender spot on my neck, just under my ear. He chuckled softly. "Perhaps I should order Prest to—"

With an exasperated snort, I turned in his arms and kissed him, winding my arm around his neck, pulling him down so that I could claim his mouth. I pulled back, to see that the hint of humor was still there, a sparkle in the depths of the blue, but it faded to be replaced by an emotion that I recognized in a heartbeat.

Wonder, that we lived.

Guilt, that we had survived.

He raised his hand to brush my hair back, and then curled his fingers around the back of my neck. I shivered at his touch, as he pulled me close and kissed me again. It was long, slow, and sweet. I wrapped my arms around him, and leaned into his warmth.

He broke the kiss, and buried his face in my hair, letting his lips brush my ear. "Or maybe Rafe would—"

I stiffened, even as he chuckled. With a slight turn of my head, I gently licked his earlobe, then bit down.

He jerked, breathing hard. "Ah. Perhaps not."

I laughed.

Keir smiled, and swung me up into his arms.

"Keir," I protested, knowing that he wasn't yet fully re-

covered. But he ignored me, carrying me into our sleeping area to place me on my feet at the end of our bed.
Even that had been an effort. I could feel the barest tremble in the muscles of his arms. I stilled his hands at his
side. "Let me."

He sighed in contentment as I started to unlace his
leathers. Keir had insisted that he be armored for the
senel, but had left it to just his black leathers. I took my
time, nuzzling his face and neck as my fingers slowly exposed his skin. He was such a contrast, the hard muscles
of his arms, the calluses on his hands, the soft skin of his
stomach. There were scars, but they were as much a part
of him as anything else, and I explored it all, with fingers
and lips.

With a groan, he stopped me, and with a few quick
movements he had me naked and on the bed.

"Keir," I hadn't finished, he was still half dressed, but
he silenced me with his mouth and did his own explo-
ration, using his hands to touch every inch of my skin.
There was an urgency there, a desperation that I answered, moving under him, hungry for more.

I cried out when he moved away, but he only stood to
strip away his trous, then he was back in my arms. I'd
thought our loving would be long and slow, but the fire
between us flared bright and wild. He entered me hard
and hot and we never paused, urging each other on and
on, striving until we both cried out, shattering into a thousand bright pieces of pleasure.

Keir rolled to his side, pulling me with him, keeping
our bodies pressed tight together. We lay quiet, until our
breathing eased. My whole body tingled, heated where
his skin touched mine, cooled were the air caressed my
exposed skin.

Keir stroked my back and it was my turn to sigh in contentment as he nuzzled my ear. His hand traveled down my back to rest lightly on my ribs. "You lost flesh."

"You as well," I whispered. I moved my hand over his ribs. "It will return, as we heal." I looked at him through my lashes. "Although some heal faster than others."

Keir gave me a sly smile. "I save my strength for the important things."

I laughed, breathless with delight at his teasing.

"You light from within when you laugh, Lara." He stroked my face as I blushed. "I've missed that."

"There's been little to laugh at lately."

He nodded, and drew me closer. "Truth, Lara."

"We've lost so much." My voice broke as I thought of all that had happened.

"We've won as well," Keir offered. "We've learned more of each other, and our peoples. It's strengthened us."

"At a cost."

Keir moved us so that his body covered mine. "There is always a cost."

"I just," I swallowed hard. "So many died, and we—"

"We lived." Keir brushed the tears from my cheeks, and followed with soft kisses over my face. I clung to him, rejoicing at his touch.

Gently, softly, we explored each other, murmuring words of love and reassurance as we gave each other pleasure. The ache in my heart eased and I forgot my fear and guilt. Beyond our tent walls lay pain, problems, and death. But within these walls, within Keir's arms, lay strength, love and support. The wonder of that was evident in every touch of his lips to mine.

But more wondrous still was that he seemed to draw the same from me, craving my love as much with his heart as with his body. Making me a true partner, Warprize to his Warlord, woman to his man. Who could know that I would find that in the arms of a conquering Warlord?

Our mutual pleasure was drawn out this time, less frantic than the last, but no less sweet. Keir nuzzled my breasts, teasing me with hands and lips as he explored them. I wasn't as ample as the women warriors of the Firelanders, but Keir seemed satisfied. Goddess knew, I moaned at his touch, responding to every caress.

When he drew my nipple into his mouth, I gasped, digging my nails into his back. He chuckled, pleased at my reaction. But I'd learned well, and let my hands drift down his back, to tease the downy hairs at the base of his spine. He growled low in his throat, much to my satisfaction.

It wasn't a shattering this time, more of a slow dissolving into bliss. Keir lay there, eyes half shut, breathing heavily as I cleaned us and then pulled the bedding up over our cooling bodies. He drew me close within the warmth, and we drifted off to sleep together.

We awoke to find ourselves entwined in the darkness, the braziers glowing softly, providing just enough light to see by. It was paradise, laying in his arms, enjoying the smell of his skin and the look in his eyes. For long moments we lay there, simply content.

Keir moved first, lifting his hand to brush the damp hairs off my forehead. "I didn't know what it meant."

I blinked at him, focusing on his blue eyes, warm and sated. Probably reflecting the satisfaction in mine. I let my fingers drift over the soft skin of his chest, enjoying the feel of the sparse hairs there. "Didn't know what?"

"Didn't know what 'forever' meant."

I stiffened, uncertain and afraid. I remembered that moment so clearly, when Keir had claimed me for the second time. The wind in my hair, the ache of my bare feet, the fear that he wouldn't allow me to stay with him and the joy when he'd whispered the word 'Forever' in my ear. Did he regret his words?

He chuckled, moving his hands to stroke me, easing my tension. "No, no, my heart's fire, you misunderstand my words." Keir shifted to Xyian. "When I spoke that word, and made that pledge to you, I didn't really understand what it meant."

He shifted slightly, pulling me closer. "It doesn't just mean for years and years, for the rest of our lives. Or as we would say, to the snows and beyond."

"Oh?" I still wasn't sure what he was trying to say.

" 'Forever' means every day, every breath. Through the mistakes that we make, through the love that we share between our bodies, through illness we suffer, through sorrow, grief, and joy. All of it, Lara."

I melted against him, listening carefully, marveling at his words.

"It's the total of all our shared moments, good and bad, perfect and ugly."

I pushed up onto an elbow in order to look at his face. "Keir . . ."

He placed a finger over my lips. "What I am trying to say is that now that I do know what it means, it makes it mean so much more."

I smiled, and reached out to stroke his cheek.

He huffed out a breath in frustration. "I am a warrior," he grimaced slightly. "A barbarian in your people's eyes. My words do not flow easily, in either language." He placed his palm over my hand. "So I say this truth to you, Lara, Xylara, Daughter of Xy, Queen of Xy, Master Healer, Warprize and woman I love, I am sworn to you. Forever."

I kissed him, even as my eyes filled with tears.

Keir gave me an uncertain look. "Are those tears of joy?"

I nodded, laughing. "Oh, they are, my Keir."

"Well then?" He asked. "Don't you have something to say to me?"

"Do I?" I arched an eyebrow, trying to control my smile.

He growled, and moved, pinning me to the bed, covering my body with his. I laughed out loud, and buried my hands in his hair. "Keir of the Cat, Warrior of the Plains, Warlord of the Plains, Overlord of Xy, I say this truth to you. I am sworn to you." I paused, growing serious. "Forever. Through whatever life, and the Gods and the Elements have in store for us."

He kissed me then, intertwining our fingers together. "My heart's fire." He grinned, his white teeth flashing in the light, and then flipped us again, so that I was on top. His hands rested on my hips, fingers splayed out.

I sat up, letting the bedding fall off my shoulders. His eyes gleamed, and I raised an eyebrow. "What are you—"

He flexed beneath me, and I gasped.

Keir's smile widened. "Perhaps a riding lesson?"

I arched my back, moaning with pleasure as his hands moved my hips.

After a few days, one morning when Keir left early to judge a round of combats, I took advantage of his absence to take care of a chore. When I told Rafe and Prest what I wanted to do, Rafe paled, glancing at Prest for support. "I'm not sure this is wise."

Prest shrugged.

Rafe scowled. "You are of no help."

I stood. "I'm going to talk to him, with or without you."

Rafe heaved a rather exaggerated sigh, and followed us out of the tent.

There'd been a heavy mist hanging in the air the last few days, and this morning found a thick frost riming the grass and trees. The Goddess's Lace, we called it, the first hard frost of the season, heralding the start of winter. Soon, within a few weeks, the snows would begin. As we walked, I wondered what winter would be like on the Plains.

Most everyone was watching the contests, except those on guard duty. Prest and Rafe followed as I walked to Iften's tent, and pushed through the flap with no ceremony.

He was there, seated on a stump, eating gurt with his left hand. The right was held against his chest, close to his body. I stepped far enough in to allow Prest to enter behind me, but stopped there, since Iften's expression made it clear that I was not welcome.

"Iften."

"Xyian."

I stiffened. His tone, and choice of address was as clear an insult as I had heard. Prest put his hand on his weapon. Iften's eyes flicked, but he looked away, and spoke grudgingly. "Warprize."

Prest lowered his hand.

I cleared my throat. "Iften, I want to speak to you about your injury."

"I want nothing from you, Warprize. Not your healing, not your words."

"If you reject my care, I can't inflict it on you. You are free to make a choice, good or bad. But my oaths require that you know the consequences of your choice. So I will speak. Listen or not, as you choose."

"I will not—"

Prest spoke. "The wind will teach, if we but listen."

I looked at him, startled. It wasn't like Prest to speak up that way. The words he'd uttered sounded like a saying of some kind. But Prest's face was bland and composed.

Iften was taken aback as well. He looked at Prest, and then looked away, as if ashamed. "I will listen."

"Your arm is still badly swollen and the flesh is discolored. Your hand and fingers are numb, and it hurts to move them. There is no strength in the arm."

Iften eyed me, but made no response.

"If you don't let me set it, you may heal, but you will not heal true. You may lose all use of your hand, or never regain the strength in it again." I paused. "It is your sword arm."

He responded then, glowering in my direction.

"If you allow me to care for it, the chances are good that the arm will heal true. If you wait to see a warrior-priest, the damage maybe too great for them to fix."

"You'd cast your spells, eh, Warprize." He mocked me.

"I cast no spells, Iften. I have only the skills and knowledge of my craft. The rest is in the hands of the Goddess. Or the elements."

There was a long pause, and for a moment I held the hope that he would agree. But his face darkened, and anger flared in his eyes. I'd lost.

He spat out his fury. "I've listened, and the wind has brought me nothing. Leave."

"Fool," Prest said.

Without a thought, Iften reached for his weapon, but the pain caught him even faster as the arm began to move. He hissed, drawing the limb back against his chest.

I turned and left without another word. As we emerged and headed toward Keir's tent, I questioned Prest. "What was that?"

He smiled, the wind catching his braids. "A teaching tool."

"For children." Rafe shook his head. "For a quiet man, you can sure make someone froth at the mouth."

Prest grinned.

Rafe turned back to me. "It goes like this, Warprize.

> The wind will teach us—if we but listen.
> The stars will guide us—if we but look up.
> The waters will cool us—if we but seek it.
> The fire will warm us—if we are wary.
> Remember this, Child of the Plains.

I nodded, then looked over at Prest. "You insulted him."

Prest shrugged, but there was no grin this time. "How long, Warprize?"

"Before he loses the use?" At his nod, I continued. "It depends on the swelling. But the damage will be permanent if he doesn't get it seen to within the next week or so. And even then, I might have to re-break the bone."

Prest grunted, but he looked oddly satisfied.

The combats proved to be both unsettling and exciting.

Unsettling because these warriors went at it tooth and nail, with bare steel and grim faces. I was used to watching practice sessions, but that didn't prepare me for naked combat. True, they were to first blood, but they took the fighting deadly seriously. Each combat had a judge, usually one of the warleaders, or Keir himself.

Exciting because each combat had warriors watching, warriors who yelled out their support, their criticisms and encouragement. More mob than audience. The first one or two, I had sat there in fear, waiting for one to kill the other. But Isdra pointed out the level of skill that the warriors were using, and Yers explained that it was considered disgraceful to kill someone in these types of fights. So I started to relax. The noise was startling but the fever was catching, and I found myself yelling as well. Keir, laughing at my enthusiasm, had reminded me that it would be best if I showed no favoritism. It was hard to sit there and watch without really participating, so I spent more time in my stilltent. Because the combats accomplished more than just determining a winner: They also had warriors seeking me out for aid. The last one for today was standing before me, holding his right arm in his left hand.

"That looks deep." I reached for his arm, to see it better. The blood was oozing through his leather armor. It looked clean, thank the Goddess, and I looked up to offer reassurance.

Large brown eyes stared at me glumly through fairly long brown hair. "I made it through four rounds, Warprize, but Ander's blow went right through the leather."

If he was twenty, I'd be surprised. A warrior, and his disappointment was obvious. I turned the arm carefully, to look at it closer. "A nasty cut. Sit here, and let me see to it."

The lad shifted from foot to foot before sitting down

rather slowly. I called to Rafe, standing guard outside, then turned back to my patient. "What is your name?"

"Cadr, Warprize."

With Rafe's help, we eased the young man out of his armor. Rafe whistled when he saw the cut through the leather. "Who was your opponent?"

"Ander."

Rafe nodded. "He's a strong one. How many rounds did you make it through?"

The lad looked up. "Four, Warrior."

"Well done, to make it that far." Rafe gave me a nod, and went back out to his post.

The lad straightened at Rafe's parting words. I started to clean the arm, although it wasn't all that dirty.

"Gonna use bloodmoss?"

Startled, I look at him. "Why, yes, I think so."

He nodded. "Gils told me. Told me that the wound had to be clean." He gave the wound a critical look. "Looks clean."

"You knew Gils?"

He nodded, and used his good hand to open a pouch at his side. He pulled out a small package of bloodmoss, wrapped carefully in a clean cloth. "Gils and I were friends, Warprize." His face was stoic, but I could hear the pain in his voice. "I wanted to take his place as your guard."

"Gils wasn't my guard, Cadr. Gils was my apprentice." I choked a bit on the words.

"Guardian of your knowledge." Cadr answered quietly.

I reached for the dried leaves as I blinked back my tears. Cadr watched in silence as I packed the arm carefully, pressing it tight to the wound. The familiar moldy smell filled my nose as the plant did its work. As soon as the color changed, I pulled the leaves away to reveal the pink skin beneath it. "Favor the arm for a day, Cadr."

"I will." He adjusted his seat as he struggled into his tunic with my help. "Warprize, what Gils told me was interesting, and I'd like to learn more. Not sure I want to give up being a warrior . . ."

I looked at him and smiled. "If you want to learn more, that's fine. Come when you have time, and I'll be glad to teach you some useful things."

Cadr nodded, picked up his other bits of armor and turned to leave. But a memory came to me, something Gils had said. "Cadr?"

He turned, with an enquiring look.

"Didn't Gils tell me that you had a boil?"

He hesitated, then nodded. "I tried to deal with it myself, Warprize. Thought you'd be angry. But it's back, and bigger, and hurting."

"Drop your pants, young man." I moved to get my lances, a sense of quiet joy in my heart. Here was something I *could* cure. "I'll explain about boils while we take care of this problem."

Cadr sighed, and dropped his pants.

After dealing with Cadr's problem, I returned to the command tent. Keir was still out, but Marcus had promised to have four buckets of hot water waiting, with my soaps laid out for me, and drying cloths. Keir's people may be comfortable bathing together naked in the river but not me. While a hot bath might be out of the question, using the drain in the privy room to shower myself with warm water was the next best thing.

Rafe and Prest took up position by the tent entrance.

Marcus was waiting inside. "Everything is laid out, Warprize. If you need help with the water, call."

"I will." I turned and glared at my guards. "No interruptions."

"Even the Warlord?" Prest asked with a sly grin.

"The Warlord may enter." Actually, I was hoping the Warlord would enter. I'd not seen him most of the day. "No one else, unless they are ill."

"As the Warprize commands." Prest bowed, as Rafe and Marcus chuckled.

Once in the privy, I checked the water temperature, set my bag on a bench and started to undress. I did miss the hot baths under the castle of Water's Fall. Soaking in their warm depths was a luxury that I had taken for granted. But given the living conditions in this camp, I was grateful for what I had. Remembering the temperature of the water in the lake made me shiver.

I took my time, hoping that Keir might appear. I removed my tunic, combed out my braid, and eased my trous off. As I bent down, it seemed to me that my waist was a bit thicker than I remembered. Of course, Marcus had been feeding me on a regular basis but—

I paused, thinking back. When had I last had my courses?

The last I'd thought of it had been the day when Keir and I had eaten by the lake. I flushed at the memory of our tryst. We'd taken advantage of the sun and the water and the privacy. I'd been due then, and here I was, weeks later, with no sign of them. Admittedly, I'd been sick, which could cause a delay, but still . . .

Could I be pregnant?

I sat and stared at the tent wall for some time, thinking about it, trying to decide how I felt about the possibility. I didn't feel like I was bearing, not that I had any actual experience. But I knew the symptoms as well as any other healer, and I wasn't feeling anything along those lines. No swelling of the lower limbs, no nausea.

I thought of how Keir had played with little Meara, how the other warriors had treated the babe as gently as any Xyian. The news would bring great joy, but troubles too. The Council of Xy had made demands, conditions on my acceptance of the role of Warprize. I hadn't talked to Keir about them yet. It wasn't an issue until I was pregnant and the child was due.

Which was a falsehood on my part. I worried my lip, thinking. How do I tell him what I'd promised? Before I'd seen him with a babe, I'd thought that children meant little to these people. After all, they bore children, they left them to be raised by theas, going off to serve in the army. But then they'd shown that they treasure children much as my people do, maybe even more.

I drew a deep breath in and let it out slowly. I'd tell him when I was with child, not before. Isdra would know, she'd borne before. I could confide in her, but even as I had the thought I knew I wouldn't. It was too 'soon, and I had no desire to add to her pain, or worse, give her a false hope. I'd share the news when I was certain, not before.

Time would tell, of course, and I tried to be practical. But for just a moment, as I put my hand over my belly, a vision of a small boy with dark hair and blue eyes, dragging a wooden practice sword, flashed into my mind. He'd look so much like Keir . . .

In a bemused state, I moved to start my bath.

* * *

Of course, I was bending over, rinsing my hair, when I heard someone enter behind me.

"You came too late, my Warlord." I stood and turned to reach for another bucket of water, a teasing smile on my lips.

It wasn't Keir.

A man stood there, with wild tangled fur for hair and colored tattoos all over his face and chest. He was glaring at me, holding a long spear, with a human skull tied near the tip.

I shrieked, and heaved the bucket at him.

13

The bucket hit his chest and water splashed everywhere, but it didn't faze the wild man. He raised his spear and shook it at me, snarling and growling like an animal, his unruly hair tossing about his head.

My heart was in my throat, but I wasn't finished yet. My bag was a step away, and a large jar of boiled skunk cabbage was the first thing my fingers touched. I threw, catching him right on the head. The jar shattered, and the stinking, gooey mess exploded in the man's face. He roared in pain as it splashed into his eyes.

I darted around him, and ran through the door. My cloak was on the bed, I snatched it up to cover my nakedness, screaming for help. The man was behind me, yelling something that I didn't pause to hear. I plunged through the meeting room and out the entrance.

Rafe, Prest and Marcus were there, but I only had eyes for Keir, who was running toward us, swords in hand. I ran to meet him, as the crazy man stumbled out of the tent behind me, wiping his eyes and roaring.

Keir placed himself between us, and I took shelter behind him, clutching at the cloak. Everyone was shouting and in an uproar. But Keir's roar silenced them all. "What is the meaning of this?"

"He came in while I was bathing!" I stayed behind Keir, and wrapped the cloak tight around me. My wet hair was a mess, streaming water down my back, and the ground was cold beneath my bare feet.

"We tried to tell him, Warlord." Rafe spoke, glaring at the man. "He would not listen."

Marcus spat on the ground.

There was silence as the wild man stood there, dripping water and stinking of skunk cabbage.

"Why do you violate the privacy of the Warprize, Warrior-Priest?" Keir challenged.

That was a warrior-priest? I peeked out from behind Keir, to stare at the man. He looked no less crazed than he had before. The matted hair was thick, and there was fur braided into it. His tattoos were bright and vivid, colored in green, red, blue, and black. His cloak was a fur of some kind, and his trous looked like it needed a good scrubbing. That skull on the spear did nothing to reassure me.

The man drew himself up, and tried his best to look impressive. Ordinarily, I was sure that it worked, but it is hard to be dignified and awe inspiring when noxious stuff is dripping from your hair. I had to give him credit for try-ing, though.

"There were no bells, Warlord. A Warrior-Priest of the Plains enters where he wishes, when he wishes."

Of all the conceited, arrogant . . . I opened my mouth to reply, but Keir beat me to it. His voice vibrated with anger, but his face was impassive. "The Warprize is of Xy. Xyians do not expose their bodies to others easily. You en-tered my command tent without invitation, Warrior-priest. That privacy requires no bells. You ignored the guards placed at the entrance."

The warrior-priest glanced about, but made no re-sponse to Keir's accusation. "We were sent by the Elders from the Heart of the Plains. You failed to appear, as your messages indicated that you would, bearing a warprize."

I sucked in a breath, but Keir anticipated me. "You traveled with others? Where are they?"

The warrior-priest frowned, taken back by the abrupt change of topic. "They follow. I came ahead."

Keir turned his head, looking around. "The perimeter guards did not stop you?"

"They tried." That arrogance was back again. "What means this?"

Keir ignored him. "Prest, you and Rafe, head off the rest of his party. Tell them to keep their distance, and see my orders enforced."

"Enforced?" The warrior-priest gripped his spear tighter as Rafe and Prest ran off.

"We are isolated from others, by the command of the Warprize." Keir looked him in the eye. "You risk death entering this camp. As you were told when you crossed within."

"I see no enemy."

"Pray that you do not." Keir turned. "Lara, let me return you to our tent. You are shivering." He put his arm around me and we started walking toward the tent.

The Warrior-priest gave ground only grudgingly. "I would have a report from you, Warlord."

"I will provide the report, Warrior-priest." We both stopped at Iften's words. He was standing there, Wesren at his side.

"You are Second?" The warrior-priest asked. "Where is Simus of the Hawk?"

"Simus remained behind, upon my order." Keir growled. "I will see a tent set up for you, and will meet you there to discuss this matter."

"Your tent—"

"You are not welcome within my tent, Warrior-Priest."

I shivered at the look in those cold eyes. Keir swept me up into his arms, and Marcus reached over to flick the cloak over my bare feet. I could feel the tension in Keir's body, taught and tight under my hands.

"You are welcome within mine, Warrior-priest." Iften raised his right arm. "I would also ask that you cast your healing spells, for my arm has been injured."

"The only honorable wound I see," the warrior-priest said.

That got a reaction. The warriors around us all stiffened, placing hands on weapon hilts. But where ordinarily they would have all attacked for the insult, there was no movement beyond that. The warrior-priest looked around, and grunted slightly in satisfaction. "I will cast those spells for you."

Spells? Magical healing? I turned my head to look at the man. "Could I watch? Could I watch the spell casting?"

Eyes popped open on every face, including the Warrior-Priest's. He looked so astonished I almost laughed, but then his eyes turned mean. "No."

"But—"

The squeeze of Keir's arms warned me before the response of the warrior-priest. "You are of Xy, and offensive to the elements."

Keir bristled, and the others too were looking damned angry. The warrior-priest tossed that matted hair of his. "Come, Iften of the Pig. I will hear your truths, and heal your wound."

They walked off, Wesren but a step behind. I opened my mouth to make a comment, but Keir swept me into the sleeping area, and set me on the bed. He knelt, taking my feet in his hands and rubbing some warmth into them.

I leaned back, propping myself up with my elbows. "So, Iften is of the Pig. That explains a lot."

Keir's head jerked up, and he laughed out loud. I loved his face in that instant, happy and relaxed. But then he shook his head. "You have the word wrong. These are not the pigs of your land, Lara. These are wild boars, fierce, fleet of foot, and dangerous. Have a care when you face one."

Isdra had appeared, and stood sentry at the door, with Marcus at her side. Marcus growled. "I'm more than willing to hunt one particular boar."

Isdra nodded.

Keir kissed me. "Get dry and warm. I will deal with this."

"Keir, I'm sorry. He scared me and I didn't think, I just threw—"

Keir flashed that boyish grin. "Ugly, isn't he. They all are. And do they offer their name? Or ask permission for anything? Ah, I couldn't ask for better, my heart's fire. He reeks of that foul smelling goo."

I rolled my eyes. "And he will for some time. That odor doesn't really wash away without strong soap."

"Which will be in short supply." Keir kissed me again, then whispered in my ear. "I'm sorry I was late for your bathing. Next time, send word."

I blushed, but sat up to grab his arm as he turned to leave. "Keir, for all your pleasure he has been exposed to the plague. He needs to know the symptoms and the ways to treat—"

Keir turned back, knelt down at my feet, and took my hands. "Lara, you must understand something. He does not care, as you do. He is not a 'healer'. Warrior-priests use their magic only as it profits them."

"But if he has magic, Keir, I want to learn." I tightened my grip on his arm. "Imagine what I could do with that power? I could have healed Atira's leg, maybe even saved my father—"

"They do not share knowledge, Lara. I have doubts about their powers." Keir looked at me intently. "You must promise me that you will not attempt to talk to him, not even with all your guards with you. He despises any who are not of the Plains. But he will hate you more for the gifts you bring us. Do you understand?"

Marcus moved slightly, and I looked over at him, remembering the cold blade at my throat. I looked at Keir and nodded. "I understand. Death can come in an instant."

Keir smiled, and then lifted my hands to kiss them. "We will watch him carefully for signs of illness." He stood, looking down at me. "I will make sure that the rest of his party returns to the Plains, Lara, with messages for the Elders." He hesitated slightly. "Isdra."

"Warlord?"

"Make sure that any who tend to Meara are such as can face a warrior-priest."

I shivered at the very idea that any would harm the child. Marcus sucked in a breath and Isdra looked shocked. "Warlord, not even they would dare—"

Keir was grim, the hate in his eyes flaring. "I'll not give them a chance." He left, with a swirl of his cape. Isdra followed him out.

Marcus had drying cloths, and dropped one on my head. "See to your hair, Warprize." He knelt at my feet, and started to rub them roughly with another cloth. "I've hot kavage fresh brewed, that will warm you."

I sighed as I toweled my hair. "I certainly made a mess of things."

"A mess of that arrogant fool, yes." Marcus paused, looking up at me intently with his one eye. "But you did well, Warprize. You distracted him with what you had at hand, and used that advantage to flee."

I smiled, warmed by his praise. "Still, I angered the warrior-priest. That won't help Keir."

"There'd be no help regardless. Hisself makes no secret of his hatred."

"Because of what happened to you?" I asked quietly.

"There are other reasons." Marcus stood. "I will fetch the kavage. Be warm and dry and tucked within the bedding when I return, eh?"

He left without another word.

The next morning the final winners of the combat rounds stood before us, both smiling. I couldn't help but smile back, enjoying their obvious pride. The man, Ander by name, was older than most warriors, although clearly not as old as Epor. He was bald, with thick bushy white eyebrows and hazel eyes. The woman, Yveni, was tall and thin, her skin as black as Simus's. I'd seen her around before. Her hair was black and cropped close to her skull, and her brown eyes had flecks of gold.

"Heyla!" Keir called out, and the crowd around us returned his call with a loud shout of approval.

"Behold, the last two that contest for the position of the Warprize's guard. They both meet with my approval, and so the winner of this combat shall have the position."

Another cry of approval went up. Keir had met with each of the candidates the night before, talking to them about their duties and responsibilities. The man he knew from other campaigns. The woman had battle experience, but this was her first time under Keir's command. Yers had given them both praise and Isdra told Keir she could work with either one. Marcus hadn't had anything negative to say, other than his usual complaints.

"But this position requires one who is sharp of skill and wits. Who can both attack and protect. So, I have decided to change the rules." That brought quiet, as everyone leaned forward, intent on Keir's words. He smiled, his dark hair shining in the sun. "Marcus. Rafe."

Marcus and Rafe moved to stand together, back to back, with something in their hands. They each paced out five steps, and then knelt to press something into the ground.

"Hear now the rules for this combat. Behind each warrior is a horsehair braid, tied between two stakes, a handslength above the ground. The goal is to cut your opponent's braid. Do you understand?"

Ander and Yveni both considered the ground as Rafe

and Marcus moved away. They studied the stakes and the braids, and then took positions in front of them, facing each other.

Sal was to judge the combat, and she stepped forward at Keir's nod. "Are you ready, warriors?"

They'd barely nodded when Sal cried "Begin!" They sprang forward, their blades clashed, the crowd roared, and the fight was on.

They were both using swords and shields and moved so fast I was sure to miss something if I blinked. The location of the stakes restricted their movements. While there was no formal circle, the warriors never wandered far from their braids. Keir and I were seated on a bit of higher ground, giving us a better view. Rafe and Prest were behind me, Isdra at my side, watching with a careful eye.

Iften and the Warrior-Priest were off to one side, also using the rise to their advantage, but making sure not to come close to Keir and I. The warrior-priest had a sullen look, but Iften seemed to be awfully pleased with himself, almost happy. I narrowed my eyes, trying to get a better look at his arm, which was hanging loosely at his side. I'd been told that the healing had taken place, with the sounds of chanting coming from Iftens's tent, with clouds of purple-blue smoke billowing from the tent. But I couldn't get a very good look, with all the people in the way.

The Warrior-Priest was unhappy because Keir had warned off the rest of his party. He'd told them to return to the Plains, bearing the message concerning what had happened here. By the time he'd crawled into our bed, he'd been hoarse from the shouting. But the messages had been understood, and they departed in haste from the area. Apparently warrior-priests travel with some kind of servants, who care for their needs. Being without didn't strike the wild man's fancy.

In the morning light, my first impression still stood. The man wore only leather trous, and a ratty fur cloak. The colors in the tattoos were very bright, and I wondered how that was done. I didn't recognize any of the designs. And his hair! I thought it looked remarkably like a rat's nest, but I kept my opinion to myself. From the way people were standing upwind, he still hadn't gotten rid of the skunk smell.

I forced my attention back to the fighting. Ander and Yveni moved, considering one another, each looking for an advantage. They'd exchange ringing blows, and then break off. To my eye it seemed they were evenly matched, with no one having a true advantage over the other. Ander seemed to have a bit more power behind his blows, but Yveni had greater speed.

The fight continued, but my gaze was drawn back to Iften. Was it possible that he'd been healed? I looked back just in time to see the warrior-priest hand him something that looked like gurt, only brown in color. Iften placed it in his mouth, and started chewing.

I stiffened. His right hand, his sword arm. He'd used it with no obvious pain, grasping the food with fingers that I'd seen swollen and numb. The same arm that Isdra had broken.

How was that possible?

THWACK.

I flinched, and turned at the sound. Ander's sword had bit deep into the wood of Yveni's shield. He tugged hard, but the blade did not come loose.

Yveni moved back, trying to pull the sword from Ander's hand. He followed, trying to rock the blade from its prison. Ander concentrated on his sword, never once watching his feet. She yanked the shield back again, dancing a few paces sideways. Ander followed, intent on his weapon.

It was the laughter from the crowd that finally drew his attention, making him look up and take stock of his situation. Yveni had danced him around, moving both of them, until she stood a mere step from Ander's braid. Her sword arm was extended, the tip of her blade just under the taut braid.

Yveni grinned at him, her teeth flashing.

Ander shook his head, then laughed, raising both hands in the air.

A roar of approval went up as Yveni cut the braid.

In Xy, chess matches are quiet things. Two players, sitting at a table in silence, making moves on a board,

It was an entirely different matter for the Firelanders.

If I'd thought the crowd noisy for the combats, I wasn't prepared for the enthusiasm for this new game. Aret's idea for a living chessboard had been a good one, and the warriors chosen as pieces had decked themselves out in their very best armor, with a shine and a polish to the weapons that told me they'd been worked on for hours. They'd used armbands to designate their color, and the 'pawns' had tried to make themselves look as uniform as possible.

But under all the noise and bustle and laughter was an underlying tension. The division that I'd seen in the warleaders was starting to be seen in the army. Oh, no obvious insult was given to Keir or myself. On the surface all seemed well. But the games of chess were seen as being

Xyian, and many had decided not to participate or watch for just that reason.

Not that the game seemed Xyian any more. To my horror, the time-honored pieces known as 'castles' had been replaced. Instead, the pieces were called ehats. I hadn't heard of this change until the pieces took the board. Four warriors, two for each side, had stepped forward with fur cloaks wrapped around them, and huge horns carved from tree branches. The other warriors had to duck as they moved on the board, holding their heads low, and sweeping the area around them with their horns. Laughter filled the air as the ehats snorted and pounded the earth with their feet.

The players strode at the ends of the boards, some pacing back and forth as they shouted their moves. The crowd then would chant the words, until that 'piece' moved into its proper place.

Warleaders, warriors, and even Keir had entered the chess tourney. The games had taken days, and had absorbed everyone's attention. Keir managed to win all his games and was in the final match.

His opponent was a woman that I didn't recognize, whose name was Oone. She was a muscular, thoughtful woman, almost as big as Simus, with short red hair and brown eyes.

I was watching the game board from the rise, wrapped in a cloak against the chill wind. Prest and Yveni had the watch, and were standing behind me, acting as a wind break. The game area had been laid out with stones, and they'd managed to make the squares big enough that the knights could be mounted on horses. Which meant that the 'pieces' had to deal with some obstacles not normally found on a chess board. Still and all, it was an amazing spectacle.

Iften and the Warrior-Priest were avoiding the games, and were very vocal in their opposition. They wanted nothing to do with me, or anything remotely Xyian, which frustrated my efforts to get a good look at Iften's arm.

But I had help.

Marcus came to offer me hot kavage. "Any luck?" I asked.

"Not so far. Isdra is trying to get closer, as is Rafe. But they swear to me that it's almost as if he knows what they are trying to do."

Prest grunted. Yveni looked at him, then turned back to me. "Tell me again, why we are trying to see the Second's arm?"

"Herself is curious." Prest said.

I looked at him sharply, but his face was neutral. Some time after Yveni had won the combat, I'd found her with Keir, Rafe, Prest, Isdra and Marcus clustered together, their conversation serious and intent. They'd broke off their words as I approached, but I was certain that the quirks and foibles of one warprize had been discussed in great detail.

"Ah." Yveni nodded her understanding. "Do you wish me to try, Warprize?"

"Not yet." I sat, watching Keir make his first move in the game. Oone was intent, but quick and the game seemed to move as fast as they could call out instructions to the 'pieces and pawns'.

After a bit, Rafe and Isdra reported back, glum with their failure. I nodded, unworried. It stood to reason that Iften would know them, and anticipate their interest.

As Keir's knight advanced to take one of Oone's bishops, Cadr moved up beside me, and knelt, adjusting his boot. "I got a good look, Warprize."

"And?"

"Not sure. He has his bracers strapped tight over his leather sleeve. He is using the hand, and flexing the fingers. I thought they looked a little swollen, but I saw no sign of pain."

"Pity." Isdra said.

I kept my attention on the game, and my voice soft. "My thanks, Cadr."

He stood, and moved off into the crowd without looking back.

I settled back on my stump, and pondered what that might mean. Magical healing? I'd read about it in stories, but could the warrior-priests wield that power?

A wave of pure jealousy washed through me. To be able to heal everything with the touch of my hand. I'd give anything to be able to ease pain, mend wounds that way.

I was so lost in thought that I didn't really see the game, until the crowd cheered, and I looked up to see that Keir and Oone had reached a draw. Oone studied her remaining pieces carefully. "I could offer you a warprize."

Keir threw his head up, and glanced over in my direction. His eyes were bright, his smile so bright it took my breath. "Oh no, Oone. I have claimed my warprize, and will have no other."

I blushed bright red, warmed to the tips of my toes.

Keir looked back at his opponent, over the heads of the joyful crowd. "Oone, I think instead that your warrior-priests would leave you in this instance. What say you?"

There was much commenting on this. I frowned, a bit

puzzled. Oone still had bishops on the board at her command. Yet she was looking at them with distrust. And the warriors portraying them were standing with their arms crossed, glaring at all and sundry from beneath lowered brows.

Keir's bishops had been taken from the board, long before this. Yet he didn't have the ability to force a checkmate. It was clearly a draw. Why were they—

Oone nodded her agreement. "I concede the loss, Warlord. My warrior-priests are not to be trusted."

Stunned, I watched as the crowd erupted into cheers and Keir raised his arms in victory. I didn't understand what had just happened, but I knew somehow that it was important. What kind of power did the warrior-priests hold that they would refuse to support a leader?

Movement distracted me, as Keir was lifted on the shoulders of some of the warriors and carried high above the heads of the cheering crowd.

I cheered as well, but groaned mentally. There'd be no living with him now.

Keir had announced a mourning ceremony for the evening before we were to leave. There had been no new cases of the Sweat since Gils had died. A full forty days had passed, and we were free of our invisible enemy.

Free of the disease, but not free of its effects. These people had been changed profoundly by what had happened here, each marked in different ways by the experience. They had confronted something unknown to them, and learned new skills as a result. I knew that I too had been affected. Never again would I walk into a situation so sure that I had a solution. A loss of confidence, perhaps, or maybe more of facing the truth of my limitations that I hadn't wanted to acknowledge before.

As the sun started to sink behind the mountains, everyone began to gather for the ceremony along the shore of the lake. This time, a minimal guard had been set, for all would mourn together. I watched the sun as I stood outside the command tent, wrapped in my cloak. The gathering warriors were bringing blankets to sit on, filling in the area, sitting close together, side by side.

Keir emerged from the tent with blankets and a bundle in his arms. He'd released my guards to join the grieving, and Marcus had indicated that he would remain in the command tent with Meara. Without a word, Keir took my hand, leading me toward the rise that overlooked the edge of the lake.

I saw Iften and the Warrior-Priest standing outside Iften's tent. It almost looked as if they were hiding something, the way they looked about them as they talked. Iften threw open the tent flap and vanished inside. The Warrior-Priest walked off, disappearing behind the tent in the directions of the herds. I was surprised that they didn't join in the ceremony, but it certainly didn't bother me.

Keir stopped. I looked around to find that we weren't far from our tent, and were really at the fringes of the crowd. "Aren't we going to sit closer?" I asked.

Keir shook his head. "I think for this ceremony, we'd be better off here." He shook out one of the blankets and spread it on the ground. "Besides, we are not the focus of this gathering. The dead are."

I sat next to him, and he pulled me close, drawing another blanket over us. He leaned in, and spoke for my ear alone. "When you grow uncomfortable, we will leave."

An odd statement. I would have questioned him, but a drummer had stepped out into the clear area at the lake's edge. He sat, a large drum before him, and pounded sharply four times.

Everyone stopped talking.

Joden stepped forward, followed by four warriors, carrying small braziers. He faced the crowd, the warriors placing their burdens at the compass points around him, with Joden at the center.

Joden raised his right palm to the sky. "May the skies hear my voice. May the people remember."

The response rose. "We will remember."

Joden lowered his arm and spoke again. "Birth of fire, death of air."

One of the warriors knelt, and blew on the coals within, feeding fuel that caused flames to leap up and dance.

"Birth of water, death of earth."

The second warrior knelt, dipping her hands and letting the water trickle back into the brazier.

"Birth of earth, death of fire."

The third warrior knelt, raised a lump of dirt, breaking it up to let the clods fall back into the brazier.

"Birth of air, death of water."

The fourth warrior knelt. He too blew on coals, but the fuel he added caused a thin trail of smoke to rise up.

The four warriors stood, bowed to their elements, and melted back into the crowd.

"We gather tonight in remembrance of the dead." Joden spoke again, his voice melodic and beautiful. In the silence, every word carried, clear and firm. "All life perishes. This we know. Our bodies arise from the elements, and return to them when we fall."

The drummer started a beat then, a slow but steady pulse.

"But we are also more than our bodies. This we know. That which is within each of us, lives on. Our dead travel with us, until the snows."

Joden paused, then continued. "How can we mourn then? How can we sorrow for what must be? If our dead are with us, and we will join with them when our bodies fail, how then do we weep?"

The drummer's beat continued behind Joden's words.

"We grieve for what we lost. For the hollow place within our hearts. For the loss that is felt each time we turn to confide a secret, to share a joke, or to reach for a familiar touch."

My eyes filled. I remembered Epor, his flashing grin. Gils's serious face. Father's joy when he won at chess, his mind sharp even as his body failed.

"This is our pain, the pain of those left behind. Let us share it." Joden began to sing then, lifting his face and voice to the sky. It was the same song that he'd sung in the throne room of Water's Fall, and my tears flowed when I recognized the words.

I was not alone. Others, too, wept, clinging to those around them, offering and receiving comfort. I sheltered a bit deeper within Keir's arms and felt his rough breathing as his eyes sparkled in the fading light.

At the end of the song, Joden started a chant, similar to the one that I'd heard when I'd been ill. The phrases repeated over and over, to the rhythm of the drummer's beat.

"Death of earth, birth of water, death of water, birth of air, death of air, birth of fire, death of fire, birth of earth."

A movement caught my eye, and I turned my head to see Isdra rise and walk past us, away from the area. Her face was stoic, but her sorrow hung about her like a cloak. She staggered slightly, but walked swiftly away.

I moved to follow, but Keir held me back. "Don't."

"But she's so sad," I started, but Keir shook his head.

"Nothing you can say will ease her pain, Lara."

I eased back into his arms with a flash of guilt. I had my heart's fire. Living, breathing, sitting beside me, his arms around my waist. Isdra had lost that. Keir was right. I'd probably just remind her of her loss.

Keir drew me closer, and pointed toward the lake.

Two cloaked warriors stood, and were making their way down to stand at Joden's side. He bowed to them, and they dropped their cloaks. Each was dressed in plain black tunic and trous, no armor or weapons. Joden stepped back to stand at the drummer's side. As the last of the chant faded, the standing warriors threw back their heads, and wailed, lifting their arms and crying out. They started to dance, using their bodies to express their grief, tearing at their clothing until they were nearly naked, crying out for their loss and pain.

The drumbeat grew faster, and their wails turned angry, now howling their rage to the skies. The crowd joined in, shouting and cursing the elements and the skies. Even Keir spit out a curse. The emotion startled me, but I felt my anger too, at a disease that I knew little about and had no way to defeat.

The man kicked over the brazier of fire, and stomped out the flames. The woman overturned the brazier of water, and then did the same to the one with the earth, stomping the clods flat to the ground.

The brazier of air received the same treatment. Their

hands moved to dissipate the smoke that rose from the coals. Their angry howls filled the air, and with a final beat of the drum, they dropped to their knees, and embraced one another.

I was crying openly now, sobbing in my anger and pain. Keir produced the bundle of clean cloths he'd brought from the tent. I fumbled with one to clean my face, when the silence was broken by another drum beat, and Joden, calling out to the people.

"Death and pain are a part of life. But not all of it, People of the Plains! Joy is also there, to be enjoyed and shared! Rejoice!"

I looked up to see the dancers moving, embracing one another, kissing, rubbing their . . .

I blinked.

The drumbeat was getting faster, and the dancers moved with it, their hands stroking one another, removing their torn clothing. The man was kissing the woman's neck and . . .

Goddess.

I looked away, only to discover from the movement around me that the dancers weren't the only ones seeking 'comfort'. People were embracing their neighbors, hands reaching out, clothing being removed, caresses being exchanged. There were two men near us, and to my amazement, one reached for the other, stroking and kissing and . . .

I hid my face against Keir's chest.

He drew the blanket up over my head, chuckling softly. "My shy one."

"Keir," I whispered in his ear. "Men with men?"

He shrugged. "Each to their own preference. It's not

one I share." He helped me to my feet, then swept me up
and started toward our tent.

I pressed my face to his neck, hiding my eyes, embarrassed by what was happening, but also embarrassed at
the heat growing within me, a hunger for him, for life. I
wrapped my arms around his neck. "I'm sorry, Keir. I
know this is your way, but—"

"It is not yours." I felt the movement of his head as he
nodded his understanding. "They but celebrate life,
Lara." His breath tickled my ear.

"I don't mind celebrating life." A laugh escaped me as
he picked up his pace. "Just in the privacy of my own
tent."

"As you wish, my Warprize." His voice was low and
hungry and I felt my own desire flare within me.

We'd reached the entrance, and I was so distracted by
the look on his face that I didn't see Marcus standing
there until he spoke. "Warlord."

Keir turned, and my stomach dropped as I saw the look
on Marcus's face. "Oh no," I whispered. "Not the Sweat.
Please, Marcus, don't tell me it's returned."

"No, Lara." His face held a strange look of regret. "It's
not the disease."

They'd found Isdra sprawled on the ground, a dagger in
her stomach up to the hilt. There was a lot of blood, and
she had a puzzled expression on her face. I didn't have to
touch her to know that she was dead, but I did it anyway.
There was warmth in her flesh, but no life.

"No, no, she promised to stay with me." I cried as Keir
pulled me back to his side. Marcus had come with us, and

he'd managed to find Rafe and Prest as well. I looked at Marcus. "She promised, Marcus."

"Epor's call was stronger, Warprize."

"As it should be." The Warrior-Priest walked up. "Her place was at her bonded's side."

"I would have done the same." Keir said.

I looked at him in horror, but he met my eyes calmly. I looked away, angry at his acceptance. "Before, she was ready for it—even offered Epor's weapon to Prest. Why would she do it this way?" I scowled, wiping my tears with my hands, then turned to look at Prest. "Do you believe this?"

Prest let his eyes flicker over the crowd that had gathered, but said nothing. With a long step, he took the warclub off of Isdra's body, and walked away.

The sun was rising as we prepared to depart.

As was her preference, Isdra was given to the sky. A platform was erected, with her naked body exposed to the elements. At my insistence, they'd placed it in the center of the burned village, by the stone well. As close to where Epor had burned as I could arrange it. I'd dug through my supplies to find those few dried lavender flowers to place around her body. Joden chanted a soft, sad song in the crisp, cold air.

I stood there in the blackened ruins. I'd known, of course, that the village was being used for the pyres of the dead. But that hadn't prepared me for the sight of black cinders and ashes, spread out over such a large area. The smell of smoke seemed overwhelming. I stood next to Keir, and leaned against him. He wrapped his arm around my waist, and held me close.

Rafe and Prest were there, with Marcus. Some others were in attendance as well. Yveni was behind us, with the horses. Ander was there as well. Keir had summoned him, and asked him to take Isdra's place, and Ander had agreed.

The last notes of Joden's song hovered in the air. In the silence, we all turned and walked to our horses. The crows were already gathering as we left.

I did not look back.

With Isdra gone, I'd made the decision to send little Meara back to Xy, to Anna's care. The babe had recovered well, although she'd been quieter than normal. But she had a ready smile for all of her theas. I couldn't ask for better caretakers than the fierce warriors that had surrounded her. But despite their protests, she was a child of Xy, and I wasn't sure of her welcome in the Heart of the Plains. The comments by Iften and the warrior-priest's attitude made me nervous. Keir agreed with my decision. He'd gathered a swift group of riders to escort her back, and they had left with the dawn. I had no fears for her safety.

The command tent was being dismantled when we returned. Marcus started to complain about the way they were loading the horses before he even stopped his horse. Everyone dismounted to pitch in, and the remaining gear was loaded very quickly.

This time I was to ride by myself, and I was delighted to find that it was the same brown, with the scar on his chest. He seemed happy to see me, sticking his nose in my hair and snuffing me. Greatheart checked me over throughly, and then promptly fell asleep. He never stirred as I gathered up Gil's satchel and tied it firmly to my saddle. Tears filled my eyes, but I resolutely turned and watched as the others prepared to mount. Keir had indicated that I would be in the center of the army again, so it would be some time before we took our position.

Iften was waiting at the head of the army, ready for the command to move. I'd never seen the blond look so confident or proud. The warrior-priest was there beside him, a stony look on his face. Neither had attended the funeral. I focused hard on Iften's right hand, but he seemed to be using it normally. He was chewing something, and I assumed it was gurt.

Without any further ceremony, Keir gave the signal, and the forward scouts sprang to a gallop, taking their lead positions. Once they were out of sight, Keir gave another signal, and Uzaina started the front riders at a walk on the road. Slowly but surely, the long line of riders headed out.

I stood for a while, watching them gradually leave. Rafe and Prest had mounted already, and Yveni and Ander were close at hand. Greatheart was still fast asleep, his head hanging, ears flopping over, eyes closed. He'd put all his weight on his left leg, his right hind foot cocked behind him. I reached over to give his ears a good scratch when his head jerked up, his eyes wide. He snorted, his stance changing in a moment, on guard for an attack.

Even as I turned to look, I could hear the drumming of hooves. I fully expected to see one of the scouts, except the sound was louder, stronger . . .

There were four of them, galloping hard, sending men and horses scattering out of their way. Four warrior-priests, two men and two women, with long spears held at the ready. All were riding dressed in nothing more than trous and a long cloak. Even the women had the matted

long hair, and tattoos that covered their breasts, but one
had also added colored streamers and some kind of white
paint on her dark face. I had a moment to wince at the tattoos that covered the women's breasts. But then I realized
that their target was Keir.

I took a step to run to his side and ran smack into
Prest's horse as he moved to block me. Yveni and Ander
mounted in a heartbeat, covering my back. They formed a
circle around me, with Marcus next to me, a firm grasp on
my arm. Greatheart stood at my side as well, head held
high as if to see.

They galloped in a direct line right toward Keir. Terrified, I looked on as the warriors about him merely
watched, none taking any action to protect him. "Will no
one help him?" I whispered.

"Watch." Marcus's response was soft.

Keir stood firm, his hands at his side, facing the riders.
From the rigid lines of his back, I knew that his face was
grim. I feared to see them plunge a spear into his chest,
but at the last moment they circled him, each taking a
point equal distance from the other.

One, a warrior-priestess, pulled her horse to a stop at
the last moment, right in front of Keir. Keir didn't flinch or
step back. The rider's horse reared, flailing its hooves, as
the priestess plunged a spear into the ground at Keir's feet.

"Keir of the Cat." Her voice was shrill and piercing.
"The Elders of the Plains summon you to appear before
them, to answer for the dishonorable deaths of the warriors entrusted to you."

Keir's shoulders shifted slightly, but he made no response.

The warrior-priest to his right threw his spear, close to

Keir's feet. "Keir of the Cat. The Elders of the Plains summon you, to answer for the dishonorable deaths of a bonded couple entrusted to you."

The warrior-priestess behind him threw her spear with a scream. "Keir of the Cat. The Elders summon you, to answer for your failure to provide for the People."

Finally, the warrior-priest to his left threw his spear as well. "Keir of the Cat, The Elders summon you to challenge your claim of a warprize."

The warrior-priestess before him snarled. "The Elders will demand your life, Warlord."

With that, she spun her horse on its heels and they galloped away.

I took a deep breath even as Marcus released my arm. But what broke the silence was the sound of Iften laughing out loud, ringing like a bell. As I looked over, the blond urged his horse to a walk, moving with the warriors of the army. I had to grit my teeth at the look on his face, and that of the warrior-priest at his side. They both rode off toward the head of the army, Iften's chuckles still floating back on the breeze. And the expressions on the warriors as they rode past indicated that there were many that agreed with Iften in this matter as well. Some joined in his laughter, while many seemed to frown and shake their heads.

It was a long moment before everyone around us turned back to their tasks. But I noticed that a few were looking at Keir from the corners of their eyes and others were not looking at him at all.

The tension left my guardians, and Rafe and Prest moved their horses off. Greatheart relaxed and lowered his head, as if to go back to his nap. I looked at Marcus, who spat on the ground, and returned to his task, his expression grim.

Keir grabbed the spear before him, and with a quick jerk, broke it over his knee.

I took Greatheart's reins and tugged, leading him over to where Keir stood. Greatheart shook his head in protest, stretching his neck out as far as he could before he actually picked up his feet to follow me.

Keir was holding the spear halves, and watching the warrior-priests ride away into the distance. As I came alongside, he growled, and threw the pieces down on the ground.

We stood in silence for a bit, then he turned and looked at me intently. "This will not be easy, Lara. My enemies have been at work, taking advantage of this delay." He gave me a rueful smile. "We stand on the brink of checkmate." He looked off toward where the warrior-priests had disappeared. "You could still return to the safety of Water's Fall."

I moved closer to him. Keir turned to look, and I lifted my face and kissed him, leaning into his strength and warmth. I put everything I had into that kiss, using my mouth to reassure him as to my promise. It took a long moment before I felt him relax and bring his arms up to wrap around me.

His eyes were warm and loving when I pulled away. I smiled, and turned to mount my horse. As I settled in the saddle, Keir took a step closer, and placed his hand on my knee, looking up into my eyes. "One thing I know. I have no regret in claiming you as Warprize."

He looked so handsome in the sunlight, his hair gleaming black and teased by the wind. I looked down, arching an eyebrow. "And I have no regret making you claim me."

Keir laughed, throwing back his head, and roaring his delight.

I leaned down to caress his cheek. "No regrets. Whatever comes."

Keir nodded. My guards came up with Marcus leading Keir's black. He mounted, and without another word or look, led the way to the Plains.

Turn the page for a preview of the final
tale of Lara and Keir, coming in 2007
from Elizabeth Vaughan and Tor Romance . . .

Warlord

I was terrified.

I shifted my sweaty grip on the handle of my sword, and watched my attacker's eyes. "Watch their eyes," they'd told me. "The eyes will tell you their next move."

I stared intently at him, but his eyes told me nothing. My left arm was trembling from the weight of my shield. "Look over the rim," they'd told me. "Look over the rim, watch his eyes and react to hi—"

He came at me in an instant, rushing right for me. I managed to take his first blow on my shield and tried to stab at him with my blade, but my helmet shifted into my eyes and—

THWACK.

My arm went numb, and I cried out at the pain. My sword tumbled to the ground.

Rafe stood in front of me, horrified, staring at my arm.

"That's going to bruise," Prest commented dryly.

Rafe groaned, looking up at the skies as if for help. "The Warlord will gut me where I stand." He glared at me. "Warprize, you were supposed to block the blow!"

"I tried!" I dropped my wooden shield, and rubbed my arm. "I watched your eyes and I kept the shield up, but—"

"Too slow. She doesn't have the speed," Ander offered.

"The shield is too heavy," Yveni added. "She doesn't have the strength she needs."

"Herself doesn't have the sense the elements gave a goose."

We all turned to see Marcus riding up to our group, glaring from under his cloak. "What's all this now?"

My guards all started talking at once. I sighed, took off my helmet and shook out my braid, letting the breeze reach my damp head. Trying to be a warrior-princess is uncomfortable and sweaty.

Marcus and my four guards were arguing at the top of their lungs, Marcus covered in his cloak lest the skies be offended by his scars. He'd been injured in a battle years ago, his left ear and eye burned away. Prest, with skin of light brown and long black braids, towered over Marcus. He stood silent, as usual, his arms crossed over his chest.

Rafe, his skin even paler than normal was gesturing, trying to explain. His hair was dark against his fair skin, and his brown eyes were filled with frustration.

Anders was gesturing as well, talking at the same time. The sun gleamed on his bald head, and his thick bushy white eyebrows danced over his hazel eyes. Yveni stood as silently as Prest, tall and thin, her skin as black as any

I'd seen among the Firelanders. But she'd a smile hovering on her lips. She and Ander had replaced Epor and Isdra, who had died at Wellspring.

I heaved a sigh, and looked off in the distance.

We'd left the small village of Wellspring ten days ago, leaving behind our dead, both Xyian and Firelander. We'd resumed our trek to the land of the Firelanders, the Plains of Keir's people. Another few days ride and I would get my first glimpse of that fabled place which lay beyond the border of the Kingdom of Xy. Another few days ride, and the great valley of Xy would open up onto the wilds of the Plains.

Another few days ride, and I'd be where I never dreamed of going.

I glanced over to where the army of the Firelanders moved past us, in their long slow march to their homeland. Keir had left half of his force to secure Water's Fall and Xy itself, under the watchful eye of Simus of the Hawk. He'd brought the other half with him, to return to the Plains. It was still an impressive sight as they would past us, all on horseback, an army of fierce warriors, both men and women.

Or at least, what was left of Keir's army, after the ravages of the plague we'd suffered outside of Wellspring. We'd left our dead, to be certain, but there were still problems, still conflicts at the heart of the army. Conflicts as a result of an illness sweeping through the ranks of a people who see illness as a curse. Conflicts as a result of the presence of a Warprize in their midst and the changes that I represented to them. Conflicts that had been set aside for the rest of this journey, to be dealt with before the Council of Elders when we reached the Heart of the Plains.

We could have reached it sooner, but Keir had held the

army to a snail's pace, claiming the need to regain strength in the warriors, to hunt and replenish food supplies.

In truth, we were dawdling.

I didn't object. Keir and I had spent the last ten days together, making love at night and dealing with problems during the day. How could I object to spending time with my beloved Warlord?

The silence behind me made me aware that I was the center of attention. I turned to face an angry Marcus, who had dismounted and was glaring at me with his one good eye. "And this was your idea?"

I glared at my guards, but they all found other things to look at. I faced Marcus. "It was."

"Why?"

"Because I need to learn to protect myself." I looked at Marcus and lifted my chin. "I have to be able to protect Keir." Inside I winced even as I spoke.

"Protect Hisself?" Marcus gave me a steady look. "How so?"

I sighed, prepared for Marcus's scorn. "When we were in camp, when Iften was standing over Keir. That scared me Marcus." I gestured toward the others. "I can't be deadweight. You said yourself that the Plains are hard. I thought I could at least learn how to—" the words came hard. "How to fight."

Marcus considered me long enough that I blushed and looked away. "I know it must seem silly—"

"No, Warprize." Marcus looked off, down the valley, toward the Plains, and sighed. "Death comes in an instant, and you are learning that truth. A harsh truth, but a truth nonetheless." He shook his head. "But you are on the wrong path."

"She wants to learn." Rafe protested. "What's the harm?"

Marcus turned to face Rafe. "Let me show you." Even as the words left his mouth, he'd launched himself at Anders, with no warning or sign, so fast I never really saw him move.

What I did see was Anders ward off Marcus's dagger with his own blade, which he drew with unbelievable speed. It all happened so fast, and then they stood there, Anders at guard and Marcus making no further move.

Marcus stepped back, and bowed his head to Anders, who inclined his head in return. The weapons were sheathed, and Marcus turned back to me. "You see?"

I frowned, puzzled, and answered honestly. "No."

Marcus had a patient look on his face. "Anders had no need to think of the 'how'. He reacted. He knows the blade, knows the movements, knows in the depths of his body and blood. Has known since he cut his first teeth and his thea handed him his first blade."

I blinked. First tooth? But that was—

"You think, Warprize." Marcus continued his lecture. "You think, and then you tell your body and that delay is fatal. Never mind the weight of the shield, never mind that you—"

"You give babies weapons?"

Marcus fixed his eye on me. "What do you mean by 'babies'?"

The language again. Just when I think I know the language of the Firelanders, something new comes up. "Babies. Children that still crawl and soil their—" I bit my lip. "Like Meara, the babe we found in the village."

Marcus shook his head. "No. First teeth." He opened his mouth and showed me his teeth. "All their first tooths."

I thought for a minute. He meant the first set of baby teeth—all of them. Which meant they gave weapons to children that were roughly two and a half, maybe three years old.

"Wooden blades, Warprize. The first weapon is wooden." Marcus looked at me closely. "The first true blade is at the first true tooth. You understand?"

I nodded slowly, taking that in. Firelanders wielded steel at roughly six or seven years old.

No wonder they were so fast. It occurred to me that I was very glad I'd sent Meara back to Anna at Water's Fall.

"So." Marcus's voice called me back. "We will concentrate on what you can do. Not on what you can't."

I sighed, and let my shoulders slump. "But I can't do anything!"

"Pah." Marcus turned, and picked up the wooden sword and small shield that I had been using. "What did you do when that warrior-priest burst into your tent?"

I went and sat close to Prest, flopping down in the grass. "I screamed and ran."

"And?" Marcus asked as he seated himself. Rafe dropped down next to him, and pulled out a dagger and a sharpening stone. Anders and Yveni remained standing, on watch, standing close enough to hear.

"Hid behind Keir." I picked a stem of grass and started playing with it. "Bold warrior that I am."

Marcus snorted. "You, with your terrible memory. You have forgotten."

I looked up to see that Rafe and Prest were both grinning, as if at the memory. "What?"

Rafe answered promptly. "You threw that pot of muck at him. He was covered with it when he came out of the tent."

"Wish I'd seen that," Anders spoke, his eyes still on the horizon.

"Heyla to that," Yveni added.

Prest chuckled. "The stink clung for days." He reached over and pulled his warclub close, preparing to re-wrap the handle with the leather strips. Of course, it wasn't just any warclub. I looked away from the weapon. It brought back too many painful memories.

"So," Marcus continued. "What did you do? You alerted others that you were in trouble. You used what was at hand to distract the enemy. You fled to where there was help, and positioned yourself where your defenders could protect you."

I had forgotten. I'd whipped that jar of boiled skunk cabbage right at that warrior-priest's face before I'd fled. I sat up a little straighter. "I guess I did."

Marcus gave me a nod. "Teaching you to fight is enough to make a gurttle laugh. But teaching you to defend yourself, to respond under attack and get yourself to safety, that can be done."

I shook my head. "Marcus, I froze when I found Iften hovering over Keir with that dagger. I didn't have the sense to scream."

"Fear." Prest spoke as he concentrated on his task.

Rafe nodded, even as he honed the edge of his blade. "Fear holds you still when you need to move, and moves you when you need to be still."

"Fear makes you silent when you need to be loud and loud when you need silence," Anders said, almost reciting. I wasn't surprised; Prest had taunted Iften with a teaching rhyme back at Wellspring. It seemed they used them a lot for teaching purposes. Which also didn't surprise me—since they had no written language, everything was memorized, and their ability to do that was amazing.

"Fear closes your throat, makes it hard to breathe. Fear weakens your hand and blinds your eyes." Marcus took up the chant. "Fear is a danger. Know your fear. Face your fear."

I waited a breath, but when it was clear they were done I broke the silence. "But how do I do that?"

Prest turned his head, and smiled at me, his white teeth flashing against his dark skin. "Practice."

I should have kept silent. This warrior-princess routine was uncomfortable, sweaty, and exhausting.

We had been waiting to join the army at the very rear of the march. Keir had that little-boy smile on his face when he'd told me that I'd be moving to the rear of his forces. I was fairly sure that he wanted to make sure that he gave me my first glimpse of the Plains.

Since we were waiting anyway, I'd asked my guards to teach me to use a sword and shield. I'd thought it would be easy; after all they handled their weapons with grace and skill.

Easy to say; hard to do.

We spent the rest of the afternoon as the army passed practicing. Each of my bodyguards would play the attacker, and then I had to work with the others to protect myself. Marcus stood back and watched. When it looked like I knew how to handle the situation, Marcus called out for Prest to die, and Prest obligingly fell 'dead' at my feet.

So I learned to move with my protectors, trying to stay out of their way, and be constantly aware of the threat I was under. Marcus was a strong believer in action as opposed to talking. When I got too tired, we'd stop and talk for a bit, get a drink of water, so that I could catch my breath.

The others never even broke a sweat.

Finally, as the sun was setting, Marcus 'killed' all my

body guards, and I was facing my 'attacker' alone. Prest grinned at me as he lay dead at my feet. I looked over at Marcus, who stood there with two daggers, threatening me. "Now what?"

He tilted his head under that cloak, and glared at me. "What can you do?"

"I don't know!" Frustrated, I glared back at him.

Anders had managed to 'die' face down, and looked like he was taking a nap. "Look for a weakness," he whispered to me.

Weakness? Marcus had already proved he was deadly with those daggers, so what weakness did he have?

Marcus rolled his one eye at me.

Oh.

I darted over to his left, trying to get into his blind spot. But Marcus just pivoted to face me, keeping me in sight. I stopped, frustrated. "What good does that do?"

"Keeps him moving, keeps him from throwing his daggers," Yveni responded. She was laying on the ground, chewing a piece of grass, watching the perimeter. Rafe was seated a distance away, watching in the other direction.

"You could try rushing him, getting him to move away from you. Use our bodies to try to trip him up," Anders offered.

"Throw things," Prest added. I looked at my satchel on my hip, and nodded.

"You must take advantage of any weakness." Marcus gestured at his face. "Mine is my blind side, Warprize. If you can blind a person with one of your mixtures, do it. It may be all that stands between you and death. Yes?"

"I will, Marcus."

"More important, if all your guards are down, where else can you look for help?" Marcus growled.

I eyed him nervously. I still remembered the 'lesson' he'd given me before, when he'd overborne me to the ground, and held a dagger to my throat. "The army?"

Marcus snorted.

Rafe caught my eye and jerked his thumb in the direction of our horses.

"The horses?" I looked over where our mounts were standing, waiting patiently. They were grazing, except of course for my Greatheart. He was fast asleep, his one hip cocked to the side, his head hanging down. As usual.

"The horses." Marcus sheathed his daggers within the darkness of his cloak as the others stood, brushing themselves off. "Get to a horse, leap to its back, and it will take you out of danger."

"If she could ride." Prest said calmly.

I glared at him, but they were all smiling. It was an old joke now, but in their eyes, it was true. I wasn't born in a saddle, like the people of the Plains, and to them my riding skills were horrible. But I could ride. Leaping into a saddle, however . . .

"But that lesson can wait," Marcus announced. "Hisself will be making camp soon, and the meal will not make itself." He headed toward the horses.

Thankful for the reprieve, I followed with my guards.

Since we'd resumed our march to the Plains, Keir had made some changes to my sleeping arrangements. My tent was a bit bigger now, enough that I could stand upright in it. He'd arranged extra padding for my bedding. It was saddle blankets folded and piled high, which made a very comfortable mattress. They were made from some kind of wool that I didn't recognize, but knew from its use in camp. But the biggest change, and the best change, was that I slept within his arms every night.

When we'd left Water's Fall, Keir had continued his practice of moving up and down the length of his army, in sight of his warriors and dealing with their morale. He'd left me in the center, where he'd thought I'd be better protected. But that had meant many nights of separation.

But now, with the events of Wellspring behind us, I traveled with him. Neither one of us wanted to be apart for any length of time. He continued to work with his warriors, of course, disappearing during the day to deal with any problems that arose. But every night he returned to our bed. To my arms. To me.

This night would be no different.

Marcus bustled about, keeping an eye on the warriors that set up our tent, and cooking over an open fire at the same time. I sat close to his fire, watching as he worked. Rafe and Prest had gone off to see to their own camps but Anders and Yveni remained, keeping watch over me. Once Keir arrived, they'd leave as well. While Keir circled our tent with guards, they stayed well back now, giving me an illusion of a bit of privacy.

Firelanders had a very different attitude toward privacy then the customs I was raised with. For them bathing together and strolling nude was the custom, with no regard for modesty, even between men and women. As Joden had pointed out to me, there was little privacy to be found in the tents of the Firelanders.

I sighed. Joden was something else I didn't want to think about.

In the overnight camps, no one wasted time cutting down trees for seats. Instead, we used the saddle blankets as pads. Dirt and moisture seemed to fall right off the odd wool. Seated by the fire, with a cloak over my shoulders, I was comfortably warm. Winter had moved into the mountains, and while we were moving down onto the Plains, frost still nipped at our heels. The sky was clear, it would be cold tonight.

Marcus was cutting meat and brewing kavage and would tolerate no help from me. I was too tired to do much more than sit. So I pulled my satchel close and opened the flap. I'd been using it since—

Since Gils died.

My hands stilled on the scarred leather. Gils was the young Firelander who'd asked to be my apprentice, breaking the traditions of his people. The image of his freckled face and red curls flashed before me. He'd been so young, so eager, with dancing green eyes and that cheeky grin.

I closed my eyes, and fought my tears. *Goddess, hold him close.*

And hold the souls of Epor and Isdra. The warriors who'd entered the village with me, and were the first to face the plague. Well, Epor had. Isdra had chosen to join her bonded, on the night of the mourning ceremony. Their faces, too, flashed before me. Along with the hundreds that had died of a sickness that I couldn't prevent or cure.

If only . . .

"Here," Marcus's gruff voice interrupted my thoughts. A cup of kavage was held under my nose. "Drink. Stop thinking on the dead."

I took the cup, the dark and bitter brew steaming in the cool air. "Marcus—"

"Lara." Marcus's voice softened and I look up at him through my tears. "We have mourned the dead, and will bid them farewell on the longest night. It is enough."

"But, I miss them." I answered, wiping my eyes with my free hand. "And I regret—"

"They ride with us until the snows." Marcus responded. "Send your thoughts to them, yes. But not always the sorrow. Remember the joy as well. Like when the young'un read Simus's letter to you. Yes?"

I smiled at the memory. "Yes."

Marcus grunted in satisfaction, then returned to his work. I blew on the surface of the kavage and took a sip. The heat spread through my body, and I continued to sip, remembering Gils's eagerness, and the time I caught Epor and Isdra kissing by the well.

But there was still in ache in my heart.

The satchel had been Gils's. He'd made it from an old saddlebag, adding a thick strap and lots of pockets for 'useful things.' I'd used it since he'd died, but hadn't really cleaned it out. Just kept stuffing things in and rummaging around without really thinking about the contents. I pulled it closer, intending to empty it out and re-pack it.

"Heyla!"

Keir was coming as a gallop. The sight brought a smile to my face, for he was quite a figure, dressed in his black leathers, on his big black warhorse, framed by the setting sun. I threw back the cloak and ran to greet him.

He pulled his horse to a stop and dismounted with one swift move. His black cloak swirled out around him as he caught me in his arms, and hugged me tight, claiming my lips in a kiss. He smelled of horse and leather and himself, and I returned the kiss with passion.

He broke off with a laugh, and swung me up into his arms, striding toward our tent. I wrapped my arms around his neck, and nuzzled his ear, certain of his intent and in complete agreement.

"And what of the food?" Marcus demanded, as Keir marched past the fire to our tent.

Keir spun on his heel, and faced him. "Marcus! Want to know the best part of being a Warlord?"

Marcus's eyebrow rose.

Keir's mouth curled up slowly into a smile. "Getting what I want."

I laughed as Keir turned back toward the tent.

A growl came from behind him. "The Warlord's dinner will be dumped in the dirt if Hisself does not eat it now."

Keir paused in mid-step. From his expression, he was torn with rare indecision.

"The meal is ready now. It will be eaten now."

Keir looked at me with such a sorrowful expression in his bright blue eyes. Just then his stomach rumbled, and I laughed right out loud.

We ate, as the sky above us turned a vivid dark blue and deepened to black. The stars hung bright in the night sky, with a moon that glowed through the trees. Marcus finished refilling our mugs with kavage, and was cleaning the remains of our meal away when he asked his question. "How goes it with the warriors?"

I was seated next to Keir, leaning against his shoulder, a cloak over both of us. But I leaned back a bit to see his face as he replied.

Keir sighed. "Not as well as I could wish. Iften talks, and the warriors look at empty pack animals and empty saddle bags, and wonder if they have done the right thing in following me." He reached over to stoke my hair. "I tell my truths, but words weigh little."

I leaned over and brushed his lips with mine. There

wasn't much that I could say to that. Keir's conquest of Xy was a break in tradition for the Firelanders. Their normal practice was to raid and plunder what they could, to return to the Plains laden with spoils. But Keir wanted to change their ways, to conquer and hold, for the benefit of both peoples.

"Fools." Marcus grumbled. "They can't see past the heads of their horses."

"But Keir, that's not quite true. They've pots of fever's foe, and that bloodmoss that we gathered." I yawned. "They know more than they did before about fevers." Goddess knew that was true. We'd pots and pots of fever's foe left from treating the plague, and everyone had aided in the treatment of the sick. I'd spread the extra out, making sure that everyone had some, and were watching for signs of the plague's return. If the Sweat re-appeared in our ranks, I wanted to know. Every warrior had agreed to carry some, and keep watch.

Except Iften.

Keir gave me a thoughtful look. "That's a truth I had not considered, Lara."

I smiled at him, and then yawned again, so hard my jaw cracked and my eyes watered. My stomach was full, and I was warm and growing sleepy.

Keir leaned in, taking the cup of kavage from my hand. "You are tired tonight, beloved." He moved closer, and put his arm around me. The warmth felt good, and I leaned in, putting my head on his shoulder.

"She asked for lessons." Marcus answered softly. "She wants to be able to protect you."

"Protect me?"

I nodded, even as I felt sleep overtake me. Their voices continued, as the fire crackled. Then we were moving,

and I found myself under the blankets with Keir at my
side. I roused just enough to murmur a question in his ear.

He chuckled softly. "Warlords also learn to wait for
what they want. Sleep, Lara."

Content, I drifted off to sleep.

At some point I felt Keir slip out from under the furs. I
lifted my head, my eyes half open, to see him standing
there, talking to one of the guards. I must have made
some sort of questioning sound, for Keir turned toward
me, his eyes glittering in the faint light. He gestured for
me to return to sleep.

I let my head sink down, grateful that I didn't have to
emerge from my warm bed. I'd adopted the Firelander
custom of sleeping naked. It made more sense to my way
of thinking. Less clothing for Marcus to clean, for example. A sign of my respect for the Firelanders. Goddess
knew, Keir seemed . . . appreciative.

But as convenient as the custom was, crawling naked
from warm covers to dress in cold clothes left something
to be desired. So I lay my head back down and let sleep
take me.

Much later, I roused again when Keir slid back into bed.
He made every effort to keep the cold air from me, but his
arm brushed mine in the process.

His skin was cold.

He whispered an apology and pulled away. But I'd
have none of that. Without really opening my eyes, I
moved closer.

He was *cold*. Fool Warlord, standing outside to talk to

the guards, naked. I shifted slowly, crawling over him to press my body as close as I could.

He drew a deep breath as I covered his body with mine. A shudder ran through him as I pressed my breasts to his chest, letting my warm skin come into full contact with his chilled flesh. I lifted one hand to cup his cheek, and used the other to stroke the muscles of his upper arm.

I moved my legs between his, and tried to place my feet so that they covered his toes. With my head on his shoulder my hair spread out like a blanket over him. I hummed in pleasure at the feel of his body. The soft skin of his stomach, the coarse hairs of his legs. The occasional scar. All of it Keir. My Keir.

He relaxed beneath me, whispering thanks. I just smiled, and let my thumb trace the soft skin of his lips. The blankets and furs held the heat of our bodies and the scent of his skin.

There were sounds of movement outside, probably a change of the guards. The wind was picking up, causing the tent to vibrate a little. We were coming down out of the mountains, but the chill of winter followed at our heels. Yet within this small shelter we were warm, safe, and dry.

Gradually Keir's body warmed and I shifted off to his side, so that the poor man didn't have to bear my weight. I was careful to return to my side of the bed. Keir slept with his weapons next to him, and I'd no desire to bed that cold steel. I nestled down next to him, content with his comfort and ready to return to sleep.

But I'd warmed Keir in more than one way. . . .